The Captive Queen

The Captive Queen

A Novel of Eleanor of Aquitaine

ALISON WEIR

HUTCHINSON
LONDON

Published by Hutchinson 2010

2 4 6 8 10 9 7 5 3 1

Copyright © by Alison Weir 2010

Alison Weir has asserted her right under the Copyright, Designs
and Patents Act 1988 to be identified as the author of this work

Map by Reginald Piggott

First published in Great Britain in 2010 by
Hutchinson
Random House, 20 Vauxhall Bridge Road,
London SW1V 2SA

ww.rbooks.co.uk

Addresses for companies within The Random House Group Limited can be found at:
www.randomhouse.co.uk/offices.htm

The Random House Group Limited Reg. No. 954009

A CIP catalogue record for this book
is available from the British Library

ISBN 9780091937195

The Random House Group Limited supports The Forest Stewardship Council (FSC),
the leading international forest certification organisation. All our titles that are printed
on Greenpeace approved FSC certified paper carry the FSC logo. Our paper procurement
policy can be found at www.rbooks.co.uk/environment

FSC
Mixed Sources
Product group from well-managed
forests and other controlled sources
Cert no. SGS-COC-2061
www.fsc.org
© 1996 Forest Stewardship Council

Typeset in Bell MT by
Palimpsest Book Production Limited, Grangemouth, Stirlingshire

Printed and bound in Great Britain by Clays Ltd, St. Ives plc

For seven special little people born in 2009–10:

Henry George Marston
Charlie Andrew Preston
Isla May Weir
Maisie Isobel Flora Weir
Lara Eileen Weir
Grace Daly Robinson
Frederick Arthur Campbell Thorpe
and my goddaughter,
Eleanor Jane Borman.

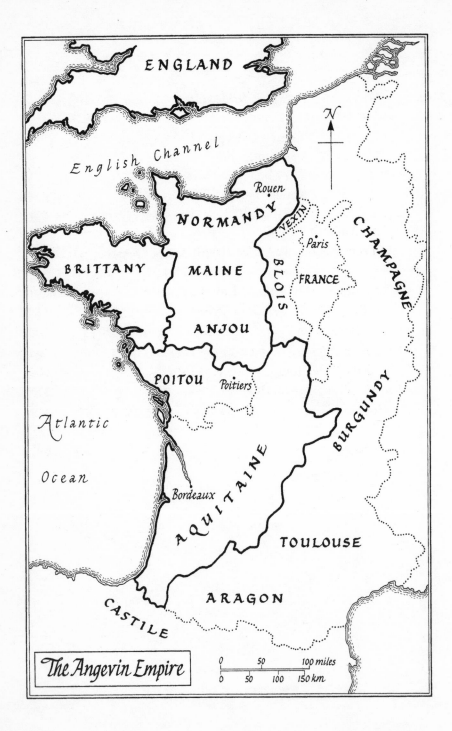

ENGLAND

English Channel

NORMANDY

Rouen

VEXIN

BLOIS

Paris

FRANCE

CHAMPAGNE

N

BRITTANY

MAINE

ANJOU

POITOU

Poitiers

Atlantic

Ocean

Bordeaux

AQUITAINE

BURGUNDY

TOULOUSE

ARAGON

CASTILE

The Angevin Empire

0   50   100 *miles*

0   50   100   150 *km*

Contents

William the Conqueror
Duke of Normandy,
King of England
1027?-1087

William II
`Rufus`
King of England
c1056-1100

Henry I
King of England
1068-1135

Adela m. Stephen,
Count of Blois

Stephen
King of England
c1097-1154

William
`the Atheling`
drowned 1120

Matilda
`the Empress`
1102-1167

m.1. Henry V,
German Emperor
2. Geoffrey Plantagenet.
Count of Anjou
1113-1151

Henry II
King of England
1133-1189

2. m.

William
Count of Poitiers
1153-1156

Henry
`the Young King`
1155-1183
m.
Marguerite
of France
1158-1198

Matilda
1156-1189
m.
Henry the Lion,
Duke of Saxony

Richard I
`the Lionheart`
King of England
1157-1199

William IX
`the Troubadour`
Duke of Aquitaine
1071-1126

| Hugh Viscount of Châtellerault | Raoul de Faye | Aenor of Châtellerault d. c1130 | m. | William X Duke of Aquitaine 1099-1137 | Raymond Prince of Antioch d. 1149 |

(bastards)
William   Joscelin

| Eleanor of Aquitaine 1122-1204 | m. 1. | Louis VII King of France 1121?-1180 | | Petronilla m. | Raoul Count of Vermandois |

| Geoffrey Duke of Brittany 1158-1186 m. Constance of Brittany | Philip d. young | Eleanor 1161-1214 m. Alfonso Infante of Castile | Joanna 1165-1199 m. William, King of Sicily | John King of England 1166-1216 | Marie 1145-1198 m. Henry Count of Champagne | Alix 1150-1198? m. Thibaut Count of Blois |

This is the worm that dieth not, the memory of things past.

St Bernard of Clairvaux, *De Consideratione*

The most persistent hate is that which doth degenerate from love.

Walter Map, *De Nugis Curialum*

Ah, cruel fate,
How swiftly joy and sorrow alternate!

Raimbaut de Vaqueyras, lyric poem

Part One
A Marriage of Lions
1151–1154

1   Paris, August 1151

'Please God, let me not betray myself,' Queen Eleanor prayed inwardly as she seated herself gracefully on the carved wooden throne next to her husband, King Louis. The royal court of France had assembled in the gloomy, cavernous hall in the Palace of the Cité, which commanded one half of the Île de la Cité on the River Seine, facing the great cathedral of Notre-Dame.

Eleanor had always hated this palace, with its grim, crumbling stone tower and dark, chilly rooms. She had tried to lighten the oppressive hall with expensive tapestries from Bourges, but it still had a stark, sombre aspect, for all the summer sunshine piercing the narrow windows. Oh, how she longed for the graceful castles of her native Aquitaine, built of light mellow stone on lushly wooded hilltops! How she longed to be in Aquitaine itself, and that other world in the sun-baked south that she had been obliged to leave behind all those years ago. But she had schooled her thoughts not to stray in that direction. If they did, she feared, she might go mad. Instead, she must fix her attention on the ceremony that was about to begin, and play her queenly role as best she could. She had failed Louis, and France, in so many ways – more than anyone could know – so she could at least contrive to look suitably decorative.

Before the King and Queen were gathered the chief lords and vassals of France, a motley band in their scarlets, russets and furs, and a bevy of tonsured churchmen, all – save for one – resplendent in voluminous, rustling robes. They were waiting to witness the ending of a war.

Louis looked drawn and tired, his cheeks still flushed with the fever that had laid him low for some weeks now, but at least, thought Eleanor, he had risen from his bed. Of course, Bernard of Clairvaux, that meddlesome abbot standing apart in his unbleached linen tunic, had told him to, and when Bernard spoke, Louis, and nearly everyone else in Christendom, invariably jumped.

She did not love Louis, but she would have done much, especially at this time when he was low in body and spirits, to spare him any hurt – and herself the shame and the fearful consequences of exposure. She had thought herself safe, that her great sin was a secret she would take with her to her grave, but now the one person who might, by a chance look or gesture, betray her and imperil her very existence was about to walk through the great doors at the end of the hall: Geoffrey, Count of Anjou – whom men called 'Plantagenet', on account of the broom flower he customarily wore in his hat.

Really, though, she thought resentfully, Louis could hardly blame her for what she had done. It was he, or rather the churchmen who dominated his life, who had condemned her to live out her miserable existence as an exile in this forbidding northern kingdom with its grey skies and dour people; and to follow a suffocating, almost monastic régime, cloistered from the world with only her ladies for company. For fourteen long years now, her life had been mostly barren of excitement and pleasure – and it was only in a few stolen moments that she had briefly known another existence. With Marcabru; with Geoffrey; and, later, with Raymond. Sweet sins that must never be disclosed outside the confessional, and certainly not to Louis, her husband. She was his queen and Geoffrey his vassal, and both had betrayed their sacred oaths.

Thus ran the Queen's tumultuous thoughts as she sat with the King on their high thrones, waiting for Geoffrey and his son Henry to arrive, so that Louis could exchange with them the kiss of peace and receive Henry's formal homage. The war was thus to be neatly concluded – except that there could be no neat conclusion to Eleanor's inner turmoil. For this was to be the first time she had set eyes on Geoffrey since that blissful, sinful autumn in Poitou, five years before.

It had not been love, and it had not lasted. But she had never been able to erase from her mind the erotic memory of herself and Geoffrey coupling gloriously between silken sheets, the candlelight a golden glow on their entwined bodies. Their coming together had been a revelation after the fumbling embarrassment of the marriage bed and the crude awakening afforded her by Marcabru; she had never dreamed that a man could give her such prolonged pleasure. It had surged again and again until she had cried out with the joy of it, and it had made her aware, as never before, of what was lacking in her union with Louis. Yet she had forced herself to forget, because Louis must never know. One suspected betrayal was enough, and that had hurt him so deeply that his heart could never be mended. Things had not been the same between them since, and all she was praying for now was the best way out of the ruins of their marriage.

And now Geoffrey was in Paris, in this very palace, and she was terrified in case either of them unwittingly gave Louis or anyone else – the all-seeing Abbot Bernard in particular – cause to wonder what had passed between them. In France, they did terrible things to queens who were found guilty of adultery. Who had not heard the dreadful old tale of Brunhilde, the wife of King Clotaire, who had been falsely accused of infidelity and murder, and torn to death by wild horses tethered to her hair, hands and feet? Eleanor shuddered whenever she thought of it. Would Louis be so merciless if he found out that she had betrayed him? She did not think so, but neither did she want to put him to the test. He must never, ever know that she had lain with Geoffrey.

Even so, fearful though she was, she could not but remember how it had been between them, and how wondrously she had been awakened to the pleasures of love . . .

No, don't think of it! she admonished herself. That way lies the danger of exposure. She even began to wonder if that wondrous pleasure had been worth the risk . . .

The trumpets were sounding. They were coming now. At any moment, Geoffrey would walk through the great door. And there he was: tall, flame-haired and intense, strength and purpose in his chiselled features, controlled vitality in his long stride. He had not changed. He was advancing towards the dais, his eyes fixed on Louis. He did not look her way. She forced herself to lift her chin and stare ahead. Virtuous ladies kept custody of their eyes, Grandmère Dangerosa had counselled her long ago; but Dangerosa herself had been no saint, and had in her time used her eyes to very good effect, to snare Eleanor's grandfather, the lusty troubadour Duke of Aquitaine. Eleanor had learned very early in life that women could wield a strange power over men, even as she did over Louis, although, God help them both, it had never been sufficient to stir his suppressed and shrinking little member to action very often.

Eleanor tried not to think of her frustration, but that was difficult when the man who had shown her how different things could be was only feet away from her, and accompanied by his eighteen-year-old son. His son! Suddenly, her eyes were no longer in custody but running amok. Henry of Anjou was slightly shorter than his father, but he more than made up for that in presence. He was magnificent, a young, red-headed lion, with a face upon which one might gaze a thousand times, yet still wish to look at again and feast one's eyes. Henry's grey eyes outshone his father's in intensity, his lips were blatantly sensual, his chest broad, his body muscular and toned already from years in the saddle and the field of battle. Despite his rugged masculinity, he moved with a feline grace and suppressed energy that hinted at a deep and powerful sexuality. His youthful maleness was irresistible, glorious. Eleanor took one look at Henry – and saw Geoffrey no more.

There was no doubt at all that her interest was returned, for, as Louis rose and embraced Geoffrey, Henry's appreciative gaze never left Eleanor: his eyes were dark with desire, mischievous with intent. Lust knifed through her. She could barely control herself. Never had she reacted so violently to any man.

With an effort, she dragged her eyes, those treacherous eyes, back to the homage that was being performed, then watched Henry, in the wake of his father, falling to his knees and placing his hands between those of the King.

'By the Lord,' he said in a deep, gravelly voice, 'I will to you be true and faithful, and love all that you love, and shun all that you shun. Nor will I ever, by will or action, through word or deed, do anything which is unpleasing to you, on condition that you will hold to me as I shall deserve, so help me God.'

Eleanor was captivated. She wanted this man. Watching him, she knew – she could not have said how – that he was destined to be hers, and that she could have him at the click of her fingers. Her resolve to end her marriage quickened and set firm.

She caught Geoffrey looking at her, but found herself staring straight through him, barely noticing the faint frown that darkened his brows as he watched her. She was thinking of how she was bound by invisible ties to the three men standing before her, that each was unaware of that fact, and that two of those ties must now be loosed. Forgetting Geoffrey would be easy: she saw with sharp clarity that she had fed off that fantasy for too long, of necessity. It had been lust, no more, embellished in her mind with the fantasies born of frustration. And she had waited for years to be free of poor Louis. The only question now was how to accomplish it.

'In the name of God, I formally invest you with the dukedom of Normandy,' Louis was intoning to Henry, then he bent forward and kissed the young man on both cheeks. The young Duke rose to his feet and stepped backwards to join his father, and both men bowed.

'We have much to thank Abbot Bernard for,' the King murmured to Eleanor, his handsome features relaxing into the sweet smile that he reserved only for his beautiful wife. 'This peace with Count Geoffrey and his son was of his making.'

More likely it was some wily strategy invented by Geoffrey, Eleanor thought, but she forbore to say anything. Even the unworldly Louis had accounted it odd that the crafty Count of Anjou had made this sudden about-turn after blaspheming in the face of the saintly Bernard. The Abbot had dared to castigate Geoffrey for backing his son, Henry FitzEmpress, in refusing to perform homage to his overlord, King Louis, for the dukedom of Normandy. Even Eleanor had been shocked.

'That boy is arrogant!' Louis was quietly fuming. 'I hear he has a temper on him that would make a saint quail. Someone needs to bridle him before he gets out of control, and his father cannot be trusted to do it, whatever fair words he speaks for my benefit.'

Eleanor was finding it difficult to say anything in reply, so smitten was she with Henry.

'I can't believe that Geoffrey was lackwitted enough to cede his duchy to that cocky young stripling,' Louis muttered, the smile fixed on his face. 'Even now, I do not trust either of them, and neither does Abbot Bernard. Whatever anyone says, I was right to refuse initially to recognise Henry as duke. Why God in His wisdom struck me down with illness just as I was about to march on them I will never understand.' He was working himself up into one of his rare but deadly furies, and Eleanor, despite herself, knew that she had to make him calm down. People were looking . . .

Louis was gripping the painted arms of his throne with white knuckles. She laid a cool hand on his.

'We must thank God for Abbot Bernard's intervention,' she murmured soothingly, recalling how Bernard had stepped in and, ignoring Geoffrey's customary swearing and bluster – God, the man had a temper on him – had in the end performed little less than a miracle in averting war.

'Aye, it was a fair bargain,' Louis conceded, his irritation subsiding. 'No one else could have extracted such terms from the Angevins.' Eleanor could only agree that Henry's offer of the Vexin, that much-disputed Norman borderland, in return for the King's acknowledgement of him as duke of Normandy, was a masterful solution to the dispute, saving everyone's face.

'Come, my Lord,' she said, 'they are all waiting. Let us entertain our visitors.'

As wine and sweetmeats were brought and served, the King and Queen and their important guests mingled with the courtiers in that vast, dismal hall. Searching for Duke Henry in the throng, hoping for the thrill of even a few words with him, just to hear once more the sound of his voice, Eleanor unwillingly found herself face-to-face with the saintly Abbot Bernard, who seemed equally dismayed by the encounter. He did not like women, it was well known, and she was convinced he was terrified of the effect they might have on him. Heavens, he even disapproved of his sister, simply because she enjoyed being married to a rich man. Eleanor had always hated Bernard, that disapproving old misery – the antipathy was mutual, of course – but now courtesy demanded that she force herself to acknowledge him. The odour of sanctity that clung to him – 'Odour indeed!' she thought – was not conducive to social conversation.

Bernard's stern, ascetic face gazed down at her. His features were emaciated, his skin stretched thin over his skull. All the world knew how greatly he fasted through love of Our Lord. There was barely anything of him.

'My Lady,' he said, bowing slightly, and was about to make his escape and move on when it suddenly struck Eleanor that he might be of use to her in her present turmoil.

'Father Abbot,' she detained him, putting on her most beseeching look, 'I am in need of your counsel.'

He stood looking silently at her, never a man to waste words. She could sense his antipathy and mistrust; he had never liked her, and had made no secret of his opinion that she was interfering and over-worldly.

'It is a matter on which I have spoken to you before,' she said in a low voice. 'It is about my marriage to the King. You know how empty and bitter my life has been, and that during all my fourteen years of living with Louis, I have borne him but two daughters. I despair of ever bearing him a son and heir, although I have prayed many times to the Virgin to grant my wish, yet I fear that God has turned His face from me.' Her voice broke in a well-timed sob as she went on, 'You yourself have questioned the validity of the marriage, and I have long doubted it too. We are too close in blood, Louis and I. We had no dispensation. Tell me, Father Abbot, what can I do to avert God's displeasure?'

'Many share your concerns, my daughter,' Bernard replied, his voice pained, as if it hurt him to have to agree with her for once. 'The barons themselves have urged the King to seek an annulment, but he is loath to lose your great domains. And, God help him, he loves you.' His lip curled.

'Love?' Eleanor retorted. 'Louis is like a child! He is an innocent, and afraid of love. He rarely comes to my bed. In faith, I married a monk, not a king!'

'That is of less consequence than your unlawful wedlock,' Bernard flared. 'Must you always be thinking of fleshly things?'

'It is fleshly things that lead to the begetting of heirs!' Eleanor snapped. 'My daughters are prevented by their sex from inheriting the crown, and if the King dies without an heir, France would be plunged into war. He should be free to remarry and father sons.'

'I will speak to him again,' Bernard said, visibly controlling his irritation. 'There are indeed many good reasons why this marriage should be dissolved.' Eleanor bit her lip, determined not to acknowledge the implied insult. Then she espied Henry of Anjou through a gap in the crowd, quaffing wine as he conversed with his father Geoffrey, and her heart missed a beat.

Bernard saw him too, and sniffed.

'I distrust those Angevins,' he said darkly. 'From the Devil they came, and to the Devil they will return. They are a cursed race. Count Geoffrey is as slippery as an eel, and I have never liked him. By his blasphemy, to my very face, he has revealed his true self. But the vengeance will be God's alone. Mark you, my Lady, Count Geoffrey will be dead within the month!'

Eleanor was struck by a fleeting chill at the Abbot's words, but she told herself that they had been born only of outrage. Then she realised that Bernard was now frowning at Henry.

'When I first saw the son, I knew a moment of terrible foreboding,' he said.

'May I ask why?' Eleanor enquired, startled.

'He is the true descendant of that diabolical woman, Melusine, the wife of the first Count of Anjou. I will tell you the story. The foolish man married her, being seduced by her beauty, and she bore him children, but she would never attend Mass. One day, he forced her to, having his knights hold fast to her cloak, but when it came to the elevation of the Host, she broke free with supernatural strength and flew shrieking out of a window, and was never seen again. There can be no doubt that she was the Devil's own daughter, who could not bear to look upon the Body of Christ.'

Eleanor smiled wryly. She had heard the tale before. 'That's just an old legend, Father Abbot. Surely you don't believe it?'

'Count Geoffrey and his son believe it,' Bernard retorted. 'They mention it often. It seems they are even proud of it.' He winced in disgust.

'I think they might have been having a joke at your expense,' she told him, remembering Geoffrey's wicked sense of humour. God only knew, he'd needed it, married to that harridan, Matilda the Empress, who had never ceased reminding him that her father had been king of England and her first husband the Holy Roman Emperor himself! And that she was wasted on a mere count!

'One should never joke about such things,' Bernard said stiffly. 'And now, my Lady, I must speak with the King.' He backed away, nodding his obeisance, evidently relieved to be quitting her company. She shrugged. Kings and princes might quail before him, but to her, Bernard of Clairvaux was just a pathetic, meddlesome, obsessive old man. And why should she waste her thoughts on him when Henry FitzEmpress was coming purposefully towards her?

What was it about a certain arrangement of features and expression that gave one person such appeal for another, she wondered, unable to tear her eyes from the young Duke's face.

'Madame the Queen, I see that the many reports of your beauty do not lie,' Henry addressed her, sketching a quick bow. Eleanor felt the lust rising again in her. God, he was beddable! What wouldn't she give for one night between the sheets with him!

'Welcome to Paris, my Lord Duke,' she said lightly. 'I am glad you have reached an accord with the King.'

'It will save a lot of bloodshed,' Henry said. She was to learn that he spoke candidly, and to the point. His eyes, however, were raking up and down her body, taking in every luscious curve beneath the clinging silk gown, with its fitted corsage and double belt that emphasised the slenderness of her waist and the swell of her hips.

'I trust you had a good journey,' Eleanor enquired, feeling a little faint with desire.

'Why don't we forget the pleasantries?' Henry said abruptly. It was rude of him, but his words excited her. His gaze bore into hers. 'We both know what this is all about,' he went on, 'so why waste time, when we could be getting better acquainted?'

Eleanor was about to ask him what he could possibly mean, or reprimand him for his unforgivable familiarity to the Queen of France, but what was the point? She wanted him as much as he clearly wanted her. Why deny it?

'I should like to get to know you,' she murmured, smiling at him boldly, and forgetting all that nonsense about custody of the eyes. 'You must forgive me if I do not know how to respond.'

'From what I've heard, you've not had much chance,' Henry said. 'King Louis is known for his, shall we say, saintliness. Apart,

11

of course, from when he is leading armies or burning towns. It is odd that such a pious man should be capable of such violence.'

Eleanor shuddered. All these years later, she could not bear to think of what had happened at Vitry. It had changed Louis for ever.

'My marriage has not been easy,' she admitted, glad to do so. Henry must not think she was in love with her husband. Once she had been, in a girlish, romantic way, but that was long years ago.

'You need a real man in your bed,' Henry told her bluntly, his eyes never leaving hers, his lips curling in a suggestive smile.

'That's what I've been trying to tell Abbot Bernard,' Eleanor said mischievously.

'Him? The watchdog of Christendom? He'd never understand,' Henry laughed. 'Do you know that, when he was young, and got his first erection from looking at a pretty girl, he jumped into an icy pond to cure himself!'

Eleanor felt herself flush with excitement at his words. So soon had they progressed to speaking of such intimate matters, it was unreal – and extremely stimulating.

'You are very self-assured for such a boy,' she said provocatively. 'Are you really only eighteen?'

'I am a man in all things that count,' Henry assured her meaningfully, slightly offended at her words.

'Are you going to prove it to me?' she invited.

'When?' he asked, his expression intent.

'I will send a message to you by one of my women,' she told him, without hesitation. 'I will let you know when and where it is safe for us to be alone together.'

'Is Louis a jealous husband?' Henry enquired.

'No, he never comes to me these days,' Eleanor revealed, her tone bitter, 'and he rarely ever did in the past. He should have entered a monastery, for he has no use for women.'

'I have heard it said that he truly loves you,' Henry probed.

'Oh, yes, I have no doubt that he does, but only in a spiritual way. He feels no need to possess me physically.'

'Then he is a fool,' Henry muttered. '*I* cannot wait.'

'I'm afraid you might have to,' Eleanor said lightly. 'I have enemies at this court. The French have always hated me.

Everything I do is wrong. I feel I am in a prison, there are so many restrictions on what I do, and they watch me, constantly. So I must be careful, or my reputation will be dragged further in the dust.'

Henry raised his eyebrows. 'Further?'

'Maybe you have heard the tales they tell of me,' Eleanor said lightly.

'I have heard one or two things that made me sit up and take notice,' he grinned. 'Or stand up and take notice, if you want the bare truth! But I have been no angel myself. We are two of a kind, my queen.'

'I only know that I have never felt like this,' Eleanor whispered, catching her breath.

'Hush, Madame,' Henry warned. 'People are looking. We have talked too long together. I will wait to hear from you.' He raised her hand and kissed it. The touch of his lips, his flesh, was like a jolt to her system.

Later that night, Eleanor sat before her mirror, gazing into its burnished silver surface. Her image stared back at her, and she looked upon her oval face with its alabaster-white skin, cherry-red rosebud lips, sensuous, heavy-lidded eyes and well-defined cheekbones, the whole framed with a cascade of coppery tresses. She marvelled that she had as yet no lines or wrinkles, yet even so, she wondered if Henry would desire her as much when he realised that, at twenty-nine, she was eleven years older than he was. But of course he must know that. The whole world knew of her great marriage to Louis; there was no secret about her age.

Setting aside her fears, she stood up and regarded her naked body in the mirror. Surely Henry would be pleased when he saw her firm, high breasts, narrow waist, flat belly and curving hips. The very thought of that steely, knowing gaze upon her nudity made her melt with need, and her fingers crept greedily down to that secret place between her legs, the place that people like Bernard regarded as forbidden to the devout: the place where, five years before, she had learned to feel rushes and crescendos of unutterable pleasure.

It was Marcabru the troubadour who had shown her how, the

incomparable Marcabru, whom she herself had invited from her native Aquitaine to the court of Paris – where his talents, such as they were, had not been appreciated. Dark and almost satanic in aspect, he had excited and awakened her with his suggestive – and very bad – poems in honour of her loveliness, and then done what Louis never had to bring her to a climax, one glorious July day in a secluded arbour in the palace gardens. But Louis' suspicions and jealousy had been aroused by Marcabru's over-familiarity in the verses he dedicated to the Queen, and he had banished him back to the south without ever realising just how far Marcabru had abused his hospitality. It had been her hunger to know that sweet fulfilment once more that had driven Eleanor into the arms of Geoffrey the following autumn.

Since then, she had learned to pleasure herself, and she did so now, hungrily, her body alive in anticipation of the joys she would share with Henry of Anjou when they could be together. And, gasping as the shudders of her release convulsed her, she promised herself that it would be soon. After all, Henry and Geoffrey would not be staying long in Paris.

'I watched you talking to the Queen,' Geoffrey said.

'We exchanged a few pleasantries,' Henry said guardedly, filling his goblet. He never discussed his dealings with women with his father.

'It looked like a lot more than that,' Geoffrey accused him. 'I know you, Henry. Remember, boy, she is the Queen of France, not some trollop you'd screw in a haystack. And we've only just made peace with her husband the King.'

'I know all that,' Henry replied mulishly. 'I'm not an idiot.'

'Convince me of that,' his father retorted. 'I saw you looking at her lustfully. And I saw her casting her unchaste eyes on you. You know, Henry, she has a reputation.'

'So rumour has it,' Henry said. 'But there is no proof. Her husband has not cast her off for infidelity. Maybe the rumours have wronged her.'

'Her husband,' Geoffrey said carefully, 'does not know the least of it, I am sure.'

'It ill becomes you to impugn her honour, Father!' Henry snapped.

'Oh, so you *are* hot for her,' Geoffrey observed drily. Then his tone hardened. 'Listen, my son. I say this for a very good reason. I absolutely forbid you to touch her. Not only is she married and the wife of your overlord, and therefore doubly prohibited to you, but' – and here the Count hesitated and looked away – 'I have known her myself.'

'I don't believe you, Father,' Henry retorted. 'You're just saying that to warn me off.'

'It's true, God help me,' Geoffrey insisted, his voice sounding wistful. 'Five years ago, I had a secret affair with her, when I was seneschal of Poitou. She was there raising support for the crusade. It was just a brief thing, nothing serious, and fortunately nothing came of it. We were never discovered.'

Henry snorted. 'So what of it? What difference does it make to me having her now? *You* clearly don't want her any more.'

'You don't understand, boy,' Geoffrey hissed, grasping Henry firmly by the shoulders. 'If you bed her, you commit incest. Such a relationship is forbidden by the Church.'

Henry glared at him and wrenched himself free.

'By the eyes of God, I care not a fig what the Church says!' he snapped. 'A lot of things are forbidden by the Church, but they go on, and neither you, my Lord, nor anyone else can stop me having my will of her – and not only my will, but a whole lot more besides. In case you've forgotten, she is the greatest heiress in Christendom.'

Geoffrey's handsome face registered shock. He leapt to his feet, sending his empty goblet clattering to the floor. 'She is married to the King of France,' he hissed.

'She can be unmarried!' Henry answered. 'I keep my eyes and ears open. Have you not heard what is being said at this court? That the marriage is invalid and should be dissolved? The barons believe it, the Queen is said to have urged it, even our friend Bernard, God damn him, is of that opinion. Only the King is obdurate.'

'He will not relinquish her domains,' Geoffrey said. 'It is too rich an inheritance to give up, so you can forget it.'

'No,' Henry defied him. 'Louis can't keep hold of Aquitaine. His authority counts for little there. They're an unruly lot, Eleanor's vassal lords. Even her father couldn't control them.'

'And you think *you* could!' Geoffrey taunted.

'I'd stand a better chance than they,' Henry assured him. 'Louis hasn't the resources. But when England is mine, along with Normandy, I will be ready and able to enforce my rule.'

'You run ahead of yourself, boy,' Geoffrey said wearily. 'There is no guarantee that England ever will be yours. God knows your mother and King Stephen fought bitterly over it for years, but Stephen is still enthroned there, despite what people say about God and His saints having slept through all the terrible years of his reign; and he has an heir, Eustace, to succeed him. Against that, the claim of your mother, a woman, however rightful, is tenuous indeed. She lost all hope of success years ago when she upset the English by her haughty ways.' His tone made it clear that he too had been alienated by them.

'That's unfair! You never loved my mother,' Henry flung at him.

'We've always cordially hated each other, you know that,' Geoffrey replied sanguinely. 'But that's beside the point. Those whom God hath joined must learn to put up with each other, or live apart, as we have. As for you, my son, just forget this hare-brained scheme to snatch Queen Eleanor from her husband. You will live to regret it, I promise you.'

'There would be no snatching involved. I know, as sure as God is God, that she would come to me quite willingly.'

'Then you're more of a fool than I'd realised,' Geoffrey spat, retrieving his goblet and striding towards the lion-shaped aqua-manile jug on the table. He poured a full measure of wine, then downed it in one go. 'You hardly know her.'

'Enough to know that I want her, and not just for her domains.' The young Duke's excited brain was racing ahead of him. 'Yet think on it, Father: were I to marry Eleanor, I'd become master of all the land from the River Loire to the Pyrenees, a mighty inheritance, perhaps the mightiest in history. I could found an empire – an Angevin empire. I would advance our House and make you proud of me. Louis would be pissing himself at the prospect!'

'Which is precisely why he won't let Eleanor go,' Geoffrey reminded him. 'Why should he effectively hand those rich domains to a vassal? If he divorces her, there'll be a stampede for her hand, which is why he's stalling. God, Henry, you can be stubborn. Just leave it alone. No good can come of it.'

'I don't call gaining half of France no good,' his son riposted.

'Then think of your immortal soul, you young fool.'

'Oh, I do think of it always, I assure you, Father,' Henry lied.

Henry closed the door and stood regarding Eleanor in the flickering light of the candles. He was wearing the same plain hunting clothes he had worn for the investiture. She, by contrast, had donned a thin loose robe of finest white samite, pinned on ear-rings of precious stones, and had her maids brush her long hair until it shone like bright molten fire. She found herself revelling in the power she could wield over Henry with her beauty and her body. She was headily aware of the diaphanous quality of her robe, the prominence of her erect nipples, and his obvious pleasure at what he was avidly devouring with his eyes.

He moved quickly towards her, throwing his belt aside and ripping off his tunic as he strode across the floor. His chest was broad, lightly covered with brown hair, darker than that on his head, and his arms and shoulders rippled with muscle. Eleanor could not stop herself. With a muted cry, she went to him, herself pulling down his *braies* to reveal his engorged penis. She was cherishing it in both hands as Henry's strong arms folded around her, crushing her against him as he pressed urgent lips to her forehead and then sought her mouth. His fingers, rough with calluses from riding, were tugging at the embroidered neckline of her robe, pulling it down around her hips, then grasping her upper arms to hold her away from him as he stared at her full breasts. Then he bent and released the robe, which fluttered to the floor around her ankles, leaving her standing there naked before him.

Lifting her up, he carried her to the waiting bed and lay down with her on the silk sheets and bolsters, his hands everywhere, caressing her until she thought she would die of the pleasure. She gave like-for-like in return, teasing and exciting him with her fingers and tongue until he could bear it no more and swiftly mounted her, thrusting deeper inside her than any lover before him, and flooding her with his desire, shouting his triumph.

Afterwards, Eleanor eagerly took his hand and guided his fingers to her clitoris, not needing to show him what to do next, for he clearly knew. Her climax, when it came, was shattering, for Henry, hard again, entered her once more at the moment of culmination. She had not believed such ecstasy possible.

It was hours before they slept. Eleanor had never before had such a vigorous and enthusiastic lover, and she quickly discovered in herself an undreamed-of capacity for pleasure in places she had barely known existed. Then came sleep, quiet and restful, and in the dawn, when she awakened, Henry's arms about her once more and his manhood insistent against her thigh.

Later, lying close to him in the afterglow of lovemaking, getting to know each other better, she knew she could never relinquish him.

Henry's grey eyes, heavy-lidded with fulfilment, were gazing into hers. His full lips twitched into a smile.

'I think,' he murmured, 'that I have never felt like this with a woman before.' His fingers, surprisingly gentle, traced her cheek. His dynamism, even after his passion had been spent, excited her.

'I feel wonderful,' she told him, her eyes holding his. 'Tell me this is more than just lust.'

'I cannot deny it's lust,' he grinned. 'In truth, you are magnificent –' He stretched out his hand and smoothed it slowly along the length of her body. 'But I want you for more than this. I want to know you, all of you. I want your mind as well as your body. I want your soul.'

'From the moment I saw you, I felt – nay, I knew – that we were destined for each other,' Eleanor ventured. 'Does that sound extravagant?'

'No,' Henry replied. 'I feel the same, and it is a delight to me that we are equal in our passion.'

It had to be destiny, Eleanor was certain. She was filled with a sense of it, and of elation. God had led this man to cross her path, this man who had the power to satisfy not only her body but also her ambition. She had known, in the moment they had joined as one, that their coming together would have far-reaching consequences, and with a sudden flash of perfect clarity, she could see what those consequences would be. She would leave Louis and break their marriage. She would go back south to Aquitaine, and reclaim it as her own. Then she would give it, with herself, as a gift to Henry. Together, with her lands joined to his coming inheritance, they could build an empire such as Christendom had never seen, and Aquitaine would become a great power in the world. And with Henry's backing, she would quell her turbulent lords and rule it wisely and well.

'Henry FitzEmpress,' she said, looking into those fathomless eyes, 'I want to be your wife.'

'And I, my Lady, want to be your husband,' he replied ardently, kissing her again. 'I know, for many speak of it, that you have doubts about your marriage, doubts shared even by the saintly Bernard. But what of Louis? Will he let you go?'

'I will talk to him,' Eleanor whispered, nuzzling his ear. 'This time he must listen.'

'You're not going to tell him about us?' Henry asked, alarmed.

'Of course not,' she said. 'I am not a fool, my heart. Do you think he would relinquish me, knowing I wanted to marry you?'

'No, I am the fool! My father often says it.'

Eleanor giggled, and began lightly stroking his hairy thigh.

'It makes sense, us marrying,' she said. 'I have long wanted my freedom, but how long would I keep it? I would be beset by fortune hunters. I could not wed just any man. But you would be my powerful protector, and I know without doubt that you would safeguard my inheritance, and help me to rule it well.'

Henry looked long and hard at her.

'It did occur to me you would think I had pursued you only for your inheritance. I think you know now that there is a little more to it than that.' He stretched luxuriously, toying with her nipples. 'Even if you were dowerless, I would want you for my wife. I mean that, Eleanor. By the eyes of God!'

'I believe you,' she answered, 'although I should hope that God has averted His eyes for the moment! Yet it has not escaped my notice that the men, money and resources that my domains could offer you would be of enormous help in gaining you England!'

Henry laughed. 'So you know about my ambitions in that direction. Of course, it is no secret.'

'And,' Eleanor went on, 'I am aware too that marrying me would make you the greatest and richest prince in the whole world.'

'Now why didn't I think of that?' Henry countered. 'Suddenly, you are infinitely more desirable!' He began kissing her, playfully at first, then with a more serious purpose.

'Wait,' Eleanor said, holding him off. 'Shall we make a promise to marry?'

He became still and regarded her solemnly. 'We shall. I, Henry FitzEmpress, take thee, Eleanor of Aquitaine, as my future wedded wife.'

Eleanor sat up in the bed, her long hair tumbling over her breasts.

'And I, Eleanor, do promise myself to thee, Henry, for ever and ever, Amen.' She beamed at him with such radiance that he caught his breath. 'Now it is decided. We will *make* it come about. You can leave Louis to me.'

'I shall have to. We depart for Anjou tomorrow. You will not fail me, my Eleanor, I know that.' Henry took her hand and kissed it. She had intuitively guessed that, plain man as he was, he made such courtly gestures but rarely, and prized it all the more for that.

'I have made up my mind,' she declared. 'Nothing shall stand in our way. But there must be the strictest secrecy. We must give Louis no clue that we intend to wed until the deed is accomplished.'

'You speak sense, for he would be bound to forbid it,' Henry commended her. 'He distrusts me as it is, for my fiefs encircle his royal demesne on most sides. I could be his greatest enemy. The prospect of my acquiring rich Aquitaine too would give him apoplexy!' He paused, frowning. 'You do realise that our marrying without his permission, as our overlord, could mean war?'

'I do,' Eleanor said calmly. 'Yet which side would have the greater chance of victory? There would be no contest. The kingdom of France is small and weak compared with the might of Aquitaine, Poitou and Normandy.'

'Might is one thing, right another,' Henry reminded her. 'Many will support Louis out of a sense of moral duty. They will argue that we acted with the greatest provocation, not to mention discourtesy. Yet if you are willing to take the risk, my Lady, how could I gainsay you?' His eyes were twinkling in anticipation of a fight with Louis.

'Some things are worth fighting for,' Eleanor declared. 'I am not afraid.'

'God, I love you,' Henry breathed, and crushed her beneath him once more.

'Go with God,' Eleanor said as, wrapping a cloak over her nudity, she kissed Henry farewell at the door of her chamber in the lightening of the sky before the dawn. 'I will send to you as soon as I am free, then I will ride south to my capital at Poitiers. Join me there as soon as you can, if you would be married to me.'

'I will not fail you,' Henry promised. 'You may count on me. I live for the day.' Again, he raised her hand to his lips.

'I do not know how I shall bear being apart from you,' Eleanor told him.

'It is only for a short time. Think on our three nights of love, and know that I will be thinking of them too, and longing for more.'

After Henry had departed, slipping into the early morning mist in search of his tethered horse, Eleanor huddled her cloak close around her and prayed fervently for a happy outcome.

'Home,' she breathed, 'I want to go home. I want this exile to end, to be among my own people, where I am loved. And with Henry FitzEmpress by my side, as Aquitaine's Duke. Together, we will usher in a new golden age. It would be joy beyond what I could ever have wished for. Dear God, hear my prayer! Oh, hear my prayer!'

2   The Loire Valley, September 1151

'I am planning a final assault on England, Father,' Henry announced as he and Geoffrey rode home along the banks of the mighty Loire, a posse of men-at-arms at their heels. It was a blazingly warm day, their clothes were sticking to them, and sweat lathered their horses. 'I have summoned my good barons of Normandy to a council of war at Angers next week.' He outlined his plans enthusiastically.

'You have done well, my son,' Geoffrey said, clapping him on the shoulder. 'Your mother will be proud of you.'

They plodded along for a mile or so, discussing the planned offensive, then Geoffrey turned to Henry, his face suddenly grave.

'I trust you have heeded my advice regarding Queen Eleanor,' he said.

'Yes,' Henry answered shortly. It was obvious that he was lying.

Geoffrey was silent.

'Nothing good could come of it,' he said at length.

'So you said, Father!' Henry retorted.

Geoffrey was silent. Beneath his hat, in which he sported his customary adornment of a broom flower, the *planta genista* after which his descendants would one day be named, he was sweating profusely.

'God, it's hot,' he said, wiping his brow. Henry, perspiring too, gazed ahead across the flat, wide plains of the Loire Valley.

'Do you fancy a swim?' he asked. 'It would cool us down. The river is shallow at Château-du-Loir, not far from here.'

'I should like that,' said Geoffrey wearily. 'And I think our escort will appreciate it too.'

At the appointed place, they dismounted and began stripping off their clothes. The men-at-arms flung themselves full-length beneath the trees to sleep in the shade, or raided their saddle-bags for food and drink. One or two disappeared into the trees to relieve themselves. The sun blazed down on the dry grass, where crickets sang in chorus and lizards darted hither and thither.

Naked, Geoffrey and Henry raced to the water's edge, then plunged into the river, swimming powerfully out into the slug-gish current. Laughing, they splashed each other vigorously, then wrestled in the rippling water. Henry was surprised to find his father's muscles iron-hard – not bad for an old man of thirty-eight, he thought. He had glimpsed too Geoffrey's impressive manhood, and wondered seriously for the first time if his father had indeed been speaking the truth about knowing Eleanor carnally, and if he had, whether he had satisfied her as well as he, Henry, had done.

Their horseplay abandoned, they swam a couple of widths of the river, then dragged themselves onto the shore, where they sat awhile in the heat, drying off, before donning their clothes.

'We will need to find a place to spend the night,' Geoffrey said. 'I should send the scouts ahead. My castle of Le Lude is at Sarthe, not far off. Let us make for there.'

After bestirring the castellan and his staff to action, they were comfortably accommodated in the fortress. Geoffrey called for a meal, then sat down at the board with Henry and their entourage to enjoy it. Lifting a silver goblet of sweet Anjou wine, he toasted the success of Henry's planned assault on England.

'I cannot fail,' Henry assured him expansively. The wine had made him bold and over-confident. He noticed his father looked flushed, but attributed it to the heat, although it was cooler in the stone fastness of the castle. Then Geoffrey waved away the plump roasted fowl, saying that he seemed to have little appetite for food in this weather. A little later, Henry, wolfing up the last of his own dinner, felt the first stirring of concern as the Count rejected a proffered bowl of fruit, then suddenly gripped the edge of the table, shuddering.

'Are you ill, Father?' he asked anxiously. Geoffrey had never, to his knowledge, known a day's sickness in his life.

'A touch of fever, my son. It is nothing.' He sounded breathless.

Henry placed his calloused palm on Geoffrey's brow. It was burning.

'I knew I should not have gone swimming in the heat,' his father said, attempting a smile. 'I must have caught a chill. It has come on suddenly.'

'You should go to bed, Sire,' Henry advised.

'I will,' Geoffrey agreed, but when he tried to get to his feet, he had not the strength, and slumped heavily against the table. Henry jumped up, in unison with four men-at-arms, and together they manhandled the sick man up the stone spiral staircase to the bedchamber above, where they laid him heavily on the fur coverlet that was spread across the wooden bed.

By now he was shivering violently, his body hot to the touch, his hands icy.

'He were a fool to go swimming in that river,' one soldier commented.

Henry glared at him. 'Strip him,' he commanded.

'Are you bloody mad?' the soldier asked him. 'He should be wrapped up warm.'

'He's warm enough. He needs to cool down,' Henry insisted. 'Get his clothes off.' Begrudgingly, the men complied, leaving Geoffrey wearing only his *braies* for modesty's sake.

'Now, fetch a basin of water and cloths,' Henry rapped. The men departed, muttering that their young lord had gone daft, and would be the death of the Count, but they complied with his orders nonetheless.

Sponging down Geoffrey's burning body, a task he took readily upon himself, for he loved his father, Henry willed him to get better.

'You are strong, Sire. You must hold fast!'

Geoffrey lay there listlessly, his eyes glazed with fever. He was muttering something, and Henry leaned down to listen. Most of it was unintelligible, but he could make out the words 'Don't, I beseech you' and 'Eleanor'. Grimly, he understood what his father was saying, and still he chose to ignore him. These were just the ramblings of a sick man.

Henry watched beside Geoffrey all night as the fever raged; he did his best to keep him cool, and turned a deaf ear to his mumblings. In the shadows, the men-at-arms kept vigil also, shaking their heads at his unorthodox treatment. But Henry had learned his wisdom from his old tutor, Master Matthew of Loudun, a very sage man who had taught him much when he was living in England, at Bristol, not just from books, but all sorts of practical knowledge. These uneducated soldiers had never had the benefit of Master Matthew's learning. His father would live, he knew it.

But Geoffrey grew worse, not better, and Henry spent much of the second night bargaining with God. If He would spare his father, then Henry would renounce Eleanor. He meant it at the time, although he had no idea as to how he could bear to give her up. God, it seemed, was listening, though, and as the sun rose, Geoffrey opened his eyes, from which the wildness had fled, and spoke lucidly for the first time since his collapse.

'My son,' he said, his face pale beneath the tan, 'will you swear that, if and when you become king of England, you will give my counties of Anjou and Maine to your brother Geoffrey?'

'Father!' cried Henry, alarmed and outraged, for he had little love for his younger siblings. 'First, you are *not* dying, so this is no time for swearing such oaths. And second, you are asking me to swear away my patrimony. I cannot do it, nor should you require it of me.'

'Boy, I *am* dying,' Geoffrey said hoarsely. 'I feel it in my bones. And I order that my body must lie unburied until you swear to do what I ask.'

'But Father, Anjou and Maine should be mine by right of birth, as your oldest son,' Henry protested.

'You have Normandy, and you will, God willing, have England.' Geoffrey's voice was weakening. 'Is that not enough? Can you not humour your dying father?'

'No,' Henry declared firmly. 'I am sorry, I cannot, for it is an unjust request.'

Geoffrey looked at him sadly.

'Then will you at least promise not to pursue the matter of the French queen? I ask only because I fear for the safety of your soul. I am done with earthly concerns.'

'I have renounced her,' Henry said truthfully, knowing that, if his father died, he would be released from that vow, God not having kept *His* part of the bargain.

'Then I can die partly content,' Geoffrey croaked, his breath coming now in shallow gasps.

'Father, do not die!' Henry cried in panic, grasping the sick man's hands and rubbing some warmth into them, then recoiling horrified as they fell limply from his fingers and Geoffrey's eyes glazed over. 'Father! Father!' He burst into noisy tears.

The soldiers, heads bowed in grief, for the Count had been a good lord to them, knelt by the bed in respect for the passing of a soul; after a moment, a dazed Henry knelt with them. It took a moment more before he realised that he was now not only duke of Normandy, but also count of Anjou and Maine, and master of a quarter of the land of France.

*

Later, Henry stood beside his father's sheeted body, which still lay on the bed on which he had died.

'He has paid his debt to Nature,' he told his men, 'and yet I cannot order his burial because I would not swear to disinherit myself.'

'But it would be a disgrace to leave your father's body to lie rotting here in this heat,' cried the castellan, knowing full well that the ever-restless Henry would soon be on his way, leaving him to deal with the problem.

'You must bury him, Sire,' the soldiers urged. 'You must swear now to what you would not swear before. You cannot leave him to stink the place out.'

'Very well,' Henry agreed, almost weeping in frustration. 'I vow to give Anjou and Maine to my brother Geoffrey. Does that satisfy you? Now let us go to Le Mans to make arrangements for my father's burial in the abbey of St Julien.' And then, he added to himself, vow or no vow, I will take firm possession of Anjou and Maine and secure the allegiance of my vassals there before setting my sights on England – and the crown that is my right. And I will marry Eleanor, with Louis' approval or without it.

3   Paris, September 1151

'Louis, you must listen to me,' Eleanor said suddenly, as they sat alone at supper in her chamber. The servants, having placed spiced rabbit, girdle bread, fruit and hard cheese on the table, had left them alone in the flickering candlelight.

Louis turned his fair head with its shorn hair towards his wife; he had cut off his beautiful long locks in penance after the burning of Vitry. There was sadness in his eyes. He knew he had lost her, this beautiful woman who had strangely captured his heart but never his body, and he feared to hear her say the words that would make the break final.

'We have known, you and I, for a long time, that there are serious doubts about the validity of our marriage,' Eleanor said carefully. A great deal hung on the outcome of this conversation, and she was determined not to let her inbred impetuousness ruin everything.

Louis' heart plummeted like a sinking stone. She looked so fine, sitting there in her bejewelled blue gown, with that glorious cloud of hair rippling over her shoulders. He could not believe she was asking him to renounce her.

'Pope Eugenius himself blessed and confirmed our union when we were in Rome,' he said quietly. 'Had you forgotten that?'

'How could I forget it?' Eleanor asked, shrinking inwardly at the memory of the beaming Pontiff beseeching them to set aside their differences and their bitterness, and then – it had been hideously embarrassing – showing them into that sumptuous bedchamber with its silken hangings and ornamental bed, and urging them to make good use of it. And they had done so, God help them, with Louis taking his usual fumbling, apologetic approach. Little Alix, now a year old, had been the result. But Louis had not touched Eleanor since. She wondered what all those French barons who blamed her for her failure to bear a son would have to say about that.

'Others, of great wisdom, have different opinions,' she said carefully, reaching for some grapes. 'Abbot Bernard for one. The Bishop of Laon for another. Bernard is adamant that our marriage is forbidden. He asks why you are so scrupulous about consanguinity when it comes to others, when everyone knows that you and I are fourth cousins. He told me he would speak to you.'

Louis' brows furrowed; he was inwardly quailing at the prospect of Bernard hectoring him yet again. He looked at Eleanor helplessly. He had stopped eating. He could not face another mouthful.

'Can't you see – God Himself has made His displeasure clear,' Eleanor went on earnestly. 'He has withheld the blessing of a son, an heir to France. Our daughters cannot inherit this kingdom, you know that as well as I. Will you risk your immortal soul, Louis, to stay in this marriage?'

'No, my Lady. I cannot fight you any more,' he said sadly. 'It seems I must heed the good Abbot's exhortations, even though they run contrary to my own wishes.' A tear trickled down his cheek. 'Did you ever love me?' he asked plaintively.

'It is because of the love I bear you that I fear for your immortal soul,' Eleanor told him, congratulating herself on this spontaneous response that so neatly side-stepped his question. 'And I fear for my own soul too.' She leaned forward. 'Louis, we must part. There is no help for it.'

The King continued to sit there in his high-backed chair, weeping silently.

'You have ever had your way of me, Eleanor,' he said at length. 'Yet have you thought what our separation will mean for me? I will lose Aquitaine, that jewel in the French crown.'

'You could never hold it,' she reminded him, cutting a sliver of cheese. 'You have not the men or the resources. You would be well rid of the responsibility.'

Louis nodded, frowning. 'You speak truth. It has proved a thankless task trying to govern your unruly lords. But do you think you can succeed where I have failed?'

'I know them,' Eleanor said, 'and they know and love me. I am their duchess.' She drained her wine goblet.

'They might not love you when you rule against them in one of their interminable disputes.'

'That is a risk any prince must take,' Eleanor replied.

'You will remarry, of course,' Louis stated. Looking at her, in all her vital beauty, he could not bear the thought of her as another man's wife. It was unendurable. She had been his prize, his ideal and, he had to admit it, his torment. She was so vital and strong, whereas he knew himself to be a poor apology for a king – and a man. He could not help it: he was afraid of the sins of the flesh. He knew he had failed Eleanor in that regard, and that that was why she wanted her freedom. He understood, of course – he had even forgiven her for her dalliance (he hoped fervently it had been nothing more) with her uncle, Raymond of Antioch, during the crusade – but he could only deplore her craving for sensual pleasures. It was what had always repelled the saintly Abbot Bernard, and Louis' old tutor and counsellor, Abbot Suger. If only Eleanor would think more on the things of the spirit rather than of the flesh . . .

'I will weigh everything carefully before committing myself to marriage again,' she was saying in a non-committal tone.

'You cannot seriously be thinking of ruling alone?' Louis asked, shocked. 'You will need a protector, a strong, wise man who will govern in your name. And one, I might remind you, who is loyal to me and would not seek to abuse his power.' Which, he thought to himself, is probably asking for the moon.

'I had thought of that,' she said evenly, 'which is why I am making no hasty decision. This has to be resolved in everyone's best interests.'

There was an uncomfortable silence. Eleanor was holding her breath, waiting.

'Then it seems I must grant your wish,' Louis capitulated. She tried to look suitably sorrowful.

'I wish it could have been otherwise,' she said gently, reaching across to lay her hand on his.

'You cannot know how deeply I wish that,' her husband replied, removing his hand and pushing his plate away, sickened at the sight of the uneaten meat congealing in its thick sauce. 'There is but one thing I ask of you, for the sake of my pride, as a king and as a man.'

'Yes?' Eleanor responded warily.

'That you allow me to initiate proceedings. Never let it be said that the King of France was abandoned by his wife.'

'I agree,' Eleanor said, biting back the retort that she was not really his wife. There was no point in making matters worse by sparring. She had got what she wanted.

'There is another thing,' Louis went on. 'I take it you have thought of our daughters.'

Eleanor *had* thought. Those two beautiful little girls with their blonde curls and wide blue eyes. Every time she looked at Marie and Alix, she marvelled that she herself had helped to create them. She loved them, of course, yet had been constrained to do so from a distance. They had never seemed like hers anyway. As the daughters of France, they had been given over at birth to a gaggle of nurses and servants, and she had not been involved in their daily care. They were far closer to Thomasine, their Lady Mistress, than they ever had been to their mother. She had rarely seen her children, and consequently had established no close bond with them.

Yet there had been precious moments, as when her daughters twined their soft arms around her neck, resting their downy little heads against her cheek as she told them stories of fairies and demons, or sang them lays of the south, learned in her girl-hood; but these had come rarely. And of course, it was better so, for one day, not far distant, those little girls would leave France for ever to be married to great lords or princes. It was the way of the world, and she had known from the first that it would not do to allow herself to become too attached to them, for she might never see them again afterwards.

For all that, she was hoping that she might have a chance to enjoy many more sweet moments with her daughters before that inevitable parting, and the opportunity to forge a closer bond with them.

'Yes, I have given them much thought,' she told Louis. 'How could I not? Marie and Alix are flesh of my flesh, and very dear to me. How will it be if I take them with me to Aquitaine, then send them back to you in a few years when you have found husbands for them?'

'Eleanor,' frowned Louis, his voice cold, 'have you forgotten that Marie and Alix are princesses of France? Their place is here, in France, with me, the King their father. My barons would never agree to them going with you.'

Eleanor blanched. 'Louis, they are but six years and one year in age. I am their mother.'

'You should have thought of that when you pressed for an annulment!' Louis said reprovingly.

'I did think of it, constantly! Is it my fault that we are too near in blood? Louis, I beg of you . . .'

'Is it not enough that I am to be deserted by the wife I love? Should I lose my children too? I tell you, Eleanor, no court in Christendom would award you custody of them, and it would kill me to have you take them away.' There were tears in Louis' eyes; his pain was not all on account of his daughters.

'So you would deprive them of their mother?' Eleanor persisted.

'They will have a stepmother before long. You said that I must remarry, remember? And I will be expected to, for the sake of the succession.'

'I realise that, but they are my children too!' Eleanor cried. 'Do not deprive me of them, I beg of you.'

'Eleanor, you know, as do I, that this is not about consanguinity,'

Louis replied sadly. 'You want your freedom, I have long been aware of that. Who is doing the depriving here?'

'I never intended that, God knows,' she sobbed, sinking to her knees. 'I know you love our girls.' They were both weeping now.

'As usual, you never think things through, Eleanor,' Louis said, resisting the urge to kneel down and comfort her. 'You just act impetuously, causing a lot of grief. I loved you – God help me, I love you still – and I feel for you. But on this issue I will not – nay, I cannot – bend. Princesses of France must be reared in France. The people would expect it. Besides, you left Marie for more than two years to go on the crusade. You insisted on coming with me, as I recall.'

'It grieved me to leave her, you must believe that. But I *had* to accompany you, Louis. My vassals would not accept you as their leader. Besides, I rarely saw Marie anyway. She did not need me. Neither of my daughters needs me. It is I who need time to get to know them, to make up to them for what I have not been.'

'Alas, I cannot grant you that,' Louis said. 'Be realistic, and understand my position.' There was a pause, a heartbeat, as his gaze held hers. 'You could always reconsider.'

'You know that I cannot,' Eleanor told him. She was trembling. The prospects of her freedom, her return to Aquitaine and a life with Henry of Anjou, not to mention the manifold benefits their marriage would bring, were too precious to her to give them up, but she had now been made devastatingly aware of just how high a price she was to pay for them. Desperately, she conjured up Henry's leonine face in her mind, trying to blot out the plaintive image of those two sweet, fair-haired little girls.

Louis shook his head. 'What a mess. We made our marriage with such high hopes.'

'We did our best,' Eleanor consoled, her mind still fixed fervently on Henry. 'But God's law must prevail.'

'I will speak to my bishops,' Louis said wearily. 'Then we must attend to the practicalities.'

'You mean the transfer of Aquitaine to me?' Eleanor asked sharply.

'Yes. There will be a peaceful withdrawal of my royal officials and French garrisons. We will go there together and oversee it. Your vassals shall attend you.'

'All those defences you built must be dismantled,' Eleanor insisted. 'My people resent them.'

'It shall be done,' Louis agreed.

Eleanor rose and went to look out of the narrow window – barely more than an arrow slit – across the broad Seine and the huddled rooftops of Paris. Above them, the inky sky was studded with stars – those same stars under which Henry of Anjou was living, breathing, waiting . . . She caught her breath suddenly, certain that she had made the right decision. She must suppress her sadness, for there was no other way for her. Her daughters were well cared for, and would barely miss her; she must love them from a distance, as she always had – except that the distance would be further. Her own future was mapped out by destiny, and there was no escaping it, even if she wanted to. She had only to contain herself in patience for some while longer, and in the meantime, she would be returning to Aquitaine, to reclaim her great inheritance. She was going home, home to the sweet, lush lands of the south, the lands of mighty rivers and verdant hills, of rich wines and fields of sunflowers; where people spoke her native tongue, the *langue d'oc*, which would sound as music after the clumsy, outlandish dialect they spoke in the north. She could not wait to be once more among her own people, quarrelsome and often violent though they were. It meant more to her to be duchess of Aquitaine than it ever had to be queen of France, or queen of the whole world, for that matter.

4   Beaugency-sur-Loire, 1152

The whispering was hushed in the vaulted hall as the princes of the Church took their seats on the stone benches, their rich robes settling in swathes of purple and black around them.

Eleanor, enthroned above them on the dais, glanced at Louis, who was staring straight ahead, his handsome features set in stern resolution. He would betray by no frown or grimace what he was feeling inside, she knew. His pride would not allow it.

It was ten days since this synod of archbishops had first

assembled. The King and Queen had attended on the first day, to plead their case and present genealogical charts showing how they were related within the forbidden degrees. Witnesses had been summoned by Louis to attest to this, and the venerable Archbishop Hugh of Sens, Primate of France, who had convened this ecclesiastical court, had questioned them all at some length, and Louis and Eleanor too, to determine whether or not they were seeking an annulment for pure motives and no other cause. That was certainly the case with the King, the Archbishop had decided – as for the Queen, who knew? Like most churchmen, he neither liked nor approved of her. She was wilful, flighty and headstrong, and France would be well rid of her. Archbishop Hugh had been mightily relieved when the Pope's decision, solicited by Abbot Bernard some weeks earlier, had arrived this morning, and he had been able to reconvene the court. Now he was rising to his feet and unravelling the scroll of parchment in his hands.

'By the authority invested in me by His Holiness Pope Eugenius,' he intoned in his softly moderated voice, 'I pronounce that the plea of consanguinity laid by our lord, King Louis, and the Lady Eleanor, Duchess of Aquitaine, be upheld, and that the marriage between them be deemed null and void.'

As the archbishops murmured their assent, and Abbot Bernard – come here specially to show his support for the annulment – looked on approvingly, Eleanor felt her heart bursting with joy, and elation welling within her. She was free, at last, after all these long years of bondage! She was liberated. In vain, she struggled to keep her face impassive, for it would not be seemly to betray the exultation seething within her. Aquitaine was hers once more. Henry FitzEmpress would be hers . . . She was free.

Bernard of Clairvaux, catching the fleeting smile of triumph on her face, frowned. Heaven only knew what this wanton woman would get up to now that she had her release. He thanked God that Louis had put her away, yet trembled at the realisation that now she was at liberty to wreak havoc on the rest of Christendom.

Archbishop Samson of Rheims, whom Louis had appointed to represent Eleanor at the synod and look to her interests, was now standing. He bowed in her direction, cleared his throat, and declared, 'My Lord King has given me assurances that the Lady Eleanor's lands will now be restored to her as she possessed them prior to her marriage. Because this union was entered into in good faith, its issue, the Princesses Marie and Alix, are to be held legitimate, and custody of them is granted to King Louis.'

Eleanor swallowed. She could hardly bear to remember the day, weeks before, when she had said farewell to her daughters. They had been playing with a puppy in their nursery, tying ribbons around his neck, feeding him morsels of meat saved from their dinner, and throwing a woollen ball for him to fetch. They had been impatient of their mother's needy embraces, anxious to get back to the game, and while Marie had looked at Eleanor with a puzzled expression when told that it might be a while before they would see her again, plump little Alix had lost interest and toddled back to the puppy. Eleanor had briefly dropped one final kiss on each blonde head, then resolutely walked out of the chamber, her eyes blind with tears. That had been her worst moment, and she had briefly wavered in her resolve – but not for long. Now she forced herself to think of the present, and heard Archbishop Samson conclude: 'Both parties are free to remarry without hindrance, so long as the Lady Eleanor remains faithful in her allegiance to King Louis as her overlord.'

'I am gratified to see that agreements have been so amicably reached on all issues,' Archbishop Hugh said. 'That being so, I grant the parties a decree of separation.' Eleanor bowed her head, not wanting the world to see the elation in her face. There had been rumours aplenty that Louis was putting her aside because of her adultery, or that she had pushed for this divorce for lascivious reasons. Well, that at least was true, she admitted, but her scruples about the marriage had been long-held, and if Bernard shared them, then she had been right to press for an end to it.

Beside her, Louis was sitting motionless, gripping the arms of his chair. He would not look her way. The court was rising, the archbishops departing in a sedate flurry of purple and furs, making their obeisances to the King as they left, the lawyers and clerks gathering parchments while murmuring to each other of the verdict. It was not every day that a royal marriage was dissolved.

Suddenly, Louis stood up and, without a word, strode after Archbishop Hugh.

'Madame the Duchess!' It was her own archbishop of Bordeaux, stepping into the breach. 'Might I be of service to you in any way?'

Eleanor beamed at him. 'Your Grace, I am grateful for your tender care of me, and for coming all this way to attend the synod.'

'What will you do now?' the Archbishop enquired.

'I am bound for Poitiers,' Eleanor told him.

'Immediately?'

'Yes. Aquitaine needs a ruler, there is much to be done, and I need to be there without delay.' She had not, of course, confided to him the most important thing she intended to accomplish in Poitiers. For that, she must wait until she was safely back in her domains.

'Then I beg of you, Madame, allow me to escort you there. My men-at-arms will offer you protection. These are dangerous times, and the greatest heiress in Christendom should not be travelling unguarded.'

'Nor will I be,' Eleanor smiled. 'My uncle, the Count of Châtellerault, and my good count of Angoulême, who makes up in loyalty for what he lacks in years, are come with their retinues to bring their duchess home. For your kindness, you are welcome to join forces and travel with us.'

'Thank you, Madame, I will,' the Archbishop said, bowing. He had seen King Louis returning, and diplomatically backed away.

Louis faced her. His grey eyes were clouded with sorrow. Eleanor took his hands.

'This is adieu, my Lord,' she said briskly. 'Not farewell, for I know we will meet again, as overlord and liege. And as friends, I trust and hope.'

Louis could barely speak.

'Forgive me,' he said humbly. 'If I had been a better husband to you, we would not now be taking our leave of each other.'

'Nay,' Eleanor protested, 'it is I who have failed as a wife. I lack the necessary meekness. I know my own faults.' She could afford to be generous now that she was no longer bound in wedlock to this man.

'I wish you well; I want you to know that,' Louis said. 'If ever I can extend good lordship to you, you have only to ask.'

'I thank you,' Eleanor smiled. 'And now I must depart. I have a long journey ahead of me, and wish to cross the Loire by nightfall. Adieu, my Lord. God keep you.'

'And may He have you in His keeping also,' Louis whispered, loosing his hands from Eleanor's. Then he watched as she stepped from the dais, sank before him in a deep curtsey, and walked out of the hall, her two damsels following.

5   Blois and Port-de-Piles, 1152

'Free at last,' Eleanor kept saying to herself, spurring on her horse and cantering south-west across the lush wide valley of the Loire, now lit by the rising moon. She had been saying it for several hours now, ever since they had set off from Beaugency that morning. 'Free. I am free!'

The Archbishop, her lords and her women were following close behind her, huddled in their thick cloaks, and on either side, carrying lighted torches, rode the helmeted men-at-arms who made up her escort. They had long ago lost sight of the sumpter mules and the carts, heavily laden with her personal possessions, so urgent was the need to move ever southwards and put a great distance between her and her party and the kingdom of France. If King Louis got wind of what she was planning, he would certainly send a force to seize her and bring her back. It was unlikely that he *would* get wind of it, of course – she had always been better than he at subterfuge – but even so, she was aware of the pressing need to make haste. And, of course, every league brought her closer to a reunion with Henry.

She had already despatched a messenger to him with the summons he had been waiting for. Now it was imperative that they both get safely and speedily to Poitiers, before the world heard of their intentions. Her lords and the Archbishop were in her confidence: they knew of her bold and daring plan.

Ahead galloped her standard bearer, his fluttering pennant announcing to all who saw it that this way came Eleanor, Duchess of Aquitaine, Countess of Poitou, and – until this morning – Queen of France. The counts had shaken their heads at her boldness in thus proclaiming her identity to the world.

'Madame, you are no longer queen, no longer under royal protection, and therefore at the mercy of any chance adventurer,' they had urged.

'They would not dare,' she had challenged, her green eyes flashing.

'Madame,' they had protested, 'you are no ordinary heiress. You own half this land of the Franks, and there are many, make no doubt, who would risk much to match with you.'

'I am already spoken for,' she declared, in a tone that brooked no further argument. 'He who would dare lay hands on the future wife of Henry FitzEmpress is a fool indeed.' As she said it, she felt a thrill of lust at the memory of Henry's strong hands on her body, hands that would take what they wanted and hold onto it, be it a woman, a duchy, even a kingdom. So she had prevailed, and there it flew, always in her sights, the silk banner embroidered with the lion of Poitou. Her own emblem. She had insisted on it.

'It will be a blessed relief not to have to sleep in that gloomy barn of a bedchamber in Paris,' she smiled at her noble lady-in-waiting, Torqueri de Bouillon, thankful that she would never again have to lie frigidly beside Louis in that great bed, both of them striving to keep as far apart as possible. 'Or with that monk I was married to!' Her smile was impish. She felt like a girl once more, for all her thirty years. And yet, she thought, smiling again and recalling the image that had gazed back at her that very morning from the burnished mirror, she still wore those years lightly: they had barely touched her. She knew she was beautiful, extraordinarily beautiful. Enough courtiers and troubadours had told her so, without flattery. And Louis, of course. He had taken pride in her loveliness, despite himself. She knew she had been his prize possession.

But not prized enough. The smile faded to a frown. She stretched in her saddle, rubbing her aching back and smoothing down her gown, fingers splayed over her tiny waist and slender hips; she could feel her flesh taut beneath the rich samite, unslackened by her two pregnancies. She turned to her lords.

'How far to the river?' she asked.

'A mile at most,' the Count of Châtellerault told her. He pointed ahead. 'Look, that is Blois in the distance.' Eleanor could see tiny pinpoints of light in the darkness, and realised that they must be flares on the château ramparts. There was a bridge across the Loire at Blois, and that was the place they were making for.

'God grant we may cross the bridge unobserved,' Eleanor muttered.

'Madame,' Torqueri said fearfully, her soft voice barely audible on the night wind, 'none of us will rest easy until you are safely back in Poitiers.'

Poitiers! Eleanor thrilled again at the name. Home. To be home at last would be bliss indeed. And when Henry kept his promise . . . She shuddered, seized with another tremor of unbidden desire. She did not fear the dangers of the journey. She would get home safely, she *must* get home . . . She felt herself invincible.

They had brought food to eat on the road. Some hours ago, she had feasted by the wayside on cold capon, white bread and the rich, sweet wine of the region. A simple meal, but delicious fare, appreciated all the more because she was in such a good mood. She was hungry at this moment, but willing to ignore the emptiness in her belly. Food was not her priority just now; they could buy more on the morrow. For the present, they must make all speed.

They were nearing Blois. Above them loomed the dark outline of the Tour de Foix, standing sentinel above the River Loire. There was a horseman galloping towards them in the dim light. It was one of the scouts who had been sent ahead to spy out the land. His mount was lathered with sweat.

'Lady,' he said breathlessly, bowing low in the saddle. 'Go no further! There is a band of armed men riding this way. They bear the device of Count Thibaut of Blois.'

'Perchance my Lord Count wishes to pay his respects and offer us hospitality,' Eleanor replied, a mischievous smile playing about her lips, since she knew that to be most unlikely, for there was bad blood between their families. But that was in the past, and supposedly forgiven and forgotten. We are all meant to be friends now, she thought, grimacing.

'Nay, Lady, by their words, which I overheard, they are planning to lie in wait for us. They were saying something about Count Thibaut having plans for you.'

'Does he indeed?' she replied grimly. 'Of course, he is a widower, so I can well imagine what they are. You have done gallantly to warn me.'

The lords and the captains were eager to be gone; their taut faces betrayed their alarm. This was what they had feared. 'Madame, we cannot risk the bridge. We must go by another way,' the Count of Angoulême urged. 'Now!'

'*À moi!*' Eleanor cried, as her forbears had done many times in the field of battle, and spurred her horse, knowing they must hurry and get away from this place if they wished to avoid disaster. She had no mind to end her days as the Countess of Blois.

Moving by stealth along the river banks, one of Eleanor's captains came upon a barge tethered to a jetty, which he gleefully appropriated. Huddled together in the sanctuary it offered, and almost crushed by such baggage as they could squeeze into the remaining space, Eleanor and her companions uttered not a word as the craft glided swiftly along the river, making its silent way towards Tours. Only when dawn broke did they relax enough to begin a debate as to which way they should now take.

'Let us make south for the Vienne, and cross the Creuse at Port-de-Piles,' Eleanor decided. On the other bank, the men-at-arms were waiting with the Archbishop, having been permitted to cross the bridge at Blois after convincing the guards that they were merely escorting his Grace back to his diocese.

The further south they rode from the Loire, the safer Eleanor felt. But as they neared Port-de-Piles, another scout came hastening towards them.

'Go no further, Lady!' he cried. 'There is an ambush lying in wait for you ahead.'

'God's teeth!' Eleanor swore, as the Archbishop winced. 'Another fortune hunter! Who is it this time?'

'I fear it is young Geoffrey of Anjou, Lady, Duke Henry's brother.'

'That young idiot? He's still wet behind the ears, surely. Well, my good angel, for that you certainly are, we will disappoint him of his quarry. My Lords!' Eleanor turned to the two counts, who were waiting grim-faced in their saddles. 'What do you suggest?'

'We should swing south, Madame, to where we can ford the Vienne, and then make a dash across country for Poitiers.'

'That makes sense,' Eleanor agreed, as the others voiced their approval of the plan, and the weary Archbishop craved leave to make his own way to Bordeaux. Having bidden the old man a quick, affectionate farewell, she wheeled around her horse and spurred it on once more, smiling to herself as she imagined young Geoffrey's fury when he discovered that she had eluded him.

'How enraged Henry will be when he learns that his little brother has plotted to supplant him!'

6   Poitiers, 1152

As the flat swathes of the Loire Valley had given way to the great plain of Poitou with its lush countryside, scattered castles, solid Romanesque churches and stone longhouses with red-tiled roofs, Eleanor's sense of elation burgeoned. It was the sight of those red tiles that had first moved her. You never saw such things in the dreary north. Soon, she would be home!

She had loosed her hair, as a gesture to her newly unwed status, and luxuriated in it streaming behind her in the warm wind that blew across from the Atlantic sea, which lay some miles to the west. Straight-backed she rode, her eager eyes on the road ahead, the road that led to her city of Poitiers. It could not be far now. She had donned her crimson *bliaut* with its fitted bodice and sweeping, gold-embroidered skirts for her home-coming, and a splendid blue mantle. And yes, there it was ahead, majestic on its promontory above the River Clain, her fair city! Here, the Romans had come in ancient times; here, Charles Martel had vanquished the Saracens long centuries before; here, in a fine church within the walls, lay the blessed relics of St Radegonde, the queenly patron saint of Poitiers. And there were her people, bursting through the gates, clamouring to greet her, their duchess come back to her own.

How they cheered as she trotted at the head of her escort through the packed streets, her standard going before her! They called down blessings on her for her beauty, and because she was one of them, and had booted out the hated French. And as she was carried into the great cathedral of St Pierre, there to give thanks for her safe homecoming, Eleanor vowed to herself that, with God's help, she would henceforth dedicate her life to her people, and never again subject them to the hateful rule of a foreigner.

After Mass on Easter Sunday, the Duchess made her way in procession to the spacious ducal apartments in the Maubergeonne Tower of the palace of Poitiers, and took her place in the high chair of her ancestors in the circular council chamber. Colourful banners hung high on the sandy stone walls, which had been crudely painted with scenes of long-past battles. The chief vassals of Aquitaine, who had gathered for the festival at the Duchess's summons, seated themselves at the long table before her.

Their eyes were on her, their newly returned duchess; they were waiting to find out what she would be like as their liege lady, and – more importantly – when she would marry. None of them had even considered the possibility of her ruling alone: she was a woman, and women were weak creatures, not fitted to wield dominion over men. Yet she was her father's daughter and they were loyal to her, most of them after their fashion, and would remain so provided she did not take a husband who would subvert their autonomy and interfere too much in the affairs of the duchy. Having just got rid of the hated French, they were unwilling to stomach another foreign interloper. But the Duchess must marry and bear heirs, of course, and she must have a strong man as her protector: they accepted that. They had all been told of her plans to marry Henry of Anjou, and were agreed that the young duke of Normandy – now also count of Anjou and Maine after his father's death – did not pose too much of a threat to them, however formidable his reputation. He would more than likely be preoccupied with this northern kingdom of England, which looked set to be his too one day – and he was young enough to be moulded to their will.

Eleanor was surveying them all as they waited for the feasting to begin. She knew, from her father, and from bitter experience, that her vassals were all but ungovernable. Away from the courts of her chief cities of Poitiers and Bordeaux, entrenched in their remote castles and hilltop fastnesses, they could thumb their noses at ducal jurisdiction. So it was best to sweeten them now by clever diplomacy and gifts – and the Lord knew she had been generous enough with those already – to keep them friendly.

'Sirs,' she began, her voice low and mellifluous, 'I have asked you here formally to inform you of the annulment of my union with King Louis, and to approve my coming marriage. You all know that I have consented to wed the Duke of Normandy, and that I must do so without the sanction of King Louis, who is overlord of us both, for he would surely refuse it.' A mischievous smile played around her lips. The lords looked at her approvingly: they understood such underhand dealings, and their resentment of the French was such that they were more than happy to overlook this blatant breach of feudal etiquette.

'Our wedding must be arranged without delay, or it might never take place at all,' Eleanor told them. 'This marriage will seriously undermine the power of France, and if King Louis discovered my plans, even he, weakling that he is, might fight. Once Henry and I are wedded and bedded, he can do nothing about it.'

'You must send again to the Duke, Madame,' her uncle, Hugh of Châtellerault, urged. 'What if your messenger has been intercepted?'

'I will despatch envoys today,' Eleanor promised, inwardly willing Henry to come soon, and wondering why he had not responded to her first message. 'And now to other business. I am resolved to cancel and annul all acts and decrees made by King Louis in Aquitaine.' The lords looked at her approvingly. So far, she was doing well. 'And,' she went on, 'I intend to replace them by charters issued in my own name, and to renew all grants and privileges. My lieges, there is much work to be done, but before we get down to business, you are my guests, and we have much to celebrate.'

At her signal, the servitors entered the chamber in a line, each bearing succulent-smelling dishes: mussels and eels in garlic and wine, salty mutton, fat chickens, the tasty local beans known as *mojettes*, ripe goat's cheeses and figs. All were offered in turn to the Duchess and her lords, as the ewerers came around the table with tall flagons of red wine. Then a toast was drunk to the happy conclusion of the marriage negotiations and the future prosperity of Poitou. Tomorrow might bring war, but for now, they would enjoy the feast!

It was May, with the palace gardens in colourful bloom, when Henry FitzEmpress rode proudly into Poitiers to claim his bride. Word of his coming had been brought ahead to Eleanor, and she was waiting with her chief vassals to greet him in the *Grande Salle* of the palace, the magnificent arcaded 'Hall of Lost Footsteps' as it was popularly known, because the chamber was so long and the beamed roof so high that the sound of a foot-fall barely carried at all.

Eleanor knew she looked her most beautiful: she had donned a vivid blue trailing *bliaut* of the finest silk tissue, patterned all over with gold *fleurs-de-lis*, and so cunningly cut and girdled that it revealed every seductive curve of her voluptuous figure. Over it, she wore a shimmering sleeveless mantle of gold, banded with exquisite embroidery. Shining gold bracelets adorned her arms, and from her ears hung pendants of glittering precious stones. Still defying the convention that constrained matrons to wear wimples covering their hair, she had on her head just a delicate circlet of wrought gold encrusted with pearls and tiny rubies, which left her copper tresses cascading freely over her shoulders and down her back. Her eyes were shining with excitement, her lips parted in anticipation . . . This marriage that she had dreamed of, with its endless, exciting possibilities, was soon to be a reality; and tonight, she would lie with Henry. At last! Her body trembled at the prospect.

And here he was, striding purposefully into the vast hall, attired in his habitual riding clothes – she was already aware that he cared little for fashion or rich robes – and wearing a jubilant smile. The sight of his face suffused her with joy. She would always remember this moment as one of the happiest of her life.

'My Lady!' Henry bowed courteously, then came briskly towards Eleanor as she rose from her throne, and jumped eagerly up the step to the dais. The touch of his flesh as he took hold of her hands set her senses on fire. She had become just a little anxious, as the weeks since their trysts in Paris turned into months, that she had imagined the attraction between them to be greater than it was, and that it would turn out to have been an illusion. That was of no moment, of course, in the making of marriages for policy, for there were powerfully compelling political reasons for this union, regardless of how she or Henry felt. But having known the sweetest passion in his arms, and pleasure that she could not have imagined possible, she thought she would die if she were to be cheated of it. Now, however, her fears had gone, for there was everything she had hoped there would be in Henry's ardent gaze and the firm, possessive grasp of his hands – and in her own response to him.

'I must apologise for my tardiness in coming to you,' Henry told her, as she gestured to him to sit beside her; already, a second throne had been set ready for Aquitaine's future duke. 'A delegation of nobles arrived from England, begging me to delay no longer in making good my claim to the throne. My supporters there are apparently losing patience. Well, I sent to tell them they will have to wait just a while yet. I have more important things to do.' He smiled at her. 'You did wonderfully well!' he said. 'I never looked to marry you so soon.'

'Louis was more amenable than I had expected,' Eleanor told him, her eyes devouring every line of his face.

'He won't be when he knows what we are plotting!' Henry laughed. 'But we can deal with that.'

'Now my lords are waiting to be presented to you,' Eleanor said, and beckoned them to come forward, one by one. They approached warily, eyeing the young Duke of Normandy with speculation. Foremost amongst them were Hugh, Count of Châtellerault, and Raoul de Faye, her mother's brothers: Hugh, serious, stammering and earnest, and the younger Raoul, witty, able, and prepared – to a point – to charm his new master. Then came eighteen-year-old William Taillefer, the handsome Count of Angoulême, so eager to prove himself to the renowned Duke of Normandy in the field and in matters of state; and after him, the loyal and chivalrous Geoffrey de Rançon, Lord of Taillebourg, whom Eleanor had long forgiven for his rash but well-meant actions during the crusade, which had led to the slaughter of seven thousand soldiers and his being sent back home in disgrace by King Louis. Henry had evidently heard of this too, for he was regarding Geoffrey warily as the man made his obeisance.

His wary look darkened to a frown when there knelt before him Hugh de Lusignan and Guy of Thouars, swarthy-skinned and black-haired, two of the most volatile of her vassals, whose notorious reputation was enough to send any overlord reaching for his sword; but they were on their best behaviour today, and observing the courtesies in deference to the Duchess's presence. She knew, though, for Louis had had enough cause to grumble about it, that these men paid only lip-service to their oaths of homage, and that their allegiance to her would go flying out of the window if it ever came between them and some land or fortress they coveted. And by the look on Henry's face, as he bade Hugh and Guy rise and be merry, he needed no warning of their perfidy.

Last, but by no means least, there came the staunch Saldebreuil of Sanzay, Constable of Aquitaine, whom she had appointed her seneschal in reward for his loyalty and staunch service. Henry smiled at him, and slapped him heartily on the shoulder as the good man bent to receive the kiss of greeting.

Eleanor was pleased to see Henry playing his part to perfection, doing his best to win over her lords by deferring to this one's wisdom and experience, or praising that one's renowned prowess in the field of battle or the tourney lists. She was amazed at his store of knowledge, especially of her domains. He had gone to a great deal of trouble to make himself accepted here. And most of them were responding in the proper manner, and saying all the right things. It was the most promising of beginnings.

Later, after the last vassal had gone back to his place and wine had been served, Eleanor led Henry and her courtiers into the gardens, where they could relax in the warm sunshine in the shade of apple and peach trees. As the nobles rested on turf benches and talked of politics and warfare, young gallants sought out the Duchess's damsels and sang songs to them, their eyes bright with the expectation of favours to come later, when the velvet summer night had stolen over the land.

Henry walked with Eleanor beside a flower-filled lawn enclosed by low trellises.

'Tell me, do you miss being a queen?' he enquired, taking her hand.

'Need you ask?' Eleanor countered. 'What I have now' – she waved her hand to indicate her throne, her lords and her surroundings, then looked him directly in the face – 'more than compensates.'

'I will make it up to you a thousandfold,' Henry promised. 'I will make you queen of England, the greatest queen that godforsaken land has ever known, I swear it. And then I will make you the sovereign lady of half Europe!'

'I have all my faith in you,' Eleanor told him, caught up in the heady excitement of this imperial vision, and exulting at the prospect of the glorious future, when all their hopes and ambitions would, God willing, be realised.

'Think of it,' Henry enthused, visibly elated. 'When England is mine, all Christendom from the Scottish border down to the Pyrenees will be under my hand! Louis will be raging with envy, but there will be nothing he can do about it. Our domains will dwarf his beggarly royal demesne.'

Our domains. Those words should have thrilled Eleanor, but coming from Henry's mouth, there was something about them that suddenly unsettled her. For all her need of him, she was suddenly aware that she did not know him well, and it was possible that, in marrying him, she might after all be surrendering her autonomy – and that of her people. Despite the warmth of the day, she felt a little chilled, but resolutely, she suppressed the thought, shocked at herself. They would be a partnership, she and Henry, from first to last, and their aims would be as one. That had been implicit from the first.

'Greatness and power,' Henry was saying, 'lie in land and a ruler's strength. Louis has neither.'

'Yet he is still our overlord,' she reminded him.

'So the fiction goes!' Henry grinned.

'I should be scandalised,' Eleanor smiled.

'Oh, I am sure you are! But remember, my dear love, you are marrying into the Devil's own family. Do not expect us Angevins to be virtuous.'

'How could I, when your brother Geoffrey tried to abduct me on the way down here?'

'What?' Henry almost roared. 'That little rabbit? I'll cut his balls off.'

Eleanor could not suppress a giggle. 'Surely you of all people don't blame him for being an opportunist, my Lord?'

'It's a family trait,' Henry muttered.

'Does our marriage find favour with your Norman lords?' Eleanor asked.

'Yes, and with those of Anjou and Maine. They know it will bring prestige to my domains, and trade too. They are all agog to see you. I sang your praises, never fear.'

'And your mother, the Empress?' Eleanor had heard a lot about the formidable Matilda.

'She is content,' Henry said shortly, with little conviction. 'She thinks it makes sound political sense for us to marry. And you will charm her, I am sure.'

'I look forward to meeting her,' Eleanor replied politely, with equally scant conviction. She wondered if Matilda was aware that her soon-to-be daughter-in-law had made the two-backed beast with her husband Geoffrey.

'I didn't come here to talk about my mother, you know,' Henry grinned. 'I'd rather discuss our immediate plans.' He lowered his voice to a seductive murmur. 'Will you bed with me tonight?'

Eleanor smiled at him, her eyes dark with desire. 'It is what I have been waiting for.'

Henry withdrew from Eleanor and, panting heavily, rolled back on his side, his hand trembling slightly as it sensuously traced the arching curve of her waist, hip and thigh. His eyes held hers, warm in the flickering candlelight. He bent forward and kissed her gently on the lips.

'I have dreamed of this,' he said breathlessly, 'through all those dreadful months of waiting. God, I hated having to wait. You have been in my heart and in my loins. I ached for you.'

'Did you ever have doubts?' Eleanor asked, resting her cheek against the curling hair that crested his broad chest, feeling his heart pounding beneath his skin.

'Not for a moment. Did you?'

'I did wonder if I had dreamed some of it,' she murmured. 'It was so unbelievable, what happened between us.'

'In the future, troubadours will sing of us and our love,' Henry predicted. Eleanor thrilled once more to hear him speak of love. She raised herself up on one elbow, her nipples teasing his ribs.

'They certainly will!' she laughed. 'Is it not quite shocking for a husband and wife to love each other? Marriage, according to our poets, sounds the death-knell to love.'

'It will not be so with us,' Henry vowed firmly.

'How could it be?' Eleanor rejoined, leaning over to kiss him and trailing her hair all over his body. Then she lay down on her side, gazing again into his eyes.

'This is bliss after bedding Louis,' she told him. 'I always had to beg him to make love to me, if only to get an heir, and then he was down on his knees praying both before and after he had done the dread deed. I feel as if I have come alive. I am free of all that! Oh, the joy of it!' She kissed Henry ardently, her tongue darting mischievously into his mouth. 'In France, I was not free. They didn't want me interfering, as they called it, in their politics. I was relegated to playing chess with my ladies, or embroidery, or telling riddles, for God's sake. I have a brain, but they wouldn't let me use it. Tell me that we won't have a conventional marriage, Henry. I couldn't bear that.'

'How could we?' he replied lazily. 'We are not conventional people.'

'You are aware that I am giving up my new-found freedom to marry you,' Eleanor ventured. 'I hope you won't forget that I am sovereign duchess of Aquitaine, even though you have the right to rule here as my husband? And to rule me – if I let you.' Her smile was full of mischief.

Henry concealed his surprise at her words and regarded her wickedly. 'That is any husband's right, as well you know! Once we're married, my fine beauty, I might shut you up in a tower or beat you if you prove to be disagreeable or deny me your bed!'

'Then I'll not go through with it!' Eleanor threatened, giggling. 'I'll be your mistress instead. You won't get an inch of my domains!' For answer, Henry began tickling her until she squealed for mercy. Then he pinioned her down and kissed her hungrily.

'At this moment, I wouldn't really care, so long as I can have you,' he muttered. 'Louis was mad to spurn you, or let you go,' he went on hoarsely, mounting her a second time, his purpose clearly urgent. 'But his loss is my gain: you are the rarest and most beautiful woman I have ever known. Now say you'll marry me, or I won't give you what you so clearly want!' The tip of his penis was teasing her sex, sending her into spasms.

'I'll marry you, on condition you allow me my sovereignty,' Eleanor demanded breathlessly.

'God, you drive a hard bargain,' Henry gasped, thrusting into her.

'Say it!' she insisted, desire flooding through her: this sparring between them was decidedly erotic. But Henry was now too preoccupied to say anything, so pressing was his need, and when he was spent, they both drifted to sleep in each other's arms, his promise ungiven.

The sun's dazzling rays were streaming through the tall windows of St Pierre's Cathedral in Poitiers. They bathed in golden light the man and woman kneeling before the high altar, receiving the Church's benediction upon their marriage. Eleanor was fully aware, as Henry took her hand and raised her to her feet, that this was an important moment in history, and that she was a participant in a deed that would have far-reaching consequences for her, for her new husband, for their descendants, and for the world at large. For this day would see the founding of an empire that promised to be one of the greatest in Christendom. The prospect was breathtaking – and a little chastening. She knew that a heavy task lay ahead of them both.

This day was also the start of a marriage – and of her cherished partnership of princes. Walking back along the nave of the cathedral with Henry, her vassals saluting and bowing as they passed, she knew she looked her radiant best, slim and seductive in her cornflower-blue *bliaut*, scarlet mantle and gauzy white veil held in place by her richly chased ducal crown. Henry too was crowned, with the coronet of the dukes of Normandy. He looked splendid in profile, straight-nosed, neatly bearded, his wavy red hair springing abundantly from his noble brow. His flushed, freckled face wore a triumphant look, and his hand was grasping hers possessively. She was his now, and since they were already one flesh, no one could divide them.

It pleased her to know that, thanks to her cunning, her magnificent Henry was now duke of Aquitaine and – at just nineteen – the mightiest prince in Europe. Together, she knew, they would make a stir in the world, greater than any royal couple before them. And as they emerged from the cathedral to acknowledge the rapturous acclaim of her people, she was again convinced of the rightness of it all – that she had made her bargain with destiny.

That night, Henry took her with even greater ardour than before, stripping away inhibitions and boundaries, and launching them on a long and sensual journey of ever-greater discovery.

'Never hold back!' he demanded. 'I want everything you can give me.'

'I am my Lord's to command now,' Eleanor answered willingly, and in that moment meant it.

'Ours is a marriage of lions,' he breathed in her ear. 'Did it occur to you? You have a lion as the symbol of Poitou, and my symbol is also a lion, inherited from my grandfather, King Henry of England. They called him "the Lion of Justice", but he's supposed to have thought up the idea after receiving the gift of a lion for his menagerie in the Tower of London.'

'I like that,' Eleanor murmured, snuggling closer to him in the warmth of the feather mattress. 'A marriage of lions. It has a chivalric ring to it.'

'It is apt in more ways than one, I think,' her husband observed as his arms tightened about her. 'Eh, my Eleanor? We are neither of us meek and mild, but strong, audacious characters, brave as lions ourselves.'

'With you beside me, I will never know fear,' she told him, pressing her smooth cheek to his bearded one, revelling in the masculine scent of him.

'We will do well together, my fair lioness!' Henry laughed, and drew her close to him once more.

7   Abbey of Fontevrault, 1152

It was with a glad heart that Eleanor paid a visit to Fontevrault in the month after her wedding.

'This abbey is a place especially dear to me,' she told Henry. 'It was founded at my grandmother's behest, and is dedicated to Our Lady.'

Henry nodded approvingly. He had heard of the fame of this double house of monks and nuns under the rule of an abbess, which had become a finishing school and retreat for royal and aristocratic ladies, and a haven of piety and contemplative prayer. It was a most unusual establishment in that its founder, a renowned Breton scholar called Robert d'Arbrissel, had wished to enhance the status of women, and had even dared to assert that they were superior to men in many ways. Leaving that strange notion aside, Henry could understand why Eleanor thought highly of Fontevrault. He had a very good opinion of it himself. It was one of the greatest bastions of piety and faith in all Christendom.

The abbey lay by a fountain, in lush woodland on the banks of the River Vienne in north Poitou, near the border with Anjou. As Eleanor entered its lofty white church, which was distinguished by a quality of light and space seen nowhere else on Earth, and which had been beautified with simple, soaring columns and elegant triforium arcades, she felt uplifted and suffused with thankfulness. The Abbess, Isabella of Anjou, who was Henry's aunt, kissed her warmly in welcome, conducted her through the tranquil cloisters and ushered her into her spacious house, which was attached to the adjoining convent of Le Grand Moutier, where the nuns lived. Almond milk, pears and sweetmeats were brought, and the two women, who had immediately felt a mutual respect and affection, sat down to enjoy some congenial conversation.

'To what do we owe the pleasure of this visit, my Lady?' Abbess Isabella asked. She was a plump, motherly woman in her mid-forties with the florid Angevin colouring, and had ruled her community for four years.

'It is a great joy to me to come to Fontevrault at this time, Mother,' Eleanor said. 'I have much for which to be grateful to God. My heart is so full, and I wish to offer thanks for the great happiness He has bestowed on me in my marriage, and for making me the instrument through which unity and peace might be achieved in Christendom.'

'We must all give thanks to God for that,' the Abbess declared. Intelligent and perceptive woman that she was, she was well aware of the hoped-for outcome of the Duchess's union with Henry FitzEmpress. 'You will join us for dinner in our refectory afterwards?' she invited.

'Most certainly, I thank you,' Eleanor smiled. 'But there is another purpose to my visit, Mother. After my marriage to my Lord Henry, I felt that divine inspiration was leading me to visit this sacred congregation. It feels as if I have been guided by God to Fontevrault, and while here, I intend to approve and confirm all the charters and gifts that my forefathers have given to this house. If you will have this drawn up on a parchment, Mother, I will affix my seal. It is a new one.' Proudly, she drew it from the embroidered purse hanging at her girdle and showed it to the Abbess. It portrayed Eleanor as Duchess of both Aquitaine and Normandy. 'See, I am holding a bird perched upon a cross; it is a sacred symbol of sovereignty.'

'If I may say so, Madame, wedlock suits you: you are looking radiant,' the Abbess observed. 'I am delighted that you have found such joy in your union with my nephew. I hear that he has ambitions to be King of England.'

'Which I have no doubt he will fulfil,' Eleanor said.

'I was in England thirty years ago, before I entered religion,' Abbess Isabella recalled. 'I was married to William, the son of King Henry, who was himself son to William the Conqueror, and grandfather to your husband. They called King Henry "the Lion of Justice". He was a lion indeed! Strong and respected as a ruler, but a terrifying man, cruel and ruthless. I can never forget what he did to his grandchildren.'

'What did he do?' Eleanor asked, thrusting away the unwelcome thought that the same violent blood ran in her own Henry.

'One of his daughters defied him, with her husband, and he had the eyes of their two little girls put out as punishment.'

Eleanor shivered. 'How vile. That's too awful to contemplate. What was his son like?'

'William? They called him "the Atheling", after the old Saxon princes before the Conquest. He was another like his father, proud, fierce and harsh-hearted. Mercifully, I was not married to him for very long.'

'Was he the prince who drowned when the White Ship sank?'

'The very same.'

'I have heard my Lord speak of his death. He said King Henry never smiled again.'

'For the King, it was a tragedy. He had no other son to succeed him. Not a legitimate one, at any rate. His bastards, of course, were legion.' The Abbess's lips twitched. 'But God in His wisdom took unto Himself my young lord, and King Henry forced his barons to swear allegiance to his daughter Matilda as his heir.'

'The Empress, my mother-in-law,' Eleanor supplied. 'Did you ever meet her?'

'No, she was then married to the Holy Roman Emperor and living in Germany. He died later on, and she married my brother Geoffrey, but she never came to visit me. By all accounts she is a strong woman. She has certainly fought hard for the kingdom that was lawfully hers.'

'And lost,' Eleanor put in. 'But my Lord will reclaim it in her name. She has ceded her rights to him. The portents are good.'

'King Stephen still lives, though,' Isabella stated.

'He is hated and despised, my Lord says. Those barons who would not accept a woman as their monarch are far more amenable to Henry, especially now that he has proved himself a ruler to be reckoned with. Tell me, Mother, what is England like?'

'They call it "the ringing isle" because there are so many churches. It is green and lovely, and a lot like France in some parts, but the weather is unpredictable. The people are insular, but hospitable. And no, before you ask, they do not have tails, as is popularly bruited here!'

Eleanor laughed. 'I never heed such nonsense!' She accepted a tiny fig pastry. 'I will look forward to seeing England someday. Oh, I wanted to tell you that my Lord and I have commissioned a window commemorating our marriage in the new stained glass. It is to be set into the east window of Poitiers Cathedral, that all who see it will remember where we were made man and wife.'

'A fitting gesture,' the Abbess said. 'And an enduring one.'

'Yet more precious to God will be my thanks and praise,' Eleanor said, swallowing the last of the pastry and rising to her feet. 'If you would excuse me, Mother, I shall go into the church now. Summon your scribes, if you would. We can have the charter written out later.'

8   Aquitaine, 1152

'Louis has summoned us,' Henry announced, bursting into Eleanor's solar and thrusting a parchment into her hands. Briefly, she perused it.

'This was addressed to both of us,' she said, anger rising, born of her fear of what Louis might do, and shock at Henry's presumption. 'You should not have broken the seal without my being there.'

'I am the Duke,' Henry stated uncompromisingly.

'And I am the Duchess!' she flared.

'And my wife,' Henry shouted. His sudden anger excited her, despite her annoyance with him. This was not the first quarrel they had had, and it would certainly not be the last, she knew that well. The only compensation was that every time, without fail, they found themselves in bed, sealing their reconciliation with passionate lovemaking.

'This is my duchy!' Eleanor insisted.

'And mine in right of our marriage. I shouldn't have to remind you that I am the ruler here now. I've told you before, Eleanor, governing is man's work, and women should not interfere.'

'You're as bad as Abbot Bernard!' she flung at him. 'You and

I are meant to be a partnership. We agreed. I am no milksop farmwife to be cast aside: I am the sovereign Duchess of Aquitaine, and I will be deferred to as such! Do you heed me?'

For answer, Henry folded her in his arms and kissed her brutally. 'This is your role now, my Lady. I do not remember agreeing to anything.'

'How dare you!' Eleanor cried, struggling free and slapping him on the cheek. 'These are my domains, and my word is law here.'

Henry recoiled. His face was thunderous, his voice menacing. 'Enough, Eleanor. Leave that for now. There are more pressing matters to consider. I came to tell you that Louis has summoned us to his court' – he unscrolled the parchment and read – 'to account for our treasonable misconduct in marrying.'

'It's bluster,' Eleanor declared, still angry. 'He cannot do anything to us.'

'I wouldn't be so complacent,' Henry frowned. 'The envoys who brought this say that their master is shocked and angered. He accuses me of basely stealing his wife—'

'As if I were a chattel to be taken against my will!' Eleanor interrupted, furious.

Henry threw her a look. 'Some of the French lords have even urged Louis to revoke the terms of your annulment,' he went on, 'or even the annulment itself. Others want us excommunicated.'

'Words!' fumed Eleanor.

'Angry men often translate words into actions,' Henry said. 'My enemies are uniting against us. Even my beloved little brother Geoffrey has declared his support for Louis. And Count Henry of Champagne, who is betrothed to your daughter Marie, is dashing off to Paris to join them. Of course, he knows very well that, if you and I have a son, Marie will not get Aquitaine. His brother, Thibaut of Blois, that whoreson who tried to abduct you, is also for Louis.'

'I heard he is to wed my little Alix when she is of age,' Eleanor said, a touch wistfully. 'I could wish it otherwise. He could not win the mother, so he settled for the daughter, the bastard!'

'It's war, no less,' Henry declared. 'I must leave for Normandy at once. The rumour is that Louis plans to attack it in my absence.'

'Then this is our first farewell,' Eleanor said, the last vestiges of her rancour evaporating. She swallowed and put on a brave smile. 'I suspect it will be the first of many, given how far-flung our domains are.'

'You knew that when you took me for a husband,' Henry said gently, tilting her chin towards his face. He kissed her long and hard, all trace of annoyance gone. 'It grieves me too, Eleanor, but it will not be for long. I will send Louis and all his cronies scuttling back to Paris with their tails between their legs. And mayhap I am leaving you with child ...'

'Then God will have smiled upon our union,' Eleanor pronounced. 'I fear it is too early to tell.'

Henry sighed. 'I could have done without all this,' he growled. 'I was planning to take an army across to England and settle matters there, but it will have to wait, yet again. At this rate, the English will get fed up with waiting and declare for the usurper Stephen after all.'

He kissed her again, then broke away.

'I must go,' he said briskly. 'Speed is essential.'

The news Henry sent Eleanor by his couriers was good. Louis had carried out his threat to invade Normandy, but Henry had advanced with such speed that several horses had dropped dead from exhaustion on the road; and with devastating compunction, he had laid waste that land called the Vexin on the Norman–French border and the demesnes of Louis' own brother, Robert of Dreux.

Next she heard, he had been in Touraine, taking some castles that his father had left to the unfraternal Geoffrey. He was winning through. Then God Himself, it seemed, intervened. Louis, Henry wrote, had collapsed with a fever and was laid up at Geoffrey's castle of Montsoreau. Eleanor smiled when she read that. It was typical of Louis to fall ill at such a crucial moment. She smiled even more broadly when she read on and learned that, right now, Henry was besieging the castle.

'The Lord Geoffrey has submitted and begged for mercy and reconciliation,' the next messenger told her, 'and the King of France has given up his cause for lost and sued for peace. He has gone back to Paris.'

How ignominious, Eleanor thought. But again, typical.

After six weeks, Henry was back in Poitiers, the magnificent victor. There was a new air of authority about him; he was now the dominant power in western Christendom, and he knew it.

Wasting no time, the returning hero took his wife to bed and had his will of her vigorously and repeatedly, to her great and unbearable joy.

'I swear to you, Eleanor,' he gasped, heaving and sweating in her eager arms, 'no assault on a fortress was ever so pleasurable. You yield delightfully!'

'Come again,' she breathed, raising her knees and clasping her ankles across his tight buttocks. He readily obliged, and soon had her crying out in ecstasy.

'Hush!' he panted, kissing her lustily. 'Your barons will think the war has broken out again!'

Eleanor held herself in speechless stillness as waves of pleasure coursed through her. Feeling Henry inside her was sheer bliss. It had been so long . . . She had barely contained her need for him. But for all her delight in their joining, she was miserably aware that he was shortly to leave her again.

'When do you depart for England?' she asked a little later, when they were lying peacefully together under the single sheet. It was a warm, balmy night, and the sky glimpsed through the narrow window was indigo-blue and bright with stars.

'Not until the end of the year,' Henry said.

'You're planning a winter campaign?' she asked, surprised.

'No, my Lady, I intend to use diplomacy this time. Of course, an army at my back will help negotiations wonderfully, because the English will know that I mean to deploy it if necessary.'

'This latest victory can only have enhanced your reputation, my brave Henry,' Eleanor murmured, kissing him. 'The English now know what they have to reckon with.'

'The English are no fools. They need a strong king, and I'm their man. The question now is how to topple Stephen and his son without causing too much unpleasantness.'

'With any luck he will have wearied of the struggle and be eager to come to terms,' Eleanor said. 'Then you can return speedily to me, my love.' She turned and twined her arms around him, rejoicing in the strength of his supine body.

'I'll be here for a while yet,' Henry said, biting her neck play-fully between words. 'It occurred to me that, before the autumn really sets in, we should make a leisurely progress through your domains, so that you can introduce me to your vassals. The ones who are speaking to you, anyway. Of course, I hope that meets with your approval, O sovereign Duchess of Aquitaine!' He was mocking her, she knew, but she did not leap to the bait. She was too overjoyed at his suggestion.

'I should love that, Henry,' she enthused. 'There are so many places I want to show you. We should start with the Limousin. It's wild country in every respect, but so beautiful, and it will do its unruly lords a power of good to be brought face-to-face with their new suzerain. They will meet their match and more!'

'Your faith in me is touching!' Henry murmured, nuzzling her ear.

'We must go to my father's hunting lodge at Talmont – he used to take us hawking there. It is where my gerfalcons are bred. I will give you one, the prize of the mews. Nothing but the best for my Lord! You must see Les Landes in Gascony – nothing but acres and acres of scrub, sand dunes and pine forests, but so wild and bracing.'

'We will ride out there together, alone,' Henry promised, catching her excitement.

'The pearl of my domains is the Périgord,' Eleanor went on. 'The valley of the Dordogne is unsurpassed for its beauty. There I will feed you on freshly dug truffles, which are glorious in omelettes, and *confit* of duck, and *foie gras* – the area is known for its wonderful food.'

'Stop, you'll have me running to fat!' Henry interrupted, laughing. 'My forbears were enormous.' He paused and looked down at her. 'So show me all, my love . . . apart from your lands!' And he ducked, choking with mirth, as Eleanor rose wrathfully up in the bed and began pounding him with her pillow.

The tour had not gone well.

'Your vassals do not like me!' Henry repeatedly complained. 'You, they defer to, and treat with respect. *I* am regarded with suspicion!' His grey eyes were narrowed in anger.

Eleanor could not refute what he said, for it was no less than the truth. Everywhere, without exception, there had been enthusiastic cheers for her and cool receptions and studied politeness for Henry. No one had actually said anything, and mercifully there had been no demonstrations, but the hostility was palpable. It made a mockery of the glorious, spacious autumnal landscapes, the sunflowers browning drowsily in the fields, the majestic rivers and spectacular crags. Henry had remarked upon none of these wonders; he had been simmering with rage.

Early on, there had been that awful day when several of Eleanor's lords had come to her privily after they had arrived in the Limousin. 'Madame the Duchess,' they had said, grim-faced, 'to you, we are devoted and loyal, never doubt it. But hear this, we owe Duke Henry no allegiance save as your husband.'

'He is your lord now,' Eleanor had said sternly, knowing how badly Henry would take this, 'and it is my will that you acknowledge him as such, and show him the customary fealty and obedience.'

'Madame, he is a foreigner, like the French. His first loyalty is not to us, but to Normandy and Anjou, and his ambitions lie in England. Many believe he means to milk Aquitaine dry to achieve his crown.'

'He does not need to,' she assured them, springing to Henry's defence. 'He has sufficient men and resources of his own! I give you my word on that.'

She had not managed to convince them, however, and she had not dared to reveal anything of this conversation to Henry. Things were bad enough, and the reluctance of her vassals to pay court to him all too plain. Inevitably, Henry's temper had become increasingly foul throughout the progress. In vain she'd tried to distract him by pointing out ancient churches and mighty castles, and to tempt him with the fine food and abundant vintages of the region, which should have been the source of much mutual enjoyment. But it had been a wasted effort. He was not going to say one good word about anything, on principle. In the end, she gave up trying.

Now, having reached gentler countryside, and traversed peaceful pastures, they were before Limoges, her chief city of the Limousin, their gaily striped tents pitched outside the massive new walls, the pride of its citizens. Henry looked up approvingly at the impressive fortifications, and his mood lightened further as he and Eleanor entered the city to the unexpectedly rapturous acclaim of the people. He expressed admiration for the great abbey and shrine of St Martial, the city's patron, and showed a genuine interest in the Romanesque splendour of the cathedral and the exquisite, richly coloured enamel plaques that he and Eleanor were given as gifts by the burghers. Limoges was famed for its enamels.

That night, they were to dine in their silken pavilion beyond the walls, with the Abbot of St Martial and the chief lords of the Limousin as guests. Eleanor's damsels had dressed her in a beautiful green Byzantine robe that set off her red hair to perfection, and as she and Henry took their places at the high table, she was starting to hope that her husband was feeling happier about the progress, and that things would be better from now on.

Given their warm welcome, Eleanor had happily anticipated a lavish feast, and had waxed lyrical about the succulent truffles produced in the Limousin, the rich game, the roast ox drizzled with sweet chestnuts, and the violet mustard, but Henry took one look at the puny duck and scrawny goose that lay on the golden platters before him and barked, 'Is this all there is to eat?'

'It is all we have, Lord,' the serving varlets stammered.

'Ask Madame the Duchess's cook to come here!' Henry demanded. 'This is mean fare indeed!'

Eleanor's master cook came hastening into the pavilion, his lugubrious face crumpled with concern. He bowed ostentatiously to her, ignoring Henry.

'Lady, I am very sorry, but this is all we have. The citizens did not send the usual supplies.'

'And why was that?' Henry snarled.

'Let me deal with this,' Eleanor murmured.

'No, my Lady, they will answer to me. Am I not the Duke of Aquitaine?' Henry's cheeks were flushed with fury.

'My Lieges, allow me to explain what has happened,' intervened the Abbot of St Martial smoothly. He was a haughty man with a chill in his manner, and for all his courtesy, he had barely concealed his resentment of his new overlord.

Henry glared at him, while Eleanor shuddered inwardly. More trouble, she thought, and just when matters were improving.

'It is customary, I fear,' the Abbot went on in his high, reedy voice, 'for food supplies to be delivered to the royal kitchens only when Madame the Duchess is lodging within the city walls.'

Henry's set expression suddenly changed dramatically. He went purple with anger. Eleanor had never seen him so enraged; was she at last going to witness the notorious Angevin temper at its worst? It seemed she was! Roaring curses on the Abbot, the citizens and – for good measure – St Martial himself, Henry lost control and, throwing himself on the floor, rolled around yelling blood-curdling oaths before finally falling quiet and grinding his teeth on the rushes that were strewn over the flag-stones. The fit lasted a full three minutes, with Eleanor looking on open-mouthed, the Abbot curling his lip in disgust at the prone, seething figure at his feet, and the aghast company craning their necks to get a better view.

After the worst excesses of his rage had subsided, Henry got dazedly to his feet and stood glowering at the sea of faces staring at him.

'Know this!' he cried in his cracked voice. 'I, Henry FitzEmpress, your duke and liege lord, will not tolerate such blatant disrespect. Nor will my Lady here.' He looked hard at Eleanor, challenging her to agree with him, and although she had been on the point of interrupting, she subsided, quelled by the menacing steel in his gaze.

'Limoges will pay dearly for this insult,' Henry announced to the silent company. 'Its walls shall be razed to the ground. No one, least of all you, my Lord Abbot, will be able in future to use them as an excuse for depriving me or your duchess of our just and reasonable dues. Now you had best get back to the city and convey my orders to your people – and see that they are obeyed! Demolition must begin tomorrow.'

Eleanor watched, appalled, as the mighty Abbot, who had up till now enjoyed great power and autonomy, was dismissed like an errant novice. She knew that Henry's anger was justified, but she also felt that his vengeance was over-harsh. Yet to appeal to him now would be disastrous – she must appear to be supporting him, and show the world that they were united in their indignation.

Later, though, in the privacy of their tent, she burned with the injustice of it all. After they had lain silent in bed for a while, she turned to him.

'What on earth were you doing?' she asked. 'People were looking at you as if you were possessed by devils.'

'Sometimes, when these rages are upon me, I think I am,' Henry muttered.

'Can you not control yourself?'

'No. Something in me explodes, and I have no power over it. Anyway, I was right to be angry. I will not be slighted like that. I will not have you slighted like that.'

'Yes, you were right,' Eleanor agreed. 'No one could blame you for being angry. I just wish you could have curbed your temper a little and not made such a spectacle of yourself.'

Henry stiffened. 'Don't you dare preach to me, Eleanor!'

'I am not. I was embarrassed. And, if I may venture to say so without your biting my head off, or throwing a tantrum, I think the punishment you handed down was severe in the extreme.'

Henry raised himself up on one muscular elbow. 'Do you? Pah! The citizens of Limoges – and your people at large – need to be taught who is master here. Stern measures are called for. It's called strategy, my dear.'

'Those walls are brand-new and strong, the latest in defences. You were admiring them yourself. They took years to build, at great cost. If you force the people to pull them down, you will be hated and resented. Could you not rescind the order and think up some other punishment?'

'I would rather be hated and resented than not have my vassals fear me,' Henry declared. 'How would it look, retracting my order? I would be seen as a weak man, whose word is not his bond, one to be cozened and wheedled out of decisions. No, Eleanor, once my mind is made up, it is made up for good. There is no point in trying to dissuade me.'

'You might have taken counsel of me first,' she protested. 'I am the Duchess, after all, and these are my people.'

'You are my wife, and your part is to obey me,' Henry flared. 'I am heartily sick of playing a subordinate role in this duchy. Now get on your back and learn who is master!'

No man had ever spoken to her like that, but Eleanor was too shocked to object as Henry forced her thighs apart and thrust himself between them, ramming his manhood into her with little care about hurting her. Not that it did hurt – not physically, anyway, for she usually thrilled to rough handling – but this was the first time that Henry had taken her in anger, or had used her body to enforce his own supremacy. Afterwards, as he slumped at her side and his heavy breathing quietened, she lay there grieving, knowing that, without her being able to help it, the balance in their relationship had altered, and fearing that it might never again be possible for them to come together as equals after this.

Henry, by contrast, seemed unaware that there had been a change. He was up early the next morning, pulling on his tunic and hose and splashing cold water on his face.

'Are you getting up?' he asked.

Eleanor gazed at him wearily from the pillow. She knew what this day must witness, and wanted no part in it.

He came towards her and sat on the bed.

'I am going to supervise the dismantling of the walls,' he said, bristling with determination. 'I want you with me, to show that we are united in our anger.'

'No,' she said firmly. Henry snorted with impatience.

'Up!' he barked. 'Get up! Like it or not, you are coming with me.' He grabbed her arms none too gently, pinching the soft flesh, and dragged her into a sitting position.

'Very well,' said Eleanor icily, realising that further protest would only result in an undignified scuffle that she could not hope to win. She slid off the bed and pulled on her shift. 'Grant me at least the courtesy of ten minutes to make myself presentable.'

Alone with her women, she asked for her black mourning gown to be brought. 'That, and a black veil – and my ducal coronet. No jewels.'

'You look like a bloody nun,' Henry exclaimed when he saw her. 'Why the weeds?'

'How perceptive you are!' she retorted. 'I am mourning the loss of my people's love.'

'Don't be so dramatic,' he scoffed.

'After yesterday's display, you are in no position to talk,' Eleanor snapped, adjusting her veil. 'Well, I am ready,' she added quickly, seeing him framing a biting reply. 'I suppose you are still insisting on this cruel, harsh order being carried out?'

'Come!' was all Henry said.

They emerged from their tent to a maelstrom of activity. Scaffolding was being erected, tools commandeered, and surly, glowering men – long lines of them – were being impressed to do the demolition work. Even the master masons, loudly protesting, had been given no choice. Women, and even children, were scurrying to and fro with huge baskets, or carrying messages conveying orders, while great carts stood ready to carry away the rubble. The atmosphere was subdued, the resentment of the people palpable. When Henry appeared, there were muffled curses.

He leaped up onto a large boulder and signalled to his men-at-arms to sound the alarum. The activity ceased, and hundreds of pairs of angry eyes turned to the stocky figure of the Duke. Eleanor, standing miserably behind him, almost shaking with resentment, could see burning hatred in those eyes – and a desire for revenge.

'People of Limoges!' Henry cried in ringing tones. 'I hope you will not forget this day, and I hope you will learn from it. When Madame the Duchess and I next visit you, I trust you will treat us with greater courtesy. And maybe you might like to rebuild these inconvenient walls so as to allow better access to your kitchens!'

There was a sullen silence. Then someone in the crowd threw a stone. It missed, but Henry was not in a forgiving mood.

'If I catch the varlet who did that, I'll have him castrated,' he threatened. 'And anyone else who thinks they can mock my justice. Now, back to work, all of you.' He jumped off the boulder and strode over to Eleanor, then, grasping her purposefully by the hand, led her along the perimeter of the plateau on which the old city was built, following the line of the doomed walls.

Behind them tramped his armed escort. The citizens saw them coming as they bent furiously to their task, not daring to slacken, for Henry's anger was still writ plain upon his face. Finally, he and Eleanor arrived at a vantage point at a safe distance from the demolition work and stood there to watch, as citizens who had lavished good money and pride, not to mention the sweat of their backs and the blood of their willing fingers, in the building of their defences, grudgingly pulled them apart, stone by stone. As the walls of Limoges began crashing to the ground in clouds of yellow dust, Eleanor felt the destruction like a physical pain. Yet her face remained impassive, for Henry was watching her, as if daring her to protest; but she would not allow him that satisfaction.

After Henry had finally let her return to their pavilion, when the choking dust became too much to bear, she just wanted to flee as far from Limoges as possible, or crawl into a hole like a badger, for she felt her citizens' grief and anger keenly, and the conviction that, in failing to save their walls, she had betrayed them. She burned with fury against Henry, and even more so when they met for dinner later, and he made no reference to the events of the day and was his usual genial self. In bed, he was once again the ardent lover, by turns demanding and tender, and Eleanor almost managed to persuade herself that all was well, but she found it hard to respond because she was deeply preoccupied with concern as to what her people now thought of her.

She could not stop brooding. It seemed to her that this marriage that she had defied the world to make had quickly become, in its own way, as much a form of captivity as her union with Louis had been in another. This was not the partnership she had planned for, but a vile durance, she told herself angrily. She had been duped, no doubt of it. Henry's passion had driven her sense of power, but now she saw that it had all been an illusion. Yes, they had had mutual aims, and he had been happy to consult and defer to her, but only when it suited him. The reality was that he had the mastery of her, by all the laws of God and man – and he was determined to assert it, even if it meant riding roughshod over her feelings and sensibilities. She seethed at her own helplessness, chafing against the invisible chains that bound her.

There were, of course, no cheers as they rode away from the destruction that was now Limoges, but the rest of the progress passed without incident, and Henry cheered up considerably when the people of Gascony showed themselves more than willing to be recruited for his English offensive, and ready to provide him with ships and supplies. He put it down to word of his strong and uncompromising rule going before him. In the future, these godforsaken southerners would think twice about defying him! Small wonder they were grovelling.

At last, they came to the Talmont, that pretty lordship nestling above the Gironde estuary on a promontory of high white cliffs. Here, Eleanor's family had built a hunting lodge, a place much beloved by her. Yet even here, her subjects' antipathy towards Henry was palpable. She cringed when, on the first day they arrived at the mews, her falconers took no pains to hide their dislike, and kept Henry waiting an unconscionable time in his saddle for a bird; and when it was brought to him, he was not best pleased to find that it was a lowly sparrowhawk – a bird deemed suitable only for priests or women – instead of the royal gerfalcon he had been expecting, and which was his right. She, on the other hand, had a most noble hawk perching on her glove. It had been horribly embarrassing, because for all the servile excuses that no suitable falcon was available, it had been quite clear that the slight was deliberate.

She said nothing. Secretly, she was gratified to see Henry so discomfited. Let him reap what he had sown!

On the surface, however, they were existing in a tacit state of truce. The weather was still good, despite the lateness of the year, and they rode out hawking daily, admired the spectacular views from the cliffs, went to Mass in the squat stone church of St Radegonde, and enjoyed each other's bodies every night. And gradually, unwillingly, Eleanor found herself succumbing again to her husband's charm and dynamism.

'I could live here quite happily,' Henry said, stretching, as they lay abed one sunny morning.

'It is beautiful in summer,' she told him, her tone still a little clipped and formal, for resentment was yet festering in her. 'There are hollyhocks everywhere.'

'Then we will come back next year,' he promised. His eyes sought hers.

'You are still angry with me about Limoges,' he said.

'You had your way. There is nothing more to say,' Eleanor shrugged, her eyes veiled.

'But you are holding aloof from me,' Henry complained. 'I fuck you every night, and in the mornings too, but I can't reach you.'

'What did you expect?' she asked. 'You have no cause to find fault with me. I played the part of submissive wife to perfection, at the risk of alienating my subjects. I allow you the use of my body whenever you want it. I am with you in bed and at board. Many couples rub along with less.'

'But we had so much more!' Henry flared.

'*We did*,' Eleanor agreed vehemently. 'It was you who decided to play the aggressive husband, you who set at naught my hopes for a partnership of equals. I am a captive in this marriage!'

'So I'm being punished,' he retorted.

'No, that is how things are now.' Eleanor made to rise from the bed, but Henry caught her wrist.

'I love you, you know,' he said urgently.

Tears welled in her eyes.

'*I love you*,' he said again, staring at her.

Slowly, she came into his arms, her body racked with uncontrollable sobs, and clung to him.

'There now,' Henry soothed. 'Now you are mine again. By the eyes of God, I will make things right between us!' As he fell to kissing her hungrily, Eleanor allowed herself to relax a little. Could things really be once more as they had been before Limoges? She had thought not, but now she saw that she must stop nurturing this resentment, and give her feelings for Henry a chance to flower again. As they were flowering now, God be thanked – or cursed, was it? – under the onslaught of his caresses . . .

Returning to Poitiers in December, Eleanor's heart was heavy. Henry was bound for England at last, and impatient to be gone.

'I should make haste,' he told her. 'I must stop at Rouen on the way to visit my Lady Mother the Empress. It's the least I can do, since she's been so generous with funds for this venture. And I want to consult her about my invasion plans.'

Eleanor fumed inwardly. He could rarely be pressed to discuss those plans with his wife, and still made no secret of his opinion that women should not interfere in politics. But clearly he was willing to make an exception for his mother.

As if reading her thoughts, Henry said, 'She is to govern Normandy while I am abroad – there is much to talk over with her. And she knows England well – and King Stephen.'

'By all accounts she knew him very well!' Eleanor said tartly.

'Don't believe those old tales,' Henry said lightly. 'But he did have a chivalrous regard for her, despite their being enemies.'

'I wonder at your naïvety!' Eleanor grimaced. He threw her a filthy look.

'Remember it's my Lady Mother of whom you are speaking,' he reminded her. 'Although I wouldn't have put it past her! She'd have eaten him for breakfast, poor weakling that he is.'

'I should like to meet her,' Eleanor said, not meaning it.

'You will, one day,' Henry told her. His disinterested tone betrayed no awareness of any possible grounds for antipathy between his mother and his wife. Eleanor wondered if he knew about her own affair with his father. He had never mentioned it, and neither would she, ever.

Henry's quick, restless mind had moved on.

'I'm leaving Anjou and Aquitaine in your hands,' he said. 'I know you will rule them both well.' Eleanor was surprised and touched, and felt not a little guilty for having jumped to unfair conclusions about him; for not only was he trusting her to look after her duchy in his absence, but also his own county of Anjou, the domain of his forefathers. He was trying to make amends, she suspected.

She smiled at him at last, her eyes brilliant.

'I will not fail you, my Lord,' she promised.

In the early hours of the morning, Eleanor awoke. It was still warm in the bedchamber, for two braziers had been left burning. In their flickering red glow, she could see Henry lying naked on his stomach beside her, the sheet tangled around his legs. He was watching her drowsily, a rare gentleness in his eyes.

'You're awake,' she whispered.

'How can a man sleep with you lying next to him?' he chuckled, feasting his eyes on her full breasts and her long limbs stretched luxuriously before him. 'There is no one like you, Eleanor. There never has been, and I doubt there ever will be.'

'So there were others before me?' she teased, really wanting to know. Henry had never spoken of any previous encounters with women, although she had heard rumours.

'Legions!' he grinned. Eleanor made to thump him with her pillow, but he stayed her hand. 'I am a man, with a man's needs. Of course there were others. But believe me when I say that none compared to you. They meant nothing.'

She believed him, yet still she felt a pang of jealousy.

Henry was regarding her closely. 'Now you tell me,' he said, 'what happened in Antioch?'

Eleanor was startled. 'What have you heard about that?' she asked warily, feeling herself flush.

'That you cuckolded Louis with Raymond, the Prince of Antioch, your own uncle, for Christ's sake, and were bundled out of the city in shame.' Henry's gimlet gaze was fixed on her face. 'Is it true?'

'Yes, it is true,' Eleanor admitted. 'You know how barren of love my marriage to Louis was. Like you, I took my pleasure where I found it – but I paid for it dearly. Louis barely spoke to me for a whole year.'

'And did you take your pleasure with anyone else?' Henry demanded to know. He was no longer bantering with her.

'Yes, twice, and that only briefly,' Eleanor replied in a low voice.

'With my father?' he asked, his expression unreadable.

'You knew?' She was shocked.

'He told me before he died. He begged me not to marry you.'

'But you defied him – and, knowing that, you did marry me.' Eleanor was incredulous.

'Of course.' Henry pulled her towards him. 'That's how much I wanted you. For you, I have defied my own father, the King of France and the Church itself!'

'The Church?' Eleanor echoed.

'Yes, my ignorant Lady. Don't you realise that your coupling with my father places us within the forbidden degrees of consanguinity, closer than you ever were to Louis?'

'I was not married to Geoffrey,' Eleanor said.

'That's immaterial. Our marriage is forbidden – or it would be if the Church had known what you'd been up to.'

Eleanor felt a shiver of fear; it was as if the carefully constructed edifice of her world had rocked slightly. She saw that, by her rash actions, she had put at risk everything she now held dear. A tremor coursed through her. Henry felt it and tightened his arms about her.

'Fear not,' he soothed. 'I won't be betraying our little secret, if you won't.'

'But what of the legality of our marriage?' Eleanor asked, shocked, seeing the foundations of their glorious future, the empire they were building, cracking and then crumbling . . .

'I care not a fig for that,' he grinned. 'We Angevins came from the Devil, remember? Why should I bother myself about a trifle like that? No one knows, so no one can question it. Should it really matter to us?'

'No,' she said after a pause. 'It matters not one whit.'

'What does matter,' Henry said purposefully, 'is this . . .' He pulled her on top of him and thrust himself up inside her, fully aroused. 'I swear to you, Eleanor, that no pope or bishop will part us. You are mine for ever, mine . . . oh, God!'

Afterwards, sated, he lay with her in his arms.

'Who was the other man?' he asked.

'The other man?' Eleanor, relaxed and contented, had no idea what he was talking about.

'You said you took your pleasure with two men besides Raymond of Antioch.'

'This sounds like an inquisition,' Eleanor said, only half joking.

'It is,' said Henry. 'I need to know. You are my wife and, God willing, will be the mother of my sons.'

'And if I tell you, will you also tell me about the women with whom you have slept?' she challenged him.

'I've forgotten most of them,' he snorted. 'They were just casual encounters. One was called Joanna, another Elgiva . . .

Oh, and perhaps I should mention Hersinde, Maud, Lucy, Ghislaine, Marie . . .' He was laughing.

'Stop!' Eleanor cried. 'You're making those names up!'

'Well, I really can't remember them all,' Henry said ruefully, playing with her hair. 'And talking to them wasn't really called for!'

'You're impossible,' Eleanor told him.

He raised himself up on one elbow to look into her face. 'There, I've told you what you wanted to know. Now you keep your part of the bargain.'

'Very well,' said Eleanor. 'It was a brief affair with a troubadour called Marcabru.'

'A troubadour?' Henry echoed, surprised, and not a little jolted. 'A low-born varlet? You might have looked higher than that!'

'You forget, I had looked higher,' Eleanor shot back. 'I was married to the King of France, no less, and much satisfaction I got from him!' She snapped her fingers. 'Marcabru showed me how to make love, and for that I will always be grateful – and so should you, for you benefit from it.'

'Did Louis ever find out?'

'He knew that Marcabru had written verses to me. He considered them over-familiar, and banished him. He assumed I shared his outrage, and I did not disabuse him of that notion – in fact, I played along with it.'

'You lied to him?' Henry asked uneasily.

'I had no cause – he never asked if I had been unfaithful. It would never have occurred to him that I would actually permit a troubadour to make love to me. You princes of the north are all alike in dismissing troubadours as being of little account, but may I remind you, Henry, that in Aquitaine they are accorded a proper respect for their talents.'

'This one certainly seems to have had talents beyond the ordinary,' Henry threw at her, not quite reassured. 'What was he like as a poet?'

'Terrible!' Eleanor replied, and suddenly they were both heaving with laughter, and the awkward moment had passed.

'I will recite you some really good troubadour poems,' she said later, when they had calmed down and were once more lying peacefully against each other. 'It would be fitting to speak of love on this last precious night before you leave.' And she began telling him about her celebrated grandfather, the talented Duke William the Ninth.

'They call him the first of the troubadours,' she said, 'and indeed, he did have a wondrous way with words. Some of his works are very bawdy, some very moving. I particularly like the one in which he says, *All the joy of the world is ours, if you and I were to love one another*. And elsewhere, *Without you I cannot live, so thirsty am I for your love.*'

'He could have written those lines for us, that good duke,' Henry observed, his calloused fingers caressing her bare arm. He bent forward and kissed her. 'What of his bawdy lyrics? I should like to hear some of them!'

'He was always chasing women in his verse, to one purpose of course, and he wrote that he usually ended up with his hands inside their cloaks.' Henry guffawed, as Eleanor went on: 'He wrote of women as horses to be mounted, yet at the same time he believed that they should be free to bestow their love freely, and not be forced into marriage.'

'That's all very well for the lower orders,' Henry opined, 'but I can't imagine my barons approving of it! We cannot have our high-born ladies sleeping with whom they please – no man could be certain that his heir was his own!'

'Yet you yourself did not object when I bestowed my love freely upon you?' Eleanor reminded him archly. 'I do not recall my holding out for marriage.'

'*We* are not ordinary mortals,' Henry told her, only half joking. 'We can defy custom and tradition, and break all the rules. We've proved that already, haven't we?' His lips were again on hers, his tongue inside her mouth. For the third time, they gave themselves up to the sweet pleasures of love, knowing that it would be long ere they tasted them again.

9   Angers and Poitiers, 1153

Eleanor was at Angers, Henry's capital of Anjou, when she discovered that she was to have a child, conceived on that glorious night. She regarded her pregnancy as proof that God looked with favour upon her irregular marriage, and bore the discomforts of morning sickness and fatigue with triumphant fortitude.

Her heart still ached for those dear little girls she had left behind in Paris. It pained her to think that there was barely the remotest chance of her seeing them now, for Louis must surely still hate her for marrying Henry, his enemy, behind his back. Yet she consoled herself with the knowledge that this new baby would compensate in some way for the loss of her daughters, and promised herself that never again would she allow any child of hers to be denied a close bond with its mother.

She missed Henry appallingly. Despite the strange changes that pregnancy wrought, she wanted him, needed him. At night, her longing for his caresses and his body inside hers was so acute that she had to bite on the sheet to stifle her unwitting moans. Yet the news from England was good. He had landed safely and been rapturously received. Sermons had been preached, proclaiming: 'Behold, the ruler cometh, and the kingdom is in his hand.' It was all stirring tidings that portended well.

Henry's objective was to march on a place called Wallingford, where his supporters were under siege in the castle, and relieve them, and as he made his exultant progress towards that place, town after town fell to him. All this Eleanor learned joyfully from the messengers Henry sent to her fairly regularly. They told her that he had shown himself jubilant at the news that she was carrying his child and that he exhorted her to take good care of herself. Eleanor smiled at his thoughtfulness. She was strong and healthy, she had borne her previous children with ease, and she bade them tell Henry so.

After the tedious and tiring early weeks, she bloomed. Her skin was soft as blossom, her hair silky and lustrous, her breasts full. Thus did an ambitious young troubadour, Bernard de Ventadour, behold her when he presented himself at her court, looking for patronage.

'Madame the Duchess,' he declared, bowing elaborately low, 'your fame is without parallel. I have made so bold as to come here in the hope that you will not turn away one of your subjects who would entertain you with his humble lays and verses.'

Eleanor warmed to his florid praise. She saw that he was a young man to whom a happy combination of wavy chestnut locks, green eyes and chiselled features lent exquisite manly beauty. Were she not so contented with her lord, she thought to herself, she might well have had seduction on her mind at this moment.

'Messire Bernard, tell us about yourself,' she invited, waving a languid hand to encompass the watching courtiers.

The young man's eyes were mellow. He was looking at her with open admiration. 'Madame, my fortune is in my songs, not my birth. I am merely the son of a kitchen maid in the household of the Viscount of Ventadour in the Limousin.'

'I know the Viscount,' Eleanor smiled. 'He and his family have long been patrons of troubadours like yourself.'

'Indeed, Madame,' Bernard agreed, looking at her a touch shiftily, she thought. 'He was kind enough to say that I had talent, and to tutor me himself in writing poetry and lyrics.'

'Then you are much indebted to him,' Eleanor observed, to a murmur of assent from the company. Again, there was that fleeting shifty look on the young troubadour's face. 'But tell me, Messire, why have you left his castle? Is it just to seek greater fame in the wider world?'

'Yes,' said Bernard de Ventadour, not now meeting her gaze. She knew he was lying. No matter, it was no concern of hers, although she was a little curious as to why he had left such a kind lord's service.

He was looking at her again, his green eyes eager.

'Well, let us hear how talented you are,' Eleanor said. 'Play for us.'

The troubadour produced his stringed vielle and sang an amusing *sirvente*, a satire on gluttonous monks, which prompted much mirth among Eleanor and her courtiers.

Clapping, Eleanor asked, 'Do you know any songs of King Arthur and Queen Guinevere?'

'Alas, my Lady, I do not, although I have read the tales of Geoffrey of Monmouth. I do know some lines from the ancient poet Ovid that might please you. They come from his work, *Ars Amatoria – The Art of Love*.' His eyes twinkled mischievously. 'Mayhap you would not understand how bold they are . . .'

'I know my Latin,' Eleanor reproved him gently. 'But play, please. We would all like to hear your naughty song!'

The troubadour, blushing, laid down his vielle and took a cithara from his pack. He began strumming an introduction, then with a smile sang in his rich voice:

> First then believe, all women may be won;
> Attempt with confidence, the work is done!
> The grasshopper shall first forbear to sing
> In summer season, or the birds in spring,
> Than woman can resist your flattering skill:
> Even she will yield, who swears she never will!
> This is the sex: they will not first begin,
> But when compelled, are pleased to suffer sin.
> Ask, that thou may enjoy; she waits for this,
> And on thy first advance depends thy bliss.

Bernard looked directly at Eleanor as he sang those last words, his meaning unmistakeable. She returned his gaze reprovingly.

'You are bold, Messire!'

'You did not like Ovid's poem, Madame?'

'I did.' She knew he was flirting with her in the accepted courtly manner: such games had become customary in this land of troubadours. It was all quite harmless, of course – or was supposed to be. A lowly squire or poet might pay his ardent addresses to the high-born lady of his choice, and she could accept – and even encourage – his adoration without tarnishing her reputation, and only rarely did it go further than that.

In Paris, when Eleanor had tried to introduce these conceits, Louis and his clerics had been shocked: they had condemned this game of courtly love as merely an excuse for committing adultery. But in Aquitaine, as Eleanor knew well, for she had grown up in the relaxed culture of the south, it was regarded as merely a sophisticated and enjoyable pastime. She thought nothing of accepting the homage and flattery of the troubadours and young men who frequented her court, for everyone understood that it was all part of an elaborate and exciting game.

Eleanor's ladies were asking for more.

'I like this Master Ovid!' declared frivolous Faydide de Toulouse.

'I have heard he is much disapproved of by some,' said beautiful Torqueri de Bouillon.

'That makes him all the more interesting!' giggled Mamille de Roucy, plump as a partridge.

'Well, Messire Bernard, can you sing some more of Ovid's verse?' Eleanor asked.

'With pleasure, Madame,' he replied warmly, and took up his cithara again.

There was a wicked glint in his eyes as he sang:

> In Love's rite
> Should man and woman equally delight.
> I hate a union that exhausts not both!
> I like to hear a voice of rapture shrill
> That bids me linger and prolongs the thrill;
> Love's climax never should be rushed, I say,
> But worked up softly, lingering all the way!

He was looking at Eleanor again as his voice died and his strumming ceased. She felt the heat bloom in her cheeks at his lewd song, which conjured up so vividly the wild, erotic nights when she had lain with Henry. Striving to control the rising ache in her loins, she joined in the applause with her ladies, all of whom were pink with excitement.

'That is a very daring song, Messire,' she reproved, but her eyes were kind. 'I think, however, that we have all enjoyed it. You shall play for us again soon.'

And he did. Suddenly, he was always there, in the dining hall, or the great chamber, or the gardens, watching her, begging permission to play for her, singing his songs of lust and dalliance. She sensed there was more to his devotion than courtly convention.

'I have written a song for you, Madame,' he announced one day, coming upon her seated under a magnolia tree, abandoned by her ladies, who were a little way off, gathering early April flowers. 'Shall you hear it?'

'I am listening,' Eleanor told him. She was gentle with him, knowing that he could hope for nothing more from her. His voice was strong and ardent:

> When the sweet breeze
> Blows hither from your dwelling,
> Methinks I feel
> A breath of Paradise!

When he finished, he was visibly shaking. Eleanor took pity on him.

'No one has ever written a song like that for me,' she told Bernard.

'Your beauty has inspired me, Madame,' he said fervently. 'You are gracious, lovely – the embodiment of all charm! With your lovely eyes and noble countenance, you are fit to crown the state of any king! Yet alas, it is I, a humble troubadour, who loves you.'

'You know you may not aspire to me,' Eleanor chided him sweetly. It was the correct, the only response.

'Say I may hope, Madame, I beg of you,' Bernard pleaded. 'Or if you will not extend to me such kindness, then give me leave to sing your praises in my verse. I swear I will not reveal the object of my adoration.' As if, she thought, suppressing a smile, it was not obvious to anyone with eyes in their head.

'Why, of course, Messire,' she said aloud, giving him her hand to kiss to show that he was dismissed. He pressed his lips to it joyfully.

After that, the court was regaled with song after song dedicated – without her name being mentioned – to the Duchess. Only a fool would have failed to realise for whom they were meant. Eleanor found such flattery irresistible. It was balm to her lonely heart to hear herself described as noble and sweet, faithful and loyal, gracious and lovely. She only wished that Henry were with her to hear it. No, she just wished Henry were with her. All she craved was his presence. But since she could not have that, there was no harm in enjoying this pleasurable little diversion and the homage of her adoring troubadour.

'When you look at me with your eyes full of fire and eloquence,

I feel the kind of joy one only experiences at Christmas or other great festivals,' Bernard effused to her, after she had graciously permitted him to walk with her on the massive castle ramparts that overlooked the River Maine, keeping her damsels at a discreet distance, yet within earshot. The wind was chilly and whipping her veil in every direction, but she had gathered her heavy mantle about her and stepped out briskly, enjoying the invigorating air. Walking, she had been told, was good for her condition.

'What have I done to deserve such devotion?' she teased.

Bernard looked at her with reproach. 'You exist, divine lady! You have been the first among my joys, and you shall be the last, so long as there is life in me.'

'Then what of Alaiz, the wife of the Viscount of Ventadour?' Eleanor teased him. At his stricken look, she smiled. 'I am well informed, as you see!' In fact, she had had inquiries made at Ventadour.

The young man continued to look crestfallen. 'It was a passing fancy, no more, Madame, I swear it . . .'

'You seduced her!' she accused him, still smiling. 'Do not deny it! It was serious enough for the Viscount to throw you out of his house and lock up his wife, whom he has now repudiated.' She frowned.

'Do not condemn me, I beg of you, my dear Lady,' Bernard pleaded. 'I was young and foolish – and she was not worth the trouble. I see that clearly now that I have beheld your face. I swear by all that is holy that I never loved her as I love you, and that from now on I will be true to you, fair queen of my heart.'

Eleanor shot him a look of disdain and strode on. He hastened to keep up with her. 'I swear it!' he cried.

She relented. 'Very well, we will speak no more of it.'

Bernard was on his knees, kissing the hem of her mantle. 'Of all women, you are the most kind and beautiful, Madame, and I would not trade your charms for even the wealthy city of Paris!'

'I should hope not,' she chided, 'for beauty, although it lies only in the eyes of the beholder, is surely priceless! Now please get up. You are making a spectacle of us both!'

They were almost at the tower door that led to the royal lodgings.

'Accept this, Madame, with my devotion,' Bernard said breathlessly, thrusting a scroll into Eleanor's hands.

'What is it?' she asked.

'Poems I have written for you,' he breathed. 'Read them, please, for they contain secret messages that only you will understand.'

Later, when she read them, she found them to be no more than further outpourings of his devotion. He declared that Tristan had never suffered such woe for the fair Yseult as he, Bernard, now suffered for his chosen lady. Eleanor smiled when she read that in her presence, he was so overcome by love, his wits fled and he had no more sense than a child. 'All I write and sing,' he vowed, 'is meant for your delight.' Poor man, she thought: he can never have what he craves. Yet it is fortunate that the rules of the game permit no mention of husbands, for I cannot be cruel and tell him that all I see is my Henry.

'God Himself has appeared to be fighting for me,' Henry had sent to tell her. He was before Wallingford at last, ready to confront the forces of King Stephen. 'But the bishops and barons are urging us to negotiate; many are of the opinion that Stephen should acknowledge me as his heir.'

'And will he, think you?' Eleanor asked the messenger.

'He might, left to himself, Lady,' the man replied, 'but the Lord Eustace, his son, is determined to stand up for his rights, so there may yet be bloodshed.'

Eleanor shivered. 'Pray God there will not,' she said sharply. She could not bear the thought of anything happening to Henry, not just for her own sake (although the Lord knew that would be bad enough), but also for the sake of the kingdom that was nearly – but not quite – within his grasp.

It was high summer, glorious August, with the golden countryside basking in the hot, unforgiving rays of the sun. She had returned to Poitiers, her capital, to give birth to her heir – and Henry's. The babe had long since quickened in her womb, and she was heavy and listless, longing for her ordeal to be over.

Her son was born with very little trouble that month, on the very day – as she later learned – that Eustace died suddenly

from food poisoning. Both events, she had no doubt, demonstrated God's approval of Henry's cause. The child was strong
and lusty with a shock of red hair, and he would be a king's son
before long, for it was now only a matter of time before the
grieving and war-weary Stephen ceded victory to Henry
FitzEmpress.

She named her son William, at Henry's insistence. It would,
he had sent to command her, please the English – or, more
importantly, the Norman barons who ruled over them – if
the future heir to England were called after King William the
Conqueror, Henry's great-grandfather, who had invaded the
kingdom and seized the crown in that memorable year 1066.
She approved the choice: William had also been the name of her
father, her grandfather and many of their forebears. Her people
would be pleased, and to please them further, she gave the child
the title count of Poitiers.

Little William thrived. Although she handed him over to the
care of a wet-nurse, since it was unthinkable that a great lady
feed her own child, she made time each day to sing and play
with him, taking delight in his progress and his gummy smiles.
This child would not be a stranger to her as Marie and Alix
had been. She would make sure of that.

William was three months old when news came from England
that Henry and Stephen had made a peaceful settlement at
Winchester, the capital city. They had agreed that Stephen would
remain on the throne for the rest of his life, and that Henry was
then peacefully to succeed him as his legitimate heir; Stephen
was even going to adopt him as his son. With the treaty
concluded and sealed, nineteen years of conflict were brought
to a joyful end.

God knows, Henry might well be his son, if the rumours
about Stephen and the Empress were true, Eleanor thought to
herself; it was only what others were saying openly. She rejoiced
in her lord's success, and she imagined how jubilantly his mother
the Empress, who had fought so hard and bitterly to topple
Stephen, would be receiving the happy news. There could be
no question now, Eleanor reflected, that God had approved of
her divorce and remarriage, for now He had ordained that she

should be a queen again, and that Henry should be master of a vast domain that stretched from the Scottish marches almost to the mighty Pyrenees. To crown it all, He had blessed them with an heir to carry on this new royal line. Her heart swelled with triumph and thankfulness. All their hopes and dreams were coming to fruition at last. Their empire would soon be a reality.

It was Christmas; the palace was adorned with boughs of greenery, the yule log burned in the hearth, and the festive meats were roasting in the vast kitchens. Her beloved had been gone from her a year now. What would I not give, she thought, to see his face, hear his voice, feel his body hard upon mine? But it could not be long now before they were reunited and the terrible, dragging months of separation were over. With this joyous prospect in mind, she presided enthusiastically over the merry celebrations, and after solemn high Mass had been celebrated in the cathedral on Christmas Day, she sat enthroned in the Hall of Lost Footsteps wearing her ducal crown, her little son crowing upon her knee, to receive the greetings of her vassals.

Soon, God willing, she would have another crown, although that would mean she must leave her beloved Aquitaine once more. This time, it would be for that far-off, war-ravaged northern kingdom with its fertile green fields, ringing church bells and cold winters, as Abbess Isabella had described.

'But I will return whenever I can, never fear,' she promised fervently, kneeling before the painted statue of the Virgin and Child in her private chapel, saying her prayers as she always did before retiring for the night.

10 Poitiers and England, 1154

The new treaty had been sealed at Westminster, and England was now at peace. Henry had sworn allegiance to Stephen, and Stephen had promised to act with his advice in future.

'God has granted a happy issue, and peace has shone forth!' the messenger told Eleanor; he had been much impressed by the ceremonies he had witnessed.

'What boundless joy for us all!' Eleanor exclaimed. 'What a happy day for England!' It cannot be long now, she told herself. I will see him soon. She willed Henry to come home. What need had he to linger now?

Henry raised himself on his forearms and looked down with distaste at the woman lying beneath him. She had a round, cheerful face, wavy fair hair that had fanned out over the straw-filled pillow, and a voluptuous body, but now that he had had his fill of her, he realised that she repelled him.

She puckered her lips, hoping he would kiss her as he used to.

'Woman, you're insatiable!' he told her, not unkindly, and, sitting up, reached for his *braies*.

'Must you go?' she asked.

'Surely the Lady of Akeny wishes to make herself ready for her husband's return,' Henry mocked.

'He rarely comes,' she said. 'Roger never loved me. He turns a blind eye to my affairs. It's his fault that people call me a strumpet, but what else can I do, when he never comes to my bed?'

Henry, who was one of the chief causes why Sir Roger de Akeny had forsaken his wife for another, was at a loss for words. What did the woman expect? He did not love her. He had nothing to offer her beyond the fairly generous allowance he paid her for their son, the child conceived of their lust during one of his earlier visits to England. Geoffrey was four now, and lay sleeping in another chamber in the Akeny manor house, which commanded a ridge at Garsington, a village that lay in rolling country to the south of Oxford. Joanna did not think it fit that Geoffrey's cot remain by her bed when Henry was in it.

Henry loved his bright little boy, who always delighted him with his quick mind and precocious speech. He was prepared to do much for him in the future, but he had tired of the child's mother long since. Yet she was unavoidably there when he went to visit his son before departing from England, and she was available and willing — so why refuse what was on offer? He had taken his casual pleasure of sundry women —

prostitutes most of them – during his time in his future kingdom, with never a thought for Eleanor, or any sense of guilt. She was his wife, he loved her and missed her deeply, but he was a man and when the urge came upon him, he could not deny it. So he had spilled his seed where he would, and the opportunities had been legion. Women were throwing themselves at him, this young, lion-like conqueror, tarts and noble ladies alike. He had taken full advantage of it. It never occurred to him that Eleanor would see this as the worst of betrayals. It was merely a physical need, like eating or pissing, and nothing to do with her.

He stood up, fastening his belt. 'I will send for Geoffrey when I am King,' he told the pouting Joanna. 'I will acknowledge him as my son and bring him up accordingly. He will be well tutored, and should go far in life.' He did not pause to wonder what Eleanor would have to say about that.

Henry was back at Westminster when his brother Geoffrey's messenger reached him.

'Well?' he barked. He was still annoyed with Geoffrey for allying with Louis, and – more importantly – impatient to be out hunting.

'My Lord,' the man said, 'my master sends you this.' He handed over a scrolled parchment. Henry broke the seal and unravelled it, then frowned.

'It's a poem,' he said, puzzled. 'Why has he sent this to me?'

'He asks that you read it, my Lord Duke.'

Henry read. It was a love poem:

> I am not one to scorn
> The boon God granted me.
> She said, in accents clear,
> Before I did depart,
> 'Your songs they please me well.'
> I would each Christian soul
> Could know my rapture then,
> For all I write and sing
> Is meant for her delight.

He looked up. 'What does this mean? Who wrote this?'

'Bernard de Ventadour, a troubadour.' The messenger, a young man with a fresh, ruddy complexion, looked embarrassed. 'Might we speak in private, Sire?'

Henry ushered him into an alcove. 'Now, what is all this about?' he asked testily.

'My Lord Geoffrey told me to say, Sire, that that poem was written for Madame the Duchess. She entertains this Bernard de Ventadour at her court. She always receives him as her guest with a warm welcome. His devotion to her is now well known, and many say he is in love with her. My master wishes you to know that his poems in her honour are sung even in Anjou and Normandy.'

Henry grabbed the messenger violently by the collar of his leather jerkin.

'What are you implying?' he hissed, his face twisted in fury.

'Nothing, Sire,' gasped the young man. 'I but repeat what my master has asked me to tell you. Out of his great love for you, he thinks you should know that people are beginning to talk. He says that he himself would never question Madame the Duchess's virtue, of course, but that others say this Bernard is her lover.'

Henry howled in rage. 'How dare they? And how dare *he* presume so far? I'll have him strung up for this! And worse!' He was shouting, and several men-at-arms who were drinking nearby turned curiously to look at their future king, exchanging glances amongst themselves. But Henry was unaware of their interest. He was remembering that Eleanor had not scrupled to take a troubadour to her bed in the past – and that she had deceived Louis over it.

'Tell me truthfully,' he growled, 'think you there is any truth in these bruits? On your honour!'

'Sire, many say there cannot be, for the Duchess's love for you, my Lord, is well known . . .'

'But others say there is!' Henry filled in, when the man fell silent.

'Some say she is in love with this Bernard.' The messenger swallowed hard.

Henry could not bear the thought. Eleanor was his, and his

alone. He was no Louis to shun her bed and turn a blind eye to her infidelities. She was his wife, his duchess and the mother of his heir.

With an effort he mastered his fears and his fury.

'You may tell your master that I will deal with this,' he said gruffly, then strode off to the scriptorium to rouse his clerks, thinking that castration might be too good for this impudent Bernard de Ventadour. Yet, gripped by fury as he was, he knew that his revenge must be more subtle than that. No breath of scandal must taint Eleanor's name – and nothing must be allowed to sully what was between them. He must take care not to perpetuate the scandal. If this matter was handled discreetly, the gossip would soon die a speedy death. Yet the pain in his heart was searing. Had Eleanor betrayed him? Had she bestowed her smiles – or, God forbid, more – on this piddling poet? He must search out the truth, and soon. He would know when he saw her, he was certain, but that would not be for a while: he could not leave England just yet. In the meantime, he had several weeks of mental torture to endure, imagining her in another man's arms, rousing the interloper to passion as only she knew how, using all the tricks she had practised on himself. Not to be borne!

At first, he thought of murder. Covert and efficient, the body thrown in a river under cover of darkness, leaving no trace. Yet reluctantly, his innate sense of justice – which would one day make him a great king – asserted itself, and his fevered brain conjured up another plan.

'I have been summoned to England, Madame,' Bernard said, rising from his elegant bow.

'To England?' She looked at her ladies, who seemed as puzzled as she did herself.

'Yes, Madame. My Lord Duke wishes me to compose martial tunes for my lyre, to entertain his knights.' He looked downcast – almost desperate.

'It seems your fame has spread,' Eleanor said uneasily, wondering what else Henry had heard. Surely he had his hands full enough in England without going to the trouble of sending for a troubadour to entertain his knights?

'That is what the Duke's messenger told me, Madame. But alas, I cannot bear to leave here, or say farewell to the person who is the most dear to me.'

'When the Duke sends such a summons, you may not ignore it,' Eleanor said. 'His patronage will be most valuable to you and add to your fame. You are a fortunate man.' Truth to tell, Bernard's excessive displays of devotion were becoming a little exhausting, and she would not be sorry to see him go, for what had begun as a pleasant interlude was now becoming merely prolonged tedium, and a little embarrassing. Besides, she would soon be reunited with Henry. When the spring came, he had sent to say, he hoped to return to her. She was counting down the days until then.

Bernard was miserably aware that Eleanor was making no protest at his going to England, and hurt to realise that she was not even showing any sorrow. In the privacy of his chamber, he wept bitter tears over her unkindness and the prospect of being parted from her, this wondrous being whose presence was so essential to his happiness. He tried to console himself with the notion that she was merely protecting herself by being so distant to him – after all, his love for her was a secret, and she would not betray it by showing emotion in public – and even ended up convincing himself that this separation would secretly be as distressing for her as it was for him.

When he arrived, London was overcast, freezing, and deep in snow. To a man of the south like Bernard, it felt like the edge of the world. Mourning the tragedy of his exile, he looked at the ice-bound river banks and thought longingly of far-off Aquitaine, and its beautiful duchess – and suddenly, miraculously, it seemed as if those banks were crowded with flowers, red, white and yellow, in a glorious sunburst of colour. He could almost smell their scent, and felt faint with longing. Then he looked again, and the illusion had gone. He was convinced it had been a good omen that presaged his speedy return to his lady.

His need became an obsession. When he thought of Eleanor, his heart filled with joy and misery in equal measure. He was a man possessed. Shivering in his meagre lodging in the shadow of Westminster Abbey, he composed song after song in her honour, as he waited for the Duke's summons to Westminster.

When it came, Bernard was disconcerted to find that Henry FitzEmpress – a steely-eyed, hawk-like, terrifying young man – did not seem to be interested in discussing the martial songs he had summoned Bernard to write. Instead, he began firing questions at him about his life at the court of Poitiers.

'Does Madame the Duchess welcome many troubadours like yourself?' he enquired aggressively, almost accusingly, Bernard thought. He had met with his Duke in the lofty, magnificent stone hall that adjoined the King's palace; it had been built, he had learned, by the Conqueror's son, King William Rufus, just over fifty years before – and, like everywhere else in this godforsaken city, it was freezing.

'Yes, my Lord. Her court is an academy of great culture,' Bernard enthused, shivering.

'And she has singled you out for special favour?' Henry went on.

'She has been most kind to me, a humble poet,' Bernard nodded happily.

'How kind?' Henry snapped. 'I have heard disquieting rumours about you. Now I want the truth!' His face was suddenly puce with anger, his voice menacing.

Bernard quailed before him. Now the awful realisation dawned, and he knew exactly why he had been summoned to England. Poor lady, he thought: this man surely is the Devil's spawn, as people say.

'Sire, as God is my witness,' he declared hotly, 'I have never compromised Madame the Duchess's honour. It is more dear to me than my life. And she, sweet lady, would never condescend so far, I know it. She is much too virtuous. I beg you to believe me, Sire.'

Henry looked at him hard. He wanted – needed – to believe him.

'These poems, though,' he said. 'They speak of love.'

'Unrequited, Sire,' Bernard told him, then pulled himself up. What was he saying? This harsh young man did not seem to understand the conventions of courtly love, so he hastened to explain. 'In my land, it is permissible for a humble minstrel like myself to pay his addresses to the lady he loves, however exalted she be, or even wed to another. He might love her, but he would be most fortunate indeed if that love were ever reciprocated. I am devoted to Madame the Duchess, I do not deny it, but I never dared hope for her favours. I am content, as are many, to worship from afar. It is the custom. My Lady has proved a most kind mistress to her servant, but that has been all, I assure you. I have been like a man without hope, sighing with love for her.'

'You dare to stand before me, Bernard de Ventadour, and brazenly tell me you are in love with my wife?' Henry was incandescent with rage.

'In my country, such things are accounted no insult to either wife or husband,' Bernard explained desperately. 'It is permitted for the poet or the squire to bestow his devotion on some great lady, and hope for her favours, be they ever so small. There is no shame or evil in it.'

'And in my country, they would cut your balls off if you were so impertinent!' Henry hissed.

'I have been a madman,' Bernard said fearfully. His face was ashen.

The Duke looked at him, fury and contempt mingling in his expression. Bernard quailed, terrified of what he would do.

'You need to be taught a lesson,' Henry growled. 'Guards! Take this varlet to the Abbot of Westminster and tell him to lock him in a cell and feed him on bread and water to cool his blood, while I decide what to do with him.'

Strong hands laid hold of the unfortunate troubadour, pinioning him, and he was marched away forthwith, struggling and wailing, beseeching his lord to have pity on him. Henry watched him go, grim-visaged. He had been so consumed with jealousy that he had come near to killing the wretch in cold blood. It was best for Bernard de Ventadour that he was out of the Duke's sight.

Bernard had been three days fretting and weeping in his freezing cell before Henry calmed down and relented. Having thought the matter over with a cooler head, he had decided that the wretched man was clearly harmless; he himself could not, if he were honest, imagine Eleanor ever wasting her time on him.

He sent orders to Westminster Abbey, commanding that his prisoner be brought before him, and when the trembling troubadour arrived, shivering in a coarse, chafing monk's habit, the Duke strode up and down for a bit, then came to a halt before him.

'Don't worry, I won't make a eunuch of you,' he barked. 'My Lady has told me something of you troubadours, but evidently I was not listening properly. I had not realised that such – games – were customary in Aquitaine. Well, henceforth, things will be different. I rule Aquitaine now. In future, kindly address your poems to some whore or serving girl.'

Bernard visibly slumped in relief, yet had the temerity to look grieved. 'My Lord has not understood the custom.'

'*My Lord* has some choice words to say about that custom,' Henry flared. 'Now, to business. My knights are waiting to be entertained, so I suggest you put on some decent clothes and go and get your lyre.'

Bernard was only too glad to scuttle out of his master's presence. But he did not relish his new duties, and pined still for Aquitaine. A week later, encountering the Duke in the gardens, and spurred by the courage born of desperation, he threw himself to his knees.

'Sire,' he entreated, 'how long am I to stay here in England?'

'Until I say you can depart,' Henry said.

'But it is so cold here, and the court is a rough, unfriendly place. There are no ladies to lighten it.'

'The Queen is dead, so what did you expect? The King does not need ladies to attend upon him!' his master retorted.

'I beg of you, Sire, allow me to go home to Poitiers, where I can mingle with fair and courteous ladies and chevaliers!' the troubadour pleaded.

'No!' Henry barked. 'You must stay here, if only for the sake of my Lady's reputation. And do not ask me again, for the answer will be the same.'

11 Rouen, 1154

As Eleanor's colourful cavalcade wended its stately way through the wooded hills of the Haute-Seine towards Rouen, the capital city of the dukes of Normandy, she could barely contain her excitement. The news brought back to her by the outriders that she had sent ahead, impatient to be at the centre of things, was excellent.

'Lady, the Lord Duke has returned triumphantly to his duchy and is even now lodged in his palace!'

'Lady, he has been received with joy and honour by his mother, the Lady Empress, and his brothers, and by all the people of Normandy, Anjou and Maine!'

They would be celebrating in Poitou also, at Eleanor's behest, but she had not stayed to participate. At the first news that Henry had crossed the English Channel, she had hastily gathered together a retinue, settled her little son in a horse litter with his nurses, and travelled north. Now she was approaching Henry's greatest city – for he had chosen to make it his seat of government for all his domains – and her mind was in joyous turmoil, her body tense and alive with desire. It had been sixteen long, dragging months since she had laid eyes on him, her beloved lord, and now it was only a matter of minutes before they would be reunited.

Had she been anticipating a private reunion, with just the two of them present, she would have been delirious with anticipation. Even a public reunion on familiar ground would have set her heart beating wildly. But she and Henry were to be restored to each other not only in the presence of his entire court, but also under – she anticipated – the eagle eye of his mother, the formidable Matilda. This would be her first encounter with her mother-in-law, and she was dreading it. Hence her mixed – and very turbulent – emotions.

Before her lay the fair and bustling city, set among murmuring streams, meadows and woods, and encircled by strong walls. As Eleanor rode through the massive stone gates, a slender, elegant figure in rich red silk on a dancing white horse, the people cheered. They had a warm affection for their Duchess, for she had brought great lands and prestige to their Duke, and done her duty by presenting him with an heir. And just look at him, tiny William, Count of Poitiers, gurgling and pointing on his nurse's lap as he was borne into Rouen in his fine litter. The delighted citizens waved back. Such a sturdy child, and strong! He would be another like his sire, they told each other.

Eleanor passed through narrow, cobbled streets lined with the timbered houses of prosperous merchants and fine churches. Presently, she saw before her the impressive Romanesque cathedral of Notre-Dame, with its high, tiered tower dedicated to St Romain. Inside, she was told, were the tombs of Henry's ancestors, the early dukes of Normandy, right back to the Viking Rollo, who had seized the duchy in the tenth century. Impatient though she was to see her lord and to have her meeting with his mother over and done with, she graciously acceded to the citizens' pleas that she enter the cathedral and marvel at its glories.

When she emerged, her eyes dazzled by sunlight after the gloom of the dimly lit interior, she became aware of the crowds parting for a small party of horsemen who were riding towards her across the market square, their hooves clattering on the cobbles. She squinted at them as they pulled up a few feet away, then as their leader dismounted, she recognised the wonderfully familiar hunting attire and realised, her heart leaping with joy, that it was Henry, come to welcome her. Shaking with excitement, she sank to her knees as he approached.

'Eleanor, you should not kneel to me!' he exclaimed, grasping her delicate hands in his strong ones, and raising her to her feet. She looked at him and marvelled. A youth had gone away sixteen months before, and come back a man. A new maturity cloaked him with ease, and invested him with greater authority and assurance. At twenty-one, Henry was battle-hardened, taut of muscle, ferocious with energy. His cropped red head jutted forward from his bull-neck, as he bent and kissed her full on the lips.

'You are most welcome, my Lady,' he beamed, his voice cracked and husky as he spoke the formal words of greeting suitable for such a public occasion. It was wonderful to hear that voice again, to see his face, and to have him near her. Battling surges of lust and the need to cry joyous tears, Eleanor gladly placed her hand on his as he led her to her mount. It was obvious from Henry's expression that he was as delighted to see his wife as she was to see her husband; he was grinning broadly, and there was a highly suggestive glint in his eyes that promised glorious bedsports later. But for now, they were duke and duchess, reunited, and must show themselves to their cheering people.

Eleanor's smile was becoming rather fixed as, her hand still on his, Henry walked with her into the hall of the magnificent royal palace that lay in the shadow of the church of Notre-Dame des Prés, just outside the walls of Rouen. This palace was the chief residence of the Empress Matilda, and had been built by her father, King Henry of England; it was as grandly appointed as Eleanor would have expected the palace of so great a lady to be, with its imposing arcaded hall and rounded archways richly ornamented with chevrons, its silken hangings and costly tapestries, and all the luxurious accoutrements of a royal and imperial household.

Matilda herself was very grand too. There were two thrones on the dais, and she was standing erect and proud before one of them, a tall, regal woman in her early fifties, wearing a purple robe girdled with gold and a snowy white wimple held in place by a circlet studded with amethysts. Her face was still handsome, despite its hawk-like nose and the faint lines that bore witness to the many disappointments she had suffered in her life. As Eleanor drew near, she saw there could be no doubting that she was Henry's mother – or that she was regarding her approaching daughter-in-law with undisguised disapproval.

Eleanor sank into a deep obeisance.

'Welcome to Rouen, Madame,' the Empress said in a cool voice. 'Please rise.' She turned to Henry. 'My son!' she said, with more warmth, and raised her face for the expected dutiful kiss.

'Mother, where is Eleanor to sit?' Henry muttered, ignoring her and jerking his head at the two thrones.

'I will have a chair brought,' the Empress said. She signalled to her steward.

She means to slight me, Eleanor thought. She wishes to show me who is mistress here. She knew I was coming, yet she conveniently forgot to have a third throne set ready.

Aloud, she said, smiling, 'My Lady Empress, I am most happy to meet you, especially on this happy occasion. You must be overjoyed that Henry's invasion of England has led to such a successful conclusion.'

The Empress bristled faintly. Was Eleanor implying that Henry had succeeded where she, for all her efforts, had failed? 'He has indeed done well in championing and vindicating my cause, for England was always rightfully mine,' she declared frostily. 'But I happily cede my claim to him, for I will never return to that godforsaken island . . .'

Henry cut her off in mid-flow. Clearly he had heard this before, and had no mind to listen to another tirade against King Stephen, his adoptive father, whom he had found himself quite liking, after having been brought up to regard him as the arch-enemy, and little worse than the Devil himself on the general scale of wickedness.

'You are of much greater use to me here, ruling Normandy in my absence, Mother,' he said. 'And when I have England under my hand, as well as Aquitaine and my other domains, I will need your help and support more than ever.'

Matilda looked somewhat mollified. Just then, the third chair was brought and placed next to Henry's. It was lower-backed than his, but Eleanor swallowed the insult and sat down on it, not waiting for the Empress, as the highest in rank, to be seated first. Henry covered her hand with his and squeezed it, which made her feel a little better, but she knew already that the battle lines had been drawn.

'I have a surprise for you both,' she told her husband and his mother, then nodded at Torqueri de Bouillon, who briefly disappeared, came back with little William wriggling in her arms, and handed him to Eleanor.

'My Lord, let me introduce your heir, the Count of Poitiers!' Eleanor announced triumphantly.

Henry's face was ecstatic as he took the child, marvelling at the infant's chubby limbs and the red curls that were so like his own.

'What a grip!' he grinned, as William grabbed his finger in his tiny fist. 'That's a sword grip, my son! That augurs well for the future. This boy will hold onto his own.' Even the Empress's steely gaze softened. Then Henry rose to his feet and held William high above his head, much to the child's delight.

'Madame my mother, my Lady, my Lords and barons all. Behold my son, William, who will one day rule this duchy –

and England and Aquitaine too, God willing. When he is older, I will bring him to you so that you may swear fealty to him, but in the meantime, I thank God for the gift of such a fine boy, and entrust him to the excellent care of his mother.' As the company cheered lustily, he passed William back to Eleanor.

'He looks like your father,' the Empress said to Henry.

'And his beautiful mother!' Henry replied. 'Eleanor has done well, has she not, in bearing me such a strong son?'

Matilda smiled faintly. 'You are both to be congratulated,' she said stiffly. 'Now, send the child back to his nurse, as our lords and bishops are waiting to be presented to the Duchess.'

They dined in private that evening, just the three of them, in the Empress's solar. After spreading the cloth, the servitors brought napkins, wine cups and dishes, all offered on bended knee. Then round cakes of wheaten bread marked with crosses were served, followed by the best that Normandy could offer: gigots of lamb and succulent duckling, sole in a cream sauce, spiced apples with jugs of thick cream and a platter of the Pont l'Évêque and Livarot cheeses that tasted like ambrosia to Eleanor. When the servitors had withdrawn, the talk was mostly of England and Normandy, and by the time the fruit and spiced wine appeared, Eleanor was growing tired of being ignored.

'Have you ever visited Aquitaine, Madame?' she asked Matilda.

'No,' Matilda said. 'Henry, did you go to Oxford? I had a horrid time there.'

'Yes, Mother, I did, but we were speaking of Aquitaine. It is a land of great beauty.' Oh, so you did notice, Eleanor thought, a trifle resentfully.

'I have no desire to go there,' Matilda said. 'I have heard that the lords there are violent and uncontrollable.' She shot a look at Eleanor.

'It has ever been so,' Eleanor said. 'That is because Aquitaine has massive rocky hills and rivers, and each lord thinks he is a king in his own valley. They have always fought amongst themselves, but I trust that now, thanks to their love for me and my Lord's reputation as a strong ruler, they will not be so disobedient. My cities of Poitiers and Bordeaux are always safe and quiet, and there we enjoy a good standard of living. My duchy is a land of great abbeys and churches, and the arts and letters are thriving.'

'By that, I take it you are referring to your troubadours,' her mother-in-law said, her tone dismissive. 'I have heard that they sing only of love and its trivialities.'

'Love is not trivial,' Eleanor defied her. 'In Aquitaine, it is an important part of life. And women are valued there as nowhere else. Believe me, Madame, I know. I have lived in France—'

'Where women are required to be virtuous and live in subjection to their husbands!' the Empress cut in.

Henry, toying with his wine cup, glanced at his mother in mock surprise, wondering when she had ever lived in virtuous subjection to his father. But Matilda was a woman on a mission and did not notice.

'I dare say,' she was commenting to a frozen-faced Eleanor, 'that you would not understand that, coming from Aquitaine, which, I am told, is little better than one vast brothel!'

Eleanor's temper flared, but Henry was there before her. He had been sitting at the head of the table, listening to the exchange between his wife and his mother with amused interest, but now it had gone far enough.

'Are you suggesting that Eleanor is less than virtuous?' he barked, his blood up. 'Remember she is my wife!'

His mother looked as wrathful as he did. 'I'm not only suggesting it, I know it!' she retorted. 'Either this woman has deceived you, my son, or you have lost all sense of respect for me in bringing her here and forcing me to receive her.'

Eleanor rose. 'I am leaving,' she said hotly. 'I will not be spoken of like that.'

'Will you deny, then, that you were Geoffrey's mistress?' the Empress flung at her. Eleanor paused in her flight, drawing in her breath, and there was an awful silence before she found the words to reply. Henry's expression was, as so often, unreadable.

'I will not deny it,' she said, her cheeks burning, 'but know this, Madame, that he told me he was unhappily married and that you had no more use for each other as man and woman. Do you deny *that?*'

'My relations with Geoffrey are no business of yours. What

you did was wrong, and it was even more wrong of you to marry my son, knowing you had been his father's leman.'

'That's enough,' snarled Henry. 'I will hear no more. And you, Mother, must keep what you know to yourself, if you wish to retain what power is left to you in the world – and my filial devotion.' His tone was sarcastic.

Matilda got to her feet. 'You must both live with your consciences. It is not I who have committed the sin of incest. Mark me, there will be a reckoning one day. God is not to be mocked. And there's no need to threaten me, Henry. I had already decided that discretion was essential – do you think I would bring shame on myself by publicly announcing that my late-lamented husband had an affair with a woman who is the scandal of Christendom? Don't think I haven't heard the rumours—'

'Enough!' bellowed Henry, flushing with rage.

'You're right, I've had enough,' spat Eleanor, and gathering up her mantle, she swept regally out of the room.

'Well, I hope you're pleased with yourself, Mother,' Henry said, his gaze thunderous.

'Your marriage made good political sense, I grant you that,' Matilda muttered. 'But I can only deplore the fact that your wife has a stained reputation, and that she betrayed me with my husband, your own father. And that she has the brazen nerve to come here and expect to be honourably received.'

'Mother,' Henry said quietly, leaning forward and glaring directly into her eyes. 'Perhaps you did not hear me or understand, but Eleanor is my wife, and you will treat her with respect, as I do. I love her, I love her to distraction, and you had best get used to that. It matters not to me that she has strayed from virtue in the past, for I have done the same myself, often, and so am not fit to judge her. But I know that she loves me and that she has been true to me, so let that be an end to it.'

'You are a besotted fool!' she told him. 'And one day you will realise it. You are so much your father's son, headstrong and impulsive.'

'I am your son too, Mother,' Henry reminded her.

'No, Henry, you come from the Devil's stock, and more's the

pity, for the Devil takes care of his own. Now go. Leave me, I am weary.'

'Very well. Shall I crave your nightly blessing, my Lady Mother?' Henry jeered. 'No, don't bother. Since I'm descended from the Devil, it won't do me any good. What I want from you, rather, is a truce. You don't have to be friends with Eleanor – even I, besotted fool that you say I am, wouldn't ask that – but I want you always to treat her with the respect due to her rank and to my wife, if that is at all possible. Is that understood?'

Matilda said nothing. Her expression was glacial.

'I'm waiting,' Henry said pleasantly.

'Very well,' was the tight-lipped reply. 'Just make sure that I see her as little as possible.'

'I should imagine she wouldn't want to see you at all,' said Henry.

'I'm really sorry, Eleanor,' Henry said, climbing into bed and taking her in his arms. 'I especially regret that my mother decided to poison our reunion with her vitriol – and my first meeting with young William.' He kissed her. 'He's wonderful, isn't he? Me to the life!'

'I love you, Henry,' Eleanor murmured, feeling vulnerable, and resting her head on his chest, taking comfort from his strength. Then she forgot all about Matilda as the familiar and much longed-for melting sensation coursed through her body, and she gave herself up to her husband's delightful caresses – although not for long. As needy as she, he mounted her swiftly.

'God, it's so good to hold you again!' he cried, and then could say no more as passion overtook him. Eleanor's desire was no less urgent, and as they lost control in unison, rolling between the sheets, grabbing and devouring each other, she thought she would die of the pleasure. Afterwards, lying together in blissful euphoria, kissing gently and sensuously, they gazed at each other in wonder, shaken by the depth of their passion.

'I pray you never have to leave me for so long again,' Eleanor said, low, touching Henry's cheek.

'I think I shall have to, if that's what I'll be coming home to!' he teased, grinning. 'By the eyes of God, woman, you are a marvel! No one has ever made me feel like this.' He was being serious now.

'And shall make you feel even better . . .' Eleanor promised, sliding sensuously down the bed. 'How like you this, my dear heart? And this?'

'Eleanor, you're insatiable!' Henry groaned, stretching with pleasure, and chuckled, 'Do you realise that for this you could end up doing penance for three years?'

Eleanor momentarily stopped what she was doing. '*If* I confessed it,' she murmured, 'but in truth, I consider it to be no sin.' She resumed where she had left off.

'Then we shall burn together in Hell, and be damned!' Henry gasped.

In the morning, the Duke was up early, anxious to be out hunting. He would never lie late in bed, but was always restless to be gone.

'He makes a martyrdom of the sport,' his mother complained. She had complied with Henry's demand, and there was an unspoken, if uneasy, truce between her and Eleanor when they met in the chapel before breakfast and bowed warily to each other.

'She had actually sent a message asking me if I wished to accompany her to Mass,' Eleanor told Henry on his return.

'And did you?'

'Of course. She will never have cause to call me undutiful.' She set down the illuminated book she had been reading.

'Henry—'

'What's that?' Henry interrupted, looking admiringly at the book with its bejewelled silver cover. He had an insatiable curiosity.

'It is *The Deeds of the Counts of Anjou*,' Eleanor told him. 'I am learning all about your forebears.'

Henry sniffed. 'It might put you off me for life! They were troublesome bastards, the lot of them.'

'It does make for very interesting reading,' Eleanor smiled. 'And it explains a lot of things!'

'Hah!' cried Henry. 'Don't paint me with the same brush. Although if you listen to Abbot Bernard, I'm worse than all of them put together.'

'So he told me!' she laughed, then her face grew serious. 'Henry, how long are we to sojourn in Normandy?'

'I'm not sure,' Henry said warily. 'I wanted to talk to you.'

'You said six weeks.' The prospect of a longer stay with her dragon of a mother-in-law was more than she could stomach.

'I know, but I have just had news from Aquitaine. Some of your vassals are in rebellion. I want you to remain here while I go and teach them a lesson.'

'Rebellion?' Eleanor echoed.

'It seems they don't like me,' Henry muttered, 'but it's nothing major.'

'I could quell them,' she told him. 'They will listen to me.'

'And that's precisely why I am going in your stead, so that they learn to listen to me as well.'

'Henry, I insist—'

'Eleanor, my mind is made up. Don't worry, my Lady Mother won't eat you up while I'm gone. She's got enough of the statesman in her to appreciate the folly of upsetting me, when her power here derives from me.'

'But Henry, you need her to govern Normandy, and she knows it,' Eleanor protested. 'That's an empty threat. She has no need to fear you.'

'Yes, but she has every need to fear you,' Henry retorted. 'Normandy has a duchess now – why should she not rule it in my absence?'

'And when we are summoned to England? I don't want to stay here!'

'I have many dependable Norman barons, my sweetheart. No, never fear, my mother will behave herself. And you have your ladies and young William to occupy you.'

'You make it sound as if that should be enough to content me,' Eleanor complained. 'Take me with you. Let us not be parted again.'

'No,' Henry declared. 'It will not be for long, and war is man's work. Then we can look forward to another reunion.' He grinned at her suggestively.

Again, Eleanor experienced that hateful feeling of being trapped and helpless.

'You just don't understand, do you?' she fumed. 'I am the

Duchess of Aquitaine, and I am fitted for higher things than the company of women and babies. When there is trouble in my domains, I should be with you, putting things right. We said we would do these things *together*, Henry! And, as you seem to have forgotten already, we have just been parted for sixteen months – *sixteen months* – yet you are going to leave me again. I can't believe you would even think of that, not after last night.'

Henry came to her and caught her roughly in his arms.

'Do you think I want to leave you?' He sighed. 'Ah, Eleanor, in an ideal world we would be together always, but I have vast domains to rule, and that means I must continually be on the move. Listen. I know you for an intelligent woman, and I do value your political ability, but I need to assert my authority in Aquitaine, and I need to do it alone. When those godforsaken vassals of yours have learned who's in charge, we will rule the duchy as equals. In the meantime, all I ask is that you stay here in safety with our son.'

'Very well then,' Eleanor conceded after a pause, still simmering, 'but summon me as soon as you can.'

'No, I will return to you here,' Henry said.

'But why?' she asked in dismay.

'There is news from England,' Henry said. 'I have not yet had a chance to tell you or my mother. King Stephen is ill; it can now only be a matter of time. We must hold ourselves in readiness, and for that reason we should stay here in Normandy. It is only a short distance across the Channel from England.'

'But you are going south,' Eleanor pointed out. 'What if the summons comes while you are away?'

'I shall ride like the wind and be here in ten minutes!' Henry chuckled. 'And I'll bring your rebellious vassals with me. The promise of rich pickings in England might make them like me more.'

12 Rouen, 1154

It was late October. In the solar of the royal palace, the two richly garbed royal ladies sat sewing by a brazier. The wind was howling outside, and the colourful tapestries on the walls stirred in the draught from the slit windows.

'Bring me more silks,' the Empress commanded, and her waiting woman scuttled away. Another appeared with goblets of cognac, which she placed on the table.

'I wish there was news of Henry,' Eleanor said, taking a sip. 'Oh, that's warming.'

'I expect the weather is as bad in the Vexin as it is here,' Matilda said. Her manner towards her daughter-in-law was still merely polite, but months of familiarity had eroded the sharp edge of the glacier. Thrown together by virtue of their rank, both women had had to make the best of it.

'I worry about Henry. He is still not over his illness.' Eleanor shuddered as she recalled her beloved's close brush with death the month before, after he had been laid low with a rampant, burning fever. Thanks to his vigorous constitution, and no thanks to his inept doctors, he had pulled through, but not before his wife and his mother had suffered some searingly anxious moments.

'I worry too, but it is imperative that he puts down this revolt,' Matilda said.

'I know that, Madame, but he was still suffering fits of the shivers the night before he left.' And he had been too fatigued to make love.

'I know my son. He is strong, and a fighter. He will recover. But he hates being ill and, as you have no doubt discovered, he will never admit to any weakness, nor will he be told what to do.' The Empress smiled dourly, then turned her gimlet gaze on the younger woman. 'You have heard the news about your former husband, King Louis?'

'That he has remarried – yes,' Eleanor said, rising to throw another log on the brazier. 'I wish him nothing but happiness – and his bride nothing but fortitude.'

'They are saying that this Castilian princess, Constance, won him by her modesty,' Matilda murmured, 'and that his subjects think he is better married than he had been.'

Eleanor ignored the barbs. She had grown too used to them. 'More likely he was won by the prospect of a rich dowry from her father, King Alfonso,' she retorted. 'At least he has now made peace with Henry and stopped calling himself duke of Aquitaine. That really did irk me!'

She shifted in her chair, and rested her hands on her swollen belly. She was five months gone with child, and finding the waiting tedious. She longed to be back in the saddle, riding in the fresh air, her hawk on her glove.

Suddenly, Mamille de Roucy burst into the room, her rosy round face flushed with excitement. The Empress frowned at her deplorable lack of ceremony, but the damsel did not notice.

'Mesdames, there is a messenger arrived from England, much travel-stained! He says he is come from Archbishop Theobald, and must see the Duke urgently.'

Eleanor sat bolt upright. The Empress looked at her, and in the two pairs of eyes that met, hope was springing.

'Did you tell him that Duke Henry is not here?' Eleanor asked.

'I did, Madame. He is asking to see you instead.'

'Then send him in.'

Eleanor rose, a proud and regal figure in her scarlet gown of fine wool with long hanging oversleeves. Her head was bare, her long hair plaited and bound around the slim gold filet that denoted her rank. Thus did the exhausted messenger see her when he was shown into her presence. His admiring glance paid tribute to the beauty of her face and the voluptuousness of her fecund body. He fell to his knees before her.

'Lady, allow me to be the first to salute you as queen of England!' he cried. 'King Stephen, whom God assoil, has departed this life. He died on the twenty-fifth day of October.'

'Praise be to God,' Matilda breathed exultantly, crossing herself. Eleanor did likewise, not being quite able to take in the glad tidings. She was a queen again, queen of that strange northern land beyond the sea, of which she had heard so many tales. Everything that she and Henry had schemed and hoped for had come to pass.

'I thank you for bringing me this news,' she told the messenger, giving him her hand to kiss. 'The Duke – nay, the King! – must be informed at once. I pray you, refresh yourself in the kitchens, then make all haste to the Vexin to my Lord, and bid him return without delay, so that he may hasten to take possession of his kingdom. God speed you!'

When the man had gone, Eleanor turned to her mother-in-law, who had also risen to her feet. The Empress had a rapt expression on her handsome face.

'So God has been just at last,' she said. 'These nineteen long winters of the usurper's rule I have prayed for this and beseeched Him to uphold my rights. Now He has spoken, and my son will wear the crown that I fought over so long and bitterly.' Her eyes were shining.

'Madame, I rejoice in this happy ending to your struggle,' Eleanor said sincerely. In this moment of triumph, she could afford to be generous to her enemy. Impelled by a shared sense of jubilation, the two women embraced and kissed, each planting cool lips on the other's cheek.

'Come,' Eleanor said, taking the initiative. 'We must assemble our little court and tell them the glad news. Then we shall gather a retinue and go to the cathedral and give thanks.' And she swept out of the chamber, her woollen skirts trailing regally behind her, and for the first time daring to take precedence before the Empress.

There was much to be done while they waited for Henry. Letters to be sent, announcing his accession, provision made for the governance of Aquitaine in its rulers' absence, and administrative matters to be dealt with, for the duchy of Normandy was to be left in Matilda's capable hands. Eleanor had, as a matter of courtesy, invited Matilda to come to England with her and Henry, but she had declined, much to her daughter-in-law's relief.

'I will never set foot there again,' the older woman had stoutly declared, 'not after they insulted me so horribly, and drove me out – me, their rightful queen!'

Eleanor had heard that it had been Matilda's insufferable haughtiness and arrogance that had driven the English to abandon her cause, but she said nothing of this.

'If you change your mind, Madame, or even if you come only for the coronation, you will be very welcome,' she said courteously, then turned to receive a travel-weary messenger who had just come from Henry.

'Is my Lord on his way?' she asked.

'No, Lady, he is besieging a castle.'

'What?' Eleanor could not believe her ears.

'Lady, he says he must teach his rebels a lesson, and will not be deterred from his purpose, neither by the news he is to be a king, nor by pleas for him to come quickly. And he sends also to say that, when he is victorious in the Vexin, he must put his affairs in order elsewhere before joining you.'

'He speaks sense,' Matilda ventured to say. 'There is no point in going to England and leaving unrest in Normandy. England can wait a bit. Archbishop Theobald is a sound man, and is keeping things in order. By all accounts, the English are pleased that Henry is now their king, so we can expect little trouble there.'

'I just wish he were here with me, to share this triumph,' Eleanor said wistfully, rubbing her aching back. She turned back to the messenger. 'Is my Lord in good health?'

'Never better, Lady,' the messenger replied cheerily, and relief coursed through her. That was one blessing, at least. She dismissed the man, then summoned her seamstress.

'You should rest, Eleanor,' Matilda said. 'Remember your condition.'

'Did you, Madame?' Eleanor asked.

The Empress had to smile.

'No, I was not very good at heeding the advice of my women, or the midwives,' she admitted. 'Pregnancy was a great trial to me. Once I had borne Geoffrey three sons, I told him that was enough. No more.' Her tone grew cooler and faded. Saying Geoffrey's name had reminded her of how Eleanor and Geoffrey had betrayed her, and of the reason for it. She was sage and just enough to admit that it was partly her fault, but she found it hard to forgive. Geoffrey had been her husband, and they had both dishonoured her by their rutting together. Yet she had come to concede that Eleanor had dignity and intelligence, and she was aware of a grudging admiration for her. She had made Henry the greatest prince in Christendom, this errant daughter-in-law of hers, and she would make a fine queen. That was enough to earn Matilda's acceptance. But she knew she would never, ever like Eleanor, or approve of her – that much was certain.

*

When Henry did finally return, he found his wife, his mother and the whole court immersed in a flurry of preparations for the journey to England.

'What's all this?' he asked, astonished, coming into Eleanor's chamber at noon with a sore head, after a night spent celebrating his accession with his barons, then in joyful reunion with his lady. There, on the bed, on the table, on stools and on every available surface, were heaped piles of clothes, fine garments of silk, linen and wool, many of them richly embroidered, gowns, *bliauts*, cloaks, chemises . . . Red-cheeked damsels were hastening to and fro, stowing some of the stuff away in chests, or adding even more items to the piles.

'We are packing.' Eleanor was swirling about before her mirror in a rich mantle lined with ermine. Henry looked at her admiringly as he came up behind her.

'I see you are dressed like a queen already,' he complimented her, pulling her hair aside and kissing her on the neck. 'We make a handsome couple, eh?' he added, looking at their joint reflection.

'If you would take the trouble to dress a little more like a king, we'd make a very handsome couple,' Eleanor said tartly, as she swivelled out of his grasp and offloaded the mantle into the arms of Mamille. Henry looked down ruefully at his hunting clothes; he rarely wore anything else, and only donned state robes when it was necessary to impress on formal occasions. The riding gear was clean and of good cloth, but mended in places. He had wielded the needle himself, as Eleanor watched in astonishment. 'Why can't you ask your valet to do that for you?' she had asked. 'That's no job for the Duke of Normandy and Aquitaine!' 'Why, when I can do it myself?' Henry had replied. She secretly applauded his lack of grandeur. It made him all the more approachable. You knew where you stood with him. There was no false façade.

Henry threw himself on the bed, shoving aside a pile of veils, and began munching an apple.

'Mind those veils!' Eleanor cried, and hastened to rescue them. 'Torqueri spent a long time hemming and pressing these,' she reproved. 'And get your muddy boots off the bed!'

Crunching, Henry amiably complied.

'Exactly how many veils are there?' he enquired, eyeing the great pile.

'Too many to count,' Eleanor said, distracted. 'Florine and Faydide, have you packed my shoes?'

'All fourteen pairs,' Florine told her.

'And the forty-two gowns,' Faydide added.

'Forty-two?' Henry echoed. 'You don't need forty-two gowns.'

'I must impress our new subjects,' she answered.

'They'll be accusing us of extravagance,' he muttered.

'The warm undershirts, Madame,' Torqueri said. Henry eyed them suspiciously. Eleanor caught his expression.

'I have heard that it can be freezing cold in England,' she said. 'These are to wear beneath my gowns, over my chemise.'

'For one awful moment, I thought you were going to wear them in bed!' Henry grinned. The ladies giggled.

'I might yet do so, if England is as bitter in December as they say,' Eleanor warned.

'Over my dead body,' Henry growled.

'It might be!' she laughed. 'How are your preparations progressing?'

'I'm all packed, and the escort is assembling,' he told her. 'I am taking the usual rabble of barons and bishops – they all want a share of the booty. It'll be hard restraining them when they get to Westminster. I had to include my brother Geoffrey, the little bastard – my mother insisted.'

Eleanor groaned. 'That troublemaker? You'll need to keep an eye on him.'

'He's harmless enough, just a pissing nuisance. But to make up for it, my love, I have summoned your sister to join you.'

'Petronilla?' An image of a tall, fair young woman with haunted eyes and a fragile mien sprang to mind. 'That was most thoughtful. I have not seen her for years. Henry, you are so good to me.'

'Since my mother is to stay here, I realised that you would be without female company of your own rank in England,' Henry explained, gratified to see her so pleased. 'I gather there was some scandal,' he added lightly, throwing the apple core out of the window and reaching for a wine flagon. 'I was quite young at the time, and the adults wouldn't talk about it. Was she a naughty girl, your sister? I have heard that she is very beautiful – although not as beautiful as you,' he added quickly.

'Pour me some wine too, please,' Eleanor said, dismissing her women and sitting down on the only corner of the bed that was not occupied by Henry and heaps of clothing. 'I need to relax for a bit.'

'Here, put that stuff on the chests and rest here with me,' Henry offered, extending his arm invitingly and winking. 'You are tiring yourself. You must think of the child.'

'Which is precisely what you won't be doing if I lie down next to you!' Eleanor chided. 'Remember, the Church forbids lovemaking during pregnancy.'

'Bah!' chortled Henry. 'You weren't saying that last night, if I remember aright.'

'I don't see any harm in it,' Eleanor said. 'Neither do I see how a lot of celibate clerics, all of them terrified of women, are qualified to pronounce on such matters.'

'They'd burn you for heresy if they heard that!' Henry laughed. 'They think that sex is only for procreation, and that once you've procreated, there's no further excuse for doing it.'

'How little they know,' Eleanor smiled. 'It may sound blasphemous, but when you are inside me, it's almost a spiritual experience – a communion of both souls and bodies, if you will.'

'What are you trying to do to me?' Henry asked in mock anguish, pointing to the erection that was visibly stirring beneath his tunic.

'Control yourself!' Eleanor reproved him, feigning displeasure. 'Not now, please. I'm supposed to be resting. And I was going to tell you about Petronilla.' Henry made a face, but settled down to listen.

'It was over ten years ago,' Eleanor began, settling herself comfortably against the bolster. 'My sister was only sixteen at the time, and very headstrong. She fell in love with Count Raoul of Vermandois.'

'Surely he was too old for her?' Henry interrupted.

'Yes, by thirty-five years, but it didn't seem to matter as she was completely infatuated, as was he.'

'Randy old goat!'

'Must you always see love in terms of sex?' Eleanor made an exasperated face, but her eyes were twinkling.

'You've never complained,' Henry grinned, and lifted her hand to kiss it.

'Well,' Eleanor went on, appreciating the gesture, 'as it happens, you are right, because Raoul was certainly deep in lust. Unfortunately, he was married to the sister of that awful Thibaut, Count of Blois, who tried to abduct me, remember?'

'As if I could forget that bastard,' Henry frowned.

'I never liked him anyway,' Eleanor continued, 'and at the time, for reasons of his own, he was refusing all homage to Louis, and so to pay him back, I encouraged Raoul to seek an annulment. That wasn't difficult, as he and Thibaut were enemies. Anyway, Raoul left his wife, and Louis appointed three bishops to annul the marriage and marry him to Petronilla. Then all hell broke loose! Thibaut took his sister's part and complained to the Pope, and of course Abbot Bernard had to stick his nose in, telling His Holiness and anyone else who was listening that the sacrament of marriage had been undermined and the House of Blois insulted.'

'And what happened?' Henry asked.

'Raoul was ordered by the Pope to return to his wife. You should have seen Petronilla – she was beside herself with grief. But Raoul stood by her, and refused to leave her. For that, they were both excommunicated. Louis sprang to Raoul's defence, and went to war against Thibaut. He had many good reasons to, believe me. It was during that war that the massacre of Vitry took place.'

'I heard about that,' Henry said.

'All Christendom does,' Eleanor sighed. 'It was just awful. Louis was blamed, but he never meant for it to happen. When the townsfolk barred their gates against him, he had his men launch flaming arrows at the castle, which was made of wood. It caught fire, and the defenders perished, so Louis' men were able to force an entry into the town. That was all planned. But the soldiers went berserk; their captains could not control them. They laid about them with swords and torches, and soon all the buildings were ablaze. In the streets, it was a bloodbath. Those people who managed to escape took refuge in the cathedral, thinking they would be safe there, poor fools.'

'Don't tell me the saintly Louis ordered the cathedral to be fired,' Henry interrupted.

'No, he was some way off, watching in horror from a hill outside the town. It was the wind – it blew the flames towards the cathedral, and they engulfed it at terrifying speed. Fifteen hundred people died that day, women, children, the old and the sick. It was terrible.' She turned haunted eyes to Henry.

'You saw it?' he asked, his face grim.

'No, I was in Paris, but I had to deal with Louis on his return. He was stricken. He had seen it all; he'd heard the screams of those poor trapped people, and smelt their burning flesh.' She winced. 'He'd watched helplessly as the roof caved in and those wretched souls perished. He felt it was his fault, although he never intended for such a dreadful thing to happen.' She remembered him ashen-faced and shaking, unable to speak, lying sick and mute in his bed for two days. 'After that, he was never the same. He was weighed down by guilt. He even cut off his long fair hair that I had always liked, and took to wearing a monk's robes.'

'I suppose sex was out of the question,' Henry said wryly, in an attempt to lighten the mood. Eleanor smiled at him.

'It was usually out of the question!'

'So did Louis ever forgive himself?'

'I think it was more a case of accepting that God had forgiven him,' Eleanor recalled, 'and that only happened during the crusade, when we visited Jerusalem and he received absolution at the tomb of Our Saviour.'

'And what of Petronilla?' Henry wanted to know.

'Well, after more fighting and arguing, Abbot Bernard brought about a peace between Louis and Thibaut, and eventually Petronilla's marriage to Raoul was confirmed by the Pope. That was a relief! But her happiness lasted no more than ten years. When Louis and I divorced, Raoul decided that he no longer wanted to be married to the sister of the King's ex-wife; there was no advantage in it for him. More to the point, he had fallen for another woman, much to Petronilla's grief. Despite her tears and protests, he divorced her, and took custody of their three young children. Losing them has been dreadful for her. Her little boy suffers from a nasty skin disease, poor child, and she worries fearfully about him. Petronilla's lot has not been a happy one.'

But Petronilla, when she arrived, looking like a paler, plumper replica of her sister, was cheerful at the prospect of being reunited with Eleanor, and excited to be going to England for the coronation. Putting on a brave face to mask the ever-present sorrow she felt at being parted from her children, she made much of young William, who gurgled with delight whenever his aunt approached. Petronilla threw herself with vigour into the preparations for the coming voyage to England, and she and Eleanor spent many a happy hour reminiscing on their childhood and making plans for the future. Before long, though, it dawned on Eleanor that Petronilla's cheerfulness was largely the result of her increasing dependence on the fruit of the vine, but her sister had had such a difficult life, with her happiness having been cruelly snatched from her along with her little ones, that she could not bring herself to remonstrate with her long-dead father.

In Petronilla's wake, again at Henry's behest, had come Eleanor's two bastard half-brothers, William and Joscelin, whom he had appointed to join her household knights. Eleanor thanked Henry appreciatively for his thoughtfulness, and warmly embraced the two eager young men, who so much resembled her long-dead father.

At last, the great retinues were gathered, and Henry and Eleanor formally bade farewell to the Empress Matilda and set off on the road to Barfleur, where their ships were waiting to transport them to England.

13 Normandy and England, 1154

'This should make a good impression on my new subjects!' Henry declared, turning and waving an expansive hand at the long procession of magnates and bishops, each with their retinues and baggage carts, that trailed into the distance behind them. Inwardly, Eleanor rather thought that the English might see the King's great train as a pack of scavengers come to bleed their country dry, but she was confident that Henry's reputation was such that his followers would heed the honourable lead he intended to give them, and deal honestly with his new subjects.

She smiled up at him from her litter; she was too far advanced in pregnancy to ride beside him, and not relishing being jolted along the rutted tracks that passed for roads, but she was making light of her discomfort and trying to relax on the piled cushions beneath her, pulling her fur-lined cloak closer about her to protect herself from the freezing wind. She would not complain, she had resolved, because she knew Henry wanted to get to England as quickly as possible, and she just wanted the long journey to be over.

It was when they were making an overnight stop in Caen that Henry espied Bernard de Ventadour skulking among the varlets of his household.

'What's *he* doing here?' he muttered to himself, and beckoned the troubadour over. Bernard, who had been hoping that his master had not seen him and was on the point of fleeing, had the grace to look terrified.

'Sire?' he almost squeaked.

'I thought I told you not to leave England without my permission!' Henry said fiercely.

'I-I know, Sire, but your whole retinue was returning with you, and your knights needed entertaining . . .'

'Blast my knights!' Henry roared. 'You disobeyed me, you scum.'

The troubadour quailed.

'Now hear this,' Henry went on, 'and never disobey me again, or you will rue it painfully. You are to leave here now, without delay.'

'But Sire, where shall I go?' asked Bernard.

'Anywhere but here!'

'But I cannot go back to Ventadour . . .'

'No, that you cannot, and my good lady has told me why.' Henry had the satisfaction of seeing the young man wince. 'You'll have to find somewhere else.'

Tears filled Bernard's eyes. 'This is a great grief to me, Sire,' he wept. 'I know not what to do or where to go.'

'Take my advice and go as far away as possible. You might try your talents with the Count of Toulouse.'

'Sire, may I speak frankly?' Bernard was frantic.

Henry folded his arms and looked at him. 'I'm waiting,' he said brusquely.

'There is a lady, Sire—'

'By God there is!' Henry erupted.

'Nay, Sire, not Madame the Duchess – another lady.' Bernard hung his head.

'Hah!' Henry pointed at him. 'Another lady! You don't waste much time.' And he doubled up with laughter.

'Sire, I love her, and could never leave her . . .'

Henry stopped laughing.

'Toulouse!' he barked. 'Get your gear and go. And let me not see your face again.'

Bernard scuttled away. There was no lady; his heart was broken and he knew himself defeated. That night, lodged at an evil-smelling inn, he hastily composed a poem to Eleanor, in which he mournfully sang her praises for the last time and told her that her lord had forced him to leave her. Then he gave it to his servant, who galloped off in search of the royal cavalcade. Eleanor, reading the grubby parchment two days later, sighed in exasperation, then screwed it up and threw it in the River Vire.

Henry peered over the stone parapet of the tower of St Nicholas's Church, the wind and rain lashing his face and soaking his short woollen cloak. Below him, the shallow waters of the port of Barfleur churned and seethed in the storm, and there was not a soul to be seen in the prosperous little village; the inhabitants, grasping lot though they were, had all retreated to their houses in the teeth of bad weather.

'How much longer are we to be holed up here?' he fumed to the ship's master.

'I beg ye, be patient, Lord King,' the weather-beaten man shouted against the gale. 'Them currents down there can be mighty swift. Ye'll have heard of the White Ship.'

Henry had heard of it, too many times, from his mother, whose brother had gone down with it on that terrible night thirty-four years before, and he'd heard it again over the past few days, from the mariners, who always seemed to relish recounting tales of disaster. Of course, if the White Ship hadn't sunk, drowning the heir to England, he wouldn't be standing here now, waiting to take possession of that kingdom. And standing here was all he seemed to be doing; he was almost stamping with impatience.

'By the eyes of God, it's not far to sail!' he argued. 'Do you realise, man, that England has been without a king for six weeks? Why, my very throne might be in jeopardy because of this delay.'

'Lord King,' the master said evenly, 'it is not me that commands the heavens.'

'No,' Henry muttered, 'but when *I* command you to set forth, I expect to be obeyed. That's five times you have defied me now.'

'And it might be five times I've saved your life, Lord King,' the man replied sagely. 'Better for England to have a king across the sea than no king at all.'

There was no arguing with that, but Henry was not in the mood to be put off by wise words of caution.

'Thank you for your consideration,' he snapped sarcastically. 'God knows, we might be here for ever. No, my mind is made up. We sail today.'

The mariner was about to protest again when Queen Eleanor, her heavily pregnant figure swathed in a black hooded mantle, suddenly appeared at the tower door.

'I had to get some air,' she said, turning her face up to the elements, not minding the buffeting wind and smattering rain-drops. 'They've lit so many braziers I am suffocating in my chamber. Petronilla especially feels the cold. God's blood, it's wild, this weather!'

She battled her way through the tempest to Henry, who folded his arms around her.

'My Lady, our ship's master here is unwilling to put to sea,' he told her, 'but I am of a mind to brave the elements and be on our way.'

'That's madness, Lord King,' the master cried, 'especially with the Lady Queen near her time.'

'Well, my Lady?' Henry asked, ignoring him. 'What do you say?'

'A little weather never bothered me,' Eleanor replied, more cheerfully and bravely than she felt. She knew that Henry would have his way, whatever anyone said, so it was prudent to make the best of things – although that sky looked black and angry, and the gusts were fearsome . . .

'I would not put you through this,' he told her, 'or young William, but God knows what's happening in England without me. Is Archbishop Theobald truly the man to keep those unruly English barons in check?'

'The last reports suggested he was doing brilliantly,' Eleanor reminded him.

'Yes, but for how long?' Henry fretted. He knew, none better, how those same barons had defied the weak Stephen: how they had built their castles without waiting for his licence, then terrorised the countryside, using the civil war as a pretext for unspeakable depredations and atrocities. No, his mind was made up. There was greater risk in staying here than in braving the sea.

Eleanor thought she would never see daylight again, shut up as she was with her women in this pitching, stinking cabin with its alarmingly creaking timbers. Outside, the unforgiving Channel continued its howling, relentless assault, surging against the vessel's sides and tossing it mercilessly on the crashing waves. The wind screamed, and the ship rolled, and every time it did, the ladies emitted little shrieks or threw up once more into the overflowing basins.

'In future all I will ever ask you for, O Lord, is for my feet to be on dry land,' Eleanor prayed silently, as she lay on her wooden cot, clutching at the side for dear life, and trying to ignore the heaving of her own stomach. Beside her lay little William, tight in the crook of her arm, and in her swollen belly the babe kicked, affrighted no doubt by the unaccustomed tumult.

She could hear men shouting above the storm, and the tethered horses neighing and rearing in terror. The baggage stored in the hold was inexorably sliding about as the ship lurched from side to side, and ominous thumps announced its latest whereabouts. She had not seen Henry once since they had set sail, for the master had been firm about the women keeping to their quarters, and for all she knew – or cared, she told herself – her husband could have gone overboard. He might at least have come to enquire how she was coping in this hell.

She buried her nose in the rough pillow to escape the stench of vomit and the latrine pail. How long had they been at sea?

She had utterly lost track of time, and only knew that they had all endured hours of torture locked in this foetid cabin. In the next cot, Petronilla was weeping noisily. She had consumed a lot of wine in a hurry before forcibly being persuaded to board the ship, and had paid dearly for it since, but it had loosed her tongue, and her terrified ramblings were threatening to drive the other women hysterical.

'We're going to die,' she moaned. 'I will never see my sweet babes again.' This only provoked more frightened sobs and squeals. Any minute now, they would all be wailing uncontrollably.

'Enough!' Eleanor said sternly. 'Sailors face these storms all the time, and survive them.' She was gratified to hear herself sounding more confident than she felt. The women subsided, suppressing their cries and their fears. She spoke more gently to them then, offering words of comfort and reassurance that she wished she could believe herself.

The night hours – presumably it *was* night – seemed endless. For most of them, Eleanor remained in that twilight state between sleeping and waking, too strung-up to fall into slumber and so attain the oblivion she craved. At one point, though, she must have nodded off, for when she next came to, a watery light was penetrating the oiled linen stretched over the single window, and the sea had miraculously stilled. God had answered her prayer.

She offered little William her breast; mercifully, he was his usual, sunny self, unfazed by the terrible hours they had just endured; how blissful it must be, she thought, to be so young and innocent that one has no conception of the perils and dangers of this world. She kissed her son's soft, downy head, feeling for the hundredth time that sweet surge of all-consuming maternal love, this time coupled with thankfulness that both of them had been safely delivered from the tempest. As soon as they made land, she promised, she would seek out the nearest church and express her heartfelt gratefulness to God.

She rose, shook her women awake, and made them fetch royal garments and an ivory comb from the iron-banded chest that housed her most prized possessions and had not therefore been entrusted to the hold. This day she must dress like a queen, for she and Henry were setting foot for the first time in their new kingdom, and their subjects would surely come crowding to greet them. She donned her rich Byzantine robe, which fell in stately folds over her high belly, and let her long hair fall regally loose under a simple gold circlet. Then she emerged from the noisome cabin into the fresh, cold morning air, to find Henry standing not a few feet away at the ship's side, looking across a calm estuary to wide, sandy beaches and a vast expanse of woodland beyond.

'My Lady,' he said, doffing his cap. His barons and clerics bowed courteously as Eleanor came to join him. She noticed he had forsaken his customary hunting gear for a fashionable tunic ornamented with wide bands of embroidery, worn beneath the short cloak he had recently made popular, earning himself the nickname 'Curtmantle'. His coppery hair curled endearingly around his ears beneath the ducal crown of Normandy. He looked every inch the King, with his high, majestic features and erect mien, and her earlier resentment was forgotten in the heady joy of the moment: she was grateful to be alive, and proud to be standing beside him as his consort.

There was no one to greet them when they disembarked. Of course, no one knew when or where to expect them. They were, for the moment, a small party, because the other ships had been scattered in the storm and had hopefully made land further along the coast.

'We ride at once to our capital city of Winchester to secure the royal treasure and receive the homage of our English barons!' Henry announced to his company, and himself led the way on his magnificent battle charger. 'The others had instructions to meet up with us there if we got separated,' he explained to Eleanor. 'I have sent ahead to Archbishop Theobald, commanding him to summon the magnates.'

It was a cold day, but bright with winter sunshine. The land lay damp and glistening after the storm, and the litter's wheels made sucking noises as they were dragged resisting through the mud on the waterlogged roads. The Abbess Isabella had been right, Eleanor reflected, looking out eagerly from her litter: this kingdom of England did look a lot like Normandy and the Île de France. It was green and well wooded, gently undulating with shady glades, glittering streams, heaths and moorland. For most of their journey, though, they were riding through a great forest, its dense trees – mighty oaks, as well as chestnut, ash and beech – bare of leaves. Here and there, deer could be glimpsed in the distance, and solid, sturdy little ponies, most of them bay, brown or grey.

'Good hunting hereabouts!' Henry enthused. 'This is the New Forest, established by William the Conqueror, purely for the pleasures of the chase. The forest laws he laid down are very strict. None must poach the King's deer on pain of death – or, in his day, mutilation.'

'Mutilation?' Eleanor's eyebrows shot up.

'My great-grandfather was a just but harsh king. He abolished hanging, but replaced it with castration or mutilation.' Henry grinned. 'It was very effective, of course. In those days, you could walk from one end of the kingdom to the other with your bosom full of gold, and no man would dare molest you.'

'That's hardly surprising!' Eleanor giggled.

'My great-uncle, King William Rufus, was shot dead with an arrow in this very forest,' Henry went on. 'He had fallen out with the Church, and was generally unpopular. Some said he preferred boys to women, and the bishops, God bless them, got themselves all worked up over the extravagant clothes he and his courtiers liked to wear. His death was supposed to have been a tragic accident, with a man called Tyrell shooting the King instead of the beast he said he was aiming for, but I often wonder.'

'You think he was murdered?' Eleanor asked.

'It's more than possible,' Henry said slowly, 'although it's not the done thing to accuse one's own grandfather of regicide!'

'King Henry was responsible?'

'Well, he got the crown by it. Didn't wait for the formalities – he immediately raced off to Winchester to lay hands on the royal treasure, much as we are doing now, my Queen, although perhaps not with the same urgency!'

When the forest gave way to farmland, the track took them alongside acres of fields divided into a patchwork of strips; each serf would be working his own strips of land as well as those of the local lord to whom he was bound. As the royal cavalcade passed through a succession of small villages, every one with its stone manor house and squat church surrounded by a cluster of thatched cottages of wattle-and-daub, the country folk came running to see them, curious as to whom these richly clad, and clearly important, strangers were. Henry greeted them all, with that common touch that came so easily to him. He listened to their grievances, shook his head over their gruesome stories of the terrible years of King Stephen's reign, and promised that he would ensure justice for all. They cheered him heartily, hailing him almost as their saviour, as the rustic priests ran out of their glebe houses to bless him, and women and children approached Eleanor with small offerings of hard apples, black bread and cider.

Everywhere they went, they heard the ringing of church bells, that ringing for which England was famous. Once the news of the King's coming was known, every village rang its bells in celebration, to signal this momentous event to the next parish. As the royal procession passed through each rural community, it left in its wake jubilant peasants dancing and carousing for joy.

Very soon, they found themselves approaching Winchester, that great walled city dominated by its ancient cathedral, its fine abbeys and the imposing castle built by the Conqueror. This, Henry told Eleanor, was the city of Alfred the Great, the renowned Saxon hero-king, whose bones lay buried in the cathedral not far from those of the little-lamented William Rufus. And here, coming towards them, was the worthy Archbishop Theobald, riding on his mule to greet his king, a mighty entourage of barons and prelates at his back, all craning their necks anxiously to get a good sight of the young man who would now rule over them.

'My Lord King!' Theobald saluted Henry, then dismounted and, leaning on his crozier, went down on his creaky old knees in the muddy road.

'My Lord Archbishop!' Henry cried in ringing tones, leaping off his horse and hastening to raise the old man to his feet. They exchanged the customary kiss of peace and welcome, then Henry smiled graciously – and not a little calculatingly – at the magnates, who had dismounted from their saddles and made their obeisances as one.

'Rise, my Lords!' he commanded. 'Greetings to you all. I thank you for coming.' Turning to the Archbishop, he said, 'You have done well, your Grace, to have kept this realm in quietness these past six weeks. Tell me, is it true that no one has dared to dispute my succession?'

Theobald beamed. He was a devout soul, but also a competent and shrewd man of business, clearly respected by all. 'It is true, Sire. These lords here have all remained at peace for love of the King to come. And, to be frank with you, none dared do other than good, for you are held in great awe. Your reputation has gone before you.'

Henry nodded, well satisfied, then assisted Eleanor out of her litter and presented Theobald to her.

'My Lady, in truth, we are astonished to see you all here safe and sound,' the Archbishop told her. 'It is a miracle you survived that terrible storm. And I may tell you,' he added in a lower tone, the hint of a smile playing on his lips, 'that our barons here are quaking like a bed of reeds in the wind for fear of your husband. They think him almost superhuman to have defied the elements to come here.'

It was a good beginning. Enthroned in the Conqueror's great hall in the castle, Henry FitzEmpress received the homage of the lords and clergy, with Eleanor watching from a smaller chair of estate, her ladies gathered about her, their number now including several English noblewomen who had travelled to the capital with their husbands. It was a day of rejoicing and goodwill, with the English barons displaying an uncharacteristic admiration and respect for their new king, and the common folk singing his praises in the streets.

After a comfortable night spent sleeping soundly beside Eleanor in the castle's luxurious painted chamber, his hand resting proprietorially on her pregnant belly, Henry was keen to make an early start. He was anxious to get to London, and be crowned at Westminster without further delay. Then the real business of ruling England could begin.

London was frost-bound, but packed with exuberant citizens and visitors, come to witness the spectacle of the coronation. Nestling proudly beside the mighty River Thames, the City was smaller than Paris, Eleanor discovered, but equally impressive, and fully deserving of its reputation as one of the noblest and most celebrated cities of the world. Henry was full of praise for its defences, its stout walls, its strategic position on the River Thames, and its three dominant fortresses, Baynard's Castle, Montfitchet Castle and the famous Tower of London, the Conqueror's chief stronghold.

They approached through prosperous suburbs of fine houses and beautiful gardens, and, entering the City from the west, by Newgate, rode in procession through slippery, narrow streets lined with waving and applauding crowds. Everyone was huddled in cloaks and furs, but even in the bitter cold, London was vibrant and exciting, its people warm and welcoming. They hailed their new king as 'Henry the Peacemaker', and when they saw sturdy little William clasped in his mother's arms as they were borne along in her horse-litter, they cheered wildly.

Eleanor was torn between acknowledging their acclaim and gazing in awe at the sights of the City – the great cathedral of St Paul, the fine Guildhall, the numerous monasteries and churches with their gaily jangling bells, the prosperous inns with their bunches of evergreens hanging above the doors, and the maze of streets packed with wooden houses painted red, blue or black. In Cheapside, she was itching to take a closer look at the fine shops with their luxury goods on display: she caught tantalising glimpses of gorgeous silks from Damascus, enamels from Limoges – a reminder of her own fair city, which brought a pang to her heart – and the famed, home-crafted goldsmiths' work, which was of the finest quality. Eleanor made a mental note to place some orders with the merchants here at the earliest opportunity.

Eventually, they left the City by Oystergate and traversed London Bridge to the Surrey shore of the Thames and the palace of Bermondsey, where they were to lodge, since the King's residence at Westminster had been vandalised and was awaiting refurbishment. It had been decided that they would remain at Bermondsey for the Christmas court and the birth of Eleanor's child, which was expected in February.

When, late that night, she finally escaped the exuberant and rowdy celebrations in the great hall, Eleanor sank down in her bed exhausted, as her women folded her clothes away into chests, blew out most of the candles and closed the door quietly behind them. It had been an overwhelming day, and her mind was full of myriad impressions of London, and of this land of which she was now queen. She felt elated – and yet a little trapped, like an exile, for she knew she could not hope to return to Aquitaine for some time. Her place now was here, in England, by Henry's side; but part of her heart – the part that was not his – remained in the south. A tear trickled onto the pillow as she lay in the dark, the babe kicking inside her, and homesickness engulfing her as never before. Maybe it was the fact that that treacherous expanse of sea separated her from her homeland; when she had lived in Paris with Louis, or in Normandy or Anjou, her domains had been just a few days' ride away. Now they seemed far, far distant.

Resolutely, she put the thought away. She must be strong, for Henry, for their children, living and unborn, and for the people of England, who needed a just and strong ruler. And when, the next day, she walked in procession with the King into the magnificent abbey at Westminster, none would have guessed at her inner qualms. She looked every inch the Queen, Henry thought, his eyes roving approvingly over her elaborately gauffered white silk *bliaut* embroidered with gold trellis-work and clasped with a heavy emerald, and her sweeping blue mantle powdered with gold crescents and lined in rose brocade. Her hair was flowing loose, like molten copper, over her shoulders, and over it she wore a veil of the thinnest gauze, edged with gold. Most satisfying of all, Henry felt, was her obvious fecundity, manifest in the unmistakeable rounded contours of her ripened breasts and high belly; it was, after all, the first duty of a queen to be fruitful.

Eleanor gazed up at Henry's rugged features, the straight nose, the jutting jaw, the full lips – and loved him anew. There was no mistaking his majesty, as he strode in measured paces up the nave, resplendent in his scarlet dalmatic with its border of gold *passement* around the neck and its diapered weave; beneath it, he was wearing a blue tunic, and beneath that, a bleached linen alb. His long cloak billowed out behind him as he walked. His curly red head was bare in readiness for the great ceremonies to come. He looked the perfect image of a king.

The abbey was thronged with the estates of the realm, the lords and the clergy, brilliantly attired in their silks and brocades. The long coronation ritual was infused with mystery and grandeur, such as sent tremors tingling down the spines of those who heard its timeless rubric. Eleanor thrilled to hear the psalm that Henry himself had chosen as a tribute to his beautiful consort; she, unmistakeably, was his 'queen in gold of Ophir', and she was exhorted to forget her own people and her father's house. In their place, she was told, 'The King will desire your beauty; he is your lord, pay homage to him.' At that moment, she would gladly have cast herself down in abasement for love of him, for thus proclaiming his devotion to the world.

When Henry was lifted into his throne by the prelates, and the crown was placed on his head by Archbishop Theobald, there were resounding shouts of joy and acclaim from those watching. Then it was Eleanor's turn, and she could not but think – as the consort's diadem was placed on her bent head – that this was a far happier crowning than she had experienced with Louis, all those years ago, in Notre-Dame in Paris, when, as a fifteen-year-old girl, she had experienced no sense of a great destiny. And there was to be further rejoicing, for afterwards, as the royal couple emerged from the abbey, mounted their horses and rode through London, the citizens ran alongside crying, '*Waes hail!*' and '*Vivat Rex!*' – 'Long live the King!' It brought tears to Eleanor's eyes, and made her heart feel near to bursting with jubilation.

Part Two
This Turbulent Priest
1155–1171

14 Westminster, 1155

Eleanor awoke to the sun streaming through the glazed windows of her bedchamber. The June day was going to be beautiful, and she looked forward to walking in the palace orchards with her ladies and courtiers. She would take two-year-old William with her, and four-month-old Henry, a handsome, adventurous baby who never cried, and who resembled his father in looks and character. Both infants had been presented to the barons and clergy at Wallingford, where the lords had sworn allegiance to little William as the heir to England. Young Henry, his father had declared, would one day have Anjou.

At the thought of her husband, Eleanor frowned. She was uncomfortably aware that the space beside her in the bed was conspicuously empty, and would be so for some weeks to come. Having vigorously set his new kingdom in order, and made ambitious plans for the future, Henry was away hunting in Oxfordshire with his new friend and chancellor, Thomas Becket.

Becket was everywhere these days, with an elegant finger in every pie. Eleanor still found it hard to credit that this hitherto-unknown and relatively lowly fellow could so quickly have been advanced so high. It was just six months ago, only that long, that Archbishop Theobald had presented his most promising clerk to the King at the Christmas court.

'My Lord King, may I warmly recommend my servant Thomas Becket for the vacant office of chancellor of England,' he had said, indicating the tall, dark, elegant man at his side. Eleanor had watched Thomas Becket fall to his knees before Henry, had been aware of her husband, expansive with good wine, warmly greeting the clerk.

'Welcome to my court, Thomas,' he had said, regarding him speculatively. 'My Lord Archbishop here has given me glowing reports of your abilities. Do you think you can serve me as well as you have served him? Are you worthy of the high office for which he has recommended you?'

Thomas Becket had bowed his head. 'My prince, I will dedicate myself utterly to you,' he vowed. 'I will make myself worthy of your trust.' Coming from most other people, the words might have sounded extravagant, flattering, empty, but when the clerk raised his handsome face to his king and smiled, his apparent sincerity was striking. Either he was a good actor, or he was that rare breed of man whose word is his bond, and whose integrity shines clear. Eleanor still was not sure, but in that moment, she had seen Henry take an instant liking to Thomas Becket, witnessed the rapport that immediately sprang up between the two men, and felt faintly uneasy when the King unhesitatingly raised the newcomer to his feet and approved the appointment almost at once.

'But you hardly know this man,' she had ventured to remonstrate later, when they were alone.

'I take him on Theobald's recommendation,' Henry had answered reasonably. 'He is a shrewd judge of character.'

Eleanor had since come to wonder if even the sage Archbishop could make a mistake – or if she was being unfair to the newcomer. Becket, thirty-six, well educated, intelligent and able, and of good Norman stock, coming from a wealthy London family, was – on the surface – the ideal administrator and diplomat, as he had already proved on several occasions. She had learned that, even before he'd come to Henry's notice, he had taken minor orders and rendered valuable service to his mentor, Theobald, who had rewarded him with rich church livings and benefices. Becket's meteoric rise had made him the object of other men's envy, and the jealous back-biters at court were already whispering that he had grown lax and idle in his parochial duties, and too ambitious and over-worldly for a cleric. What Becket sought, it seemed to those – including the Queen – who jealously kept him in their sights, was power, wealth and glory.

She supposed, to be fair, that her overt suspicion of Becket was the reason why Henry had not initially told her that he was going hunting with his new friend. When he had informed her, without offering any reason, that he would be away for a few days, and she had unthinkingly asked where he was bound, he had glibly told her that he was going to make sure that the castles of certain barons who had given trouble during the anarchy of Stephen's reign had been dismantled, as he had ordered; but he had looked like a small boy playing truant from his lessons.

She'd smelled a rat then. Something was not right. He was lying to her! She knew it.

'Where are these castles?' she had pressed him.

'In the Midlands.' Again, she sensed he was making it up. And the lie was easily exposed, for only hours afterwards she had heard the Justiciar speaking of the King's hunting trip.

'I thought you were going to inspect fortifications,' she had challenged Henry.

'I am,' he said. 'Is a man not allowed to combine business with pleasure?'

It was a less-than-satisfactory answer, and it left Eleanor wondering why Henry had felt the need to be so evasive. It was only when she saw Becket riding away with him, chatting and laughing, that the truth dawned on her. He had wanted to get away and spend time with his friend, and had thought his wife would not approve; that she might feel slighted because he should prefer her company to Becket's.

He would have been right. She did feel slighted. She also feared that there was something wrong about all this. What were they up to? Wenching? Whoring? Drinking? No, that could not be – Becket never drank, nor did he frequent women. Even so, Eleanor could not suppress her conviction that something odd was going on.

Who would ever have thought that Henry would desert her for the company of a member of his own sex? But that was what he had done. There had been no falling out between husband and wife. Indeed, Henry was as ardent a lover as ever on the nights he came to her bed; yet it had gradually dawned on her that he now preferred to spend his waking hours with Becket – the insidious Becket, who had become his indispensable comrade and adviser in such a breathtakingly short time.

Her mind in tumult, Eleanor thrust aside the Byssine silk

coverlet, pulled back the bed curtains, and slipped out of bed, padding across the green-and-red tiled floor to the garderobe in the fastness of the thick stone wall. There, having relieved herself, she took a loose robe from its peg and went to rouse the two damsels in attendance, who were sleeping on bench beds along the chamber wall. Her eye was drawn, as it often was, to the new tapestry woven in vivid blues and reds, which hung high on the pale stone wall above the fireplace – a real innovation, this last, a hearth built into the wall. It was the very latest thing, and Eleanor was hoping to persuade Henry to have more constructed in his castles and palaces. So far, though, he had shown scant interest in the idea, for material luxuries meant little to him, but Eleanor was not giving up yet. She liked her creature comforts.

The tapestry depicted the Wheel of Fortune, an ever-present reminder of the ultimate futility of striving for earthly happiness. She wondered now why she had chosen it, and thought that she might one day replace it with something more cheerful – a scene from one of the legends of King Arthur, perhaps, or the romance of Tristan and Yseult, tales she had long loved.

She had only days before taken up residence in the newly renovated palace of Westminster, a strong and beautiful complex of honey-coloured buildings surrounded and protected by a mighty outwork and stone bastions. The palace rose majestically above the broad, rippling Thames, and was surrounded by woodlands to the west and a teeming suburb to the east, with Westminster Abbey opposite. Eleanor had already been to pay her respects at the tomb of its founder, the Saxon King Edward the Confessor, whom many now accounted a saint. That was hardly surprising, Eleanor thought smiling, when he had refused to bed his wife and get an heir because of his piety!

The Queen's bedchamber, solar and bower were in the fine new royal apartments built by King Stephen. To the south, nearer the river bank, lay the older part of the palace raised by William Rufus, and now given over to the royal departments of state, the Treasury, Chancery and Exchequer. Rufus's huge hall adjoined it; it was reputed to be the largest hall in Europe. Henry was planning to set up a court here, where his justices would implement his laws. He had also spoken to Eleanor of his idea of appointing jurors – twelve good, true men – to decide verdicts, in place of trial by ordeal or combat. She was so proud of him when he showed such passion for good government and the welfare of his subjects.

After Mass, Eleanor broke her fast with bread, fruit and ale, then conferred with her steward about the appointment of a master cook; the food in England, she had discovered, left much to be desired. After that, she summoned her clerks, listened to petitions, and dictated letters. Henry had always trusted her to deal with routine business in his absence. 'By English law,' he had told her after the coronation, 'you, the Queen, are a sharer in my imperial kingship.' She had been thrilled to hear him say that.

Business done, she and her ladies amused themselves by making music, one of Eleanor's favourite pastimes. Mamille played the pipe, Torqueri the tabor, and Petronilla the harp, as Eleanor strummed a cithara. The others joined in clapping, and before long someone suggested they dance. Soon, they were carolling around the bower, skirts and veils flying.

Eleanor reflected that they were very lucky to enjoy lives of such leisure and luxury. The Queen's lodgings were a haven of retreat from Henry's chaotic court, and beautifully appointed, with her chambers boasting every comfort: fine carved furniture, carpets imported from the Orient, plump cushions and silken hangings, even glass in the windows. She supposed she must thank Becket for that. Only weeks before, during the first days of spring, she had grown impatient of staying at the dark, cramped palace of Bermondsey, and had urged Henry to put in hand restoration works at Westminster. Henry himself had conceived great plans for Westminster, so he'd willingly agreed and immediately appointed Becket to oversee the refurbishment. Becket had thrown himself into the task with his usual enthusiasm and flair, and in a matter of just weeks, the great palace had been transformed, down to the very last detail. Nothing had been overlooked.

Despite her reservations, she had found Becket easy to work with, and had grudgingly admired his smooth efficiency. He had deferred to her in every possible way. Would Madam the Queen prefer this damask or that silk? Should he order silver or gold candlesticks for her chapel? Maybe her chair of estate was too high, and he should obtain a footstool? Was the canopy of estate to her liking? She was sufficiently fair-minded to admit that she had had no cause for complaint.

And yet . . . she could not like him. There was something about the man that repelled her, something she could not define, which was strange, because Becket was exceptionally good-looking, with his proud, finely chiselled features, and Eleanor usually responded warmly to handsome men. But there was a coldness about him when he was in her presence, a coldness that was never apparent when he was in Henry's company, and she sensed also an aversion to herself, for all his courtesy. Maybe he was aware of her resentment, which would not be surprising, for she found it hard to unbend to him as she did to most other people. But she felt it was more than that. It was almost as if they were rivals.

It had soon seemed to Eleanor that Becket stood with the King as Joseph had with Pharaoh.

'He is too smooth in his dealings,' she'd said carefully to Henry. She had to tread cautiously because he would hear no criticism of his friend. She forbore to add that she suspected Becket of also being self-seeking and manipulative, and that – the antipathy between them aside – there was something about him that offended her, something she could not explain, even to herself.

'Is that a fault?' Henry had asked. 'He has great talent and boundless energy, which he is willing to expend in my service.'

'He is vain and ambitious,' Eleanor persisted. 'The good Archbishop looks to him as a champion of the Church, but he is far too worldly in my opinion.'

'I want him to champion *me*,' Henry had said defiantly.

Since then, that was exactly what Becket had done, serving his new master in every way he could, and making himself indispensable. And Henry had quickly grown to love him, this man who was fifteen years his senior; indeed, he had become increasingly in thrall to him, treating him as a brother and an equal – and, Eleanor wondered, perhaps finding in him a substitute for the father he had loved and lost.

'If you ask me,' Henry's real brother, the obnoxious Geoffrey, had scowled, 'there's more than is seemly in this friendship.'

They had been seated late at the dinner board at Bermondsey, watching Henry and Becket chatting animatedly with a group of young barons. The King's love for his new friend was evident in his open countenance, his warm regard and his bodily demeanour. Eleanor, who did not shock easily, rounded furiously on Geoffrey.

'That is preposterous,' she hissed. 'The King is a paragon of manhood in every respect – and I should know!'

Yet alone in her chamber, that night – for Henry was still carousing with Becket and their cronies – Geoffrey's words had played on her mind, despite her ready dismissal of them. Could the virile young man who had bedded her passionately no less than three times the previous evening, and on countless occasions before – and who had boasted of his previous affairs with women – have suddenly become attracted to a man? To this pernicious Becket? It was inconceivable.

Inconceivable or not, she'd lain there torturing herself. She'd heard of men who were so lusty, and so lacking in morals, that they would fuck anything that moved, women, men, children, even animals. She could not believe that Henry, lecherous as he was, was so mired in filth that he could stoop so low. But if one listened to the teachings of the sterner clerics, men who indulged in this kind of fornication were irrevocably damned for all eternity, condemned both in Heaven and on Earth. People were not as tolerant these days as they once had been, and she had even heard that some poor wretches who had committed these grievous sins had been burned at the stake for heresy. She could not imagine her husband being one of their kind, or doing anything to merit such punishment.

But the doubt would not be stilled. When Henry had finally lurched into bed, drunk and smelling of wine, she'd turned to him in what had become desperation.

'Henry, have you been staying up late with Becket *again*?' Her voice sounded shrill, shrewish.

'What if I have?' he muttered, slurring his words slightly. 'Thomas is my friend. He is witty c-company. We have some good times together.'

'You spend too much time with him,' she accused him. 'People are beginning to talk.'

'They're just envious,' Henry grunted.

'No, it's not that,' she said slowly.

'Then what?' His jaw jutted forward.

'They are saying that it is not seemly, this friendship.'

'What?' Henry roared. 'Who is saying this? Who has such an evil mind? I'll have him strung up, I'll . . .'

'It's Geoffrey,' Eleanor told him.

'By the eyes of God, what gets into that Devil's spawn?' Henry spat, still outraged. 'How dare he say such things, and to you, my wife? He will pay for it, by God, he will pay for it.'

'Oh, leave him be,' Eleanor said, relief flooding through her, for Henry's reaction had convinced her that her irrational fears were groundless. 'He is just jealous. Perhaps he thinks *he* should be your chancellor.'

'Heaven forbid,' fumed Henry. 'That's it. I'm packing him off to Normandy tomorrow. Our revered Lady Mother can keep an eye on him. And for now, Eleanor, I intend to prove to you just how wrong that whoreson Geoffrey was!'

'You are too good to me, Sire,' Becket protested, looking up from the document he had just read.

'Think nothing of it,' Henry said. 'Those revenues will help you to live in the style to which my chancellor should be accustomed.'

'I am not worthy,' his friend declared. 'I have not merited such largesse from you.'

'Nonsense!' Henry snorted, getting up to pour himself more wine. They were in his solar, and had just finished going through the day's business. It was after the last account parchments had been rolled away that Henry had presented Becket with his gift. It was a grant of several manors with a good yield in rent – and it was not the first such grant that Becket had received.

'You know your courtiers grow envious of me,' the Chancellor said slowly, relaxing his lean frame in his chair. 'I've heard them complaining that there is none my equal save the King alone.'

'Bah!' Henry scoffed. 'None of them have half your talent, or your energy. Do you want some of this?' He came over and handed his friend a jewelled goblet.

'I see you are using my gift,' Becket said.

'Splendid, aren't they?' Henry observed, holding up his own goblet to the light.

'I had them sent especially from Spain,' Becket told him. 'It was the least I could do, given how generous you have been to me.' He was regarding the younger man with obvious affection.

'Thomas, you have earned it a thousandfold!' Henry retorted. 'I want no false modesty.'

Becket smiled, absently fingering the sumptuous silk of his tunic. 'I cannot tell you how much I value your friendship, my prince.'

'That makes two of us.' Henry's voice was gruff. Truth to tell, he could not have said, even to himself, what it was about Becket that drew him, and he often asked himself how, in such a short time, he had come to love this man. He could only explain it by telling himself that they were kindred spirits, that they shared the same interests, and that Thomas's company was enormously stimulating.

'We must plan another feast,' he said, as an idea was born. 'We'll have it at your house and invite my jealous courtiers. Let them see me giving you all the honour and favour that you merit.'

'Would that be wise?' Becket wondered. 'It might be a better idea to hold the feast here, in the palace, since your barons are always grumbling that there is little enough pomp and ceremony at court, and it would look as if you were doing them an honour too.'

'I'm bored by pomp and ceremony,' Henry retorted. 'Still, you have a point. And there won't be much pomp and ceremony when the nobility of England are in their cups!' He chuckled at the thought. 'Do you remember them last time, sprawling in the rushes and groping the wenches?'

The chuckle became a belly laugh, and Becket smiled too.

'You plan it, Thomas,' Henry said. 'You're good at these things.'

'What of the ladies? Shall I invite the Queen?' Becket asked.

Henry grinned at him.

'Better not! We'd have to be on our best behaviour, and she'll only complain when we all get drunk.'

'When *you* get drunk, my prince,' Becket corrected.

'I'll make a man of you yet, my friend!' Henry jested.

Eleanor no longer worried that there might be anything more than friendship on Henry's part for Becket, but she knew that they were unusually – and disturbingly – close. This was not the kind of comradeship that flourished between fighting men thrown together on military campaigns, but a sort of thraldom, in which Henry hung upon Becket's every word, and preferred his advice to everyone else's. She had gradually become painfully aware that she was being supplanted, that her husband no longer sought her counsel first, and that he was spending more time with Becket than he did with her. He came to her bed frequently enough, though, and paid her every courtesy out of it, and on the surface all was well between them, but she sensed, more strongly than ever now, that in every other way that counted, Becket was her rival.

It seemed that he was deliberately trying to usurp her place in Henry's affections – and in the affairs of the realm. There had been that crucial matter of patronage. From the time Eleanor had first come to England, she had been deluged with petitions and requests by those who knew her to be influential with the King, and it had pleased and flattered her to know that she had the power to change the lives of others for the better. But, only a month ago, it had been made plain to her that her enjoyment of that power was under threat.

Becket had come upon her as she sat with her clerks, going through the latest pleas from her petitioners. They had made two piles of the parchments – one for those to be ignored, and one for those that the Queen would lay before the King, with her own recommendations. But suddenly, almost symbolically, a shadow loomed over the table and the documents, and when she looked up, she saw Becket standing before her. In the fleeting second before he made his bow, she had seen the contempt in his eyes.

'What can I do for you, my Lord Chancellor?' she had asked courteously.

'I think, Madam the Queen, that it is more a case of what I can do for you,' he had answered, refusing to meet her gaze, but fixing his eyes on the parchments. 'With your leave, I will look after these petitions.'

She was shocked, outraged! The petitions were addressed to her, and it was her privilege, as queen, to deal with them. How dare this upstart deacon insult her so?

Even the clerks were gawping at Becket's presumption. One man's jaw had dropped in shock.

Fury blazed in Eleanor's eyes as she rose from her chair. 'My Lord Chancellor, you are new to your office, and quite obviously have much to learn,' she said in clipped tones. 'You will not be aware that these are petitions meant for the King, and that they have been sent to me, his queen, by right, in the hope that I can persuade him to grant them.'

Becket's response was infuriating. He merely smiled and held out his hand. 'On the contrary, Madam the Queen, I think you will find that the King wishes me to deal with them. If you would like to ask him, I'm sure he will confirm that.'

She was speechless. Never had she been so slighted, not even by those dismissive old clerics at Louis' court.

'Leave them here,' she said, her voice steely. 'I command it. I will indeed speak with the King. Now you have my leave to go.'

Had she imagined it, or had Becket actually shrugged before he withdrew, bowing and giving that maddening, contemptuous smile? He would not get away with his insolence, she vowed, as she hastened in rage to seek out her husband.

She found Henry soaking in his bath, humming to himself as he was washed by his valets. As she burst into the chamber, almost breathing fire, he waved the men away, frowning.

'Sweet Eleanor, what is wrong?' he cried, as he rose and reached for a towel to cover his nakedness. But Eleanor wasn't interested in his body at that moment.

'It's your Lord Chancellor, that insolent man Becket!' she seethed. 'He has dared to demand that I turn over my petitions to him. He says that you wish it!'

Henry's face flushed, and not with the steam from the tub. There was an awful silence. Eleanor stared at him, horrified.

'It's true,' she accused him, unable quite to believe it. 'You do wish it.'

Henry found his voice. Tying the towel around his waist, he came to her and put his arms around her. His skin was damp and he smelt sharply of the fresh herbs that had scented his bathwater.

'Forgive me,' he said. 'Thomas suggested that he might be of help with the petitions, and I thought it a good idea, especially since you have the children now, a royal household to run, and many other duties.'

'A queen's role is not all domestic!' Eleanor flared. 'It is my royal privilege to exercise patronage and use my influence, and you know how much I value that.'

'It is of no matter,' Henry hastened to reassure her. 'I will thank Thomas for his thoughtfulness, and tell him that you will continue to deal with the petitions as before.' He bent and kissed her, clasping her face in his hands. 'There – does that pacify you, my beautiful termagant?'

It was easy to say that it did, and so end the quarrel, but Eleanor had come away with the feeling that Henry had been a fool in allowing Becket his head in this matter, and the even greater conviction that she was now – willingly or not – engaged in a power struggle with the Chancellor, who was clearly out to subvert her influence, supplant her in the King's counsels, and have her relegated to the domestic sphere, where he obviously thought women belonged. And the awful truth was that Henry could not see it! He thought Becket was merely being kind. She could have howled with frustration.

But she had won the first round in the contest, and at least she knew her enemy, whose smile was rather more forced when they next came face to face; and she was resolved to fight him with all the subtle weapons at her disposal. She'd known it would be a secret struggle, no doubt of it, because Henry did not understand subtlety, and she would be fighting Becket on his own terms. It had not been long, however, before she realised, to her dismay, that she was losing the battle.

Becket was clever. He was unfailingly faultless in his manner towards Eleanor, and took care never to scant the respect due to her as his queen. She was always invited with the King to his house in London, a splendid establishment provided and maintained by Henry, and as palatial as any of the royal residences. In fact, the first time she had seen it, she had felt indignant that this upstart chancellor should be living in even more regal state than his master. But she had sat there with a smile fixed on her face, dining off gold plate laden with the finest fare, drinking from crystal glasses encrusted with gems that glittered in the flickering light from the great silver candelabra, and served by the sons of nobles, who had been sent to Becket's household to be schooled in courtesy, martial arts and those things that befitted fledgling aristocrats. She had graced the table, holding her own in the lively and witty conversation that flowed around it, yet aware that her opinions counted for very little with her host, whose courtesies belied his shut-off look whenever she ventured to hold forth.

She watched him covertly all the time, this tall, slender clerk, with his dark hair, his finely chiselled features and his aquiline nose, watched him charming barons and prelates alike, talking of anything and everything from hawking and chess to the business of the kingdom, his eyes alight with zeal as he spoke of his plans for the future. And Henry was captivated, hanging on every word. Seeing them together, you would have thought that Becket was the King, in his magnificent robes of silk and brocade, not Henry, in his plain woollen cloth tunic and short mantle, or his accustomed hunting gear. Eleanor thought Becket's vanity and taste bordered on effeminacy, and she was inexplicably repulsed by his small, tapering hands, which were like a woman's. She did not want those hands to touch her, and tried not to recoil when the Chancellor bowed before her on greeting and took her hand in his own to kiss.

Not that Becket's hands would have touched women very often, she thought. It was well known that he had taken a vow of chastity in youth, and that he avoided encounters with the fair sex if he could. She had sensed his aversion to herself, and noticed that he kept his converse with the ladies to a courteous minimum. She often wondered if he did prefer his own sex, as rumour had covertly speculated. But one thing was certain – he was not promiscuous in the least, and that was something she did not have to worry about: Becket, unlike many other courtiers, would never seek to be Henry's accomplice in fleshly pleasures, encouraging him to go whoring or to frequent brothels. It was a small thing to be grateful for.

At the moment when Eleanor was dancing with her ladies at Westminster, Henry and Becket were riding south from Oxford, talking animatedly of yet another hunting trip they were planning, this time to the New Forest; it was to take place as soon as Henry and Eleanor had returned from their coming great progress through England, to see – and be seen by – their new subjects.

'We will stay at my hunting lodge at New Park, near Lyndhurst,' Henry declared. 'Perhaps you would like to come too?' he jested to the little boy who was perched before him on his saddle. He winced as he remembered Joanna de Akeny's tears as she had given up young Geoffrey into his father's care; he never had been able to deal with a weeping woman. Anxious to escape, he had assured her that he would look after the lad well, and that a great future lay ahead of him as the King's bastard son, for sons, whichever side of the blanket they were born, could be great assets to a king. Joanna had wept again, this time tears of gratitude.

'Sire, have you considered how the Queen might react when you arrive with Master Geoffrey?' Thomas had enquired gently, as soon as they were on the road. He had not anticipated this hunting jaunt encompassing a visit to Henry's former leman, and had been rather astonished to find that Henry had intended it as cover for taking custody of his son. He could only deplore Henry's morals – or lack of them. His king had no self-control!

Henry had considered, briefly, but it had not occurred to him that Eleanor would be offended by a bastard child who had been conceived and born before they had even met.

'I doubt it will concern her very much,' he replied. 'The boy is no threat to her or the children she has borne me.'

'Women can be sensitive about such things,' Thomas said. 'She might take your acknowledgement of Master Geoffrey as an insult to herself.' He forbore to add that Eleanor might react even more violently were she to find out about Henry's covert dalliance with Avice de Stafford, one of her damsels. Henry had boasted of this conquest to Thomas while in his cups one night – although now he probably had no recollection of ever mentioning it. Thomas shuddered at the thought of Henry and Avice together, much as he had shuddered several times during the past months, whenever Henry had casually referred to other amorous exploits, all of them casual encounters, and none of them troubling his conscience. Becket was well aware, as Eleanor was not, that the King's reputation was already such that the barons had taken to keeping their womenfolk out of his way.

'The Queen is a woman of the world,' Henry declared confidently. 'She is not easily outraged.' Thomas knew this too; he had not forgotten what he had heard in Archbishop Theobald's household, from his friend John of Salisbury, who had worked for the Papal Curia when Eleanor was trying to obtain a divorce from Louis. John had confided to him several interesting, even scandalous, pieces of information that he could never repeat. And there had been colourful rumours going the rounds for years. Becket had heard them repeatedly, from many people. If ever a man needed evidence that women were frail creatures, what Thomas had learned of Eleanor would suffice.

'Do you think me a fool to acknowledge my son?' Henry asked, fixing his steely gaze on his friend.

'I should have advised discretion,' Thomas said candidly. 'But it is a private matter for my Lord himself to decide.'

'I intend to advance the boy. He could prove useful to me in time. I remember my bastard uncle, Robert of Gloucester. He was a rock of support to my mother in her quarrel with Stephen.'

Becket glanced down at the child; the boy was listening intently. He had intelligent eyes. A child to watch, certainly. Henry was right.

'Might I suggest a career in the Church?' he ventured. 'Although his bastardy might be a bar to high ecclesiastical office.'

'Popes can be bought,' Henry said. 'I could make young Geoffrey here archbishop of Canterbury! Or even chancellor, when you are in your dotage, Thomas!' He winked, then began chuckling. 'My barons won't approve, of course!'

'Then they will have to do as the Queen must, and put up

with it,' was the apposite rejoinder. The King smiled ruefully. As ever, Thomas had got his measure.

'I think the Queen does not like me,' Thomas said.

'Nonsense!' Henry replied. 'You have been a staunch friend and a great support to me. How could she not like you?'

'I fear she resents my influence. I suspect she would like to be first in your counsels.'

'I dare say she would,' Henry said, 'but she is a woman, with a woman's limitations, although she is more able than most. She has no need to be jealous. I sleep with her, don't I?' Becket winced, but Henry did not notice. 'And I allow her considerable power. I trust her to rule in my absence, and even when I am here, she can issue writs and official documents under her own name and seal. I've even told her she can sit in my courts and dispense justice if she wants, and settle disputes on request. So why should she resent you?'

'Then mayhap I have imagined her resentment,' Thomas conceded, keeping his doubts to himself. He suspected that Eleanor already regarded him as a rival. God knew, that was how he regarded her.

'The Queen knows you are invaluable to me,' Henry went on. 'Where else would I find a man of such diligence and industry, experienced in affairs, and able to discharge the duties of his office to the praise of all? Who else is such a staunch friend to me? Thomas, I tell you, you are my right-hand man. I put all my trust in you. Together, we will make this kingdom great!'

'My Lord flatters me,' Thomas said, with that slow, gentle smile that was so endearing. 'I am ever happy to be of service with my small talents.'

'You speak like a courtier!' Henry scoffed. 'Accept praise where it is due, man. You earned it by your merits.'

They rode on companionably for some time, past the peasants toiling on their strips of land, and beasts grazing in the fields, with Henry pointing out butterflies, cows and pigs to the inquisitive Geoffrey, and answering his persistent, incisive questions.

'This child is clever!' he announced delightedly. 'He wants to know everything. Young William is all bombast and will make a great warrior, but this one has a brain.'

'I shouldn't let the Queen hear you saying that!' Thomas warned.

Henry laughed, then drew his habitual short mantle around him. It was unseasonably cold for June. He felt a momentary yearning for the warmer climes of Anjou and Aquitaine.

Presently, the sky darkened and it began to rain. Soon, it was sheeting down and, fearful of being soaked to the skin, they tethered their horses under a tree and sought shelter in a church porch, huddling in their cloaks. Suddenly, they realised that they were sharing their sanctuary with a beggar, shivering in his meagre wet rags. He regarded them hopefully, as if he had guessed they were persons of some importance.

'Who is that man?' Geoffrey asked.

'He is a poor vagrant,' Henry explained. The poor vagrant continued to regard him with speculative eyes. The King turned to his friend.

'Would it not be an act of merit to set the boy an example and give that poor old man a warm cloak to shield him from the rain?' he asked, a glint of mischief in his eye.

'It would,' Thomas agreed, missing the glint, and thinking this was uncharacteristically generous of Henry.

'Yours be the merit then!' the King announced gleefully, and, whipping Becket's expensive cloak from his shoulders, thrust it at the astounded beggar, who gathered it around him and scuttled off without a word, leaving Thomas with no choice but to accept his loss; but he was angered and shocked, realising in that moment that Henry could be unthinkingly cruel. It was the first time he had felt anything other than love for the younger man, and he was further grieved with Henry for making him feel that way. As he stood there, shivering in the damp porch, it even occurred to him to wonder how far his unpredictable master, in times to come, might put their friendship to the test.

Eleanor stared as her husband stood before her, giving the strange little boy a push in her direction.

'Bow to the Queen,' he instructed, as the black-haired child stood there uncertainly. Henry grabbed him by the collar and jerked his head forward. 'Like that!' he said. 'Eleanor, this is

Geoffrey. He is my natural son, born before our marriage. I have brought him to court to receive an education, and to be company for our boys.'

Eleanor froze. She knew that kings and lords took mistresses as a matter of right and sired bastards unthinkingly, especially those whose arranged marriages were unhappy. Her father and grandfather had done it, and to prove it her two illegitimate brothers were even now in her household, eating her out of house and home. No prude herself, she knew too that Henry had had mistresses in the past, and accepted that, but being confronted with the living evidence of his rutting with other women was a shock to her. In a flash, she realised what the true purpose of the hunting expedition had been.

'I bid you welcome, Master Geoffrey,' she said coolly, stiffly on her dignity. It had been impressed on her as a child, by Grandmère Dangerosa, that a wife never upbraided her husband for his infidelities, but maintained a lofty silence. That was all very well, but only up to a point. There were questions that had to be asked.

'Who is his mother?' she asked lightly, as if this were a normal conversation to be having with her husband.

'The lady of the manor of Akeny in Oxfordshire,' Henry told her, his tone defensive. 'I was lonely on my forays into England. I took my comfort where I could. I'm sure you can understand that.'

'I can,' she replied, her tone softening a little. 'How old is Geoffrey?'

'He is five years old.'

Eleanor relaxed a little. The child smiled at her winningly. 'I can read, Lady,' he told her proudly.

'Can you now?' she responded, warming to his sunny nature despite herself.

'He is a marvel,' Henry declared, clearly bursting with pride, 'and will be a fitting playmate for William and Henry, who will benefit by his example.'

Eleanor, still schooling herself to the dignified acceptance that Dangerosa had enjoined, rang the tinkling little bell she kept for summoning her damsels.

'Welcome to court, Master Geoffrey,' she said. 'I hope you

will be happy here.' She told herself she could hardly blame this little lad for his father's sins, and that Henry had in no way betrayed her; he had just omitted to tell her of the boy's existence. When Torqueri arrived, she instructed her: 'This is Master Geoffrey, our Lord the King's son. Take him to the nursery and tell them to treat him with honour, and kindness, for he may be missing his mother.'

Hiding her astonishment, Torqueri took Geoffrey's hand and led him away.

'We have a new litter of puppies,' she could be heard saying. 'The Lord William will enjoy showing them to you.'

When they had gone, Eleanor looked at Henry.

'Am I to expect any other additions to my children's household?' she asked.

'No,' Henry lied, knowing there might one day be several moments of reckoning in regard to a number of other bastards he had carelessly sired, but confident that he could bluff his way through them if or when the time came.

He rose and walked over to his queen; he still found her utterly beautiful with her coppery locks loose, her deep-set green eyes regarding him seductively – he thought – and her full lips ripe for loving. He bent and kissed her.

'You are my Lady,' he whispered hoarsely. 'You have my heart. None can touch you.' It was true, and he meant it absolutely. Frantically fucking Avice de Stafford in a garderobe when overcome by lust did not count at all against his sexual cherishing of his wife. He tightened his arms around her, wanting her urgently.

'Send your women away,' he murmured in her ear. 'I can hear them clucking in your bedchamber. I want to be alone with you, and get another heir to England!'

An hour later, as they lay peacefully entwined between the tumbled sheets, Henry gazed down at his lovely Eleanor and traced a trail with his rough fingers from her breast to her hip.

'If only all my other kingly duties were as pleasant!' he grinned.

'And my queenly ones!' she smiled back.

Henry caught sight of the hourglass on the table and frowned. 'My God, I had best go. I'm already late for a meeting with my barons of the Exchequer to discuss improving the coinage.' He stood up and stretched, the sunlight from the window anointing his muscular, naked body. Eleanor gazed at him lazily, admiring the perfection of his broad shoulders and taut buttocks.

'Will you join me for dinner tonight, my Lady?' he asked, pulling on his clothes.

Now it was Eleanor's turn to grimace.

'If the food is palatable,' she said. These days Henry was busy all the time, and didn't care too much what he ate, usually gobbling it up and leaving the table within five minutes. Consequently, the fare served at his court was poor, and she had taken to having her own meals prepared by her own cook, and eating them with Petronilla and her chief ladies in her solar. When he had leisure, Henry would join her, but, as he had explained, a king had to have a visible presence at his court, so it was expedient that he made it his usual habit to dine in the great hall with his household. On feast days and holy days, though, Eleanor always took her place there at Henry's side, and put up with the appalling food. This day was neither feast day nor holy day, but she sensed that he wanted her to be with him after that ecstatic session in bed, and knew that she should seize the moment.

'I will expressly order my cooks to make sure that it is to your liking,' he promised, pulling on his boots. 'And we will have some music, to delight you.'

'You delight me,' she told him, rising in all her naked beauty and clasping her arms about his neck.

'Witch!' he growled, kissing her. 'Would you detain me with your wiles? What of the coinage? My barons await me.'

'They can wait a little longer,' Eleanor purred, employing her tongue to artful effect and pulling him down with her once more on the bed.

At the board of the Exchequer, the lords sat looking at each other and drumming the table with impatient fingers, watching the sand drizzling slowly through the hourglass, and wondering what had become of their king.

At his place at the high table on the dais, Becket, watching Henry's unruly barons arriving – half-drunk already – for dinner, reflected that his friend John of Salisbury had been right when he'd compared the English court to ancient Babylon. All scandal, debauchery and frivolity were here, encouraged by sensuous music and bawdy mimes and dramas. He had heard that they were to have some entertainment later this evening – more ribaldry, he supposed – but that was fortuitous in a way, since it would ensure that the King actually sat down to eat, and everybody else could finish their meal – although, thought Becket with distaste, perhaps that was not such a boon.

He could only disapprove of the excesses he witnessed at court, and regretted that Henry did nothing to curb them. But, of course, the King would do no such thing, for he indulged in such excesses too, swearing, drinking himself into oblivion and whoring with the best of them. It was not dignified behaviour in a king. That was why Becket was happier when he could enter-tain Henry in his own house, and afford him the elegance, luxury and sophistication that were deplorably lacking at court. He sensed, though, that Henry cared far less for these things than he did, and that the person who gained the most pleasure from them was himself. It flattered his vanity to be able to lavish such bounty on his king, and show him how things *should* be done.

The company rose to its feet – or tried its best to do so – as Henry entered the hall, holding the Queen by the hand. They'll have to be on their best behaviour now, Becket thought, amused, knowing how Eleanor was a stickler for observing the courte-sies. Someone belched loudly, and she glared, quelling the unfortunate culprit, who hung his head in unaccustomed shame.

Henry escorted her to her seat at his right hand; Becket, standing to his left, bowed as she sat down. He heard her murmur to her husband, 'Your barons could at least comb their hair before they come to table. They're a disgrace.'

As Becket suppressed a smile, Henry looked about him, slightly puzzled.

'I hadn't noticed,' he said. 'As long as they serve me well and do as I tell them, their appearance matters not one jot to me. But since it obviously does to you . . .' He rose to his feet and raised one hand.

'Silence!' he bawled, above the hubbub, and upwards of fifty faces turned towards him.

'I have a new edict for you,' he announced, smirking. 'At the express wish of the Queen, no man is henceforth to come into her presence with his hair uncombed. And that means you, my Lord of Arundel!' He frowned disapprovingly at an earl who was engrossed in picking nits out of his greasy locks. The fastidious Becket shuddered.

Everyone laughed, even Eleanor. Then she noticed that there were no napkins on the table, and grimaced.

'Summon the ewerer,' she murmured to the steward, as Henry sat down beside her. He made a face, and smirked as, presently, reasonably clean napkins were brought and distributed along the tables.

'Anything else you would like, my Lady?' he asked, only half-joking.

'No, thank you. I am looking forward to the culinary delights in store for me!' Eleanor replied, recalling the green, rancid meat she had been served the last time she had dined in the palace hall. Even the garlic sauce that smothered it had not disguised the foul taste and smell. But tonight, Henry had assured her, she would have a feast fit for the Queen she was.

The chief butler and his acolytes came in with great flagons of wine, and a thick, murky brew of indeterminate colour was poured into Eleanor's goblet. She sipped it warily. It was horrible, greasy and foul, and tasted like soot. Almost banging down her goblet, she decided to treat herself to some quality wine from her city of Bordeaux when she returned to her chamber. Next to her, Henry was imbibing thirstily, but she was aware of Becket also disdaining to drink. A faint pucker of distaste pursed his thin lips. It wasn't often that Eleanor found herself and Becket to be kindred spirits.

The first course was the wild boar that Henry had killed while out hunting that very morning, so it was fresh, and only slightly overcooked. The second course was trout, long-dead. Eleanor smelt one whiff and recoiled in disgust.

'That fish cannot be less than four days old!' she complained.

Henry took a mouthful. 'Hmm, it is a bit off.'

'Sire, it is so off that it should be food only for worms,' Becket said. 'I marvel that the King is so badly served.'

Eleanor bit back a mischievous suggestion that Becket take on the cooking for the court in addition to all his other duties. She knew he was speaking the truth, and that he was supporting her, but she felt he had no right to be saying such things, which amounted effectively to a criticism of his master.

'Tell them to send something else,' Henry commanded, 'or I will be paying a visit to the kitchens.' After thirty minutes, a dish of jugged hare arrived, along with some capons in saffron sauce. Eleanor tasted both cautiously, but they were equally delicious. A plump partridge followed.

'It's remarkable how the threat of a royal inspection can work wonders,' Henry observed drily.

The Abbot of Winchester, who was in London on business, and the King's guest, by virtue of his standing, sampled the partridge and complimented his sovereign on his table. 'Our bishop allows us only ten courses at meals,' he lamented, clearly anticipating more to come. Henry stared at him.

'Perish your bishop!' he exclaimed. 'In my court, we are satisfied with three courses. In a moment, the tablecloth will be lifted, so hurry up and finish, as we have some minstrels waiting to play for us. From Germany, you understand. They have come a long way.'

The portly Abbot looked crestfallen and hastened to eat up his partridge, as if it might be snatched from him at any moment. Eleanor tried to hide a smile.

When Becket, as the King's chaplain, had risen to thank God for His bounty, the minstrels were ushered in.

'They are called *minnesingers*,' Henry said. 'The German equivalent of your troubadours, Eleanor. I trust they are more respectful.' Eleanor chose to ignore the barb. Henry never had come to terms with the troubadour culture in which she was steeped.

The lead singer was a beautiful young man with long red hair, full lips and sad eyes. He fixed them boldly on Eleanor as he rose from an elaborate bow.

'This for you, *meine Königin*,' he announced. A hush fell on the court as he began singing, his voice as poignant as his expression, his words imbued with yearning and erotic meaning:

The sweet young Queen
Draws the thoughts of all upon her,
As sirens lure the witless mariners
Upon the reef.
If all the world were mine
From the seashore to the Rhine,
That price were not too high
To have England's queen lie
Close in my arms.

There was a stunned pause as the singer fell silent. Drunk as they were, Henry's courtiers had seen their master's face darken, and were refraining from applauding in case of provoking his notorious temper. Eleanor sat tense in her chair, relishing the tribute paid to her in the song, and smiling fixedly, yet graciously, at the young singer, as courtesy – and the best traditions of the south – demanded. She did not dare look at her husband.

'You are bold, minstrel,' Henry said at last. 'Over-bold, methinks.'

'Lord King, I mean no offence,' the young man protested, clearly surprised that anyone should take his song amiss. 'The beauty of the Queen is sung of even in my land. Her fame is great. Our young men sigh for a glimpse of her.'

'Yes, yes, so it appears,' said Henry testily. 'Well, you can stop sighing and play us something more appropriate. And remember, minstrel' – he leaned forward menacingly – 'the only arms in which this beautiful queen will ever lie are mine!'

There was general mirth as the discomfited youth bowed and hastily launched into a well-known song about the heroic Chevalier Roland, which was much more to the martial taste of the barons and knights present, who clapped and roared their approval. Eleanor now ventured to look Henry's way and, to her astonishment, found him smiling at her.

'Yon bold fellow has some nerve, but he has put me in mind of how fortunate I am!' he said, taking her hand and kissing it. 'Will you lie close in my arms tonight, my Lady?'

It was at that moment that Eleanor caught sight of Becket's face over Henry's shoulder, and saw the fleeting, anguished look of naked longing and pain that was quickly masked by the

Chancellor's usual suave, aloof expression. Becket had been looking at Henry; he could not but have seen the courtly gesture and heard what the King had said.

So that's how things are, Eleanor thought to herself. He suffers an unrequited love, a love to which he dare not ever own up, for he knows it is forbidden, and that it will never be returned; and he is sworn to chastity. But he is jealous. He knows that this is one part of Henry's life over which he cannot hold sway; that in the final reckoning, I will always be the victor. Yet strangely, she felt no sense of triumph – only sadness, for the sterility and emptiness of her rival's existence.

Henry was leaning over and nuzzling her neck. She watched Becket murmur his excuses, bow and leave the hall, his young attendants scrambling to follow him.

15 Wallingford, 1156

Eleanor sometimes wondered what she was doing, riding around England seven months into her latest pregnancy, issuing writs and charters, and ensuring that the kingdom was efficiently governed during Henry's latest absence. He was in Normandy, paying homage to Louis for Aquitaine at last, and curbing the ambitions of little brother Geoffrey, which even the formidable Empress had failed to hold in check.

Eleanor had with her a sizeable retinue, which included her sons, her sister Petronilla and her half-brothers, William and Joscelin. They were now lodged at Wallingford, in the impregnable castle that had been of such strategic importance during Stephen's wars, but had now been given to the Queen as part of her dower.

Already, Eleanor's brothers were becoming restive. They had made no secret of the fact that they disliked England. It was too cold, and the food was ghastly. Soon, they warned her, by her leave, they would return to the sunnier climes of Aquitaine. That gave her a pang. She always tried her best not to think of her own land, knowing that it might be many moons, and probably years, before she saw it again. Understanding their homesickness, she had told William and Joscelin that they might depart whenever they wished, with her blessing; she would not keep them here against her will. She knew they would go soon. They were not creatures of the court, but men of property who had fiefdoms to look after. She would be sorry to see them go, but glad for them, all the same.

Eleanor was resting in her bower with her feet up, reading letters, when Petronilla, a little blurred at the edges with wine as she so often was these days, knocked and entered.

'Eleanor, I think you should come and see young William. He has developed a fever in this last hour, and the nurse is a little concerned.'

Weary and ungainly as she was, Eleanor got clumsily but hastily to her feet, her heart full of fear. Children died young – it was a common occurrence – and she had only yesterday given thanks to God for being blessed with such healthy boys. Had she been too complacent? Had there been some symptom she had missed? She had last seen William after dinner; he had seemed well enough then, had eaten up every morsel, so she had been told. Maybe she was over-reacting – but she did not think so. She had appointed the best nurse to be had, and if *she* was concerned enough to summon her mistress, when usually she dealt competently with childish ailments herself, then there must indeed be cause for worry.

As swiftly as she could, she ascended the turret stairs to the princes' apartments on the topmost floor of the keep, a weepy Petronilla lurching in her wake. Bursting into the boys' bedchamber, she found William lying hot and sweating beneath the rich covers, surrounded by his own nurse and Young Henry's, the rockers who tended Henry's cradle, and the nursery servants. As they all stood aside to allow the Queen to approach the bed, she could see from their expressions that her alarm was justified. In the far corner, the bastard Geoffrey stood taking it all in, his little face taut with fright. There was much love between him and his half-brothers.

'William, sweeting,' Eleanor said, sinking to her knees and clasping her son's freezing, limp hand. He did not respond. The fever was at its height, and he was barely conscious, moaning fitfully in his stupor, his red curls on the pillow wet with perspiration. This could not be happening! He had been well and thriving only hours before!

Eleanor felt her son's brow. It was burning.

'When did this come on?' she asked, her voice abrupt with terror.

'An hour ago, Lady,' Alice, William's nurse, replied. There were tears of distress – and fear – in her eyes. 'Young ones of that age – he's not yet three – take ill quickly; they're up and down like windmills.'

'He's so hot!' Eleanor cried, running her hands over the small body, frantic to do something to alleviate her child's plight. 'We must uncover him.'

'That be dangerous,' Alice frowned, aghast. 'He'd catch cold and it could kill him.'

'Then what are we to do?' the Queen almost sobbed, gathering her child to her breast and rocking him in her arms. 'Oh, my boy, my little boy! Get better for Mother, please!' She turned desperately to the attendants. 'Have the physicians been sent for?'

'They are here,' said Petronilla, her face white, her voice shaking. 'And the chaplain.'

At mention of the chaplain, Eleanor began to tremble, and tightened her arms around William's fevered body. His head was against her shoulder, damp and tousled; his eyes were closed. How could her sweet, innocent child be struck down so rapidly? It was like a nightmare from which she would surely soon wake.

The physicians gathered by the bed. They laid the child flat, pulled back the covers and took turns to examine the patient, their faces grave.

'It is an imbalance of the humours, my Lady,' one pronounced. 'We could try bleeding him, although it might be best to let him sweat it out.'

'I will make up a remedy of caraway, cucumber and liquorice,' said a second. 'They are all trusted cures for fever.'

William was tossing fitfully. Eleanor felt his brow again. It was hot. Her hands roved searchingly over his restless little form, and touched dry heat; he was burning up, and no longer seemed to be aware of her. She was praying inwardly, desperately bargaining with God, willing Him to restore her son to health.

'I will promise anything, Lord,' she vowed, 'anything at all, in return for his life.'

Just then, William's body stiffened, and his limbs went rigid. His head jerked back, and as his arms and legs began to convulse alarmingly, his skin seemed to drain of blood, and took on a blue tinge.

'Dear God, *do* something!' Eleanor screamed at the doctors in panic.

'It is the fever, my Lady,' they told her helplessly, with tears in their eyes. 'It has reached its crisis. We can but wait for it to pass. The Lord William is in God's hands now.'

The terrifying jerking ceased almost as suddenly as it had begun. William's body went limp, and mercifully he lay at peace, his breathing shallow.

'Thank God!' Eleanor sobbed, collapsing to her knees by the little bed and clasping the child tightly, rocking him gently in her arms for what seemed like an eternity, not daring to let him go. Behind her, the physicians were shaking their heads. They had seen the tiny hand fall lifeless onto the coverlet. It was only when Eleanor had finally laid her son gently back on the pillow that she realised he had gone from her for ever.

16 Rouen, 1160 – Four Years Later

Eleanor smiled despite herself, as the fair-haired little girl, unsteady in her feet, was escorted by her guardian, the Chief Justiciar of Normandy, up to the altar rails of the cathedral of Notre-Dame. There, awaiting her, stood her bridegroom, the Lord Henry, heir to England, Normandy and Anjou, fidgeting in his best tunic and cloak, his silky red curls crowned with a small gold circlet. His father, King Henry, was smiling too, well satisfied with this new marriage alliance, and, standing beside him, the Empress was nodding her approval. This was a fitting match for her grandson.

The bride, not quite three years old, performed a wobbly curtsey to the King and Queen and, at the bidding of the Justiciar, placed her hand in that of the Lord Henry. Then the Papal Legate stepped forward and began intoning the marriage service.

Eleanor watched, her younger children at her side. Matilda, who had been born during that terrible time of mourning for poor William, was the physical image of her grandmother, for whom she had been named, yet a much gentler soul. Her pleasant, placid round face was framed by the copper-gold locks of her race. She was a good, dutiful girl, and one day, she would make some lucky prince a fine wife.

Geoffrey, two years old, black-haired, handsome and wilful, clung to Eleanor's hand. As the King's third living son, he was already aware of the need to assert himself against his older brothers, and knew that he came lowest in their pecking order. But he has the tenacity to hold his own, and to make his mark, Eleanor thought. No one will make a fool of my Geoffrey.

Behind her, firmly constrained by his nurse, the plump and motherly Hodierna, fidgeted Henry and Eleanor's middle son, three-year-old Richard, a handsome, robust and vigorous little boy with angelic features and the Plantagenet red hair and temper. If any of the Queen's children could be said to have replaced her precious William, it was Richard. When they had laid him in her arms, bloody and bawling after he had come bursting from her womb, ready to take on the world, she had looked upon him and instantly fallen in love. It was wrong, she knew, but he was by far her favourite of all her brood. She could not help it. She loved him so fiercely that it almost hurt, and lived in dread that anything evil would befall him. It was inexplicable, but her fears for him were far greater than her fears for her other children. She had not realised it was possible for a mother to feel such love.

There was an old, cryptic prophecy of Merlin's, so legend had it, which predicted that 'the Eagle of the Broken Covenant' would rejoice in her third nesting. Since Richard's birth, Eleanor had often wondered if she was the eagle the magician had foretold; an eagle whose wings had stretched out over two kingdoms. And could her divorce from Louis be the broken covenant? Richard was her third son; she rejoiced in him already, but the prophecy indicated that she would have even more cause to do so in the fullness of time. One day, Henry had agreed, Richard would succeed her in Aquitaine. She could not have imagined anything more fitting, or a better cause for rejoicing.

She would not allow herself, on this happy day, to think of the two sons who were missing from her brood. Little William was a constant ache of longing in her heart; the memory of him always brought tears to her eyes. She would repeatedly relive the shock of his death as if it had happened yesterday; the pain of her loss never got any better. And little Philip, dead before his navel healed. He was a poignant ghost, a fleeting joy in her life, who had also been cruelly snatched away.

Resolutely, she put away her painful memories and looked on smiling as her eldest son made his wedding vows. Young Henry was a true knight in the making, but headstrong and unruly, needing a firm hand. She could tell he was impatient to be back in the palace courtyard, playing with the royal wards who were his companions, skirmishing with wooden swords and shields, or competing noisily with miniature bows and arrows. This marriage would make little difference to his life, for the Princess Marguerite would be brought up away from the court – although that was a sore point with Eleanor – and taught those things that were deemed fitting for girls, as well as the duties of a future queen.

Eleanor was struck by how much like Louis the little girl was. The same fair hair, the fine features, the gentle charm. Pray God she shows more spirit, she thought. Marguerite was Louis' daughter by his second wife, Constance, and ever since her birth, Henry had schemed to marry her to his heir. If Louis died without a son to succeed him, Marguerite would be his co-heiress with her half-sisters, Eleanor's daughters, Marie and Alix. There could be rich pickings for the husbands of those princesses, and even a kingdom to be won, if might could triumph over right. That was Henry's long-term ambition and hope . . .

It was Becket who had gone to Paris and negotiated the new alliance – Becket, with his magnificent escort and lavish gifts to impress and sweeten the French. He had been received like a visiting prince. The immediate benefit of the marriage alliance had been a new peace between Henry and Louis, who were now the very best of friends, all past wrongs and differences forgotten. Henry had paid a state visit to the French King in Paris, and they had even gone away together on a pilgrimage through Normandy to Mont Saint-Michel. The baby Marguerite had by then been handed over by her mother to Henry, and

Louis had visited her in the castle at Neubourg, where he pronounced himself more than satisfied with the arrangements made for her care.

These arrangements had been the one jarring note in the negotiations. Eleanor could not forget it. Henry might have been forgiven for the past, but *she* clearly had not. Louis had insisted that under no circumstances was his daughter to be brought up by Queen Eleanor. It was for that reason that the child had been placed under the guardianship of the kindly Justiciar of Normandy, Robert of Neubourg.

Eleanor had been furious.

'Does he think me morally unfit, or a bad mother?' she had stormed at Henry in the privacy of their chamber. 'That I will corrupt his daughter, or not look after her properly?'

'Let it be, Eleanor,' Henry had said wearily. 'What is important is this alliance. Neither Thomas nor I wanted to jeopardise it by arguing the matter. Marguerite is Louis' daughter, and he must do as he thinks best regarding her care.'

'He has insulted me!' Eleanor raged, 'and you and your beloved Thomas are letting him get away with it.'

Henry eyed her balefully. 'Your animosity towards Thomas is beside the point – and irrational, as I keep telling you.'

'Your mother doesn't think so,' Eleanor told him. 'She disapproves of him as heartily as I do, and makes no bones about saying so, yet you do not dismiss her criticisms as irrational.'

'Not to her face,' Henry muttered. 'I owe my Lady Mother some filial respect, but there are times when I can do without her advice. And yours, my Lady!'

And there the matter had been left. Eleanor had had to swallow her pride and accept the ban on her involvement in Marguerite's upbringing, and she had long guessed that she would never woo Henry away from Becket, although it was not for want of trying. Becket was the chief counsellor to the King now, the man whose advice Henry took before all other, and indeed, the most powerful subject in the realm. There was no gainsaying him.

Louis knew nothing of this wedding. He had not expected it to take place for some years, but Henry, with his usual bull-headed determination, had gone ahead regardless.

'There is news from France,' he had told Eleanor. 'Queen Constance has died in childbed.'

Eleanor stared at him. 'God rest her,' she said at length, genuinely grieved for Constance's little girl, who had been so cruelly bereaved. 'Poor Marguerite.'

'She barely remembers her mother,' Henry stated, 'so the loss will not affect her too greatly.' Eleanor reflected that this was probably true, but even so . . .

'Did Constance die giving Louis a son?' she asked.

'No, another girl. Alys, I think her name is. Thomas did tell me. He also heard that Louis did not mourn his wife greatly, but complained about the frightening superfluity of his daughters – as well he may! The news is that he plans to marry again this very month.'

'Good God, he doesn't waste time!' Eleanor exclaimed. 'Constance can hardly have been cold before he thought to replace her in his bed. Not that he would have done so for carnal reasons, knowing Louis. He must be desperate for an heir. Who is she, this new bride?'

'Adela of Champagne,' Henry told her. 'She is the sister of the Counts of Champagne and Blois, who, I am told, are soon to marry your daughters by Louis. In effect, Louis has taken to wife the sister of his future sons-in-law. It's blatantly incestuous!' He spat out the words as his brow puckered. 'I don't welcome this marriage. If Adela bears a son, it's goodbye to my hopes in France. And even if she doesn't, her brothers are my enemies, and they may make trouble between Louis and me. Nothing would please them better than to see this alliance broken. And if that happens, Louis will get to keep the Vexin.' That rich Norman borderland was Marguerite's dowry; Henry had ceded it to Louis some years before, and was now delighted at the prospect of getting it back. 'There is no time to lose!'

Immediately, Henry had summoned Marguerite to Rouen, quickly procured a dispensation from the Pope, and set in train brisk preparations for the wedding.

The nuptial Mass over, the King and Queen headed the procession that followed the newly wed infants back up the nave and out into the chilly, brittle November sunshine. Crowds had gathered, and blessings were called down upon the two children, who made such a pretty tableau standing there in their gorgeous robes, holding hands and smiling shyly. There were sentimental sighs and aahs from the people, who were well aware that these two little ones represented the future. Then the men-at-arms stepped forward, and a path was made through the crowds, as it was time to go back to the palace for the wedding feast.

The King seated himself at the high table, with the Queen on his left and Young Henry and Marguerite in the place of honour on his right, next to the Empress, while the Princess Matilda, somewhat overawed by the grand occasion, sat gravely between Eleanor and Becket. The tiny French princess was evidently enjoying herself, clapping at the capers of the Empress's jester and cramming tasty morsels of food into her rosebud of a mouth.

'How think you King Louis will react when he hears of his daughter's marriage, my son?' the Empress asked, as the first course was brought in.

'He cannot complain,' Henry said smugly. 'The contract has been signed, and his consent to the nuptials is implicit in it. There was no need to consult him at all.'

'*He* might not agree with that,' Eleanor put in, helping herself to some roast pork from a golden salver. 'This won't be the first time we have deceived him over a marriage, my Lord!' She smiled at Henry archly.

'Ah, but in this case he has given his consent, in writing. There's no arguing with that.'

Becket leaned across.

'He might feel that he has been insulted, Sire. He could say that the terms of the treaty have been breached, and withhold the dowry.'

'I think not,' Henry said, grinning wickedly. 'I have already sent to the Knights Templar, who have been keeping custody of the Vexin, and they have willingly agreed to surrender it to me. And I have decided to take Marguerite into my own household now that she is married to my son. She will be a hostage against any reprisals that Louis might contemplate.'

Eleanor's head jerked up at that. 'And who will be in charge of her upbringing?' she asked.

Henry laid his hand on hers. 'Why, you, of course!' he said with a wink.

'But that is against King Louis' express wishes,' the Empress said, before Eleanor could answer.

'I will not have my wife slighted,' Henry declared. 'And who better to be as a mother to our new daughter?'

'You did not say that before!' Eleanor fumed later, when they were in bed and Henry had laid purposeful hands on her, thrusting his knee between her legs. 'You have only made this decision because it suits you to do so. My feelings don't come into it.'

'Yes they do,' he said, mounting her. 'And yes, it makes good political sense to have Marguerite with us, in your care. I knew it would please you.' Eleanor was about to argue that he had missed the whole point of her complaint when Henry's mouth came down hard on hers, and he entered her forcefully. Despite herself, she was swept along by the familiar tide of ecstasy, and had no choice but to give herself up to it completely. As so many times before, they made violent love, rolling in the bed, clinging together and kissing as hungrily as if their lives depended upon it.

Lying spent in Henry's arms afterwards, Eleanor felt such a surge of love for this complex, difficult man that it was like an emotional orgasm, leaving her breathless and near to tears. Involuntarily, she clung to Henry as if she could never let go, and found herself wishing that things could always be this perfect between them.

When she was calm again, they lay there replete, just looking at each other, with Henry's rough hand resting lightly on her breast. We don't need words, she thought. We have been married for eight years, and still it can be so good. She basked in the knowledge that her body continued to captivate Henry, and that, for all her thirty-eight years, she was yet a beautiful woman. Despite his dependence on the ever-present Becket, Henry still needed her. She had been at his side all through that great progress of England they had made three years earlier; she had seen the wild northern shires and witnessed the submission of the Scots; she had been with Henry when they had renounced the wearing of their crowns in Worcester Cathedral, sharing in that act of humility in honour of the crucified Christ; she had ruled England for eight months after that progress, when Henry had been absent in France; and she had shared her husband's joy and pride in their growing family, and borne the pain of his grief and her own in their terrible loss. She had never forgotten Henry's ravaged face when she had come face-to-face with him at Saumur in Anjou, five months after William's death. Later, back in England, she had wept with him before the little tomb in Reading Abbey, where their son had been laid to rest at the feet of his great-grandsire, the first King Henry. It was the heritage of these shared experiences, and the enduring rapture of their physical love, that had become the bedrock of their marriage.

Henry was sleeping now, snoring lightly against her shoulder. Her eyes wandered the length of his body, feasting upon strong limbs and toned muscles. Louis had looked defenceless in slumber, but not Henry. He was like a dormant lion. She wished they could be back in Poitiers together, as they had been the year before. They had lain night after night in her richly hung chamber in the Maubergeonne Tower, exploring new ways to make love, and sleeping late in the mornings. In Rouen, she was always the guest of the Empress, and felt she was there on sufferance; but in Poitiers, she was the Duchess – never mind her queenship – and could fully be herself on her home terri-tory. How she yearned for the wild, summer-kissed beauty of her domains! That was where she truly belonged, not in these chilly northern lands, where the freedoms of the south were so much frowned upon.

Henry, however, had been in Poitiers for a purpose. In fact, it had been her idea that he should attempt to enforce her ances-tral rights to the southern province of Toulouse. But she had set herself up for some prolonged grief, for she had been left fretting in her tower while he rode south at the head of a large army – and she was still fretting, months later, when he rode back in a foul mood, having failed in his purpose. For as soon as he had laid siege to the city of Toulouse, Louis had come to its defence, and Henry could hardly fight the overlord with whom he had so recently made that advantageous alliance. So he had been thwarted of Toulouse, and thereafter had stayed in Normandy, dealing with pressing affairs there and sulking. Eleanor he had sent back to England, where once again she found herself ruling as regent, touring the kingdom, issuing writs and dispensing justice. And there she had remained until Henry had summoned her back to Normandy for the wedding.

Louis would not make too much trouble, she was certain of that. He might bluster and protest at the marrying of his daughter without his knowledge, but he knew that Henry FitzEmpress was more than a match for him, so it was fairly safe to say that Henry would get away with what he had so impudently done.

17 Domfront, 1161

Eleanor bit on the sheet and bore down hard, her chin pressed against her chest. The pain was unendurable, and the need to scream overpowering, but even *in extremis*, she remembered that she was queen of England and duchess of Normandy and Aquitaine, and must behave as her dignity required.

'Nearly there, Lady,' the midwife said. 'One more push.'

Eleanor somehow found the strength to make a final effort. This was her ninth confinement, and she had never suffered such a difficult travail; all her previous babes had slipped out easily into the world with the minimum of trouble and fuss. But she had not had an easy pregnancy, what with one problem or another to deal with – and no end to it in sight.

She pushed – and the tiny head emerged into the midwife's capable hands, followed by a slippery shoulder – and then the rest of this new little stranger.

'A fair princess, Lady!' the midwife announced, beaming, as the infant started squealing. Eleanor, almost drained of energy, took her daughter into her arms, and found herself gazing at the very mirror image of herself.

'There's no doubt as to what *your* name will be, little one,' she smiled, kissing the crumpled face. 'You will be Eleanor, like me.' Henry could never object to that.

Relaxing in bed after the birth, too elated at the safe delivery of so pretty a daughter to sleep, Eleanor recalled how her husband had said that, unlike poor Louis, he was rich in sons and would welcome a girl, because girls could be married off for policy or profit. It was true, but she sometimes wished that Henry would stop seeing his children as pawns to be moved about in some giant game of political chess. There was no doubting that he loved them, but it grieved her that he could speak of disposing of them profitably without a qualm. Marrying off a daughter often meant sending her far away to a distant land – and the pain of a parting that might be for ever.

She was not pleased with Henry. She felt he had behaved with less than his usual wisdom in recent months. It had all begun when news of the death of Archbishop Theobald had reached them in Rouen, brought by Gilbert Foliot, the Bishop of Hereford. Henry had been shocked and grieved.

'Theobald was my true friend,' he said. 'I owe my kingdom to his support.'

'God rest him, the good man,' Eleanor murmured, crossing herself. 'He has earned his place in Heaven.'

The Empress had got to her feet stiffly – she suffered miseries from painful joints these days – and rested a hand on her son's shoulder.

'He must be replaced,' she counselled. 'England cannot long be without an archbishop of Canterbury.'

'I agree, Sire,' Bishop Foliot chimed in. He was a portly, bushy-browed ecclesiastic, a traditionalist who was much respected for his integrity and learning. Eleanor had always admired his directness and fearless honesty. You always knew where you were with him.

'Yes, but who could fill Theobald's shoes?' Henry asked, obviously reluctant to have to consider replacing his old friend.

The answer was obvious, Eleanor felt: it could be none other than Foliot himself. He would be an outstanding choice, having all the requisite qualities and experience.

Matilda evidently felt the same, for she too was looking hopefully at Foliot.

'You have not far to seek, my son,' she said.

'Indeed, I have not,' Henry answered her, his eyes lighting

up, but not on the expectant Bishop. 'Thomas Becket shall be my archbishop.'

'Thomas Becket?' echoed three dissonant voices in unison. Oh, no, Eleanor thought; Becket would be a disaster. He was far too preoccupied with earthly glories, and insufferable enough as it was.

'Have you gone mad, Henry?' the Empress cried, abandoning her customary self-control and deference. 'He is too worldly a man for high ecclesiastical office.'

'That is exactly what I was going to say, Sire,' chimed in Foliot. 'And he is not even ordained a priest.'

'Then show me a better candidate,' Henry challenged.

'I said before, you have not far to look,' the Empress bristled.

'I want an archbishop who is on my side, and prepared to work with me, not against me,' Henry declared.

'My Lord King, all your bishops are *on your side*, as you put it,' Foliot said smoothly, unruffled by the implied slur. 'And, unless I am very much mistaken, none has ever worked against you. We are loyal to a man, depend upon it.'

'True, very true – to a point!' Henry rounded on him. 'But, if put to the test, your first loyalty would be to the Church. Am I correct?'

'It would be to God,' Foliot stated firmly.

'Well, I can't argue with that,' Henry sniffed, with a rueful smile. 'As long as God is on my side, at least. Anyway, the matter must wait. Louis is threatening war, although I doubt he will exert himself greatly. Even so, I must strengthen my defences on the Norman border, in case he tries to take back the Vexin. And then I have to go south to Aquitaine, for there is trouble in Gascony – again.'

'To Aquitaine?' Eleanor had echoed, joyfully. 'I will go with you, my Lord! I can stay in Bordeaux.' It would be wonderful to see her domains again, to feel once more the heat of the southern sun, hear the lays of the troubadours and the summer buzzing of the crickets, taste succulent duck and rich truffles, and see the majestic hills and sparkling rivers of her homeland.

'No,' Henry said.

*

162

It had been that adamant refusal, and what followed, far more than the matter of Canterbury, that had driven a wedge between them. She had insisted, she had cajoled, she had begged, but Henry had proved immovable, arguing that her condition prevented her from travelling far. That was a nonsense, she countered, arguing that, during her earlier pregnancies, she had journeyed hundreds of miles around England during his absences, right up to her ninth month. She was as strong as an ox, she told him, and had never felt better. But still he had refused. And soon it was to become clear why.

She had stayed in Rouen with the Empress, fretting at her enforced idleness and wishing beyond hope that she was in Poitiers and Gascony with Henry. He sent messengers fairly regularly, though, with news and solicitous enquiries as to her health, and the first tidings of his venture were good. He had besieged and taken the strong castle of Castillon-sur-Agen within just one week, and the rebel lords had been so overawed – utterly terrified, in fact – by this feat that all resistance had quickly melted away.

It was the next reports from Henry that made Eleanor see red. She had left her uncle, Raoul de Faye, in charge of her domains, but Henry had made it quite clear to Raoul, when he saw him in Poitiers, that he had a poor opinion of Raoul's ability to function effectively as the Duchess's deputy, and had over-ruled him on several important matters. Raoul, in turn, had written to Eleanor to voice his protest and warn her that her subjects were up in arms about it, complaining that the Duke was infringing on their liberties. And they had even more cause to gripe when Henry began installing his own Norman admin-istrators in positions of influence.

As soon as she heard of this, Eleanor had written to him in furious haste, demanding to know what he thought he was doing. He replied briskly that it was desirable that Aquitaine, like Normandy and England, should have strong, centralised govern-ment, and that he meant to enforce it upon her unruly, whoreson barons if it was the last thing he did! Which it might be, she thought savagely.

At the same time, a further letter arrived from Raoul. 'The people have withdrawn from their allegiance to the King of the English,' he wrote, deliberately omitting to refer to Henry as Duke of Aquitaine, his proper title in the duchy. 'They complain that he has pruned their liberties. They have even approached the legates of the Pope, showing them a chart of lineage and asking them to dissolve your marriage to the King on the grounds of consanguinity.'

When she read this, Eleanor's blood ran cold. Beside herself with frustration, she took the letter and sought out the Empress, thrusting it in front of her.

'See what your son has done!' she cried.

Matilda said not a word, but read the parchment. 'I should not worry yourself, Eleanor,' she said coolly. 'The legates will not dare to offend the King; they are only in Aquitaine because they seek his support for their master, Pope Alexander.'

'I am aware of that,' Eleanor retorted. 'What angers me is that Henry has once more alienated my subjects – and gone against my wishes.'

'Strong measures are never popular,' Matilda observed, 'but sometimes they are necessary. Your Aquitainian lords are a menace, you must admit.'

'I will write to Henry,' Eleanor fumed. 'I will protest at his interference in my domains. How dare he!'

'Because he has every right,' Matilda pointed out. 'He is your lord, and he is their duke.'

'He should have consulted me!' Eleanor raged.

'He does not need to,' Matilda told her. Eleanor sensed she was enjoying seeing her daughter-in-law discountenanced. She snatched back her letter, swept out of the room, and dashed off a response to Henry, castigating him for his folly, and for arousing the ire of her subjects.

His reply made her want to howl with rage. He had ignored all her complaints! There was not a word in justification or apology. He wrote only that the legates, who were falling over themselves to humour him, had told him that the Pope had agreed to canonise King Edward the Confessor. He himself, he continued, was still in Poitiers, where he had inspected the building work at the cathedral and found it satisfactory; she might like to know that he had ordered the building of a new church, new city walls, new bridges, a market place and shops, and that he was having the great hall of her palace refurbished, with bigger windows.

Her heart lay cold, like a stone in her breast. All this he had put in hand without consulting her – and he had ducked out of discussing the larger issues. Was it for this that she had wed him? What had become of their shared vision for the future, their marriage of lions? Henry's behaviour was a betrayal of their marriage and all it stood for. It was not to be borne! So here she was, lying in with her new daughter, her heart torn between love for this exquisite child and a burning resentment against its father.

18 Bayeux, 1161

Henry had sent to say he would rejoin her in Bayeux, and there she resentfully repaired with her children and their nurses, thankfully leaving the unsympathetic Empress in Rouen. During the days before Henry's arrival, to distract herself from the coming confrontation that she must have with him, she took Young Henry and Richard to see the glories of the cathedral of Notre-Dame, where they were shown a wonderful old strip of embroidery depicting the whole story of William the Conqueror's invasion of England in 1066. It was hanging in the apse of the church, and the little boys stood there marvelling at the colourful, lifelike figures of the soldiers and horses, staring open-mouthed at the battle scenes, and listening entranced as Eleanor recounted to them the stirring story of the Conquest.

'There is King Harold, with an arrow piercing his eye,' she said, pointing. 'And there he is, being felled to the ground with an axe.'

'I'm going to be a soldier when I grow up, and I'm going to kill people with axes!' Henry boasted.

'No, I am!' cried Richard fiercely, not to be outdone. Eleanor rejoiced that these boys of hers had such spirit.

'You both will be soldiers,' she said firmly. 'Very brave soldiers, like your father.'

Mollified, the two lads contented themselves with buffeting each other surreptitiously.

'Come now,' said their mother, aware of the watching clergy exchanging disapproving glances. 'We must offer prayers for your father's safe return.' Firmly, she guided them into a side chapel and pushed them down to their knees, constraining them to quietness.

Husband and wife faced each other across the castle courtyard, as Henry clattered in at the head of his retinue and leaped off his horse at the dismounting block, where Eleanor was standing waiting for him, her children attending with her ladies and the knights of her household.

'Welcome back, my Lord,' she said, her face expressionless as she offered the customary stirrup cup and waited for Henry to greet her. He brushed her lips briefly, then stood back, looking at her quizzically, his face weather-beaten and tanned, his unruly hair more close-cropped than usual.

'My Lady,' he said formally, raising her hand for a second kiss. 'I am well pleased to see you, and looking forward to meeting my new daughter!'

Eleanor beckoned, and the nurse stepped forward with the infant, who regarded the big, strange man solemnly for a moment, then broke into a gummy smile.

'You're a little beauty, aren't you?' Henry murmured, taking her into his arms and touching her downy head gently with his lips. He looked up at his wife. 'You have done well,' he said, in a softer voice. 'Princes will be clamouring for her hand, if she fulfils this early promise. She is just like you.'

Eleanor accepted his compliments with the barest hint of a smile.

'Won't you come within, my Lord, and take some refreshment after your journey?' she asked formally, taking the baby and handing her back to her nurse. The other children now ran forward, clamouring to greet their father, and after boisterous greetings, they entered the castle together.

Later, when dinner was over and their offspring were in bed, Henry came alone to Eleanor's solar, where she served him strong cider distilled from the apples that grew plentifully in this part of Normandy.

'Nectar!' he pronounced. 'My, that's potent!'

'Henry, we need to talk,' Eleanor began, bracing herself.

'Indeed, we do,' he said quickly. 'The Archbishop of Rouen has just had a word. He is fretting about Young Henry's education.'

'Is he? Why?'

'He is concerned that the heir to England is still living with his mother and has not even begun his lessons.'

'I have taught him much!' Eleanor exclaimed indignantly, immediately on the defensive, and fearful of what Henry was about to propose.

'Yes, *I* know that, but it wouldn't count with our friend the Archbishop. He was going on at some length about how I was different from other kings, who are all rude and uncultivated, in his opinion at any rate. He was waffling on about how my wisdom and prudence – as he put it, God bless him – had been informed by the literature I read in my youth, and he told me that my bishops unanimously agree that my heir should apply himself to letters, so that he can be my true successor.'

'And so?' Eleanor asked warily.

'Well, I take his point. Young Henry is now six, and it's time he was sent away to be educated.'

It was indeed the custom for princes and sons of the nobility to be placed in great aristocratic households to be nurtured and schooled away from their parents, mothers and fathers being accounted too loving and indulgent to do the job properly. Eleanor knew this, and accepted it. It was just that, the time now having come, she was devastated at the thought of being parted from any of her children. She had kept Young Henry close to her all his life; given what had befallen two of his brothers, she could hardly bear him out of her sight. Parting from him would be like losing a limb. How would he fare without her? Who would tend to his hurts, or calm his fears, or kiss him goodnight? She could not bear the thought of him crying into his pillow, alone and homesick.

Henry said gently, 'I know it will be hard for you, but you must realise that a boy cannot grow to manhood tied to his mother's apron strings. He has to learn to be independent, to fight his own battles and to grow brave and strong as befits a warrior. But you *will* see him from time to time, more than most mothers see their sons. I have hit upon the ideal arrangement.'

'You have?' Eleanor asked, unable to hide the eagerness in her voice.

'Yes.' Henry smiled at her. 'He is to be placed with my Lord Chancellor, my devoted Thomas.'

'Becket?' Eleanor echoed sharply.

'Yes, Becket. Why not? He has a great household, into which he has already accepted several noble boys. They will be companions for Young Henry. He will be well looked after.'

Eleanor was about to protest, but she could see the wisdom in the plan. Becket was often in attendance upon the King, and she and Henry were frequent guests at his table. Her lord was right: there would indeed be plenty of opportunities for her to see her child.

'When will he go?' she enquired.

'After Christmas,' Henry informed her.

She had three weeks, she reckoned quickly, before they took Henry from her. She vowed to herself that she would spend every possible moment with him. This was going to be far worse than parting from Marie and Alix had been. She had had so little to do with them, those sweet girls, had been kept at a distance, and never got to know them well. But Young Henry had been with her from birth, and she loved him fiercely; not quite as much as she adored Richard – her lion cub, as she thought of him – but deeply and protectively. Yet it would not be goodbye, she told herself resolutely. She must not think of the parting as final; she would see her son again, soon enough. And she would still have Richard, and Geoffrey, of course: if she could help it, she would never let her darling Richard be taken from her. He was to be her heir, so surely she would have some say in his upbringing. They would have to snatch Richard over her dead body.

'It is a wise decision,' she said evenly, conceding defeat. 'But there was something else I wished to discuss with you, and that is what you have done in Aquitaine. '

'Aquitaine is quiet now,' Henry said, his tone final, indicating that that was an end to the matter.

'Quiet, but seething under the surface, so I hear,' Eleanor persisted.

'From your Uncle Raoul? I didn't notice *him* keeping your unruly vassals in check!' Henry smirked unpleasantly.

'No one has ever succeeded in doing that, not even my father or my grandfather,' Eleanor snapped. 'The geography of my lands does not lend itself to unity, can't you see that?'

Henry rose and began pacing up and down the room.

'Well, I'm not content with my authority extending only to the regions around Poitiers and Bordeaux,' he told her. 'With my officials in place, answering directly to me, I intend to bring some order to your domains.'

'You are alienating *my* subjects by doing that!' Eleanor flared. 'They resent having strangers lording it over them. Things were bad enough before, when Louis sent in his Frenchmen to rule in his name; when I went home and they were sent away, the people rejoiced. It was very moving to see that. It meant everything to them to be governed by their own. Henry, I want my subjects to love you, but if you persist in this folly, they will only hate you.'

Henry had been listening with an irritated expression. He stopped his pacing by the door, and turned to face her.

'I'm not doing it to win popularity,' he declared. 'I mean to have your vassals bend to my will, like it or not. *They* must recognise my authority, and *you* must support me in enforcing it.'

'Then you must go about it a different way!' Eleanor flung at him.

'No one says *must* to me,' he snarled. 'I don't take orders from you, or anyone. You are in no position to dictate to me, Eleanor. Might I remind you that a wife's duty is to obey her husband, to rear his children, and to warm his bed when he so desires. And there it ends.'

'If you think I'm in any mood to warm your bed after you've insulted my intelligence, then let me put you straight now!' Eleanor riposted, her face flushed with anger.

'Please yourself!' Henry said testily, and went out of the room, leaving Eleanor wanting to scream with frustration. She could never win with him. He was utterly incapable of seeing her point of view and, once his mind was made up, there was no moving him.

The King stormed down the spiral stairs and into the great hall of the castle, nearly colliding with two of the Queen's ladies, who were making their way up to her chamber with their arms full of freshly laundered veils and chemises, smelling of sweet herbs. One of the ladies looked him boldly in the eye. She had a heart-shaped face set off to perfection by the widow's wimple that framed her chin and her rosy cheeks. He knew who she was – what man didn't? Rohese de Clare, Countess of Lincoln, had the reputation of being the most beautiful woman in England. It was well known that, during the five years since her husband's death, she had resisted all offers of remarriage, and it was also bruited that that was because she enjoyed taking her pleasure where she listed, although Henry was of the opinion that people *would* say such things about such a lovely widow.

Now he was not so sure. His eyes locked for a moment with the Countess's, then the moment passed, and she and her companion dipped into quick curtseys and hurried on. But his blood was up. He was furious with Eleanor for questioning his rights in Aquitaine – *again* – and powerfully intrigued by the enigmatic Rohese. He had long admired her from afar, but he had never quite seen in those slanting green eyes and pouting lips what other men had. There was something almost child-like about the woman, although the look she had just given him had been anything but child-like. Now he could see what it was that had made her so admired – and the promise in that brief moment of eye contact had fired his imagination.

That evening, after supper, he sought her out, and finally came upon her standing, wrapped in her cloak, gazing out over the battlements at the green fields of the Cotentin below.

'I thought you would come, my Lord King,' she said in a modulated, mellow voice. Again, her eyes met his, boldly, vibrant with promise.

'People speak truth when they say you are beautiful,' Henry told her. 'My wife is beautiful too, but in a different way, and I like variety.'

She came to him then, and he folded her in his strong arms. Both of them were trembling with desire.

'I want you,' Henry muttered gruffly against her veil. His hands delved inside her cloak, roved eagerly over firm breasts and hips. Rohese parted those full lips for him to kiss, and he obliged, tenderly at first, then hungrily, devouringly . . .

When they had taken their fill of each other, Henry returned alone to his bedchamber thinking how marvellous it had been simply to swive a woman without the added complications of having to enter into any other congress or pay heed to her whims. He loved Eleanor, there was no question about that in his mind, but she would insist on prolonging these endless, fruitless power struggles, and interfering in matters that were not her concern. He valued her judgement, of course he did, but only up to a point. She was a woman, God damn her, and as his wife, she owed him due obedience; he thought he had been unusually generous in allowing her some say in the governance of his domains.

He was still angry with her. Her denying him her bed yet rankled. Not that he would have sought it after their quarrel, but it was his right! It infuriated him that she had such scant regard for his rights. Sleeping with the beautiful Rohese had been his means of taking revenge on her, and he meant to go on exacting that sweet revenge. Even if Eleanor never got to know about it, he would enjoy his victory in private!

He lay down in his bed. His body was sated and ready for sleep, but his mind was strangely ill at ease. He was a plain man, a direct man, so this puzzled him. It would not have occurred to him to feel guilty for betraying his wife.

It was some time, in fact, before he realised that what he was feeling was an odd sense of loss.

19 Falaise, 1162

They were keeping Easter at Falaise, the birthplace of the Conqueror, and the court was lodged in the massive fortress that dominated the town from its high position on the escarpment overlooking the River Ante.

'This was where King William's father, Duke Robert the Magnificent, was staying when he espied the woman Herleva,' Henry told Eleanor, as they stood in the bailey staring up at the great buttressed keep with its Romanesque windows. 'She was extraordinarily beautiful.' When he mentioned Herleva, he was thinking of Rohese.

'I heard he was called Robert the Devil,' Eleanor said wryly.

'Indeed he was, at least to begin with,' Henry grinned. 'You see, I am doubly descended from the Devil!'

Eleanor made a face. 'I can believe that!' she said, a touch tartly. 'Wasn't Herleva meant to be washing clothes in the river at the time?'

'She was, or so the story goes. She was a tanner's daughter from the town. The Duke saw her and fell in love instantly. She bore him two children. He couldn't marry her, of course, as he had a wife already, so their son was called William the Bastard before his victories earned him the name of Conqueror.'

They strolled around the bailey and entered the little Chapel of St Prix, where Henry pointed to an iron-studded door.

'That leads to the crypt, where I store some of my treasure. There are only two keys. I have one – and Thomas has the other.'

At the mention of Becket, Eleanor frowned. If anyone should have held the second key, it was herself, but again, Becket had usurped her.

'I wanted to talk to you about Thomas,' Henry said. They sat down on a stone bench beneath the window. 'I have made up my mind that he is to be my Archbishop,' he said. 'No, wait!' He held up a hand to still her unvoiced protest. 'Thomas is my friend, and loyal to me. The Church has become too powerful, and I have radical plans for reforming the abuses within it. I know he will support me.'

'What makes you so sure?' Eleanor asked, her expression troubled.

'His unstinting and faithful service over these past seven years speaks for itself,' Henry said warmly. 'With my true Thomas as archbishop, I foresee no trouble in implementing these very necessary reforms.'

'Then you have made up your mind,' Eleanor stated, knowing

that nothing she could say would make any difference. She knew too, in her bones, that Henry was making a bad decision for all the wrong reasons, and feared that no good would come of it. Others, wiser than herself – among them the Empress Matilda and Bishop Foliot – had voiced their concerns, but Henry had paid them no heed. Well, he must go to Hell in his own way.

'I *have* made up my mind,' Henry said firmly. 'You could at least look cheerful about it!'

She smiled distantly. 'Let us hope that your confidence in Thomas is justified.'

'Oh, it will be, it will be,' he assured her blithely.

They were enthroned on the dais in the hall when Becket came in response to Henry's summons. Eleanor noticed how regally he was dressed, his embroidered scarlet tunic and blue cloak in stark contrast to the plain, mended garb of his master. But Henry had never cared much for the trappings of majesty. He let Becket be his ambassador in such things: Becket's magnificence could proclaim the wealth and status of the King of England.

Henry leaped up from his throne and embraced his chancellor warmly.

'Thomas, I have a mission for you.'

'Yes, my Lord?' Becket's handsome face bore an eager look, as if he could not wait to hear about this latest duty that Henry was now to require of him.

'First, I want to ask after your adopted son, the Lord Henry. How is he?' the King enquired.

'He is well, my Lord, and his diligence at his studies is indeed praiseworthy, although I dare say he would rather be learning swordplay than attending to his letters,' Becket smiled.

'I pray you, my Lord Chancellor, remember his mother to him,' Eleanor said wistfully.

'Rest assured, my Lady, that he includes you in his daily prayers without fail,' he told her, then turned back to the King. 'Does this mission concern my adopted son?' he asked.

'Yes. I want you to take him to England and have the barons swear fealty to him as my heir,' Henry commanded. 'You are to leave at once, so that the ceremony can take place at

Whitsun, but first, have the boy brought here now to say farewell to us.'

'If my Lord will grant me leave,' Becket said, bowing and departing.

Eleanor was thrilled. She was to see her son, albeit briefly. It had been four long months since she had set eyes on him.

When Becket returned later, bringing the seven-year-old Henry with him, Eleanor noticed the change in the boy at once. He seemed taller, more self-assured; on greeting, it became clear that there was, for the first time, a palpable distance between him and his mother. He bowed gracefully over her hand, and stood a little stiffly when she opened up her arms to embrace him. His father's boisterous hug he bore more readily, and it was brought home to her that, in her son's eyes, she had diminished in importance, although his courtesy towards her was faultless. It nearly broke her heart, but she remained smiling, and resolutely kept her distance.

'I see you have taught the lad courtly manners!' Henry observed, ruffling his offspring's red curls. 'Well, my Lord Henry. You are to go to England to receive the homage of my barons, as my heir. All you have to do is sit there and look happy about it. Just remember you are not king yet!'

They all laughed, but there was an excited and defiant glint in the boy's eyes that rode ill with the humility he was supposed to show to his royal father. Eleanor alone noticed it, and felt a fleeting chill in her heart. Was her son, young as he was, ambitious to fill that father's shoes? Had Henry's words brought home to him the reality of his great destiny? Both of them had done their best to prepare Young Henry for eventual kingship, but maybe he had not quite understood what it would really mean – until now. Or maybe he was just excited at the prospect of a sea voyage and of being made to feel important, as any young boy would be. She shrugged off her fears. She really was over-reacting, a bad habit of hers. It was the prospect of yet another parting from her son that was making her so sensitive, undoubtedly.

'Go and make ready, my young Lord,' Becket was saying. 'And walk! A future king does not run, but maintains a dignified pace.'

Henry burst out laughing. 'I think *I* ought to take some lessons in kingship from you, Thomas!'

Becket bestowed that slow, attractive smile of his. 'I too will go and prepare for the journey, my Lord.'

'Wait,' Henry said. 'You do not yet fully comprehend your mission.'

'My Lord?' Becket, for once, looked slightly bewildered.

'It is my intention,' Henry said, gazing upon him affectionately, 'that you should become archbishop of Canterbury.'

A look of horror fixed itself on Becket's face. He stood there, seemingly unable to speak. Eleanor had never seen him so discomposed.

'My Lord,' he whispered, his voice hoarse with shock, 'do not do this, I beg of you.'

The smile froze on the King's face.

'Come now, Thomas. Surely you can see the wisdom in my decision,' he said evenly.

'Lord King,' Becket replied desperately, 'I beseech you to reconsider, for many good reasons. I know that, if you make me archbishop, you will demand many things of me – things I might be unable to grant. Allow me to speak plainly. Already, it is said that you presume much in matters affecting the Church. If you seek to push through reforms that conflict with the honour of the Church, I would be bound to oppose them.'

'But Thomas, you have said yourself that the Church is in need of reform,' Henry protested.

'As your chancellor, I might voice such an opinion, but as archbishop of Canterbury, I would be in a difficult position. And my enemies would be waiting to exploit that, to drive a wedge between us. Sire, England is not lacking in good churchmen who could ably fill Archbishop Theobald's shoes. There is Bishop Foliot, for one, although I have never liked him; yet he would be the ideal choice. I am not even a priest, and I have never celebrated a mass!'

'It's no good, Thomas, my mind is made up,' Henry declared, with an air of finality. 'I have thought long on this, over many months, and I *know* that you are the right man for the office. And you know, as well as I do, that you can be ordained priest one day, and consecrated archbishop the next. I promise you, we will work together for the good of the Church – and of England. Now, no more arguments.'

Becket knew when he was defeated. He stood there miserably, looking as heavy-hearted as a man who has just been sentenced to some terrible fate. Not for the first time, Eleanor felt pity for him. She knew his arguments were well founded, knew too that he would be at a disadvantage from the start. But both he and she were powerless to gainsay Henry once his mind was made up.

Becket had risen from his departing bow when the King bade him pause.

'I will have letters prepared, informing my English barons and bishops of my decision,' he said. 'I must stay here in Normandy, but my son will be a witness to your enthronement.'

'Very well, Sire,' Becket said, his voice unsteady, his face hollow. Eleanor was torn between elation that her son was formally to be recognized as the heir to England, and dismay at Henry's folly in believing that his friend would be able to render him unstinting loyalty once he was safely installed at Canterbury.

The court was still at Falaise when, in May, reports reached Normandy of Becket's formal nomination as archbishop in the presence of the Lord Henry and the King's justices; then came the news of his ordination as a priest, and his consecration in Canterbury Cathedral the very next day. He had been overcome with emotion, it was said, and wept when the archbishop's mitre was placed on his head. Eleanor wondered uncharitably if he had done that for effect; he had a great sense of occasion, she knew, and a flair for the dramatic gesture. It appealed to his vanity.

The next news was brought by an unexpected visitor, the new archbishop's secretary, John of Salisbury. Eleanor had long known of John by reputation. He had studied in Paris and worked in the Papal Curia before entering the household of Archbishop Theobald, by which time he had become famous as a man of letters, and he was now accounted one of the greatest scholars and thinkers of his time.

'He has no great opinion of me!' Henry grimaced, after John had been announced and they were waiting for him to come into their presence. 'He thinks my court too frivolous.'

'He sounds a lot like Abbot Bernard,' Eleanor observed drily, thinking of that austere old terror who had long since gone to his heavenly reward.

'I think it was Abbot Bernard who recommended our friend John to Archbishop Theobald,' Henry told her.

A tall, dignified cleric in his early forties was ushered into the solar. John of Salisbury was known to be high-minded and uncompromising, yet his manner towards his King could not be faulted.

'Greetings, John,' Henry said.

'Greetings, Sire. I trust that you and the Queen are in health. My Lord Archbishop sends his fealty and his love, and has charged me to give you this.' He held out a richly embroidered purse with drawstrings and placed it in Henry's hands. Henry looked dumbstruck.

'The great seal of England?' he queried, in apparent disbelief.

'The very same, Sire,' John replied gravely. 'My master has sent me to tender his resignation as chancellor. He begs you to excuse him, but he wishes from now on to devote his life wholly to the Church.'

'What?' Henry was ashen, and also angered. 'I need him both as my chancellor and as my archbishop.'

John of Salisbury regarded his king with something akin to pity. 'My master has said that the burdens of both offices are too heavy for him to bear.'

'Does he no longer care to be in my service?' Henry burst out. There were tears in his eyes. Eleanor could not bear to look at him, or to witness his crushing disappointment, which seemed almost akin to a betrayal.

'Lord King, he has changed. You would not credit it.'

'In what way has he changed?' Eleanor asked sharply.

'A miraculous transformation took place just after his consecration, my Lady.'

'Miraculous?' echoed Henry. Eleanor, remembering how Becket had always revelled in playing his roles to the hilt, thought that perhaps John should have said 'calculated' instead.

'As soon as he put on those robes, reserved at God's command for the highest of His servants, my Lord Archbishop changed not only his apparel, but the whole cast of his mind. Overnight, he who had been a courtier, statesman and soldier, a worldly man by any standards, became a holy man, an ascetic even. He has changed from a patron of play-actors and a follower of hounds to a shepherd of souls.'

'Thomas? An ascetic?' Henry could not believe what he was hearing. He looked utterly bewildered. Eleanor said nothing. She was thinking that, having ceased to be the patron of play-actors, Becket seemed to have become one. She could not credit that this transformation was sincere, let alone miraculous. Becket had never done things by halves.

'Yes, Sire,' John was saying. 'He has so completely abandoned the world that all men are marvelling at the change in him. He has cast aside his elegant robes for a monk's habit, and beneath it he wears a hair shirt, to keep himself in mind of the frailty of the flesh; my Lord, it swarms with vermin. He drinks only water that has been used to boil hay. He has sold all his worldly goods, and now performs great acts of charity and humility. He washes the feet of thirteen beggars every day, and gives them alms. He asks his monks to whip his bare back in penance for his sins. His nights are spent sleepless in vigil.'

Henry was listening to all this with his mouth agape. It seemed incredible to him, who loved Becket, but not to Eleanor, who did not, and who viewed him with suspicion. She sensed that Becket was revelling in his new role, and enjoying the fame it was bringing him. How else could such a radical change be explained?

The King, still stunned, summoned Bishop Foliot and made John of Salisbury repeat to him what he had said of Becket's transformation. Foliot, the only bishop who had opposed Becket's election, looked grimly sceptical.

'My Lord King, you have wrought a miracle,' he said drily. 'Out of a soldier and a courtier, you have made an archbishop. And a saintly one, it seems.'

Eleanor made a face. The Bishop looked at her, realising that she was shrewder than he had hitherto supposed.

Henry was crestfallen. 'I know not what to think,' he said. 'I feel as if I have been abandoned. I feel as if I have lost a friend.'

20 Woodstock, 1163

Eleanor was walking with her children in the park that surrounded the royal manor of Woodstock. Earlier, they had visited the menagerie that had been established there by their father, and young Richard and Geoffrey had been enthralled to see the caged lions, leopards, lynxes and camels that had been sent as gifts to the King by foreign princes.

Matilda and little Eleanor had been particularly taken with a curious stick-backed beast.

'Hedgehog!' Eleanor cried in delight.

'No,' her mother said, 'it's a porcupine.'

They stood watching it rootling about for a few more minutes, then Richard dragged them back to see the lions, shouting, 'Raaarr!! Raaarr!' Eleanor smiled lovingly upon him, then her thoughts strayed to her eldest son, whom she still missed painfully. He had remained in Becket's household, and she had not seen him since February, when she had organised a little festival for his eighth birthday. But it had fallen somewhat flat. He was very grand now, Young Henry, too old to be thrilled by birthday treats, and all too conscious that he was his father's heir.

The July sun was warm, and when they returned to the Queen's enclosed garden, a pretty arbour made enchanting with its flowery mead of delicate, heavenly colours, and its laden fruit trees, they were served ale that had been hung in buckets to cool in the moat. There Henry joined them, fresh from hunting deer in the park. He was feeling particularly pleased with himself for, only the day before, every one of the princes of Wales had come to Woodstock to pay homage to him, following his vigorous suppression of a Welsh rising in the spring.

When the children's nurses had taken them back to the manor house to have their supper, Henry and Eleanor sat on a stone bench, basking in the late-afternoon haze, and talking of his ambitious plans to enforce law and order in his kingdom. This was his cherished project, and he had been working on it from the moment of his accession.

'What worries me the most is the increase in crimes committed by the clergy,' he said. 'And the law, as it stands, allows them to get away with it!'

This was a topic long familiar to Eleanor. She had heard him grumble about it many times before. But there was a new determination in his voice when he spoke again. 'I intend to put an end to this anomaly,' he declared.

He could never have guessed, she was to think, years later, looking back on this summer's day, how brutally that resolve would impact upon his life.

'It's wrong, and it must be ended,' Henry went on. 'If a lay person commits a crime, they end up in my courts and are punished according to their desserts, and often severely. That is the law of the land, and it is just. I have seen to that.' He got up and began pacing up and down in his usual restless manner. 'But anyone in holy orders, even the lowliest clerk, if he commits a crime, be it murder or theft or rape, can claim benefit of clergy and be tried in the Church courts. And you know what that means.'

'The Church is not allowed to shed blood,' Eleanor said.

'Exactly. So it imposes the lightest penalties. Murder a man, and as long as you've got a tonsure, you get three hail Maries! But if you or I were to commit murder, Eleanor, we would be hanged.' Henry's face was flushed with anger. This issue really rankled with him, and had done for a long time. She suspected there was only one reason why he had not decided to act until now, and that was because he had not wanted to provoke a quarrel with Becket. Relations between them since Henry's return to England had been at first wary and then amicable, but increasingly there was a distance between them that had never been there in the past, and she guessed that Henry grieved for what he had lost, and feared to upset the equilibrium of what remained of the friendship. Even so, either he had become sufficiently vexed by the matter of the criminous clerks, as he called it, to put Becket to the test, or he had managed to convince himself that his beloved Thomas really was on his side.

'No, my love, I have decided,' Henry was saying. 'All offenders must be tried in the royal courts, without exception.'

He sat down, and Eleanor laid her hand on his. It was becoming increasingly rare for them to share such private moments of tenderness these days. Henry was always too busy with the many cares and duties that went with ruling such vast and far-flung domains, while she, for her part, was preoccupied with the demands of her growing family. And above all that, they existed in a state of truce, skirting around the issues that divided them. It did not make for intimacy.

'Some will see that as an attack on the Church itself,' she said.

'I know that. I expect some resistance. But I am determined to have my way.' Henry's jaw was thrust forward, his grey eyes steely with determination. It would be a brave man who defied him.

The next night, he came to her in some anger and distress.

'Thomas defied me!' he raged. 'We were in council, and in order to replenish my treasury, which keeps emptying at an alarming rate, I proposed that the profits from revenue collected in the shires by my sheriffs be diverted to the crown. It's a thoroughly reasonable proposal, but what did my Lord Archbishop do? He opposed it. He defied me openly. He made me look a fool!' Henry was almost shouting.

'What did your barons say?' Eleanor asked gently.

'They supported Thomas. Bastards, the lot of them!' His face was puce.

Eleanor, shaking her head in despair, snuffed some candles, took off her nightrobe and slipped naked into bed.

'Perhaps my Lord Archbishop wishes to show that he can assert his authority as primate of England,' she suggested, as casually as she could. Privately, she wondered if Becket had got wind of the bigger issue that was soon to be made public, and was testing the water to see how much support he might expect to gain.

Henry sat down heavily on the bed and began stripping off his clothes. At thirty, he was still broad-chested and muscular, but he had the beginnings of a paunch, the consequence of enjoying too much of the good, sweet wines of Anjou.

'Does he indeed? Well, I'll not let him best me again!' he vowed, and climbed in beside her. 'But let us not waste time on Thomas. I came here for another purpose.' Gathering her in strong arms, he kissed her avidly, and she marvelled at how her body still had the power to arouse him. She was forty-one now, and there was the lightest silvering of grey in her still-thick hair. Faint lines ringed her eyes, her lips were not as full as they had been once, and her jaw less defined; her breasts were soft from too many pregnancies, and her stomach rounded. Yet she still knew how to tease and please Henry, and her eager fingers and tongue could always find ways to bring him quickly to the point of ecstasy, as she was proceeding to do now, rejoicing to feel his penis grow instantly hard in her hand, and feeling her own surge of pleasure at his touch. They came together, as they always did, in a mad fervour of passion, and when it had subsided, Eleanor lay slick and hot, with Henry's weight upon her, marvelling at how they could still take such joy in each other after eleven years of marriage and seven children.

Presently, Henry fell asleep, his arm flung across Eleanor in its usual position. When he awoke in the small hours, the candle had burned down, and in its dwindling light he lay gazing at his wife, recalling their lovemaking. She was still a magnificent woman, he reflected, and he still loved her. He might make secret trysts with Rohese de Clare – indeed, he was so captivated by her erotic appeal that he could not give her up – but Eleanor had his heart, and often his body, which was something of a marvel to him. When he was with her like this, he could forget for a space how deeply Thomas had wounded him by betraying their friendship. Never in history, he told himself, had a prince done so much for a subject, only to have it cast back in his face. It was as if Thomas was determined to assert his authority above that of his king! *That* Henry could not – and would not – tolerate. If there was to be a power struggle between them, then so be it. But why should Thomas wish to initiate such a thing, when he owed so much to Henry, and after they had enjoyed the most enriching of friendships? Dear God, Henry thought, must he keep torturing himself by remembering those heady days when he and Thomas had been close and carefree, heedless of the storms that were swirling threat-eningly on the horizon? He had loved Thomas, loved him as a brother, and he had believed that Thomas had returned that love. It seemed he had been wrong about that, devastatingly wrong. And at the very thought, Henry of England buried his lion-like head in the pillow and wept.

Eleanor awoke in darkness and lay there gazing through the high, narrow window at the starry night sky. A light, warm breeze drifted across the pillow, gently stirring the tendrils of her hair. England's climate might be as cold as that in northern France, but the summer months could be delightful, although not as blazingly hot and glorious as in Aquitaine. For the thou-sandth time, she struggled to suppress a longing for the land of her birth. It had been four seemingly endless years since she had been in Poitiers, and longer since she had seen the vast golden swathes of the south. Soon, she must contrive to go back, make any excuse. Her mind was full of plans.

Suddenly, she became aware of a harsh, muffled sobbing, and realised to her horror that it was coming from the pillow next to hers, and that Henry was weeping. She had rarely seen her tough, strong husband cry, and was at a loss to know what to do. Should she pretend she was asleep and hadn't heard? Would it embarrass him to have her witness his vulnerability? Or should she follow her instincts and comfort him, as she comforted her sons when they came to her in tears for some childish hurt?

He had his back to her. She reached out a tentative hand and placed it on his bare shoulder.

'Henry? What is the matter?' she whispered.

He froze for a moment, then his shoulders slumped and he dragged his forearm over his eyes.

'I am betrayed,' he murmured brokenly, 'betrayed by the one who has the most cause to love me.'

For answer, Eleanor drew him into her arms, pulling his head against her breasts. Normally, such intimate contact would inflame his desire, but not tonight. He just lay there, his eyes closed, sunk in misery.

'Henry,' she said at length, 'you should not let Thomas affect you so. He is not worthy of this mindless devotion.' That roused him, and he drew back and stared at her through the gloom.

'Thomas was the best servant a king ever had,' he said hotly, 'and the best friend. You never liked him. You've always been jealous of him – admit it!'

'I admit I resented his hold on you,' Eleanor said carefully, anxious not to make this situation any worse than it was. 'I wanted you to seek *my* advice and opinions, not his. That was only natural. Yet it did seem to me – and others – that you were in thrall to him, and that worried me, because I feared you would one day find him wanting in some way, as is sadly the case now. And I was not the only person who felt you had advanced him too greatly, as you well know.'

'I am not in thrall to him,' Henry snapped. 'What rot!'

'Then why are you so hurt?'

'I feel betrayed!' he blurted out. 'Anyone would, if they had done as much for someone as I have for Thomas, and then had it thrown back in their face!'

'Then let anger be your guide, not hurt,' Eleanor urged. 'You have his measure now. You will be prepared when he thwarts you again, and displays such base ingratitude – as he will! Do not let him get away with it a second time.'

'It's not as simple as that,' Henry said, a tear trickling down his cheek. 'I loved that man like a brother, yet suddenly he is my enemy.'

'Oh, Henry, can you not see what others see?' Eleanor sighed. 'Love can make us blind to others' faults. Always remember, whatever he does, you are his king. He owes you fealty and duty. You must swallow your pain and make him obey you, as all your other subjects are bound to do.'

'You don't understand at all, do you, Eleanor?' Henry was almost shouting. 'He has a higher allegiance than his duty to me. He tells me he has God on his side, and I can't fight God!'

'Thomas is a man, for all that he is an archbishop,' Eleanor flung back passionately, 'and it's as a man that you must deal with him, on the level. All this boasting of putting God first is more of his play-acting, yet you could never see it. He's revelling in this role and playing power games with you. And you're letting him do it!'

'Enough!' howled Henry, his face ravaged in the moonlight. 'I won't listen to your venom. You always hated Thomas.'

'It's not venom, it's common sense!' she cried. 'You would see it if you weren't so besotted with this man! By God's blood, Henry, if I didn't know better, I'd swear that you love him in the way that he loves you.'

He stared at her, shocked into silence for a moment. 'What do you mean by that?' he asked, slowly, menacingly.

'I saw it years ago,' she went on, 'and if I could see it, then others must have seen it too. The way he looked at you. He *wanted* you, Henry. It was glaringly obvious. If you hadn't been so blinded by love for him, you'd have known.'

The slap landed stingingly on her cheek, leaving her as shocked as he. Henry had never raised a hand to her before, unlike many other husbands she had heard of.

'You are truly sick in your mind if you think such things,' Henry snarled. 'I can only think it's your foul jealousy that has led you to make such vile allegations.'

'Believe that if you wish,' Eleanor said quietly, her palm pressed to her burning cheek. 'I will say nothing more, for I know that what I am convinced is the truth is painful. But when he hurts you again, Henry, I will be here. I love you. *I* would do nothing to harm you or betray you.'

In later years, she was to look back on those words with bitter regret, and to that night as one that marked a turning point in their relationship. Suddenly, she had become the enemy too, for daring to probe the raw place within her husband's heart. He had come to her for comfort, and she had only made matters worse. She was overwhelmed with the hopelessness of it all. Thomas Becket was still standing between them, more potent as an adversary than he had ever been as a friend.

21 Westminster, 1163

Henry stood up and there was an instant hush. The barons and bishops who had gathered for this meeting of the Great Council were packed into every cranny of the lofty, stone-vaulted chamber, and all were craning forward to hear him speak.

The word was that something momentous – and controversial – was in the wind.

'My Lords,' the King began, 'I am minded to address a legal anomaly in my realm: the issue of criminous clerks, those who have been leniently sentenced by the Church courts because they have claimed benefit of clergy. It seems, good sirs, that these men, because they are in holy orders, are literally getting away with murder in some cases, and I will not tolerate it any longer!'

There was general murmuring at this, and a few 'ayes' from the barons, while Archbishop Becket and the prelates sat stony-faced.

'I am resolved to require the Church courts to hand over those offenders who have broken *my* laws to *my* courts for corporal punishment!' Henry declared firmly. 'This is no new thing, my Lords, but a return to the customs of King Henry, whom you all honour as "the Lion of Justice".'

There were a few puzzled faces, as people struggled – and failed – to recall the first Henry enforcing such a law. The King smiled grimly to himself. In truth, he had made that bit up, hoping he would not be challenged on that point.

He sat down in his chair of estate, glaring at his councillors, almost daring them to disagree with him. 'Well, my Lords? What say you?' he rapped out.

Becket rose to his feet. His face was thunderous.

'Lord King, like everyone else here present, I am aware of abuses within the Church courts. But as your archbishop, and primate of all England, I cannot sanction any infringement of the authority and liberties of the Church.'

Henry's expression was glacial. He sat rigid on his throne, gripping its wooden arms. 'Are you defying me, my Lord of Canterbury?' he asked, his tone intimidating. But Becket stood his ground.

'Lord King, when you raised me to be archbishop, you conferred on me a sacred trust. I would be betraying that trust if I failed to protect the Church's immunity from secular inter-ference.'

'You are practised at betrayals, priest,' Henry muttered. A few caught his words and exchanged speculative glances. The expression on Becket's face revealed that he had heard them too. He swallowed, then regained his composure.

'I am utterly opposed to this proposed reform, Lord King,' he stated, then looked sternly at his bishops, challenging them to support him. Some gazed at the floor, others seemed suddenly to have discovered something fascinating about their episcopal rings.

Bishop Gilbert Foliot stood up.

'I am with you, Lord King,' he announced defiantly. 'It is the spirit of the law that counts, not the letter, be that law human or divine.'

'Thank you, my Lord of Hereford,' Henry said, gratified. 'At least one of my clerics has some sense. What do the rest of you say? Who is for me?'

To a man, the barons raised their hands, and a few bishops tremulously followed suit. Becket rounded on them.

'Whom do you serve first, God or the King?' he barked. Across the chamber, his eyes met Henry's. There was hatred in both men's faces, and, in the King's, pain also. But Becket was a man on a mission. He knew himself to be in the right. Earthly friendship must give place before the honour of God and His Church.

'I command you to oppose this so-called reform,' he instructed his clergy. 'Every one of you, without exception.'

'Be careful, Thomas,' Henry growled. Becket ignored him.

'Those opposing, stand up!' he commanded. 'There is more at issue here than your obedience to the King. You have your immortal souls to consider.'

No one moved for a moment, then one bishop stood up, followed by another, and another, until they were all standing, apart from Bishop Foliot, who remained resolutely seated.

'My Lord Bishop of Hereford?' Becket prompted. 'I hope you are thinking of God, and of your conscience.'

'God and my conscience are in complete agreement,' Foliot retorted, folding his arms across his ample paunch.

'Very well,' Becket said in a dissatisfied voice.

'Enough of this charade!' Henry snarled. 'You, my bishops – you will all swear obedience to the ancient customs of this realm. I command it!'

'But that would mean us swearing to uphold this law that you say King Henry passed,' Becket said.

'It is my right to require such an oath,' Henry told him firmly. 'My laws must be upheld, and if my bishops don't set a good example, what hope in Hell is there for the rest of us?'

Wincing at the King's casual mention of Hell, Becket turned to his colleagues. 'You must take the oath, as your duty to the King requires,' he told them, 'but you must add the words "saving our order". Is that clear?'

'By the eyes of God!' Henry thundered. 'Let me hear no word of your order! I demand absolute and express agreement to my laws.'

'Then, in all conscience, my King, I cannot require the bishops to take this oath,' Becket insisted. At that, Henry saw red. Shaking with anger, he got up and strode furiously from the chamber.

All of a sudden, there were frenzied sounds of activity from the palace courtyard below, the shouts of agitated men, the whinnying of horses, the trundling of carts.

'Get your women to pack,' Henry told Eleanor, as he burst into her chamber.

'What has happened?' she asked, rising to her feet and letting her embroidery fall to the floor. Little Matilda and Eleanor abandoned their skittles and looked up at their father warily. His rages terrified them. Mamille, seeing their anxious faces, set down her goblet, knelt on the floor and rolled the ball, in an attempt to distract them.

'It's Becket!' Henry hissed. 'He defied me again! In council, in front of all my lords, temporal and spiritual. He took the part of his criminous clerks; he opposed my reforms; and he forbade the bishops to swear an oath upholding my laws. Such defiance is treason!'

Eleanor poured him some wine and handed it to him, forbearing to speak. He gulped it back and resumed his tirade. 'It is not to be borne! He shall pay for this.'

'What will you do?' Eleanor asked. She had resolved never to criticise Becket again, but to remain quietly supportive of Henry when he needed her to be. That way, she hoped to repair the damage she had done on that awful night in July.

Henry sat down heavily in her vacated chair, staring into the fire, breathing furiously. When at last he spoke, his voice was calmer, deadlier. 'For a start, I'll confiscate the rich manors and castles I bestowed on him when he was chancellor. He'll find out what the loss of my favour must mean to him.'

He got up and began pacing. His daughters, at their mother's nod, scuttled out of the way and retreated to the safety of the window seat, where they sat watching him fearfully. Eleanor smiled at them encouragingly, then turned back to their father.

'Is it right that, after what he has done, Thomas still has care of our son, your heir?' she enquired.

'No, by God, it is not right!' Henry stormed. 'I will remove the boy from his household at once.'

'Let him come back to me,' she urged, but he looked at her as if she were mad.

'He is eight now, and far too old to be governed by women,' he said dismissively. 'He shall have his own establishment and servants.'

Eleanor quelled her surging disappointment, and reasoned that this would be more fitting for a king's son.

'As long as I may see him from time to time,' she said hopefully.

'Of course,' Henry told her, but his mind was clearly on other things, festering over Becket's betrayal. He was like a man possessed. She longed to comfort him, but knew very well that he would not welcome it.

'Shall I still get packed?' she asked. 'Are we leaving here?'

Henry sighed. His rage was subsiding, now that he had thought of the means to have his revenge. 'No. Forget it. I spoke in haste. I'll go hunting tomorrow, and no doubt I'll feel better afterwards. Then I'll be able to think clearly and decide what to do next.'

'You had better go down and tell them to unload the carts and the sumpter mules,' she smiled.

'I'll be popular!' he said, with a tired smile, as he left her.

The highest in the land had gathered in the barrel-vaulted gloom of Westminster Abbey. Candles flickering in their tall sconces illuminated the faces of the great and the good, here to witness this momentous event. Word had recently come from Rome: the Pope had spoken. Nearly a hundred years after his death, King

Edward the Confessor was now officially a saint, and Henry, in honour of his canonisation, had built him a glorious shrine. Today, his remains were to be translated to their splendid new resting place, a masterpiece of stone, Purbeck marble and mosaic, surmounted by an intricately carved wooden canopy.

The court and all the lords of England, spiritual and temporal, were crammed into the Confessor's new chapel and its precincts. Eleanor was standing in her place of honour at the front with the King and their children, glad to have her eldest son at her side for once. Young Henry had grown in height and dignity these last years, and now wore his exalted status like a mantle. They had Becket to thank for that, she could not but admit it.

Becket was here too today, which was why the atmosphere in the abbey was so tense. He and Henry had faced each other across the floor of decorated tiles, and the air between them had almost crackled with hostility. Yet on the surface, all was genial, with king and archbishop exchanging the kiss of greeting, and Becket proceeding to conduct the long service with grave dedication, his clever, chiselled face set in a lofty, detached expression.

Beside Eleanor, Richard fidgeted. He never could stand still, loving to be off riding his palfrey or practising the swordplay at which he was becoming so adept. But his mother's warning hand on his shoulder quelled his restlessness. How like his father he was, Eleanor thought. Her gaze swept her other children, who were all on their honour to behave composedly. They were standing solemnly, overawed by the august gathering and the sense of occasion that inspired the stately proceedings.

Henry watched the ritual with narrowed, steely eyes. He had longed for this day, could not do enough to honour the memory of this saint whose canonisation he had pressed for so passion-ately – and now it was all spoilt by the presence of Thomas Becket. Damn him, he thought, as fresh rage infused him. What was the matter with Thomas? It seemed he was deliberately doing everything in his power to provoke his king. Take that matter of William of Eynsford, one of Henry's vassals. It had been but a petty dispute over some land, but my Lord Archbishop must take umbrage and excommunicate the man! He'd *known* that would infuriate Henry, but it hadn't deterred him. What was Thomas trying to prove? That he was more powerful than the King?

Receiving a surreptitious nudge from Eleanor, Henry realised he had forgotten where he was and why he was here. He pulled himself up: this business of Becket was becoming an obsession. Get public opinion on your side, his mother, the Empress, had written. Well, he would do that. But first, he must try to focus his mind on the present.

They were opening the vault now. Sixty years before, the monks of Westminster had lifted the lid and found the Confessor's corpse whole and uncorrupted. Henry was glad he had ordered the Abbot secretly to peek into the sarcophagus to confirm that it was still intact, if only for the sake of his daughters, whose eyes were wide with apprehension; Matilda had her hand to her mouth. Young Geoffrey, he noted, was watching it all with avid interest, unshrinking. A clever boy, Geoffrey, fearless and cunning; he would go far, his father thought proudly.

There was a reverent hush as the corpse of the saint was gradually exposed in its cloth-of-gold vestments, its skin parchment-like and brown, the eyes sunken, the nose still firm. After the King and Queen and the peers had had a chance to view it, it was wrapped in precious silk cloths, then reverently lifted into its dazzling new gold coffin encrusted with gems, which Henry and his principal barons hoisted onto their shoulders and conveyed in solemn procession through the abbey cloisters before reverently placing it in its new shrine. Then the *Te Deum Laudamus* was sung in joyful celebration.

The ceremony over, the King bowed low before St Edward's shrine, swept unseeing past Archbishop Becket, and led the way out of the church. He should have felt jubilant on this great occasion, but all he wanted to do was weep.

22 Berkhamsted, 1163

It was Christmas Eve, and the Yule log had just been dragged into the great hall by several beefy serfs, while the castle servants were busily picking out the best branches from the great piles of evergreens that were strewn across the floor; these would be used to decorate the hall. The younger royal children scampered among them, full of excitement, eager not to miss out on the festive fun. They had already been shooed out of the kitchens, where the Christmas brawn was seething in its pan, and great joints of meat were roasting over the spits.

Upstairs, the King burst into the Queen's bower with his usual lack of ceremony. He wore a look of triumph.

'He has submitted!' he announced, without preamble. 'He has sworn to uphold the ancient customs of England – without qualification!'

Eleanor stood up, laid down the rose silk *bliaut* she was embroidering as a gift for young Matilda, and smiled.

'I think we have Bishop Foliot to thank for that,' she said. Henry had cunningly translated Foliot to the important See of London, so that he would be on hand to advise his king and lead the opposition to Becket. One by one, persuaded by Foliot's eloquent arguments, the bishops had gone over to Henry.

'And the Pope!' the King cried jubilantly. 'Don't forget Alexander needs my support. He ordered Thomas to submit, and told him he could expect no help from Rome if he did not. So Becket is defeated on all sides. Eleanor, this is the best Yuletide gift I could have received!'

Eleanor twined her arms around his neck; these days, they were not so openly demonstrative towards each other as they once had been, but she was so pleased to see Henry's face lit up by his victory that she could not help herself. She knew he was reluctant to display his inner hurts to her nowadays, yet he would not despise her sharing his victory. But although he briefly returned the embrace, he soon disentangled himself and went to warm his hands by the fire. They were rougher than ever now, scabbed and calloused from hours spent in the saddle, gripping worn leather reins.

He stood with his back to her. She could not – thank God! – know that he had just come from the arms of Rohese, that Thomas's messenger had encountered him as he'd left her chamber. He had been too spent to respond to Eleanor, too focused on Thomas's submission.

He turned around.

'Thomas showed good taste when he did up this place,' he said slowly, looking at the rich hues of the expensive hangings, the decorated floor tiles, the painted and gilded furniture and the delicate iron-work on the window bars and the fire screen. Eleanor agreed with him. She too had been conscious of the all-pervading, unseen presence of Becket in this castle, once bestowed so lovingly, which Henry had taken from him. Was there no escape from the man? She feared she would scream if she heard the name Thomas Becket again. He dominated their lives to an unacceptable extent. If only Henry had not been so besotted with him! She bit down the need to lash out verbally.

Henry was looking at her – a touch shiftily, she felt. Was he embarrassed by his obsession with Becket? Had it occurred to him that he ought to draw a line under this finished friendship, that it was unfair to her to prolong the agony any further? Evidently not, for when he spoke again, it became clear that his mind could focus only on one thing – or one person, to be more exact.

'Of course, I only have Thomas's promise privately, in a letter,' Henry said. 'He must submit publicly to my authority.'

'Is that wise?' Eleanor asked, taking up her embroidery again. 'He must feel he has been humiliated enough.'

'It is necessary,' Henry said coldly. 'He must be seen to submit, then my bishops will know without a doubt where their allegiance should lie.'

'I am sure you know best,' Eleanor said sourly, unable to help herself. Let be! Let be! she was crying inwardly.

Henry came to stand in front of her, looking down sardonically.

'Oh, I do,' he said softly. 'And I hope you will be there to see it happen.'

'You may count on that,' she replied briskly. 'And now, let us think of our children, and our guests, and do all honour to this season of Christ's birth.' And put Becket out of your mind. Those words lay unsaid, like a sword between them.

23 Clarendon, 1164

Eleanor seated herself beside Henry, huddling inside the heavy folds of the gold-banded crimson mantle that swept the floor around her feet, and extending one gloved hand to straighten the circlet that held her linen veil in place. They were enthroned in the spacious hall at Clarendon, the magnificent royal hunting lodge near Salisbury. The lords and clergy were swathed in furs against the January chill, and as soon as the King had sat down, they settled with a rustling of silks on their benches. Archbishop Becket sat slightly apart, his face grim beneath his bejewelled mitre, his white hand clenched around the staff of his crozier.

Henry leaned across to Eleanor.

'This should be plain sailing,' he murmured. 'I have already taken counsel of my civil and canon lawyers, and they tell me that my Lord of Canterbury has no grounds whatsoever for opposing my proposals.'

'I pray God that he will see it that way too, and that we can have an end to this quarrel,' Eleanor said low, her fingers mindlessly pleating the rich imperial silk of her *bliaut*.

Henry bristled. 'It was not of *my* making. I merely seek to extend the same justice to all my subjects. But let us not waste time. They're all waiting.' He sat up straight in his seat.

'My Lords,' he began in a ringing voice, 'I have summoned you today to ask for your endorsement of a new code of sixteen laws, in which are enshrined the ancient customs of this realm. I am happy to tell you all that our good friend here, Archbishop Becket, has already sworn to uphold these customs, so you need have no qualms about approving them.'

Becket's expression was unreadable; it seemed he was keeping a tight rein on himself. But then he would, Eleanor thought: everything he did was studied, lacking in spontaneity. She did not believe he would acquiesce as meekly as Henry anticipated. He would be looking for a loophole. He would not go down without a fight.

The Archdeacon of Canterbury, who was acting as Henry's unofficial chancellor, since no one of Becket's stature and abilities could be found to fill his shoes, stood up and unscrolled the parchment on which were listed the new laws. There was a lot of nodding and a few ayes from the company as they listened intently to the first two articles, and Becket seemed to relax a little. So far, it was all just a reiteration of the old and familiar customs, as Henry had said.

Henry was watching Becket too, a mischievous twinkle in his eyes. Eleanor wondered what game he was playing. Almost certainly, he had something up his sleeve.

She did not have to wait long to find out, for the Archdeacon
– a man who was not stupid, and who knew he was about to
summon up a tempest – cleared his throat and read article three,
as Henry sat smiling complacently.

'The King has decreed that, henceforth, criminous clerks be
handed over to the royal courts for sentencing.'

Becket leaped to his feet.

'Lord King, there is not, nor ever has been, any law in this
realm to that effect!' he protested. The bishops looked unhappily
at each other.

'Be that as it may, there is such a law now,' Henry said softly,
his tone menacing.

'It is laid down in Holy Scripture: render unto Caesar those
things that are Caesar's, and to God the things that are His,'
Becket rejoined. The bishops were now writhing in distress.

'You have sworn to obey me!' Henry snarled.

'I swore to uphold the *ancient* laws of this land,' Becket flung
back. 'You have duped me, Sire – and all of us.'

'How dare you!' roared Henry, rising, trembling with fury.
'Swear, priest! By God, you will swear!'

Becket ignored him. He turned to the assembled clergy and
addressed them. 'My Lords Spiritual, you know very well that
these new laws encompass not just the laws of the late King
Henry, but also this new, pernicious law of the King's, made
plain to you just now, and contrary to the honour of God and
His Church. I therefore command you, on your allegiance to me
and to our Heavenly Father, not to accede to these unjust
demands.'

'What of your allegiance to me, your king!' Henry bawled, as
the bishops began murmuring their assent, and Eleanor began
to fear that her husband would soon be throwing himself on
the floor, howling in ungovernable rage. 'By the eyes of God,'
he roared, his hand flying to his scabbard, 'must I obtain that
obedience at sword-point?'

'Lord King, these are men of God,' Becket flung back at him,
extending his arms in a protective gesture, like a shepherd
shielding his sheep. His eyes, direct and challenging, locked with
Henry's bloodshot ones and held them. It was Henry who looked
away first, but not before Becket had espied the tear that had

trickled down his cheek, which he quickly wiped away with his sleeve on the pretext of blowing his nose. He did not see the look of regret and compassion that fleetingly softened the Archbishop's basilisk gaze.

'Are you going to continue to defy me, Thomas?' Henry asked hoarsely, quieter now.

'No, my King,' Becket replied. 'If you asked it, I would perjure myself.'

'There will be no need,' Henry said, his mood lightening as he sensed victory. 'Just say you will swear to my laws. That's all that's needed. It's really very simple.'

'Saving your pardon, Sire, I will swear in good faith to uphold these laws, and I will order my bishops here to do the same. But I deeply regret I cannot put my seal to this parchment.'

'Just swear, that's all I ask,' Henry conceded. He thinks he has won, Eleanor thought, that he has outmanoeuvred friend Becket. But I fear this is only the beginning. She bent her head as tears welled in her own eyes. She could see her future mapped out, the long, tortuous years ahead, overshadowed by this difficult, contentious, self-important priest, with herself losing Henry in the process, and Henry losing his very soul, until the grave swallowed them all up. It was an unbearable prospect.

Becket had sworn, and his clergy with him. But he went about the palace with lowering face and bitter eyes. One day, entering the chapel ahead of her ladies, Eleanor was horrified to see a man, naked to the waist, kneeling on the chancel steps. His exposed back was criss-crossed with bloody lacerations, and as she watched, unable to tear her eyes away from this grisly vision, she saw the barbed discipline flung again and again over his shoulder, flagellating and tearing his white skin. At her gasp, he flung the whip down on the tiles, his head jerking round. It was Becket, his face a mask of grief. She stared at him for a long moment, then hastened away, shooing her tardy women before her so that they should not intrude on the Archbishop's private hell.

Word soon got around that Becket regretted what he had done and was punishing himself with heavy penances. He even tried to flee the kingdom, but was halted by the King's officers on the very seashore.

'We can't have the Primate of England sulking in France,' Henry sneered, his face dark with anger. 'How would that look?'

'I would let him go,' said Bishop Foliot, his bushy brows creased in a frown. 'The Pope could not approve of him deserting his flock, and I have little doubt he would agree to your replacing Becket with someone more amenable.'

'I could not agree with you more, my Lord Bishop,' Eleanor put in. 'We have heard enough of this priest!'

'You speak truth, Foliot. Thomas must go,' Henry agreed. Eleanor looked at him in surprise.

'All your bishops will support you,' Foliot assured him. 'He is too unstable for high office in the Church. He is bringing it into disrepute!'

'He has gone out of his way to undermine my new laws,' Henry fumed. 'Well, I will use them to get rid of him. I have decided to have him arraigned for the misuse of moneys entrusted to him as chancellor. Let's see if that doesn't shift him!'

'Was there a misuse of moneys?' Foliot asked.

'No, but it will serve our purpose!' Henry said grimly.

Eleanor was watching him. He was a man on a quest, driven by a zealous desire for revenge. Only a man who had loved so deeply could hate this much, and yet . . . She was sure that he was still hurting, deep inside, and that no cure, be it revenge or reconciliation, would ever heal the gaping wound of Becket's betrayal.

24 Northampton, 1164

'As archbishop of Canterbury, I am not subject to the jurisdiction of the King!' Becket's normally impassive face was flushed with fury.

Henry leaned forward on his throne.

'Thomas, you have not been charged as an archbishop, but as my former chancellor,' he explained, pleasantly enough. 'Now, if you would be so good as to account to me and this court for the disposition of the moneys that passed through your hands back then, we can clear this matter up.'

Becket looked at him in hatred.

'I think you are out to ruin me, Sire!' he breathed.

'I?' enquired Henry. 'I thought the spur was on the other boot.'

Becket pursed his lips, then turned to the clergy, seated by order of rank on the benches behind him. 'My Lords Spiritual,' he cried, 'I beseech you, advise and help me! I ask for your support.' There was an embarrassed shuffling, as the ecclesiastics shifted position, looked down at their feet, and generally tried to avoid meeting his pleading eyes. Only Bishop Foliot fixed his gaze directly on the Archbishop.

'By your folly, you have brought yourself to this!' he accused Becket. 'But if you will submit to the King, as he lawfully requires, then you will have our perfect allegiance.'

Becket looked profoundly shocked.

'Lord King,' he said, turning back to Henry, who was glaring at him implacably, 'might I have time to consider my position and prepare an answer for you?'

'Of course,' Henry replied. 'I am not a monster. I'm a reasonable man. But don't even think of leaving the kingdom! Have I your word on that?'

'Yes, Sire,' Becket replied, meekly enough. 'You have my word.'

Eleanor was kneeling in the chapel. The candles on the altar illuminated in warm tones the painted statue of the Virgin and Child, and it seemed that Mary was smiling sadly in poignant reproach.

On the *prie-dieu* before the Queen lay the letter she had received that day, a formal missive from Louis, informing her of the marriages of their daughters, Marie to the Count of Champagne, and Alix to his brother, the Count of Blois. Her first reaction had been disbelief that her little girls were now young women of nineteen and fourteen, and married to boot!

She rarely thought of them these days, and could barely remember their faces now, although of course they would have changed much in the years since she had seen them – and yet she was astonished to find that she was deeply upset at not having been invited to their weddings. The reason, she knew, was not far to seek: Louis still thought her a bad, uncaring mother, who had abandoned her little girls without a thought to marry her lover. Well, she would prove him wrong. She would write to her daughters and express her joy in their marriages and her warm wishes for their future. There must be an end to this silence. She owed them some share of the kind of deep and abiding love she felt for her other children, the children she had been allowed to nurture from birth. She would write today. Even if there was no reply, she would have salved her conscience.

Eleanor was in her customary place of honour beside Henry when Becket was again summoned to court. She heard his sharp intake of breath when the Archbishop made a dramatic entrance, clothed in his rich vestments and carrying his episcopal cross, which was normally borne before him by one of his monks.

'Why is he doing that?' she whispered, shocked at Becket's aggressive stance, when he should have been suing for Henry's favour.

'I think he is claiming the Church's protection against my ill will,' Henry muttered dourly. Bishop Foliot, seated within earshot at the end of the nearest bench, looked up and said, quite audibly, 'He was always a fool, and always will be!' Becket glared at him.

'Well, Thomas, what have you got to say for yourself?' Henry asked, his grey eyes bearing down on his former friend.

'Lord King, I am come to remind you that you yourself have long since released me from all my liabilities as chancellor,' Becket told him with a defiant stare.

'God's blood, man! Are you to deny my justice at every turn?' Henry blustered.

'I think, Sire, that there is less in this of justice than malice,' Becket retorted, and as Henry roared oaths at him, he swooped down on his bishops. 'I forbid you to sit in judgement on me!' he shouted at them.

Henry leaped to his feet. Eleanor found herself gripping the arms of her throne; she could have killed Becket with her bare hands. How dare he provoke Henry in this way? Henry, who had done so much for him, and loved him too well.

Henry stepped off the dais and bounded forward until he was standing toe-to-toe with Becket.

'You have gone too far this time, Thomas!' he snarled. 'Now, my Lords and Bishops, you see his venom plainly. He defies not only his king, but the Pope himself. Now, listen. You will all write to His Holiness and inform him that this priest has breached his sworn oath to uphold the laws of England; and you will request that he be deposed from his office.'

There was a stunned silence as Becket gathered his wits.

'You have planned this, haven't you?' he flung at the King's retreating back, at which Henry, mounting the dais on the way back to his throne, rounded on him, shaking with rage.

'You –' he spluttered, barely able to speak. 'You viper! My Lords, let us proceed to the judgement at once. This priest is condemned out of his own mouth.'

'I will not hear it!' Becket thundered. 'You have no right. God alone can judge me!' And holding aloft his great golden cross, he stalked from the hall to furious cries of 'Traitor! Traitor!'

Eleanor could not sleep. The momentous events of the day kept playing on her mind, and at length she rose from her bed, wrapped herself in a fur-lined robe, stoked up the glowing coals in the brazier and settled herself on the stone seat in the window embrasure, gazing out at the stars that glittered over the dark, sleeping town. Her chamber overlooked the curtain wall of the castle, and on the bailey side, in the courtyard, the sentries had built up a bonfire, at which they were warming their hands as they stamped their feet on the damp earth. A solitary soldier was patrolling the walls; she watched him casting a cursory glance over the distant landscape before disappearing through the door that led to the opposite tower and the continuing wall walk beyond it.

It was then that she espied two dark, hooded figures emerging on the outer side of the castle. They must have come through the now-unguarded postern gate that was almost directly below her. She peered at them with interest, then realised they were monks. What business they had to be about after curfew she could only imagine: maybe they had been summoned from the nearby priory to attend someone in the castle who was sick, or maybe they were two members of Archbishop Becket's entourage escaping for a stolen hour to the taverns and brothels of Northampton. As the figures disappeared into the night, Eleanor forgot about them and, dousing the candle, climbed wearily back between the sheets. She thought she could sleep now.

'Becket has fled,' Henry said, a week later, climbing into bed beside Eleanor. Suddenly awake, aroused by the import of his words, she was surprised to find him in her chamber; these days, he did not come to her as often as she would have liked, and he had been so drunk at dinner that she'd feared he might collapse in a stupor where he sat. But soon she realised that he had not come seeking her body, but to talk over this latest outrage of Becket's.

'So he has gone,' she said. She was not surprised. Nothing Becket could do surprised her now.

'Yes. He disguised himself as a monk and fled across the Channel. He thinks he is safe – but I have not finished with him yet!' Henry's voice came out as a hiss.

'You are well rid of him,' she said tartly.

'That may be so, but is England well rid of its archbishop?' Henry retorted. He had a point, she conceded.

She sighed. She was truly pleased to see him. She had missed the warmth of him lying next to her, the sudden passion that sprang up between them, the drowsy peace and contentment that came after their coupling. She knew she was advancing helplessly into middle age, that the burnished beauty of her youth really was beginning to fade, and that Henry was yet a man in the vigour of his prime. He was highly sexed – as she had good cause to know – and she had often wondered if he sought sexual release anywhere else. She had no proof, but her common sense – and the odd, careless whispers of gossip she had not been meant to overhear – told her it was more than likely. Nevertheless, she could not bear to dwell on the possi-bility of her husband being unfaithful. But it was coming to something, she reflected bitterly, when he came to her bed primarily to talk about the friend who had become his most bitter enemy.

Well, she would not be defeated in the bedroom by Becket! She was a woman of experience and she had weapons at her disposal. Smiling welcomingly at Henry, she raised herself up on one elbow, letting her chemise fall open to reveal her voluptuous breasts.

'Would you prefer to talk?' she murmured, but Henry's troubled eyes, deep pools of grey fire, had suddenly lit up, and he reached for her, burying his face in her neck, biting her hungrily as his hands roved over her body. He was not a man to waste time, and within seconds, they had locked together in the old, familiar way, lust igniting powerfully as so many times before. All that Eleanor wanted at this moment was for him to be entirely hers, to feel him inside her, and never let him go.

When, later, they had slid apart, and Henry lay catching his breath beside her, she turned her face to his.

'Becket was disguised as a monk, you say?'

'Yes,' Henry grunted.

'It's strange,' Eleanor recalled, 'but some nights back – it was the night after you confronted Becket – I was watching from my window and I saw two monks leaving the castle. I did wonder what they were doing. You don't think . . . ?'

'My God, that must have been him!' Henry cried, sitting up suddenly. 'He left that very night. Why didn't you say anything?'

'There was nothing to say. I thought them of little consequence. I had no idea, in fact I'd forgotten all about them until now.' Eleanor realised she was stammering.

'Of course,' Henry relented, subsiding onto the pillows beside her. 'How could you have known?' His body was tense, rigid, his attitude no longer that of a lover but of a man in pain. 'By God, I will find him,' he muttered. 'There is not a place in all Christendom where he can hide from me.'

She had lost him once more. His thoughts were clearly over the sea with his Thomas. He was obsessing again over how he could carry on the fight with his renegade archbishop. He was lying there, his troubled grey eyes staring up at the vaulted ceiling, unaware that she was still there beside him. It was useless. Her heart heavy, she rolled over, turned her back to him and pretended to go to sleep.

25 Marlborough Castle, 1164–5

Another Christmas, and here they were in the Great Tower of Marlborough Castle, perched high on its mound on the edge of Savernake Forest, where Henry was hoping for some good hunting. Geoffrey, Henry's bastard, now fourteen, had just drawn the bean from his slice of the traditional cake, and was in consequence proclaimed Lord of Misrule for the evening. He had begun his sovereignty by issuing the most daring forfeits, and was even now challenging every handsome man in the room to kiss the cheek of the Queen.

'That should narrow the field!' Eleanor laughed. She loved the levity of the Yuletide season.

'By God, I'll have their balls if they show the slightest scanting of respect!' Henry growled good-naturedly.

It was a shame that the French envoys timed their arrival just now, when the court was at its merriest. A page came and whispered in the King's ear, and his grin faded.

'I'll be back shortly,' he told his wife, and she watched as he threaded his way through the revellers, absent-mindedly ruffling his giggling daughter Eleanor's auburn curls on the way. After waiting in vain for an hour for him to return, the Queen could bear it no longer, but murmured her excuses and hastened up the spiral stair to the King's solar, the sounds of jollity receding as she ascended. There was a light under the wooden door. He was there, as she had expected. She turned the iron ring. As she entered the room, Henry turned a ravaged face to her.

'What has happened?' she asked, forbearing to go to him, and horribly aware of the aching distance between them.

'Louis!' he snapped. 'He has offered Thomas his support and asked His Holiness not to heed any unjust accusations against him.' He got up and began stamping up and down the room, working himself into an incandescent rage. 'But Thomas had got to the Pope first, and do you know what he did? He complained that I had harassed him!'

'But Henry, the Pope is on your side and always has been,' Eleanor soothed.

'Not any more!' Henry's mouth was twisted in an ugly, anguished grimace. 'He has threatened me with excommunication!' he roared. 'By the eyes of God, that priest will be the death of me! I will tolerate him no longer. Let them do their damned worst! I'm going to bed.'

He was beyond consolation, beside himself with anger and pain. His face red and livid, he tore the cap from his head, threw it on the floor, then unbuckled his belt and tossed it to the far side of the room. Nearly weeping with frustration, he shrugged off his cloak and his fine, long robes, donned in honour of the season, and kicked off his *braies*; then, naked and trembling, he ripped the silken coverlet from his bed, and sat down heavily on it, his hands and face working in distress. Overcome with frustration, he suddenly clawed back the sheet, grabbed a handful of straw from his mattress and, stuffing it in his mouth, as if to stop himself from howling out loud, began chewing it voraciously.

'Henry . . .' Eleanor began, but he flung out an arm to silence her, his out-thrust jaw chomping, his face a mask of agony. Then he got up, walked to the fire and spat out the straw. 'Just go,' he said.

He remained in a foul mood throughout the festivities, his anger at Becket, Louis and the Pope gnawing at him remorselessly. On St Stephen's Day, Eleanor attempted yet again to talk to him, but he silenced her with a glare. No one could reach him; he was too deeply sunk in ire and misery. That evening, deeply concerned for him, she decided to try again. She found him calmer, however. He was sealing a document, which he then handed to one of his clerks.

'This is my revenge!' he declared.

'What is?' she asked, wondering what on earth it could be, and if it would provoke more trouble.

'An order for the banishment of every one of Thomas's relatives from England,' Henry said, with grim satisfaction.

'But they have done nothing wrong! And there are many of them, women, children, old folk.' Eleanor was appalled.

'About four hundred, I think,' Henry said, with some satis-faction. 'They will be stripped of all their possessions and deported. Let them beg for their food!'

'Henry, I beg of you, rescind that order!' she pleaded, falling on her knees. 'It is cruel, it is vindictive, and it is born purely of unbridled passion, which is unbecoming in a king of your wisdom.'

He stared coldly down at her. 'Get up. It's no use, Eleanor. These tactics are necessary. Thomas is in Rome, beyond my reach, but this should bring him hurrying back. Let him see the consequences of his defiance; let him feel the heat of my anger, and know what it is to be my enemy.'

Eleanor rose to her feet, shot him a withering look, and was about to leave when Henry grabbed her hand.

'I have thought of a way to force Pope Alexander and King Louis to abandon Becket,' he said. 'You had better hear about it, as it concerns our daughters.'

'Our daughters?' Eleanor echoed. 'How can they be involved? What new scheme is this?'

'I intend to make an alliance with the German Emperor, Frederick Barbarossa,' Henry revealed smugly. 'That will put the noses of His Holiness and King Louis out of joint, I can tell you, because our friend the Emperor is Louis' enemy, and he has supported Alexander's rival, the antipope Victor. I'll wager that Louis and Alexander will do anything to stop me from allying with Frederick, and that the very prospect of it will make them shit themselves and drop Becket like a hot cake!'

'But where do our daughters fit into this?' Eleanor asked, wondering if this plan was as foolproof as it sounded.

'I have proposed that the alliance be cemented by two marriage treaties,' Henry explained. 'It is my intention that Matilda marry the Emperor's greatest vassal and ally, Henry the Lion, Duke of Saxony, while Eleanor will wed the Emperor's young son, Frederick. I have written requesting the Emperor to send his envoys to Rouen to draw up the agreements. I hope to meet them there in February.'

'Are your plans so far advanced?' Eleanor asked, utterly dismayed at this news and at the prospect of losing two more daughters – cherished daughters this time – and furious that

Henry had said nothing of this business until now, when he must have been planning it for weeks. 'Did you not think to discuss it with me first? They are my children too.'

'I am discussing it with you now,' Henry said. 'You of all people know very well that kings marry their daughters for policy. These are advantageous marriages that will benefit us all.'

'You are using our daughters to be revenged on Becket!' Eleanor cried.

'That would be one advantage of the treaty,' Henry admitted, 'but there would be many others.'

'I do hope so!' she retorted. 'And when are you sending our little girls to Germany? Henry, they are so young! Eleanor is but three.'

'That is to be decided, but it will not be for a while yet,' Henry told her.

'Then I must be grateful for that small mercy,' Eleanor hissed, and hastened from the room before the tears fell.

She stood her ground all through January and into February. She would not go to Normandy to witness the selling of her daughters in a hopeless cause. She was adamant about that. Henry shrugged and did not bother to argue with her.

'You can stay here in England,' he said.

'I shall go to Winchester with the children,' she told him. 'Then perhaps I might travel a little. Shall I act as regent for you?'

'No,' Henry replied crushingly. 'My justiciar can act in my absence.'

She hid her distress and wondered — not for the first time — why he was increasingly reluctant of late to allow her any autonomy in state affairs. At one time, he unhesitatingly would have relied upon her to rule in his absence, but that had been before this distance had opened out between them. It was four years now since she had issued a writ in her own name. It was all Becket's fault, she believed. Becket had been the sole cause of the discord between them.

'When the treaty is signed, I want you to summon the Great Council to Westminster to confirm it,' Henry commanded her.

'I shall then send the Emperor's envoys to pay their respects to you in England, and to meet Matilda and Eleanor. You will receive them with all honour. I know you will not fail me.' His tone was aggressive.

'You can rely on me,' Eleanor said coolly. 'I know how these things are done.'

On the last night before Henry's departure for Normandy, he came to her bed and took his pleasure of her, little caring whether or not he was welcome. She lay beneath him, wishing she could give him more, but her heart was too bitter against him. She did not like the man he had become, the vengeful, petty man who could use his own daughters to score points against his enemies. She grieved to find his heart closed to her, to have him treat her as an adversary and, worse than that, a mere chattel he could use at will. It seemed that no one could oppose Henry these days: he would not brook it. You were either for him or against him.

They said their farewells in public the next morning, Eleanor standing by Henry's great charger with the warming stirrup cup.

'God speed you, my Lord,' she said formally.

'Join me as soon as you can,' he said, bending down in the saddle to kiss her hand. Then he wheeled his horse around and was off, clattering through the gatehouse, his motley retinue and cumbersome baggage train lumbering in his wake.

26 Rouen and Angers, 1165

It was May before Eleanor was reunited with Henry in Rouen, and by then she knew she was pregnant again. He was delighted by the news, but it only saddened her, for this was the first of her children not to have been conceived in love. Yet she supposed the infant would be as precious to her as the others when it arrived.

She was shocked by the change in the Empress. The elder Matilda had aged much in the years since they had last met, and she was now quite frail and stiff in her joints. Eleanor had brought with her Richard and the younger Matilda, and she had to enjoin them quite sternly not to behave so boisterously around their grandmother.

The Empress had mellowed with the years. There was little left of the antipathy she had once shown towards her daughter-in-law. Eleanor found it comforting to sit with the older woman and confide her opinions of the quarrel between Henry and Becket, and she was gratified to have her own position bolstered by the old lady's wise views, robustly expressed.

'That man has written repeatedly to me, claiming that Henry is hell-bent on persecuting the Church,' she revealed. 'Of course, he got no satisfaction from me. I ignored all his letters.'

'It is Henry who worries me,' Eleanor confessed.

'Henry was a fool to advance Becket,' the Empress declared, sipping delicately at her wine cup.

'He is obsessed with him. He will not listen to reason.'

'But Henry is right!' his mother said sharply. 'He has good reason to be angry. Becket is a menace, and he appears deliberately to have provoked Henry from the moment of his consecration.' She leaned forward, her faded blue eyes steely beneath paper-thin lids. 'This issue of the criminous clerks – it is all wrong, and must be stopped. Becket is a fool to take his stand on that.'

'I know, but it seems to me he has taken his stand on so many things that we have all lost sight of what the quarrel was originally about.' Eleanor sighed. 'I have done my best to support Henry, truly I have, but he does not appear to need my support. I too am the enemy these days. I have criticised his need for vengeance too often.'

'You were right to do so,' Matilda pronounced. 'Someone needs to keep my son in check. He is too passionate and headstrong for his own good.' She leaned her bewimpled head back against her chair. 'Alas, I fear this will end badly. It goes on relentlessly.'

'It dominates our lives to an unacceptable extent,' Eleanor told her. 'It has spoiled my marriage. I pray God it is resolved soon.'

'Amen to that,' the Empress murmured. 'But I suspect it will not be.'

*

Eleanor spent a mere fortnight with Henry before he was off on his horse again, bound this time for Wales, to teach a lesson to the Welsh princes who had united to cast off his rule.

His mood had been kinder these past few days. She wondered if his mother had said anything to make him treat her more tenderly. He had come to her bed every night, and they had made love frequently – not as fervently as they once had, but with something of their former passion, and a sense of close-ness. Eleanor dared to hope that, if things went on like this, they would in time recapture some of the joy they had once taken in each other.

She knew for certain that matters were mending between them when Henry told her, two days before he left, that he was entrusting the government of Anjou and Maine to her while he was overseas.

'I want you to go to Angers,' he said. 'Take up residence there; be a visible presence in my dominions.' It was wonderful – and heartening – to have him pay her such a compliment.

She went, her heart singing, to Angers. Once installed in the massive fortress that dominated the town, she sent to Poitiers, requesting that her faithful uncle, Raoul de Faye, come to join her to assist her in her great task. Henry had never had any good opinion of Raoul's abilities, but Eleanor had found him to be a true and loyal deputy these past few years, dedicated to her service and diligent at attempting – not always successfully, she had to admit – to keep her troublesome lords in check. Anyway, Henry was far away, fighting the Welsh. The decision to send for Raoul was hers to make.

Raoul came. Eleanor had never before noticed how elegant and attractive he was; for years, she had had eyes for no other man than Henry, and the two men could not have been more different. At forty-nine, Raoul was just six years her senior, and long wed to Elisabeth, the heiress of Faye-le-Vineuse, who had borne him two children. He had all the charm and humour of her mother's family, the seigneurs of Châtellerault, and Eleanor felt entirely comfortable in his company. He was courtly in his manner, ready to do her service in any capacity, and full of good advice, much of which she was happy to heed. Most important of all, he shared her tastes in music and literature, and in doing so proved himself to be a true son of the south.

The long hours they spent together discussing the affairs of Anjou and Aquitaine – how Eleanor delighted in hearing news of her own land! – lent an intimacy to their relationship. She found herself eagerly anticipating their meetings, and captivated by Raoul's wicked smile and sharp wit. He was capable of saying the most outrageous things – court gossip was his speciality, particularly the amorous exploits of the Queen's ladies – and she enjoyed his earthy turns of phrase. She found herself laughing a lot of the time she was in his company – something she had not done very much with Henry in recent years. It was all exceedingly pleasant.

She was aware, of course, of something flowering between them. She knew instinctively that Raoul wanted more from her than an uncle should expect of a niece, but she could hardly blame him for that. Her scandalous affair with another uncle, Raymond of Antioch, was universally notorious, and gossip about it had been circulating for years. Raoul would surely have heard it, and perhaps concluded that Eleanor would not be averse to a similar dalliance with him. The idea amused her, although she did not consider it seriously. She was content to enjoy flirting with him, indulging in the old familiar game of courtly love – so much a part of their common culture – and keeping him tantalisingly at arm's length. There was no harm in that, was there?

There were, of course, more serious moments, such as the times when they discussed the problem of Becket.

'I have never met him, but I know I would detest him,' Raoul declared loyally. 'He is a dangerous man, and the King your husband is well rid of him.'

'But he is *not* rid of him, that's just the point!' Eleanor exclaimed. 'However far away he may be, Becket is a constant presence in our lives, stirring up trouble.'

'If I were the King, I would find a way to silence him,' declared Raoul.

'And think what a furore that would cause!' Eleanor rejoined.

'It could be managed . . . discreetly,' he suggested. She wondered if this was a game, if he was really in earnest.

'And tongues would wag. No, my dear uncle, it wouldn't work. And Henry would never agree to it. He has many vices, but murder is not one of them.'

'Forgive me, I spoke only in his interests,' Raoul hastened to assure her. 'I would rid him of that bastard archbishop if I could.' The hostility in his voice was palpable.

'Why do *you* hate Becket so?' Eleanor asked curiously.

'Because he has been the cause of your pain,' Raoul answered, his hand closing on hers.

They were alone, in her solar, seated at the table with a bank of scrolls and tally sticks before them and the sun streaming in through the windows. Eleanor silently withdrew her hand.

'You are still very beautiful,' Raoul said softly. 'You have a fine bone structure that will never age. You are incredible.'

'Flatterer!' she smiled.

'It is the truth. I know beauty when I see it.'

She laughed. 'You expect me to believe that – me, an old married woman, pregnant with her tenth child? Look at me, Raoul!'

He did, intently, his deep-set, dark eyes full of yearning, and suddenly they were no longer laughing.

'It is now, especially, that you should be cherished,' he said. 'Does the King your husband cherish you as he should, sweet niece?'

'Henry cannot help the fact that the Welsh are in rebellion,' she answered lightly.

'But if he *were* here, would he be cherishing you as you deserve?' her uncle persisted.

'Of course,' Eleanor answered, although her voice betrayed a certain lack of conviction. The recent renewal of the bonds she shared with Henry was too fragile, too precious to be taken for granted. He had never been one to cosset her when she was carrying his children, but then she herself had not encouraged it, preferring to carry on much as normal. Raoul, on the other hand, was a troubadour at heart, a ladies' man in every sense, courtly and extravagantly devoted. He would not understand how she and Henry functioned together. He didn't like Henry anyway, never had – and now he had an ulterior motive for finding fault with him.

He was frowning, still looking at her intently.

'You know he is unfaithful to you,' he said. His words hit her like a slap in the face. She reeled inwardly from the blow. Coming out of the blue, it forced her to confront a truth she had long feared to face. She had *wondered* countless times if, when they were apart, Henry took his pleasure where he would, but she had had no proof. And there had been those rumours she had heard . . . She had made herself dismiss them as mere gossip. Yet now, it all made sense; and there was no surprise in her. Of course Henry had been unfaithful. How could she ever have doubted it?

'Explain exactly what you mean by that!' she demanded, rising and going over to the window, keeping her back to Raoul so that he should not see how profoundly he had shocked her. If what he said were true, she would not want to look a fool – the poor, ignorant wife, the last to find out. Already, she feared, she had betrayed herself by her violent response.

Raoul swallowed. He had not expected her to react so explosively. He had thought only to cozen from her an admission of what she already knew, so that they could forget Henry and proceed to amorous matters. Clearly he had miscalculated. Still, he had said the words now and, hurt her though he knew he must, he had no choice but to qualify them.

'When he was in Poitiers, there were women,' he said, swallowing again. 'He made no secret of it. They were whores, brought up from the town. Everyone was drunk. It was the same each night.'

Eleanor took a deep breath. It was not as bad as she had feared. She was surprised to find that she was not as hurt by these casual betrayals as she would have expected. What she had feared most, could not have tolerated, emotionally, and as a wife and queen, was her husband becoming involved with one particular woman. It was almost a relief to hear that Henry had resorted to whores.

'Well, he is a man!' she said, as lightly as she could, and turned to face Raoul with a brittle smile. 'Women learn to shut their eyes to such things. They mean nothing.'

Raoul guessed she was putting on a brave face, and resolved not to repeat what Henry had said in his cups about a beautiful mistress called Rohese . . .

He stood up and put his arms around her. He knew it was unfair to take advantage of her when she was so vulnerable, yet he could not help himself. She was still lovely, even in her maturity, and he wanted her. But although there was a brief moment when he thought she would yield, she gaily disentangled herself.

'Raoul, my life is complicated enough, not so much by other women, as by another man!' she told him. 'And no, there's no need to look so shocked. It is nothing like that, at least on Henry's part.'

'You mean Becket . . . ?' Raoul was staggered.

'I would swear to it. I could understand if it *was* that; it's Henry being in thrall to him that is beyond me. He's never explained it satisfactorily, and I don't suppose he knows himself why Becket has this hold over him.'

'Becket is older,' Raoul ventured. 'Mayhap Henry reveres him as a father figure, or elder brother. Maybe there is something in Becket that Henry would like to be.'

'Or maybe he gave Henry the kind of companionship that I could not,' Eleanor added bitterly.

'I don't think it has anything to do with you,' Raoul comforted her.

'Oh, yes, it does! As soon as Becket came to prominence, I was second in importance to Henry. Before that, everything had been wonderful between us. We were a formidable partnership. That all finished with Becket. There are moments when it's there again, just within my grasp, but not for long. Always that man intrudes. And another thing. My Lord Bishop of Poitiers is here. I expect that this matter he wishes to discuss with me concerns him too. Raoul, I am going to give him an audience in a few minutes. I want you to be there when he comes.'

'You know I will,' Raoul said, gently touching her cheek.

'Raoul!' she reproved. 'You know there can be nothing between us.'

'Ah, but I may live in hope, like a true troubadour,' he smiled sadly.

Eleanor received Jean aux Bellesmains, Bishop of Poitiers, in her solar. She was seated in her high-backed chair, her yellow samite skirts fanned out at her feet, a gold coronet on her snowy veil. Behind her stood Raoul, his hand grasping the finial on her chair-back.

The Bishop bustled in self-importantly. Eleanor remembered that he had been with Becket in Archbishop Theobald's household, that they had become friends, and that, even though he owed his bishopric to Henry, Jean aux Bellesmains had stayed staunchly loyal to Becket. She sensed that this interview wasn't going to be easy, but sat there smiling pleasantly, asking how she could be of service.

'Madame the Duchess, I come on behalf of his Grace the Archbishop of Canterbury,' the Bishop said grandly, almost as if he were throwing down a gauntlet. 'He sends his duty and affection to you, his dear daughter in Christ, and begs you most earnestly to intervene on his behalf in this quarrel with the King your husband.'

As Eleanor caught Raoul's sharp intake of breath, she quickly collected her wits. She had not expected Becket to approach her, of all people.

'I am flattered that his Grace believes I could help him,' she answered, 'but he cannot but be cognisant of the fact that, since he and my husband became such *good friends*, my influence has declined.'

Before she could say anything further, Raoul interrupted. 'The Archbishop, of all people, should know that a wife's first duty is to her husband, and that to him she owes obedience. How, then, could she intervene on behalf of the man who has deliberately defied him and made himself his enemy?'

Eleanor's face briefly registered amused surprise. Not an hour before, Raoul had been doing his best to make her forget her duty to her husband!

The Bishop flushed with anger. 'Surely one's first duty is to God, my Lord of Faye?'

'Let's leave God out of this,' Raoul retorted. 'This is about one man's vanity.'

'It is about far more than that, and you know it!' Jean aux Bellesmains turned to Eleanor. 'Madame, I did not come here hoping for much. But if you would consent only to act as a messenger—'

'No! How can you ask that of her?' Raoul interrupted.

The Bishop glared at him. 'Can you not let Madame the Duchess answer for herself, my Lord?'

'Yes, Raoul, please allow me to speak,' Eleanor insisted. 'My Lord Bishop, it is my greatest desire to see my husband at peace with all his subjects. But, as my Lord here has said, it would not be appropriate for me to become involved in this quarrel. All I can do is pray every day for its happy resolution.'

The Bishop shot her a withering look.

'In truth, I am not surprised, Madame. I myself told his Grace that he could hope for neither aid nor counsel from you, and John of Salisbury said the same. He shares Becket's exile, you know, and his many privations. But I see you have put all your faith in my Lord here, and that he is hostile to his Grace.'

'How dare you speak to me like that!' Eleanor flared. 'You are impertinent, my Lord Bishop. You would not address me thus if the Duke were here, or so insult his deputy.'

Jean aux Bellesmains bristled with outrage, which loosened his tongue.

'Maybe you have not heard what people are saying, Madame, and maybe I would be doing you both a kindness by informing you. There are conjectures that grow day by day in regard to the influence that my Lord of Faye here appears to wield over you. Some say they deserve credence. I say, have a care to your reputation.'

Eleanor stood up, quivering with rage. 'I have never in my life been so insulted!' she hissed. 'You will quit my presence right now, my Lord Bishop, and never come back until you have abased yourself and craved my pardon for the baseless accusations you have made. Rest assured, my Lord shall hear of them. He will not be pleased. In fact, if I were you, I would make sure I was not in Poitiers when he returns there.'

The Bishop stared at her aghast.

'Madame, in my disappointment, I forgot myself,' he babbled. 'I apologise unreservedly! I make a thousand apologies! I lay myself at your feet . . .'

'That will not be necessary,' Eleanor said coldly; privately, she would have loved to see this pompous fool grovelling on his knees. 'I accept your apologies – and I will hear no more of these calumnies, you understand?'

When he had backed out of the room, assuring her of his love, loyalty and discretion, Eleanor turned to Raoul.

'You heard what he said, my uncle.' Her face was serious. 'I pray you, keep a wise distance. And please don't speak for me in future!'

'Eleanor, I would die to serve you!' Raoul protested.

'You might well, if Henry gets word of this!' she told him, with a grim smile.

27 Bredelais Castle, the Welsh Border, 1165

Henry slowed his horse to a trot. He had far outgalloped his companions, who were some way behind with the huntsmen, carrying with them the game they had caught that day. Ahead, in the distance, loomed the castle of Bredelais, the home of their host, Sir Walter de Clifford, whose services in the so-far-unsuccessful campaign against the Welsh rebels had nevertheless been admirable. But the tide seemed to be turning, thank God, and, flushed with success, both in the field of battle and in the chase, Henry was in a holiday mood, looking forward to a merry supper with his genial host and his lordly companions.

Behind him, he could hear faint shouts and guffaws. Close by, a cuckoo called. It was the early evening of a glorious summer day, with the sun sinking to the west in a blaze of gold and roseate hues. God, but it was warm. He had long since stripped off his tunic and stuffed it in his saddle-bag, and wore only his shirt and hose. He trotted along whistling, feeling as if he had not a care in the world. He even thought he might ask for a bath to be prepared on his return. That should set them scuttling!

He steered his mount through some woodland, keeping the castle always in his view through the trees, and emerged on to a grassy meadow, a vast green expanse that swept up to the moat. There was a girl there, kneeling in the long grass, her tight-laced dress a vivid blue against the emerald sward. She had her back to him, so he could not see her face. Long fair tresses rippled unbound and uncovered over her shoulders, proclaiming her a maiden as yet untouched, and her fine raiment bore testament to her gentle birth. She was gathering flowers, and made, in all, a pretty, fetching sight.

His eye roving on the slender lines of her body and hips, Henry felt the familiar upsurge of lust. He had not been so aroused by a woman in a long time. Rohese he had abandoned months before, tired to satiety of her all-too-familiar charms. Eleanor was in Angers, pestering him with demands for aid against some rebellious vassals, and no doubt bitching about Becket to anyone who would listen. Try as he might, he could not recapture the happiness he had once shared with her. There had been a fleeting resurgence of it, back in the spring, but it had as briefly waned, at least on his part. He could not forgive Eleanor her hostility to Thomas, her searching questions, her neediness. He loved her still, and knew he always would, but not in the way she wanted. It grieved him, but there it was. Something that had died could not be brought to life again.

He was thirty-two, a man in his prime, even if he was putting on a bit of weight, and naturally there had been women, plenty of them, conquered, used, then as quickly forgotten. But now that he had seen this exquisite young girl, it came to him in a blinding instant that something precious had long been absent from his life, and that he needed far more than a quick roll in the hay with any easy trollop.

But this was no hoyden to be pursued for his gratification: this, he guessed, must be one of the daughters of his host, who had a large brood that included five strapping sons. He wondered why he hadn't seen her the night before, when Lady de Clifford had presented her family to her king.

The girl had heard his horse approaching. She turned around suddenly, and the flowers spilt from her lap, scattering in a riot of delicate colours over her gown and the grass. She was utterly enchanting. Her skin was like cream, her lips full and round like dark cherries, her cheeks flushed with surprise, her eyes the blue of cornflowers. As she rose, her gown settled becomingly; the jewelled girdle wound around her waist and hips revealed a slim figure, the low, scooped neckline and tight bodice accentuated small, high breasts. Henry felt his erection harden. He must have her, God, he must have her!

Of course, she would have no idea who he was. She had not met him the night before. As he slowed his horse to a standstill, she was already backing away, the flowers forgotten.

'Fair maiden, have no fear!' he called gently. 'I am your king, and your father's guest. I wish you no harm.' I wish you in my bed. That was what he really wanted to say to her.

The girl looked flustered. Her creamy cheeks blushed strawberry red, and she sank into a curtsey. 'Sire, I beg your pardon!' Her voice was low and melodious, with a delightful Welsh accent. Henry heard it, and was utterly lost.

'Up!' he instructed, with a winning smile, dismounting beside her. 'No need to stand on ceremony, fair maiden. What is your name?'

'I am Rosamund,' she told him. 'Rosamund de Clifford.'

'Rosamund,' he repeated. '*Rosa mundi*. The rose of the world. A beautiful name, in English or Latin.'

She said nothing, but just kept on blushing. Henry held out his arm to her and, leading his horse by the reins, proceeded to walk with her towards the castle drawbridge, where the sentries could be seen dozing at their posts in the heat. The touch of her small hand on his skin was heaven.

'Tell me, Rosamund, why were you not here to greet me last night?' Henry probed.

'Lord King, I returned only this day from the good nuns of Godstow, with whom I have lived these past three years.'

Henry was intrigued. 'Am I to understand that your parents intended to make a nun of you?'

'No, Lord King, they wished me to receive a virtuous education that would serve me well when God sees fit to send me a husband.'

'Very wise, very wise. You are far too pretty to spend your life in a cloister!'

Rosamund blushed becomingly again.

'How old are you, my little nun?' Henry teased.

'I am fourteen, Lord King.'

'And have you come home to be married?'

'I know not, Sire.'

Henry was captivated – and dismayed. He had lusted before after virgins from good families, and it had always ended badly, with irate fathers summarily shoving their daughters into convents or hastily marrying them off. Most of the females Henry had bedded over the years were either married women, or whores – or his wife. He knew very well that Rosamund was virtually beyond his reach – unless he proved himself the monster he always claimed jokingly not to be. He knew very well that no decent man worthy of his knighthood – or his kingship – would so dishonour a maiden of noble birth, for that would irrevocably ruin her chances in the marriage market and sully her reputation for ever. Men who were not as decent might not scruple to do so, but Henry now had daughters of his own, and would have cheerfully run through any bastard who ventured to compromise their honour. He told himself he could not do such a thing to sweet Rosamund, or to her father, his loyal and likeable host.

But just then he glimpsed Rosamund peeping coyly at him from under her lashes. Her artless look betrayed her. She found him attractive, he would swear to it! She might well be amenable . . . In which case, he would not, could not, feel so guilty about robbing her of her maidenhead. He realised – for he was, as he liked to boast, a plain man, always brutally honest with himself – that, dismally soon, all his chivalrous scruples were falling by the wayside. It could only be Rosamund's fault: with that shy glance, she had disarmed him. By the eyes of God, he wanted her!

Of course, he had to relinquish her arm when he brought her to her father's castle, and let her lady mother – gushingly grateful to her king for escorting the girl home safely – cart Rosamund off to her chamber so that she could wash and change her clothes for the feast that was planned for the evening. It pained him to let her go, but he murmured a few gracious words, then retired to submit to the attentions of his valet.

Later, seated at the place of honour at the high table, he selected a chicken leg from a proffered platter, gnawed upon it absent-mindedly, then turned to Sir Walter.

'I met your daughter Rosamund today,' he said, striving to

make himself heard above the chatter and laughter. 'I thought her a most virtuous young lady.'

Sir Walter looked along the board, beyond his great, strapping sons, to where Rosamund sat with her sisters. Henry's eyes followed; they had been straying in that direction all evening. The girl's eyes were modestly downcast as she ate her food daintily, but her golden tresses fanned over her shoulders and breast like a burnished cape, and her lips were ripe for kissing. She looked a picture of beauty, and Henry found himself aching with desire – yet again.

'Aye, Sire,' Sir Walter said complacently. 'She's a good girl. The nuns have done well with her. I'll have to find her a husband soon.'

'She is not yet spoken for?' Not that it made much difference. She soon would be. Any man worthy of the name would snap her up in a trice.

'No, Sire. I have many children to settle in matrimony.'

'I know all about that!' Henry smiled. 'I have many of my own.' But the recall of them did not act as a deterrent, and he paused for a moment, plotting frantically. 'How would it be if Rosamund came to court to wait upon the Queen? She would be well looked after, and I myself would take an interest in finding a suitable match for her.' Never a truer word had been spoken, he mused.

'Lord King, I would be honoured!' effused a surprised Sir Walter. 'And my daughter too, depend on it.'

'Queen Eleanor is in Anjou just now,' Henry said, 'but some of her English ladies are at Woodstock, awaiting her return. I myself am bound for there when my Welsh rebels have been taught some respect.' It was a lie, but Sir Walter was not to know that. 'I and my men would happily escort your daughter to Woodstock, or you could arrange for her to travel in the company of your own men-at-arms later on.'

As Henry had anticipated, the proud, ambitious father jumped at his offer, and so it was decided that Rosamund should go to Woodstock.

It had been that easy.

That night, Henry lay awake, aware that what he was about to do was a great sin and an even greater wrong. Yet he was unable to help himself: he could not resist the allure of Rosamund. He *had* to have her – he was mad to have her. His penis throbbed insistently at the very thought of her. He could think of nothing else.

A little voice at the back of his mind warned him there would be a reckoning. He did not doubt it, but he did not care. The devil in him, that diabolical legacy of his heritage, was driving him on, urging him to take what he wanted. He would defy the world, if need be, to have this girl. It was as bad as that.

When the time came to leave for Woodstock, early in September, there were no tearful goodbyes, unlike three years before, when Rosamund had first gone to Godstow; she had now grown used to being apart from her family. Like a lamb borne to the proverbial slaughter, she went meekly with Henry, her manner trusting and respectful. If she suspected that there was more to this than her going to serve the Queen, she gave no sign.

28 Woodstock Palace, 1165

Rosamund looked around the sunny, whitewashed stone bower with delight. It occupied the top floor of a turret, and at the bottom of the spiral stair a low wooden door opened onto a pretty pleasaunce, or garden, made colourful with violets, columbines and roses around a lush greensward, shaded with hornbeam, hazel and ash trees. She had beheld that with wonder, and when she saw the chamber that had been prepared for her, her cornflower-blue eyes widened even further. This was a bower fit for a queen. In fact, although she was not to know it, it was the Queen's. The bed had silken drapes, bleached cotton sheets and a bright chequered coverlet. There was a window-seat cut into the thickness of the wall, a chest supporting great golden candlesticks of an intricate design, a fine oak chair and two stools on the tiled floor, and carved pegs on the wall for her gowns.

Henry watched with pleasure from the doorway as his desired one exclaimed at her good fortune.

'Lord King, do all the Queen's ladies live in such luxury?' she asked. Her manner towards him was always deferential. His gaze lingered on her.

'No,' he said at length. 'This is especially for you, because you are beautiful.'

'But what will the other ladies say?' She looked frightened.

'Nothing, my sweet. There are no other ladies!' He grinned at her.

'I don't understand.' She looked at him in puzzlement.

Henry hesitated. One false move now, and all might be lost. Was it best to be honest with her? Or to keep up the charade a little longer, and give her feelings for him more time to grow and flourish.

He did not think he could wait that long. Already, people were looking askance at them both and whispering. On the way here, his retinue had apparently assumed that he was escorting her back to Godstow – or so he had gathered from remarks he had overheard. There had been genuine astonishment, followed by dark and disapproving looks, when he brought her to Woodstock. But he was beyond caring. He was the King, and his actions were not to be questioned.

His conscience told him that he could give up the idea now and send the girl back, unsullied in body and reputation, to her father. It was not too late to do the honourable thing. But that devil, the devil that ruled his sexual impulses, was rampant in him, and not to be gainsaid. He crossed the floor and put his arms around Rosamund.

'I want you to stay here with me,' he said hoarsely, as he felt her body stiffen. His own was stiffening too, not out of alarm, but from lust. He felt he was in paradise, holding her so close. He had not wanted a woman so much since he had first set eyes on Eleanor. He thrust the thought of Eleanor away, quickly.

'Lord King, I beg of you . . .' Rosamund whispered, her breath coming in little gasps. 'It would be wrong!'

'Is loving someone so very wrong?' Henry asked. 'I think I have loved you since the moment I saw you. Your father gave me permission to bring you here – and here we are.' And may God forgive me the deception, he thought. The devil in him stirred again.

'My father? I thought I was to serve the Queen, Sire?' Her eyes were wide with incomprehension.

'And so you are, in due course. But your father knows that royal favour and preferment can be won in many different ways,' Henry said. 'He has entrusted you to my care, and I have undertaken to find you a husband.' Perish the thought! 'But for now, all I want is to serve you, and make you mine. Will you be mine, Rosamund?'

He saw, to his consternation, that she was weeping.

'Do not cry, sweeting,' he murmured, stroking her hair. 'All will be well, you have my word on it. I will cherish and protect you, never fear.'

He tipped her chin upwards with his finger and looked down into her wet blue eyes. God, how lovely she was!

'Could you love me a little?' he asked her. 'I think you do!'

She stared at him, as if she were drinking him in. 'I do not know,' she whispered. 'I cannot. It would be wrong. I find it hard to believe that my father meant for me to become your leman, Lord King. I cannot bring dishonour on my house. It would be a sin, and we would both burn in Hell for it.'

'Fairy tales for children!' Henry scoffed. 'But even if there were a hell, I would gladly burn in it for all eternity for just one night with you.'

'There *is* a hell!' she assured him, with some spirit.

'What a little nun they have made of you,' he teased, pressing her closer to him. 'Listen, Rosamund, the only hell is the one we make for ourselves on this earth. The rest is just a myth put about by the Church to frighten us into being good.'

She recoiled from him, and he let her go.

'I fear that is blasphemy, Lord King,' she whispered.

'It's one of my many vices,' he replied cheerfully.

'I must not gainsay you, Sire, but I think you are in error.' She looked like a terrified rabbit. Henry roared with laughter.

'There speaks the abbess in the making!' he chuckled. 'Well, virtuous maiden, I will leave you to your chaste bed. We will talk some more tomorrow.' In truth, his desire had subsided with his laughter, but he knew when to leave well alone. He raised her hand and kissed it in courtly fashion, then gazed up into her incredible eyes.

'Until then, fair Rosamund,' he said, and was gone.

*

Rosamund had not known until now what it was to want a man. In fact, having been living in a convent since she was eleven, she was more or less ignorant of what passed within the marriage bed; she only knew that it was rather naughty, and that you had to let your husband do this naughty thing without complaining or resisting. This she had learned from the whispered confidences of the other girls of gentle birth entrusted to Godstow's care.

She had grown up knowing that a suitable husband would one day be found for her, and had always imagined – if she thought about it at all – that he would be around the same age as herself, which was nonsense, really, because plenty of her kind ended up with older – or even ageing – spouses.

But here was the King, old enough to be her father, a loud, rough, brisk and in some ways alarming man, and something inside her was responding strangely and powerfully to him. He was not handsome like the knights in tales of chivalry, but stocky and thick-set, with a tousled head of red hair, a rough man, but attractive in that foreign, Gallic way, with an overpowering physical presence. Like Eleanor, fourteen years before, Rosamund had looked once, and fallen headily for him.

If this wanting feeling, this uncontrollable tension between her thighs, this sudden sweet awareness of her body, was desire, then all of a sudden, she could understand why people did mad things for love: why knights fought dragons, or maidens languished in towers . . . or convent-educated girls compromised their virtue, as, yes, even she was tempted to do.

She had said all the right things, all the things that a virtuous girl should say to an over-bold, predatory male. She had put up a convincing display of maidenly modesty. Yet underneath it all, there had been the urgent and enchanting dictates of her body, compelling her to surrender, and the excited response of a young mind flattered that a king should say he loved her. It was an irresistible combination. She did not delude herself that she loved the King in return; immature though she was, she suspected that he might well have used the word 'love' merely to cozen her. She had no idea what love really felt like. Certainly it did not appear to exist between most of the married couples she had seen. She had been taught that it was a wife's duty to love the husband chosen for her, but that was not the kind of love that drove men to distraction, or sent them on quests, or made them fight duels.

Her mind was in a ferment. What if this were the only opportunity she would ever have of knowing that kind of love? Should she not seize it with both hands, and follow the demands of the flesh?

She fell asleep wondering what it would be like to lie in the arms of the King of England.

29 Angers, 1165

Eleanor was lying in after her confinement, cradling her newborn daughter, Joanna, in her arms, when a letter arrived from Champagne. She opened it with trembling fingers, supporting the baby against her shoulder, and read the neat, pointed script of some unknown clerk. Her daughter Marie politely sent her greetings, and enquired after her mother's health. She herself was well and happy, and wished Madame the Queen to know that she remembered her in her prayers.

That was all, but it was something, and it was more than she had received from Alix, who could not have remembered her in any case. It was but little, but it was something – something she could build on.

30 Woodstock, 1165–6

The siege did not last long. When the last defence had been torn down, Henry came to Rosamund in her silken bower, and she received him with open arms. She was tight when he entered her, and gasped a little as her maidenhead fractured, but thereafter she twined herself sinuously around him as if she would never let go. Afterwards, he lay there with his head on her breasts, stroking her firm, flat belly and thinking that it was a long time since he had experienced such joy with a woman. Pleasure, yes – but not this surging tide of delight and well-being. Once, he had known a similar joy with Eleanor, and something of that survived still, when they were together; but when he was apart from her, he felt detached and even hostile.

He would not think of Eleanor now, not when his fair Rosamund lay beneath him, his for the taking again as soon as he had caught his breath and rested a bit. Rosamund, whose blonde tresses lay tangled across them both, tickling his cheek, and whose straight limbs with their pearly sheen lay stretched out with abandon. His fingers crept to the cleft of her sex, parted it, and slid further, as her eyes widened in surprise and she began to moan with unexpected pleasure. God, she was beautiful, he thought, raising himself on one muscular elbow and raking her with his gaze as his kneading became more insistent – beautiful in a different way from Eleanor, for there was a fragility about Rosamund, and an innate delicacy. She was aptly named, with her petal-soft skin and her rosy cheeks! He knew he could never bear to be parted from her.

Henry could not leave Rosamund alone. He kept wanting her, at all hours of the day and night, and exulted in the breathless fervour with which she returned his ardour. Yet, so young and inexperienced was his love, for all her growing artfulness in bed, that every time they made love it seemed like the first time – as if he were deflowering her all over again. It was utterly irresistible!

He tarried at Woodstock all through the autumn, kept Christmas there, then made excuses to stay until the spring. He called in masons and master builders to construct a new tower for his lady, and gardeners to lay out a labyrinth for her delight, planting the young hedges of yew and briar in an intricate circular pattern. He knew that the time would come when he must leave Rosamund, and that she would be lonely and in need of recreation, and with the summer coming, this maze would divert her and the damsels he had appointed to wait on her. It never occurred to him that, one day, it would become the source of many rumours and legends.

When he wasn't dallying in bed with Rosamund, Henry was hard at work formulating his planned legal reforms, and in the depths of winter, he went to meet with his Great Council at Clarendon, where his new Constitutions, as he was pleased to call them, became law. One in particular gave him great satisfaction, for it meant that Becket's criminous clerks would no longer be entitled to claim benefit of clergy. Henry had won his long, hard battle – but he doubted he had won the war.

The wounds dealt by Thomas still festered. Lying awake at night, he would torment himself by reliving the heady days of their friendship, or engage in bitter disputes with the absent Archbishop, saying all the clever things he wished he had said at the time. Occasionally, with Rosamund sleeping peacefully beside him, he would let the tears fall, and wonder when he would ever be free of this turmoil. He had *loved* Thomas – so why had Thomas defied and abandoned him? At such times, he would reach out for the sweet girl lying beside him and try to lose himself in her, to blot out the pain and the anger. He never discussed Becket with her; he did not want to sully her purity by unburdening himself. She was his refuge, his peace, his joy: that was all he needed from her.

He could no longer tarry: he was needed in Maine, to quell some godforsaken rebel vassals; his ships were even now waiting at Southampton.

He kissed Rosamund long and lovingly in farewell, his heart aching. God knew when he would see her again. She stood on the mounting block, slender and utterly alluring in her soft wool gown, and lifted the stirrup cup to him as he sat on his horse at the head of his retinue, ready to depart. He made himself say his last goodbye, his voice gruff with emotion. Parting with her was unbearable, tragic, not to be borne . . .

He rode south determinedly, making good time, but they had not gone far when, driven by his unspeakable need, he suddenly wheeled about and cantered back towards Woodstock, his astonished train in his wake, struggling to keep up. When they arrived, he leaped off his lathered steed, raced up the spiral stairs two at a time, and burst into Rosamund's chamber, scattering her women with a wave of his hand. As soon as the door had banged behind them, he crushed her to him, devouring her with kisses.

'I had to come back to you, to see you one more time!' he gasped.

Rosamund was momentarily too stunned to respond.

'What will people think? That I keep you from your royal duties?' she asked, sounding panicked, but letting him do with her as he would.

'I care not a fig for what they think!' Henry growled. 'All I know is that I have to have you once more before I cross the sea. I had to see your face, oh my darling!' His hands were everywhere, his eyes were drinking her in. He was desperate to bed her, could wait no longer. As they tumbled between the sheets, the outside world forgotten, downstairs in the hall and the courtyard the King's household officers and men-at-arms exchanged knowing glances, then shrugged, and grinned at each other.

31 Angers, 1166

Eleanor saw Henry and his long line of followers approaching as she was taking the air on the battlements of the castle of Angers. She paused and stared. So he had come at last. Finally, he had bestirred himself and remembered that he had a wife. There was bitterness in her heart. She had not set eyes on him in more than a year; he had not come to greet his new daughter, Joanna, and he had not even come for Christmas. That had been a cruel blow, for never before had they spent a Christmas apart, and she had still been under the impression that things had been mending between them. He could at least have thought of the children's disappointment, if not hers, she thought, aggrieved.

She had wondered if Henry had heard wanton talk of her closeness to her Uncle Raoul, or if Jean aux Bellesmains had blabbed of his damned suspicions. Or, worse still, had Raoul kept something back when he had spoken of Henry having other women? That would hardly be surprising, given her reaction. But supposing there was another woman? If a love affair was the cause of Henry abandoning his wife and family for so long, then it surely posed a serious threat to all that Eleanor held dear. The prospect was nightmarish, and she had worn herself down with wondering and playing out horrible possibilities in her mind. She wished she could let it all go and not care, but that was proving impossible.

For the thousandth time, she pulled herself up. Henry was a king, and, in the wider scale of things, women meant little to him beside his vision for his kingdom and the demands of his far-flung domains. Had that not been the case, his amours would have been notorious rather than discreet, and she would surely have known about them. He was not the kind of man to let a female sway or rule him. Even she herself, his queen, had been kept firmly in what he perceived to be her place, albeit much to her chagrin. No, Henry would not shirk his duties and obligations for so long just for the sake of a woman. And if he had heard evil gossip about his wife, he would no doubt have acted upon it, much as he had done all those years ago when he banished that poor fool, Bernard de Ventadour; he would never tolerate any hint of scandal attaching itself to his own.

Having reasoned yet again with herself, she realised that she was no nearer to understanding what was going on than she had been before, and, with her thoughts in turmoil, she smoothed her skirts, adjusted her veil and circlet, and descended the stairs to greet her husband.

They faced each other across the polished wooden table in the solar. Henry's eyes were wary. He looked almost sheepish, guilty even. Her heart plummeted, and again she wondered why he had come.

'I trust you had a good journey,' she said, for the second time, betraying how nervous she was. 'Some wine?'

Henry sat down, kicked off his boots, and gratefully accepted the goblet.

'I trust you are well, Eleanor,' he said. 'I'm sorry I couldn't get here earlier. I was at Clarendon, making sure that my new laws will be properly enforced.'

That had been back in January. It was now Easter. What had he been doing in the meantime? His ships had been waiting at Southampton for weeks.

'I regret you had all that trouble with my barons in Maine,' Henry was saying.

'I have never been treated with such contempt!' Eleanor

fumed, anger flaring at the remembrance, and momentarily distracting her from her fears. 'Your Norman captains refused to heed my orders. They said they would not take them from a woman.'

'I know, I know,' Henry admitted. 'They had no right to say that, and they will be called to account, you may depend on it. But the rebels are crushed. On my way here, I taught them a lesson they will not easily forget.'

'I am relieved to hear it,' Eleanor said tartly. She was aware that this conversation was being carried on purely on the surface, and that each was taking the measure of the other and wondering where they really stood. The air was almost crackling with the things they were leaving unsaid.

'Would you like to see our new daughter?' she asked.

'By all means,' Henry smiled, 'and our other children.' He would not meet her eyes.

'You will find them much grown,' she told him. 'It is so long since you have seen them.' It was a barb, and it hit home. She actually saw him wince.

The baby was brought by the nurse, and placed in the King's arms. Henry gazed down at the copper-haired infant on his lap, with her chubby cheeks and gummy smile, and thought how like Eleanor she was. He chuckled at her, well satisfied, and gave her his blessing, his calloused hand on her downy head.

'She's a pretty one,' he pronounced. 'Fit to be a queen, which one day, no doubt, she will be. I hear that Louis at last has a son. Are you thinking what I am thinking?'

'Am I to understand that you have abandoned your plan to marry Matilda and Eleanor in Germany?' Eleanor asked in astonishment. 'I thought you were trying to discountenance Louis to pay him back for his support of Becket?'

'I never pass up an opportunity to discountenance Louis, you know that, Eleanor!' Henry grinned, lightening the atmosphere a little. 'But I did have hopes of one day annexing France to my domains. All dashed now, of course – if that boy lives. So we rattle Louis now, while planning for the future. His son will need a wife some day, and it would be to my advantage, and that of my heirs, to have an English queen on the French throne.'

'It is a wise plan,' Eleanor had to concede.

'I think so,' he nodded. 'And as I haven't changed my mind about the alliances I have negotiated for Matilda and Eleanor, I will be putting this little one forward as the future Queen of France. It will be a great destiny for you, sweeting,' he murmured, smiling down at the baby.

'Well, I can only hope that the French court has livened up a bit by the time she gets there,' Eleanor said, her tone still tart.

'She will liven it up, I make no doubt. She has her mother's charm, I can see it.' He was placating her, she knew it.

'Charm availed me little at Louis' court,' she sniffed, unwilling to bend. 'But it would be a great match, and it could bring a more stable peace between England and France.'

'No doubt the princes of Europe are all rubbing their hands in glee in the hope of securing such a rich matrimonial prize for their daughters as the new heir to France,' Henry observed wickedly. 'But I think we have a strong advantage. I can always dangle the Vexin as a carrot!'

'They said Louis was overjoyed to have a son at last,' Eleanor recalled, remembering how, strangely, she had felt so pleased for her former husband when she'd been brought the news. He had waited an unconscionably long time – and she herself had failed him in the one thing that mattered. Now his prayers had been granted, and she was glad. 'There were great rejoicings, I heard. Much will be expected of this little prince. Already, they are calling him Philip Augustus, like the old Roman emperors.'

'I heard he was named after the month he was born, and that he'd been nicknamed "the God-Given",' Henry said. 'Well, I hope, for his sake, he doesn't take after his father with names like that! He'll have to live up to them!'

He handed the baby back to the nurse, picked up his goblet, drained it to the dregs, and reached for the flagon.

'Well, I will have one more cup of wine, and then I will change my clothes and slough off the dust of the road, and go greet my beloved barons of Anjou.' He poured the red liquid. Eleanor watched, wondering if they would ever again be close enough to get beyond the pleasantries and generalities.

'Is there any news of our friend the Archbishop?' Henry asked, his flippant tone not quite masking his obsessive interest.

'Yes, but it's not good,' Eleanor told him. 'He is still living in the abbey at Sens, and still threatening to excommunicate you. It is said that he is angered by the Constitutions of Clarendon.'

'He should get over it and accept that change is necessary,' Henry scowled. 'My patience is wearing thin.'

It's about time, Eleanor thought, but she forbore to say anything; she hesitated to disrupt this uneasy peace between them. So she just smiled and called for the nurse again, asking her to bring the other children to greet their father.

Henry came to bed her that night and paid the marriage debt. At least, that's what it felt like, a duty to be done. Never before had he seemed so uninvolved when making love to her. She lay there afterwards, sleepless and in turmoil, suspecting that what she had long dreaded had come to pass: that he no longer loved her, and all that was left to them was a marriage of convenience, which fulfilled the purpose for which it had been made. Her personal feelings were not supposed to matter, when one looked at the wider picture. But they did, oh, they did!

She looked at Henry's sleeping back, its solid form white and shadowy in the moonlight that flooded the room through the tall window. It had struck her anew, when she first saw him on his return, how manly he looked in the strength and vigour of his maturity; a little thicker about the girth, true, but still a muscular bull of a man, broad-chested and leonine of feature. How she loved and wanted him! She could not help herself. Of all the men she had known – and known in the biblical sense – none could touch him. Yet she feared he was hers no more. Her pillow was sodden with her tears.

32 Chinon, 1166

The court was staying at the Fort St George, Henry's magnificent castle of Chinon, which straddled a high spur above the River Vienne, when both the King and Queen sickened. Eleanor knew very well what was causing the familiar nausea: she was pregnant for the eleventh time, made fruitful with the seed planted that tragic night at Angers, the night when she had realised that she had lost Henry in all the ways that were most important to her. Since then, matters had not improved between them, and now it seemed that there was an unbreachable distance. They still observed the courtesies, and they talked like civilised beings; he had frequented her bed on several nights, but it was like coupling with a stranger. She knew he sensed her withdrawal from him, a retreat that was less tactical than instinctive, born of the need to protect herself. She told herself that love was not essential in a royal marriage: she was Henry's wife and queen: she was Eleanor, Duchess of Aquitaine, Queen of England, Duchess of Normandy, Countess of Anjou and Maine. She was undefeatable, a match for any light-of-love to whom her lord might take a passing fancy. She dared not let the façade drop; she must think of herself as invincible.

Henry appeared not to be troubled by her studied amenity; she believed he welcomed it, for it absolved him of any need to put things right. There was no point in him trying to do that if his heart wasn't in it. She did not want him to play a role for her: she needed his honesty, but she was damned if she would probe for it, for she feared to provoke any painful revelations. But now, here she was, pregnant with his child once more, another reason why the pretence that all was well must be maintained. And she must tell him her news.

She came upon him in their solar as he sat stitching a tear in his hunting cloak, and sat beside him on the wooden settle, struggling to suppress the rising bile in her throat. The thought of the coming months depressed her: she was weary of childbearing, had suffered it too often. She was forty-four, and she had had enough. This, she vowed, would be the final time.

'I am to have another child, Henry,' she announced quietly. He paused in his mending.

'You are not pleased,' he said.

'If I spoke the truth, no. However, it is God's will, and I must make the best of it. But I pray you, let this be our last child.' She looked at him as she spoke, but he would not meet her eyes.

'You understand my meaning,' she persisted, her heart breaking. She had the horrible, sinking feeling that she was closing a door for ever – and perhaps closing it prematurely.

Henry did not answer. The needle flew in and out.

'Henry?'

'It's your decision,' he said.

'Do you care?' she ventured, thinking that she might as well be dead, and knowing she was about to shatter the fragile equilibrium between them.

Now he did raise his head and look at her. His eyes were guarded, his expression unreadable. There was a slight flush on his bristled cheeks; was it anger? That would be something . . . Surely he would not agree, uncomplaining, to what she asked. As her husband, he could insist on claiming his rights – and who knew, a miracle could happen and they might recapture the joy they had shared. She would endure ten more pregnancies for that, if he would just intimate, by one word, that he still wanted her.

'It's your decision,' he said again, turning back to his handiwork. 'You're the one who has to bear the children. Whether I care or not is beside the point.'

'Are you accusing me of deliberately ignoring your needs?' Eleanor cried, forgetting her resolve to maintain a gentle and dignified detachment.

'I'm saying I don't need this at this time!' Henry snarled. 'I've got Thomas threatening to excommunicate me and proclaiming to the whole of Christendom that my Constitutions of Clarendon are unlawful. There's trouble in Brittany, where my vassal, Count Conan, is unable to keep order, and your Aquitainian lords are up to their usual tricks. I'm not feeling well, Eleanor, in fact I'm feeling bloody awful, and you choose this moment to tell me you don't want to sleep with me any more!'

Relief flooded through her. He was ill. That explained much. Maybe things were not so bad after all. Then the implications of his being ill hit her like a blow.

'You are ill?' she echoed. 'Why didn't you tell me, Henry? What is wrong?'

'I feel sick to my bones,' Henry said, glad to be able to offer

Eleanor an explanation – albeit a temporary one – for his coolness towards her; he could never have admitted that he no longer loved her as he had done, that there was a new love in his life now. Overburdened by cares as he was, the sweet image of Rosamund remained with him constantly, his longing for her a continual ache in his loins. If that was a sickness, then yes, he was ill. But there was more to it than that.

Thomas was threatening him with anathema. Flippant as Henry could be in regard to religion, he still feared eternal damnation, and of being cast out from the communion of the Church; where would that leave him as a ruler who held dominion over all the territories from Scotland to Aquitaine? When a man was excommunicate, all Christians were bound to shun him; he could not receive the Blessed Sacrament, or any of the consolations of his faith. He would be as a leper.

He knew, though, that it was forbidden to excommunicate a man who was sick. The Church, in her wisdom and mercy, held that the sick were weak in judgement and incapable of rational thought. It would make good sense, therefore – for so many reasons – to take to his bed and feign illness.

So he took to his bed, and had it given out that he was laid low by a mysterious malady. He even fooled his doctors, groaning and rolling his eyes in mock pain as they approached. A mystery illness indeed, they agreed, conferring privately amongst themselves. Had they not seen the King in such evident discomfort, they would have said there was nothing wrong with him.

Eleanor was at her wits' end. Henry had not thought fit to take her into his confidence, so she was terrified of him dying, and distraught at the doctors' failure to cure him. When she came to sit beside him, he affected to be all but comatose, suffering her ministrations in silence, and wishing she would go away. Nothing further had been said by either of them on the subject of their quarrel: the issue remained unresolved, although, a thousand times each day, Eleanor crucified herself for what she had said. She made bargains with God; she demanded that He heal Henry; and when He had done that, she beseeched Him that He would make things right between them.

Daily, on her knees, she nagged, pleaded with, and bullied Him as if He were one of her subjects.

Henry had lain abed for two months, and Eleanor was beginning to lose all hope of his recovery, and to worry if Young Henry was ready for the heavy task of ruling the empire, when news came from Vézelay.

'Becket has excommunicated all those who formulated the Constitutions of Clarendon,' announced the Empress, who, frail as she was, had travelled from Rouen to be with her ailing son. Wearily, she had climbed the stairs to the Queen's bower to convey the latest tidings to her exhausted daughter-in-law.

Eleanor swayed. It had come, this news they had all dreaded, the fear of which – she had begun to suspect – was one of the causes of Henry's malady.

'Sit down, Eleanor!' the Empress commanded. 'You must think of the child you carry, and take comfort from the fact that Henry is not included with the rest, on account of his illness. Even Becket did not dare to go so far.'

'Thanks be to God,' Eleanor breathed fervently, collapsing onto a stool with relief. 'We must tell Henry at once.'

They found him propped up on his pillows, partaking of a little pottage.

When they told him the news, his face contorted and he wept in such rage that they both feared he might suffer a relapse.

'The bastard! I will have him. I will ruin him! He will not defy me again, I swear it, by the eyes of God!' And then he fairly leaped out of bed, this invalid who had been almost at death's door, with all trace of his illness gone. His wife and his mother looked at each other in astonished incomprehension, then, as Henry shouted for water to wash in and clean clothes to put on, realisation gradually dawned – and, for Eleanor, the bitter understanding that he had not been ill at all, but had carried on this long-drawn-out charade without a word in her ear; that he had let her suffer prolonged anguish and fear, and not thought to alleviate her misery. How, she wondered bitterly, could things ever be right between them after this?

Henry was still yelling his head off, heedless of his mother's admonishments.

'My son, you must have a care to your health!' she enjoined him.

'There's nothing wrong with my health!' he retorted, then his furious eyes met Eleanor's appalled ones, and he had the grace to look guilty. But the moment was fleeting.

'I will write to the Pope, and to Frederick Barbarossa,' he vowed. 'I will demand that the excommunications be revoked.'

'I have no doubt His Holiness will comply,' the Empress said. 'He needs your support, and the Emperor Frederick's. I, for my part, intend to write to Becket, and give him a piece of my mind for showing such base ingratitude for all the favours you have showered upon him.'

'Thank you, Mother. Someone needs to make my Lord Archbishop see sense.'

'I shall warn him,' Matilda went on determinedly, 'that his only hope of regaining your favour lies in humbling himself and moderating his behaviour. I shall go and write the letter now, so that he may see how angry I am. And, my son, I rejoice to see you restored to health. Your recovery is no less than miraculous.' Her tone was sardonic.

When she had gone, and the sound of her footsteps had faded down the stairwell, Henry looked again at Eleanor, who had said not a word.

'I couldn't tell either of you,' he explained. 'You had to believe I was ill, so that others would be convinced.'

'You think I can't act as well as you?' she answered in an icy tone. 'You don't know the half of it!'

Henry raised one eyebrow questioningly, but did not rise to the bait. He could not be troubled with confrontations with Eleanor at this time; his mind was busy elsewhere.

'I will have that priest!' he seethed. 'I will crush him to the ground.'

33 Rennes, 1166

Eleanor was present in the cathedral of Rennes when Henry formally took possession of Brittany, having deposed his ineffectual vassal, Count Conan. It was a triumphant day, coming as it did so soon after the Pope had ordered Becket to annul his sentences of excommunication and molest his king no more.

With Henry formally invested with the insignia of the newly created duchy of Brittany, the Archbishop of Rennes now sealed the betrothal of eight-year-old Geoffrey to Conan's daughter Constance, a proud little lady of five. Try as she might, Eleanor could not take to this blonde-haired madam, with her pixie face, winged eyebrows and posturing, imperious manner. She had been spoiled and allowed her head, and Eleanor feared that Geoffrey would have his work cut out to control her in the years to come, unless she, Eleanor, took steps to discipline the little minx. And that she would do, she promised herself. Constance could have her moment today, but after that she must be taken in hand.

Eleanor gazed fondly at Geoffrey as he joined hands with his pouting betrothed. He was a dark, handsome boy, devious by nature, it was true, but clever and charming. He was to be duke of Brittany when he married, Henry had decreed, but until then, his father would hold and rule the duchy for him. It was gratifying to have the boy's future so happily and advantageously settled, and the problem of Brittany brought to such a satisfactory conclusion.

There was but one jarring note to mar this day of celebration, and that was Eleanor's nagging awareness that, although Young Henry's and Geoffrey's futures were mapped out – Henry was to have England, Anjou and Normandy – and both had been found brides, Henry had as yet made no provision for her adored Richard, his middle son.

She tackled him about this as they presided at the high table over the feast that followed the ceremonies in the cathedral.

'It more than contents me to see two of our boys settled,' she began diplomatically, 'but tell me, what plans have you for Richard?' Her eyes rested on the nine-year-old lad with the flame-red curls who sat gorging himself on some delicious Breton oysters and scallops further down the table. A strong child he was, a vigorous child, who was surely destined to make his mark. What she was really determined upon was to make him heir to all her dominions; and she believed that that was what Henry too had in mind for Richard. It would be entirely fitting.

'None yet,' Henry said, his mouth full of lamb. 'But, since you mention it, I have something in mind for Young Henry, and I should like your approval.'

'And what is that?' Eleanor asked.

'I want to make him your heir in Aquitaine.'

'No!' she cried, shocked. 'Why Henry? What of Richard? That would leave Richard with nothing!' Her face had flushed pink with fury, and a few of the revellers were looking at her curiously.

'Calm yourself,' Henry muttered. 'Do you think I would not see Richard well provided for? Does it not occur to you that it would be better to keep this empire of mine in one piece, under one ruler? There is strength in numbers, Eleanor, and by God I need all the strength I can get to keep your vassals in order. It's one thing to confront them with the duke of Aquitaine, quite another when that duke is also to be king of England, duke of Normandy, count of Maine and count of Anjou. You must see that!'

Eleanor did not. All she was aware of was the need to fight for the rights of her beloved. 'Richard is but two years younger than Henry. You know he has the makings of what it takes to rule Aquitaine, he is a true child of the south, and I want him as my heir, and to see him settled as Henry and Geoffrey are settled. It would only be fair.'

Henry turned to her, his face set. 'Trust me. I will see Richard settled.'

'With what?' she asked defiantly. 'All your domains are spoken for. What if you died after naming Henry my heir? Richard would be left landless!'

By now, a lot of the guests were watching them speculatively as they quarrelled. Eleanor saw it, but did not care. All that mattered was Richard's future. But Henry, seeing that their discord was observed, resolved to put an end to it.

'It's no use arguing, Eleanor,' he said. 'My mind is made up. I but asked for your approval as a courtesy. You know I do not need it. There is no more to be said, except that, after these celebrations are over, I intend to deal once more with your ever-impudent seigneurs, and then go to Poitiers, where I shall hold my Christmas court and present Young Henry to your people as your heir. I should like you to be there too, obviously, to show some solidarity.'

'Never!' she retorted furiously. 'I will go to England and stay there until this child is born. I will not be witness to an act that effectively disinherits Richard. Instead, I will help Matilda to prepare for her wedding journey next year.' She had decided all this on impulse, in the heat of the moment, and was wondering, even as she said it, if she would come to regret it, for going to England would mean that she would certainly not see Henry again for months. Was it wise to leave him to his own devices at a time when relations between them were so distant? She knew she might be sentencing herself to a lengthy period of emotional turmoil – but it was too late to retract. The words were now said, and she could not unsay them. Besides, she knew she had right on her side.

Henry was frowning, but he was immovable.

'You may go where you will,' he said. 'I will make the arrangements.'

34 Woodstock and Oxford, 1166

It was cold in the wilds of Oxfordshire, and there was a promise of snow in the leaden air. The sky was lowering, the skeletal trees bending before the icy wind. Eleanor sat huddled in her litter, her swollen body swathed in furs, aware that she should find some place of shelter soon, for it could not be long now before this babe was ready to greet the world.

Poor child, she thought: it had been conceived in sorrow and would be born in bitterness, for Henry had let her go without a protest, and there had been no word from him since. He was angry at her defiance, of that there could be no doubt, but she still maintained adamantly that she had a just grievance: the thought of Young Henry having Richard's inheritance was an open wound that would not heal.

She was weary of the ceaseless jostling with Henry for autonomy in her own lands, enraged with him for slighting her adored boy, and tortured by the crumbling of their marriage. It was a relief to be away from him, and yet . . . and yet, for all that, she missed him, wanted him, needed him . . . The pain was relentless. She tortured herself with speculation about the possibility that she had been supplanted by another woman. There was no proof, nothing at all, but what else could have caused such a change in Henry's manner towards her? Had he simply ceased to care for her?

She rested her head back on the silk pillows. It was no good tormenting herself with these disturbing thoughts – it was not beneficial for her, in her condition. She must think of her coming child.

They had been making for Oxford, hoping to get there by dusk, before the snow fell, but their battle with the elements had delayed them, and the Queen now had no choice but to order that they divert to Woodstock for the night. The royal hunting lodge was a favourite residence of Eleanor's; she kept a suite of rooms there, and was hoping that the steward would have maintained them in a habitable condition. She did not think she could face freezing chambers, an unaired bed or damp sheets; what she needed right now was a roaring fire, warming broth, a feather bed and the ministrations of her women. She was weary to her bones.

At last, the litter was trundled across the drawbridge, the men-at-arms clip-clopping on either side. As the little procession drew to a standstill, Eleanor parted the leather curtains of her litter, allowed her attendants to assist her to her feet – and then gaped in astonishment. For she saw that Woodstock now boasted a new, fair tower of the finest yellow stone. It was perhaps only to be expected, for Henry had been indefatigable in improving or rebuilding the royal residences, and he had spent much time here not so long ago. What *was* surprising was what lay before the tower, nestling within the curtain walls. It was some kind of enclosed garden – indeed, the most curious of pleasaunces – and it certainly had not been here when she last visited. She walked heavily towards it, almost in a daze. Henry had been here for much of last winter and spring, she remembered. Had he gone to the trouble of ordering it to be planted for her, for some future visit? And the tower? Was that for her too?

She soon saw that the pleasaunce was in fact a labyrinth, laid out in a circular design with young yews and briars; a paved path disappearing into its depths could be glimpsed at the entrance. The maze was not large, but it looked enticing, even magical – and not a little sinister – in the light of the torches carried by her people against the deepening dusk. Had Henry really gone to the trouble of having this intricate thing laid out just for her? How strange! He had had no idea that she would come here in the foreseeable future.

There was a grassy path skirting the labyrinth; one branch of it led to the tower, the other to the older hall with the King's and Queen's solars above, but Eleanor walked past that one. She had noticed a light in the tower, at one of the upper windows; it was flickering behind grisaille glass, such as was usually only found in great churches. Could some personage of importance be lodging here? Or, more likely, was some servant about his or her duties? That would account for the light.

Suddenly, a door opened and the steward materialised breathlessly out of the gathering darkness. His face was red, his manner flustered.

'My Lady, welcome, welcome!' he cried, bowing hastily. 'We had no idea you were coming. I will make all ready. I pray you, come in and get warm.' He indicated that Eleanor should go before him into the large hall at the base of the solar block, but she swept on.

'In a moment, I thank you. But first, I have a mind to see that impressive new tower,' she told him.

His face blanched. 'Madam, I should not advise it. It is, er, unfinished, and may not be safe.'

'Someone is up there!' Eleanor pointed, and strode in ungainly fashion towards the studded wooden door at the base of the tower.

'My Lady!' the steward protested, but she ignored him.

'Open the door!' she commanded. Unhappily, he did as he was bidden, and the Queen brushed past him and began climbing the spiral stairs. She was out of breath by the time she reached the first-floor chamber, and had to stop for a few moments, her hand resting on her swollen belly. Clearly, there was no one on this storey, and the steward had spoken the truth: the tower was as yet unfinished. Half-completed murals adorned the lime-

242

washed walls; the wooden floor was stacked with ladders, crocks of paint, brushes and stained rags.

When she had rested a pace, she took the stairs to the next level, a vaulted, unplastered store room containing several iron-bound chests, some stools and very little else. No one here either. Determined to satisfy her curiosity, she dragged herself up to the topmost storey, panting determinedly, and found herself outside a narrow wooden door. Light streamed from beneath it.

Eleanor took a deep breath and depressed the latch. The door swung open to reveal a pretty domestic scene. The room was warm, heated by the coals in a glowing brazier. An exquisitely beautiful young girl was sitting before a basin of chased silver, humming as she washed herself with a fine holland cloth, by the dancing light of many wax candles. She wore only a white chemise, draped around her waist, exposing her upper body. In the instant before the startled nymph gasped and covered herself, Eleanor's shrewd eyes took in the small, pink-tipped breasts, the long, straw-coloured tresses, the firm, slender arms and the damp, rose-petal skin.

'Who are you?' she asked, aghast, already dreading the answer.

'I am Rosamund de Clifford, Madam,' the girl said, her expression guarded. She had no idea who this intruder was; the woman was bundled up in a thick cloak, and the white wimple beneath it, although fine, was of a type worn by many middle- and upper-class matrons.

'And what is your business here?' Eleanor could not help her hectoring tone. She had to know who – and what – this young female was.

'I live here by order of my Lord the King,' Rosamund answered, a touch defensively. 'May I ask who it is who wishes to know?'

Eleanor could not speak. Her heart was racing in horror. Was this child – for she could be little more than that – the reason for Henry's strange, distant behaviour? Had he installed her here as his mistress? Or – her mind raced on – was this Rosamund some bastard child of his?

'I am Queen Eleanor,' she said, her voice sounding far more confident than she felt, and was gratified to see the girl gather her shift about her and drop hurriedly into an obeisance.

'My Lady, forgive me,' she bleated.

Keeping her on her knees, Eleanor placed one finger under Rosamund's chin and tilted it upwards, daring her to meet her eye, but the young chit would not look directly at her.

'I will not beat about the bush,' the Queen said. 'Tell me the truth. Are you his mistress?'

Rosamund began trembling like a frightened animal.

'Are you?' Eleanor repeated sharply.

'My Lady, forgive me!' burst out the girl, beginning to cry. Eleanor withdrew her hand as if it were scalded. She thought she would die, right then and there, she felt so sick to her stomach. He had betrayed her with this little whore. This beautiful little whore. Her hand flew protectively to the infant under her thudding heart.

'Do you realise that this is his child?' she cried accusingly.

Rosamund did not answer; she was sobbing helplessly now.

'Tears will avail you nothing,' Eleanor said coldly, wishing she too could indulge in the luxury of weeping, and marvelling that her emotions had not betrayed her further. But it was anger that was keeping her from collapsing in grief.

'Do you know what I could do to you?' Her eyes narrowed as she moved – menacingly, she hoped – closer towards the snivelling creature kneeling before her. She was filled with hatred. She wanted this girl to suffer, as she herself was suffering. 'I could have you whipped! If I had a mind to, I could call for a dagger and stab you, or have your food poisoned. Yes, Rosamund de Clifford, it would give me great pleasure to think of you, every time they bring you those choice dainties that my husband has no doubt ordered for you, wondering if your next mouthful might be your last!'

'My Lady, please, spare me!' the girl cried out. 'I did not ask for this.' But Eleanor was beside herself with rage.

'I suppose you are going to tell me that you went to him unwillingly, that he raped you,' she spat.

'No, no, it was not like that!'

'Then what *was* it like?' She did not want to – could not bear to – hear the details, but she had to know.

'My Lady will know that one does not refuse the King,' Rosamund said in a low, shaking voice. 'But . . .' – and now

Eleanor could detect a faint note of defiance – 'I did love him, and what I gave I gave willingly.'

Her words were like knives twisting in the older woman's heart.

'You loved him? How touching!'

'I did – I still do. And he loves me. He told me.'

'You are a fool!' Eleanor's voice cracked as she spat out the words. 'And you won't be the first trollop to be seduced by a man's fair speech.'

Rosamund raised wet eyes to her, eyes that now held a challenge. 'But, Madam,' she said quietly, 'he does love me. He stayed here with me all last autumn, winter and spring. He built me this tower, and a labyrinth for my pleasure. And he has commanded me to stay here and await his return.'

Eleanor was speechless. Her wrath had suddenly evaporated, swept away by shock and grief, and she knew she was about to break down. She must not do so in front of this insolent girl, must not let her see how deeply those cruel barbs had wounded her, far more than her empty threats could have frightened her adversary. Like an animal with a mortal hurt, she wanted to retreat to a dark place and die.

There were voices drifting up from the stairwell; her attendants would be wondering what was going on, were no doubt coming to find her. She must not let them see her here, a betrayed wife with her younger rival.

'Never let me set eyes on you again!' she hissed at Rosamund, then turned her back on the girl, glided from the room with as much dignity as she could muster, closing the door firmly behind her, and descended the stairs.

'The sewing women are up there,' she announced to the ladies who were climbing the stairs in search of her. 'I was admiring their skill.' She was surprised at her own composure. 'It seems that the steward was right, that many works are being carried out here. This place is wholly unfit for habitation. Like it or not, we must make for Oxford.' She knew she had to get away from Woodstock as quickly as possible. She could not endure to share a roof with Rosamund de Clifford, or even breathe the same air. She must go somewhere she could lick her wounds in peace.

'Now?' echoed her women. 'Madam, you should rest before we attempt to move on.'

'There will be an inn on the road,' Eleanor said firmly.

The King's House at Oxford was a vast complex of buildings surrounded by a strong stone wall; it looked like a fortress, but was in fact a splendid residence adorned with wall paintings in bright hues and richly appointed suites for the King and Queen. Here, in happier days long past, Eleanor's beloved Richard had been born, slipping eagerly into the world with the minimum of fuss. But this latest babe, unlike its older siblings, did not seem to want to be born, and small wonder it was, Eleanor thought, when the world was such a cruel place.

She had no heart for this labour. She pushed and she strained, but to little effect. It had been hours now, and the midwife was shaking her head in concern. It had been a great honour, being summoned at short notice to order the Queen's confinement, but the good woman was fearful for her future – and her high reputation in the town; for if mother or child were lost, almost certainly, the King would point the finger of blame at her.

Petronilla, tipsy as usual, for she had resorted to the wine flagon to banish her demons, was seated by the bed, holding Eleanor's hand and looking tragic, as the other ladies bustled around with ewers of hot water and clean, bleached towels. Petronilla knew she would be devastated if her sister died in childbed; she adored Eleanor, and relied on her for so many things; and she knew her life would be bleak without her. No one else understood why Petronilla had to drink herself into oblivion. Other people looked askance and were censorious, but not Eleanor. Eleanor had also known the pain of losing her children. She too had suffered that cruel sundering, had learned to live with empty arms and an aching heart. Petronilla knew, as few did, how Eleanor had kept on writing to those French daughters of hers, hoping to reseal a bond that had long ago been severed. She knew, too, that there had been no reply, apart from on one occasion, when hope had sprung briefly in her sister's breast; but evidently, the young Countess Marie had not thought it worth establishing a correspondence – and Petronilla supposed that one could hardly blame her.

Yes, Eleanor too had her crosses to bear – and probably more than she would admit to. Something odd had happened at Woodstock, Petronilla was sure of it. Before that, Eleanor had seemed strong and resolute, a fighter ready to take on all challengers. Now she appeared to have lost the will to live. It was incomprehensible, the change in her – and terrifying. Gulping back another sob, Petronilla reached again for her goblet.

Eleanor lay in a twilight world, enduring the ever more frequent onslaughts of pain as her contractions grew stronger, then retreating to a place where no one could reach her. She almost welcomed the agony of childbirth: it was far preferable to the agony that Henry and his whore had inflicted on her. He had inflicted this ordeal on her too, yet she would have welcomed it a thousand times had it been the result of an unsullied love between them. But that was all finished. He had betrayed her, and she was done with him. This would indeed be her last child. She knew it.

The ordeal went on for hours. They brought her holy relics to kiss, slid knives under the bed to cut the pain. None of it did any good, and, had Death come for her, she would have welcomed him. It was not until the dawn, on Christmas Eve, that the infant who was the cause – and the fruit – of her agony finally came snivelling into the world, a tragic bundle of bloodied limbs and dark-red hair.

'A boy, my Lady!' the midwife announced jubilantly, breathless with relief.

Eleanor turned her face away.

'Will you not look at him?' Petronilla asked, her heart-shaped face bleary with wine, yet full of concern.

Eleanor made herself look. The infant, wiped and swathed in a soft fleece, had been laid on the bed next to her. She contemplated its crumpled, angry little face, and watched dispassionately as it broke into mewling cries of outrage at being cast adrift into the wicked world. She wanted to feel something for it, the sad little mite; after all, it was not this babe's fault that she herself was in such misery. Yet it seemed she had nothing left to give it, no spark of loving kindness or maternal feeling. She felt dead inside. Nevertheless, this was her child, she reminded herself sternly. She must do something for it. Hesitantly, she touched the tiny, downy cheek, and gave her son her blessing.

'What is he to be called?' Petronilla asked.

'What day is it?' Eleanor asked wanly.

'Christmas Eve. Even now they are bringing in the Yule log.'

'St Stephen's Day is two days hence,' the Queen said wearily, 'but I can hardly call him after the martyr, for the English do not hold King Stephen in much repute. I mind me that the Feast of St John the Apostle and St John the Evangelist is in three days' time. I shall call him John.'

Petronilla gazed down at her new nephew.

'I pray God send you a long and happy life, my Lord John,' she said, aware that what should have been a happy occasion was, for some reason beyond her comprehension, a very sad one.

35 Argentan, Normandy, 1167

'Welcome, my Lady,' Henry said formally, bending over his queen's hand. Their eyes met coldly as she rose from her curtsey. He had put on weight in the fourteen months since she had seen him, Eleanor thought, and his curly red hair was silvered with grey; that had come as a shock, and an unwelcome reminder that they were neither of them getting any younger. Henry looked ragged at the edges, as indeed he was, for he was worn down by the cares of state, his interminable quarrel with Becket – and the recent death of his mother.

Indomitable to the end, the Empress had breathed her last in September, at Rouen, after a short illness. Eleanor could not mourn her deeply, but Henry must be missing her sorely, she guessed. Matilda had ruled Normandy for him for years, and had given him the benefit of her wise counsel in many matters. Now she was gone, and there would be a void in his world. Even so, Eleanor could not bring herself to feel much grief for him: he had wounded her too deeply.

They avoided looking at each other as Henry escorted her into the castle of Argentan, her hand resting lightly on his.

Courtiers were packed against the walls to watch them pass, their King and Queen, come together after so long to hold their Christmas court. There had been much speculation as to the true state of affairs between them, and whispered gossip about a fair maiden shut up in a tower somewhere in England, but the long separation could equally be accounted for by the demands of policy. Eleanor had been in England, preparing for her daughter Matilda's wedding to the Duke of Saxony; and Henry had been in Aquitaine, suppressing yet another revolt, and then in the Vexin, negotiating an uneasy truce with Louis.

'I have missed my children,' he muttered, as they processed into the hall, now hand-in-hand. 'I trust they are in health, and that our Matilda went cheerfully to greet her bridegroom.'

'She did,' Eleanor replied tersely, remembering the busy weeks of choosing a trousseau and packing it into twenty chests, and Matilda clinging to her, weeping, at Dover, begging her mother at least to cross the sea with her and delay the inevitable, awful moment of parting. She remembered, too, calling upon all her inner reserves of strength so that she could stay calm and positive, and let herself allow this beloved child to go alone to her destiny. Oh, how she missed her, the sensible, gentle girl. It had been like having a limb severed. But Henry would not be interested in any of that, she thought sourly. To him, his children were pawns to be pushed around on a chess board whenever it suited him.

'How is Young Henry?' she enquired, her voice like ice. She had neither forgotten nor forgiven Henry's presentation of the boy as her heir to her subjects at Poitiers the previous Christmas. She still thought it outrageous, and the matter of Richard's inheritance remained unresolved.

'You will see a change in him,' Henry said gruffly. 'He is twelve now, and already he seems to be verging on manhood. He will make a great king when the time comes.' As would Richard – the thought came unbidden to Eleanor, who said nothing. She was mentally upbraiding herself for her resentful feelings towards Young Henry, because it wasn't his fault that his father had overlooked Richard in advancing him; it was just that – well, she knew in her bones, with all a mother's instinct, that Henry was not cut out to be duke of Aquitaine. He lacked the soul of a troubadour, unlike Richard, who was already as accomplished at composing elegant lays as he was in the martial arts. Her people would understand that – look how they had loved her grandfather! – but try explaining it to Henry, she thought grimly!

'Aquitaine is the reason I have summoned you here,' Henry said, handing her courteously to her seat at the high table. It was as if he had followed her train of thought. Instantly, she was alert and on the defensive, prepared to defer for a time the matter of Rosamund de Clifford, which she had firmly resolved to broach with Henry. All the way here, sailing to Normandy in the foremost of a flotilla of seven ships, all laden with her movable goods and personal effects, she had argued with herself – agonised, rather – over whether or not to confront him with what she knew. Do it, and the thing would lie like a sword between them, severing the present from the past. Say nothing, and the pretence that all was well could be maintained, and a sort of peace achieved. A sort of peace? How could that ever be, when she knew the truth, and was bursting to challenge her husband? And so she had turned it round and round again in her mind, torturing herself, not knowing what best to do. Really, she wanted to scream and rage, to rake her claws down Henry's face and devise some apt revenge on that little bitch. But in the end she had decided that she must confront her husband with what she knew, and see what his reaction would be. Yet now, with Henry's abrupt mention of Aquitaine – she had guessed he would not have summoned her for her own sake – she was ready to set aside the matter of Rosamund, for now.

When the company was seated, and the first course had been served – a barely palatable dish of chunks of rabbit marooned in greasy gravy – Henry turned to her, his expression unreadable.

'As you know,' he said, 'I've spent the autumn riding around Aquitaine quelling rebellion. Your vassals are worse than most, and they hate me.'

'You have given them little reason to love you,' Eleanor could not resist retorting.

'It's not even worth the effort. In fact, I have given up trying to make them obey me. You've always wanted power in the duchy, haven't you, Eleanor? Well, it's your turn now.' There was a hint of dark humour in Henry's face.

'My turn?' she repeated, unable to still the excited racing of her heart.

'Yes, yours,' Henry told her, with the hint of a smile. He was enjoying disarming her. 'Your presence in Aquitaine, and the reassertion of your authority as its duchess, might make all the difference. Your rebellious subjects love you, and if they see me devolving my power on you, they might yet cease constantly opposing me.'

Eleanor could not speak. He was asking her to go back to Aquitaine as its sovereign duchess. This was what she had longed for all through the fifteen years of her marriage – no, in fact, it had been her dream ever since she was borne off to Paris, a bride of fifteen, by Louis. Aquitaine was her home, the place she wanted most of all to be, that enchanted land of the south, the land of mighty rivers, wooded valleys, wine and song. She wanted to fall to her knees and praise God for this sought-after blessing. She even felt some gratitude towards her faithless lord, although that was mixed with resentment, because he had been ignoring her urgent advice on courting her vassals for years, and had only belatedly come to this eminently sensible decision.

'Now you see why I asked you to bring all your belongings,' Henry said.

'I thought you were planning to set up home with me again,' she told him, with an acerbic smile. He had the grace to look uncomfortable.

'Eleanor, circumstances have kept us apart,' he said. And Rosamund de Clifford, she thought bitterly. 'Will you do it?' he went on. 'Will you go back to Aquitaine as its ruler?'

'Did you have to ask?' she replied.

To Eleanor's astonishment, Henry followed her up to her solar at the end of the evening. He was a little drunk after all the carousing, and they left behind them most of the barons of Normandy slumped asleep over the tables or sprawling drunk on the rushes.

'Out! Out!' Henry waved her ladies away. 'I will be the Queen's tirewoman tonight,' he told them, his speech slurred. They scattered, giggling and exchanging knowing glances. Evidently all *was* well between their master and mistress . . .

Once the chamber door had closed, Eleanor turned to face Henry.

'Why are you here?' she asked coldly. He came lurching towards her.

'You of all people should know that,' he replied. 'State business – the getting of heirs.'

'We have enough heirs,' she said, her voice strident. 'I told you, I wanted no more children. And you know very well we have nothing to say to each other.'

'I didn't come here to *say* anything,' Henry persisted, coming towards her. 'You're still a beautiful woman, Eleanor. Time was, you would have been eager to bed with me.' He was becoming petulant.

'That was a long time ago. Before Rosamund de Clifford usurped my place.' Eleanor's tone was frigid. It was only her body that betrayed her, responding involuntarily to the familiar nearness and scent of this man whom she had loved so wholeheartedly. She was shocked to realise that she still wanted him, despite the hurts he had dealt her.

But now it was out, the thing she had dreamed of saying. The gauntlet had been cast down.

Henry halted, stopped dead in his tracks, instantly sober. Lust withered and died. His eyes took on that shifty look she knew so well.

'Who told you that?' he asked, his eyes narrowing.

'No one! I saw for myself. And she told me, your little whore, how you love her, and she loves you. It was so touching I almost wept.' She felt like weeping now, but she would have died rather than let him see her cry. 'A pretty bower you've built for her at Woodstock – and that labyrinth, Henry: did you think to ward me off when I came seeking revenge, did you think I wouldn't find my way into that fine tower you've built for your leman?'

Henry was speechless with surprise: who could have predicted that, of all the houses she had to choose from in England, his wife would turn up at Woodstock? And Rosamund, the silly little fool, why had it pleased her vanity to brag of his favour and his love? With an effort he found his voice.

'I can explain,' he said, in the time-honoured manner of cheating husbands.

'I'm listening,' Eleanor answered, eyebrows raised in disbelief.

'I don't have to justify my actions to you or anyone,' Henry went on defensively, 'but for the sake of courtesy, I want you to know the truth. I did have an affair with Rosamund, I admit it, but I haven't seen her in eighteen months.'

'An affair? You told her you loved her! Or did you deceive her, much as you've deceived me?' Eleanor was in a ferment.

'No,' said Henry. 'I said I would tell you the truth.' He paused. 'The truth is that I do love her. I can't help it. I miss her desperately. And I know she returned that love – I hope she returns it still.' His voice was hoarse.

Eleanor could not speak. His brutal words echoed in her ears. I do love her, I do love her . . . It was the cruellest betrayal. She wished she could fall down and die, she wished she had never uttered the name Rosamund, she wished that Henry and his trollop were burning in the fires of Hell . . .

He had forsaken her, his ageing wife, the mother of his children, for a younger woman, as so many men did; for a woman so young and beautiful that there could be no hope of him abandoning her.

'So this is the end for us,' she stated flatly.

'That's up to you,' Henry said.

'Is this why you want me to go to Aquitaine?'

'You know me better than that,' he snorted. 'Kings can't afford the luxury of putting their pleasures before the demands of state. I want you to go to Aquitaine because your presence is needed there. It has nothing to do with Rosamund. If it did, then I would have been in Woodstock with her, instead of chasing after your rebellious vassals.'

'But, of course, it's very convenient for me to go to Aquitaine just now,' Eleanor said caustically. 'As soon as I've gone south, no doubt you will summon your whore here to rut with you.'

'No,' Henry replied, his voice leaden. 'I have to treat with Louis.' He sank down on the fur-lined counterpane that covered the bed and buried his face in his hands. 'I did not look for this to happen, Eleanor. I still love you, as my wife, you must believe that.'

'I know nothing!' she snapped. 'Or I wish I did. And I don't want to be loved as your wife. I want you to love me as you once loved me. When you were mine. Before Rosamund.'

Henry threw back his head and laughed mirthlessly. 'You've got it all wrong, Eleanor. Our marriage was made for policy, as much as for love, and I not only loved you, I lusted after you as I had lusted after no woman before you. But lust like that doesn't last. It dilutes in the marriage bed after long years of usage. I was never wholly yours, as you think. There have always been women along the way. I have a devil in me, and I can never be content with one woman, not even Rosamund. I've bedded quite a few since I left her in England. It's not in my nature to be faithful, yet I am quite capable of loving you as my wife, and of lusting after you yet – and of loving her too.'

Eleanor had been listening in mounting horror, unable to accept the magnitude of Henry's betrayal. She had wondered and speculated, all through the years; she had heard what Raoul de Faye had told her, but she had never truly believed . . . until she went to Woodstock. At the memory, the dreadful tears welled.

'You love her the way you once loved me,' she muttered, bitter.

'We are a partnership, Eleanor,' Henry was saying. 'You are Aquitaine, and I am England, Normandy and the rest. Together, we straddle much of the western world. Nothing can sunder us, not even hatred. To be invincible, we have to work together, to give a semblance of being in harmony. Our personal feelings do not count.'

'You talk very lightly of hatred!' she flung at him. 'You make a nonsense of my feelings, and then preach to me about partnership. Come, Henry; I am not a fool. You itch for that strumpet, and you want me out of the way. No, don't dispute that!'

'I will dispute it!' Henry shouted. 'I love and honour you as my wife—'

'Honour? You don't know the meaning of the word!' Eleanor

screamed, tears coursing down her cheeks, and slapped him hard across the face. 'That's for every time you've fucked where you shouldn't!' She lashed out again, her fury out of control.

Henry caught her wrists, his face a mask of wrath. His grip hurt.

'How dare you strike me, the King!' he roared.

'I struck my faithless husband,' Eleanor choked, crying helplessly now. 'Henry, you have *hurt* me, to the quick. You have betrayed my bed and my trust. You have made me realise I am old. If I felt joy at going back to rule Aquitaine, it is dead now. There can be no more joy for me in this world. You have killed it. I hope you are satisfied!'

Henry said nothing, but suddenly slid his arms tightly about her and held her until the storm of weeping had passed; she could not see his face with hers pressed wetly against his beard, and wondered why she wanted to. Even when the tears had dried and she was still, she stood there in his embrace, wanting to free herself, yet needing to be held there for ever, and dreading the moment ending. It was a bitter realisation, that the only man who could comfort her was the man who had dealt her a mortal hurt. But just then she felt him stir against her.

'No!' she declared, beginning to struggle. 'Not that. Never that.'

'You are my wife,' Henry muttered. 'It is my right.'

'Then you will have to rape me!' she spat.

'Don't tempt me,' he said, then let her go. When he spoke again, his voice was barely controlled. 'Very well. I was trying to mend things between us, but you have made yourself clear. From now on, we will observe the courtesies, and no more. You will not mind, I take it, if I indulge my lust in other beds?'

'Do as you please,' Eleanor seethed, with the desperation of one who realises she has deliberately, impulsively burned her bridges. 'I will go to Aquitaine, and we will keep up the pretence that all is well between us, if that is what you wish.'

'You know very well I wished for something rather different,' Henry told her.

'No, my Lord, it's you who have got it all wrong,' Eleanor

said, resolutely wiping away the last of her tears. 'Our marriage is dead. You cannot have us both.'

36 Fontevrault, 1168

They were riding south together, making for Fontevrault, a veritable army of lords, servants and soldiers at their heels. Henry had insisted on escorting his wife, warning her that the times were lawless and that his mailed fist stretched only so far. They travelled in hostile silence.

Eleanor was in turmoil, resentful that her joy in her yearned-for return to Aquitaine as its rightful ruler had been ruined by the dread knowledge that it effectively signalled her separation from Henry, a situation that was her doing, but in no way her fault. Every mile was taking them nearer to that parting, after which they would go their own ways – partners in a marriage, yes, but miles apart in far more than distance. She ached for inner peace, and could only pray that, once settled in her beloved domains in the south, she would find it.

There was to be more than one parting. With the King and Queen rode their children: Young Henry, now styled Count of Poitiers, fair of face and shooting up in height, wearing his royal status with all the assurance of his race. He would be remaining with his father from now on, to learn the business of government. Richard, eleven years old, long-limbed and blue-eyed, already a hardy warrior who was praised alike by the captains who drilled him in military exercises and the tutors who taught him Latin and book learning. He was to accompany his mother to Aquitaine with his brother Geoffrey, dark and handsome Geoffrey, who was patiently suffering the twittering of vain young Constance, who rode by his side; he would be wasted on her, this clever boy, Eleanor thought. Then there were the little girls, Eleanor and Joanna, copper-haired images of herself, but gentler, and far more docile and biddable.

They were very subdued today, her daughters. It had been decided, by Henry, with Eleanor's reluctant approval, that they should be brought up by the good nuns of Fontevrault until such time as they were married. Eleanor knew that there could be no better education for girls of high birth. Her family – and Henry's – had a long tradition of sending daughters to Fontevrault. But the decision had saddened her. She would miss Eleanor and Joanna, and felt that in some way she was abandoning them, much as she had abandoned two other little girls all those years before. Recently, at long last, in response to her own importunings, she had received another letter from Marie, to which she had felt constrained to reply in conventional fashion. She took pride in the knowledge that the young Countess of Champagne had inherited her own love of music and poetry, but there was no true bond there – it had been loosed long ago. It had been like writing to a stranger. She had not the will to pursue the correspondence further.

She smiled encouragingly at her daughters, as a pang gripped her heart. It was for the best that they be entrusted to the good sisters of Fontevrault, she told herself. Henry had warned her that she would have enough on her hands trying to control her rebellious vassals, and that most girls of high birth were reared by nuns. Yet she had prided herself that, contrary to the common custom of royalty, she had, for much of the time, kept all her children with her. She wondered if this consignment of Eleanor and Joanna to a convent was some form of revenge on Henry's part, or if he feared she might go behind his back and make alliances between his daughters and Aquitainian lords, to keep the latter sweet. He would not want to waste the fruit of his loins on such ingrates – she understood that.

That left young John, little more than a year old. Try as she might, Eleanor still could not bring herself to love him, this child conceived in sorrow and born in betrayal. His existence conjured up too many memories of that terrible Christmas-tide, when she had gone to Woodstock and come face-to-face with catastrophe and ruin, and then endured that bloody, agonising travail at Oxford. No, John was the fruit of a marriage in its death throes, and sometimes she could not bear to look upon him. His nurses had the care of him.

John was going to Fontevrault too. Young though he was, Eleanor had urged Henry to consider him for a career in the Church, and Henry had agreed. As the youngest of four sons, it did not seem likely that there would be much of a landed inheritance for him, so the Church seemed an obvious choice. John would be brought up as an oblate, in preparation for his ordination to the priesthood. The gift of a son to God would undoubtedly be one of the best ways of storing up treasure in Heaven, for both parents. And God knows, we need it, Eleanor thought bitterly. She would not miss her last-born; indeed, she was thankful that others would have the rearing of him. Her guilt was overwhelming.

There was one other whom she would miss, whose smile would never again gladden Eleanor's day. Poor Petronilla had died three months before, the victim of her own helpless predilection for the fruit of the grape. At the end, she had been comatose, her skin yellowed, her belly horribly distended. Eleanor had wept pitifully for her sister, but could not deny that death had come as a merciful release. But there was now an empty space in her life, which Petronilla had once filled; there were too many empty spaces, she reflected mournfully. Sadness seemed to be her lot these days.

Amiable Abbess Isabella had gone to her well-earned rest many years before, and it was her successor, Abbess Audeburge, who was waiting to receive them, her monks, nuns and lady boarders drawn up in a respectful semicircle behind her. As the royal cavalcade drew to a halt, the entire convent fell to its knees and the Abbess stepped forward. Audeburge was a capable, dynamic woman whom Eleanor had long liked and admired. She knew she could not have entrusted her children to a better guardian. And her confidence seemed to be justified, for when Eleanor and Joanna were formally committed to her care, Abbess Audeburge bent to kiss them affectionately and summoned forward two of her boarders with a parakeet and a monkey to distract her new charges, instantly winning their hearts. Then she reached out her strong, aristocratic hands to take John from his nurse, and herself removed his thumb from his mouth and gentled him, receiving a tentative smile in return. Before Eleanor knew it, the goodbyes had been said and her children spirited away by a bevy of smiling nuns.

They could not tarry. After Mass in the soaring white abbey church, Henry paid his respects to the Abbess and prepared to depart. He had planned to escort Eleanor to Poitiers and see her safely installed there, but had been warned of a serious revolt further south. The Count of Angoulême had allied with the particularly troublesome seigneurs of Lusignan and other malcontent lords, who had all risen in the latest protest against Henry's rule.

'You cannot deal with this alone,' Henry had told Eleanor, when they'd brought him the news, some little way north of Fontevrault. 'I will summon my lieges and ride south with you to Lusignan. Your presence at my side will remind these arrogant fools to whom they owe allegiance. Then *you* can return by a safe route to Poitiers, and *I* will teach your rebels a lesson.'

'They will resent it,' she had warned, in clipped tones.

'Are *you* going to face them in battle?' Henry retorted. 'Besides, in defying me, they defy you. I want to see Aquitaine settled before I leave you in charge.'

Eleanor had not answered, but rode on, tight-lipped.

37 Lusignan and Poitiers, 1168

They travelled swiftly south, towards Lusignan. As they approached, they could see its castle, nestling on a hill above the Vonne Valley. Eleanor recalled Henry telling her, in happier days, that his diabolic ancestress Melusine had commanded it to be built.

Poitiers, Eleanor's destination, lay not far to the east. As speed was essential to the frustrating of the rebels' plans, Henry, hell-bent on marching on Lusignan, was unable to escort her to her city. Instead, he had summoned Earl Patrick of Salisbury, his military governor and deputy in Aquitaine, to ensure that the Duchess reached Poitiers in safety. And here was Earl Patrick now, riding along the dusty road, a small force of men-at-arms at his heels.

Eleanor knew and liked Patrick. He had given long years of loyal service to the Empress Matilda and to King Henry, and during the year he had been in Aquitaine, he had proved himself an able, sensible ruler, forging a tactful and politic friendship with her seneschal, Raoul de Faye, and treating her vassals in a conciliatory fashion. She hoped he would stay on, after the handover of power had taken place; she would value his company and his sound advice.

But first, there was Henry. The moment of farewell had come. It would not be a final farewell, of course, but there was little likelihood of them meeting in the near future. It seemed strange, that such a great passion should meet its sorry end on a remote country track, with no formalities and no one else even being aware of the cataclysmic event that was taking place.

Henry was impatient to be gone, to fight his battle and to have the awkward moment over and done with. He reined in his restive mount, leaned across his saddle, gave Eleanor the briefest of kisses, and gruffly wished her Godspeed. She remained seated erect on her palfrey, regarding him with sad eyes, which he would not meet.

'Goodbye, my Lord,' she said softly. 'I pray God keep you safe, and that we may meet again in this world.'

Henry nodded to her – she suspected, indeed hoped, that he could not trust himself to speak – then wheeled around and shouted to his train to follow him. Eleanor watched as he rode away from her towards Lusignan, clouds of dust in his wake. Then she turned to Earl Patrick, forced a bright smile, and spurred her horse in the direction of Poitiers. Home. She was going home, after her long exile.

For all Eleanor's sorrows, it was wonderful to be back in residence in the Maubergeonne Tower. The Duchess's apartments had recently been refurbished, and were both spacious and luxurious. Eleanor walked about them hugging herself, and fingering in delight the soft squirrel counterpane on the bed and the silky fabric of the cushions. Every room was vivid with colour: deep indigo blues, forest greens and warm reds. There were hangings depicting erotic scenes of nymphs bathing in mythical streams and lovers entwined in forbidden pleasures. Vases of aquamarine glass and porphyry graced the brightly painted cupboards and windowsills. In the Duchess's solar, a silver ewer of wine had thoughtfully been placed on the wide table before the fireplace, and an ivory chess set had been left awaiting her pleasure, while in the corner of the room, a portable altar stood on an armoire that had been spread with an embroidered cloth.

Supper was a delight. Truffles! She hadn't tasted them in years, and they were as ambrosia to one who had had to put up with the less refined cuisine to be had in England. They were followed by a plate of duck roasted in its own fat, which was utterly delicious! And peaches and apricots, plump and juicy, such as were never seen in the kingdoms of the north. It was a happier homecoming than she had anticipated.

As she lay back on fine linen sheets in her bathtub, with Mamille and Torqueri and Florine washing her with herb-scented water and massaging limbs that were aching after days in the saddle, Eleanor began to unwind, and to feel a sense of well-being that had long been absent from her life. Here, she was the Duchess. She could please herself. She did not have to consider the moods and caprices of her husband. Almost, she felt a sense of liberation.

To boost her new confidence, she began ordering the finest textiles to be made into gowns and cloaks, and commissioned from the goldsmiths of Poitiers elegant jewellery – circlets, bracelets and brooches – wrought in the latest styles. Wearing her fine new attire made her feel more like her bold former self again, and helped her to slough off the feelings of worthlessness that had been the legacy of Henry's betrayal. She forced herself not to think of him, and to embrace her new life whole-heartedly. For this was what she had long wanted, she told herself. *Yet not like this, not like this!* cried her persistent inner voice.

Resolutely, she occupied herself with the business of ruling her duchy, taking a particular and genuine interest in every aspect of its welfare. Daily, she would occupy her high seat at the head of the council table, and patiently listen to the arguments and advice of her seigneurs. Important decisions always had to be referred to Henry for ratification, and there was a constant stream of messengers between Aquitaine and the north. No one, especially Eleanor, liked this alien interference in the affairs of her domains; the Duke had never been accepted by her people, and he was hated and resented. But power over her lands was his right, as her husband, and she kept reminding herself, in all fairness, that Henry was allowing her a considerable degree of autonomy.

When she was not in council, she was out riding or hawking, or spending tine with the children who were left to her. Presently, with Henry's blessing, Young Henry and his wife Marguerite travelled south to enter her household, joining Richard, Geoffrey and Constance; and with this blithe crowd of young people to cheer her, life in the palace was lively and joyful, a panacea for Eleanor's inner heartache. She was never alone; she had made sure of that, having summoned sixty ladies to wait upon her and cheer her days, and there was always dear Raoul de Faye to give her succour and advice in the business of governing – and to pay her meaningful compliments, as if he still hoped to win her favour in more intimate ways.

This was very heartening, for she was forty-six years old and given to looking anxiously in her mirror for the dreaded signs of encroaching old age. Yet the image reflected back in the burnished silver was of a fine-boned woman with lips that were still full and eyes that could flash wittily and invite to conversation . . . and more. Beneath the veil, her red-gold hair was paler than it had been, and well silvered with grey, but it was still long and luxuriant, and rippled down over breasts that were yet full and voluptuous. Maybe, thought Eleanor wistfully, just maybe, she might even take another lover, since Henry was no longer interested. But it would not be Raoul. She loved him, and depended on him, as a friend and an uncle, but she did not want him in her bed.

Patrick proved himself to be a charming and witty companion. She sensed that he liked her, and could see in his hazelnut-coloured eyes the kind of admiration she had inspired in men many times in the past. It was balm to her bruised pride. She thought that Raoul saw it too, and was jealous. But Raoul was not to nurture his jealousy for long.

The spring being glorious, with flowers budding unseasonably early, and the winds mild and gentle, Eleanor planned a hawking expedition with Earl Patrick. Word had reached them that Henry had efficiently crushed the rising at Lusignan, then ridden north to treat with Louis – the news that he had gone so far from her sparking a twinge of anguish in Eleanor's breast – and now Patrick had deemed it safe to ride out for the day.

'There have been no recent reports of any trouble,' he smiled, 'so I'll leave my armour at home, and we'll take just a small escort.'

It was good to be out in the sunshine, Eleanor found, even though her heart was heavy. She was surprised to discover herself thrilling to the sport, watching her mighty falcon soar into the blue sky and swoop with unerring precision to catch its prey, then return to her outstretched hand and settle on her glove, meekly accepting of its gay scarlet hood and the jesses with which she tethered it.

'Bravo, my Lady!' exclaimed Earl Patrick. The men-at-arms clapped and cheered admiringly from a distance; they them-selves would never be privileged enough even to touch a royal bird like Eleanor's.

The ambush, when it came, was sudden and deadly, with mounted armed men closing in on them from every side, uttering blood-curdling war cries.

'It's the Lusignans!' the Earl cried, frantic. 'À moi! À moi!'

Eleanor quickly collected herself; in that instant, she could see herself being captured and ransomed, if not worse. But as she made to gallop away, Earl Patrick, shouting orders to his men, dismounted from his horse, quick as lightning, and grabbed her bridle.

'Take my steed, my Lady, you'll not find a faster in Christendom.' Eleanor wasted not a moment in swapping mounts, as the Earl told her to make for a ruined castle a mile distant and wait for him there.

Their assailants were almost upon them as Eleanor, spurring her borrowed steed, deftly evaded them by almost flying through the only gap in their ranks, then cantered off like the wind towards safety. They would have come after her had not Earl Patrick and his escort engaged them furiously in battle. As the Queen rode away, she could hear the clash of steel and the shouts of men receding into the distance, and was in a fever of anxiety to know which way the combat was going.

Having ridden like the wind over a seemingly endless distance before reaching the sanctuary of the ruins, Eleanor stood fuming in the peace of the afternoon. How dare the Lusignans make an attempt on her person! No doubt they wished to wring concessions from Henry. Wait until he heard! Then she paused. She was ruler here now, not Henry. Undoubtedly he would come and deal with them, if summoned; he would be furious on her account, if only because she was his queen and duchess, but she decided now that she must prove to him that she did not need him, and show him that she was capable of dealing with problems efficiently by herself.

She waited an hour or so, becoming increasingly anxious. Then she heard horses' hooves, and shrank back behind some lichen-covered masonry until she could assure herself that it was her escort – or what was left of it – come to find her. She shuddered. How bad had it been?

'Lady,' called the captain, a big, florid man, and when Eleanor emerged, he dismounted, fell to his knees and spoke in a voice harsh with emotion. 'I bear heavy news. Earl Patrick is dead, stabbed in the back by the traitors as he donned his hauberk.'

'Oh, dear God!' Eleanor wailed. 'That chivalrous man! Those bastards! I will repay them, by God, for they have added grievous injury to grievous insult.' And she smote her balled fist in her palm. Then fear gripped her.

'Are they defeated, these rebels? Where are they?'

'Gone back to their castle,' the captain told her. 'It was the young knight, John the Marshal's son William, who held them off, with great courage and skill, until he himself was wounded and captured. They took him with them, my Lady, no doubt hoping for a fat ransom.'

'And they shall have it,' said Eleanor, fighting down her fury and thinking of the tall, dignified young man who had so bravely defended her. He was, she was aware, a soldier of fortune, who had made a reputation as a champion in tournaments, winning many rich prizes. She herself had watched him distinguish himself in the lists, and been much impressed.

'They are bringing Earl Patrick's body, Lady,' the captain told her, indicating a small party of his men approaching on horse-back. She froze as she espied the bloody corpse of the former governor slumped across a saddle, but resolutely she walked forward to pay all due honour to it, bowing her head in grief and respect.

'We will have him buried in Poitiers and pay for Masses to be said for his soul,' she declared, suppressing her emotion. There would be time enough for weeping later. 'Letters must be sent to his family in England.'

And so it was done, and the young William Marshal was, at length, ransomed. When he presented himself before the Duchess, brimming with gratitude, she gave him a gift of money and expressed concern about his wounds.

'They are healing, my Lady,' he said cheerfully, 'yet no thanks to Guy of Lusignan. He and his followers refused to have them dressed.' As Eleanor gasped in horror, he smiled at her. 'It is no matter, for I count it an honour to have served you thus, my Queen.'

'It is rare to find such loyalty,' Eleanor told him. 'They tell me you fought as a wild boar against dogs. I owe you much, possibly my very life. Rest assured, the King my Lord will come to hear of your valour.'

It occurred to her, as she kept a proprietorial eye on William Marshal in the weeks that followed, and her admiration for him grew, that he would make a fine mentor for Young Henry; and in due course, with the King's approval, he was appointed guardian, tutor and master of chivalry to the prince, a role that Becket had once filled. Thankfully, there was little risk of this fine knight causing such grief as Becket had. He performed his role magnificently, and Eleanor rewarded him lavishly, with horses, arms, gold and fine clothing. William was proving to be, she knew – and as her contemporaries would soon come to agree – one of the best knights who ever lived.

Henry had met with Louis and, for once, Eleanor had cause to be grateful to her former husband. They had thrashed out a peace, and Louis had given Henry wise advice regarding the disposing of his empire after his death. Her heart was immeasurably gladdened when the King's messenger brought news of the agreement that had been reached.

'The Lord Henry is to pay homage to the French King for Anjou, Maine and Brittany; the Lord Geoffrey is to hold Brittany as the Lord Henry's vassal; and the Lord Richard is to pay homage to King Louis for Aquitaine, and be betrothed to the French King's daughter, Alys.'

Richard was to have Aquitaine after all! Her prayers had been answered. Her first thought, as she went rejoicing to her chapel to give thanks, was that Henry had done this for her, as a peace offering. Then she remembered that he had ignored her pleadings and her displays of anger on numerous occasions before, and that he never did anything unless there was a political motive. The truth, she guessed, was that Louis, fearing the power of his Angevin vassals, had urged the division of Henry's domains on his death, and made that a condition of the peace. She wondered if Henry was making a virtue of expediency, and began to fear that he might well renege on the new treaty as soon as the opportunity presented itself.

She had written to Henry, informing him of the outrage committed by the Lusignans, as her duty bound her; and, as she had anticipated, he sent immediately to inform her that he was coming to teach the traitors a lesson they would never forget. She hoped that he would stop by in Poitiers to see her, so that she could thank him for settling Aquitaine on Richard, and thereby mend matters between them a little. But the next she heard, from another exhausted travel-stained messenger, was that Henry had been unexpectedly diverted from his purpose, and had had to march on Brittany to quell a rising by Eudes de Porhoët, the father of Count Conan.

'But Conan's family are our allies!' she exclaimed. 'Eudes's granddaughter Constance is married to the Lord Geoffrey. His daughter Alice is in the custody of the King, as surety for her father's friendship. This is madness.'

The royal messenger flushed and looked at her somewhat shiftily, she thought.

'You must tell me what has happened,' she commanded, her tone sharpened by alarm.

The man looked at his feet and twisted his felt hat in his hands.

'It is said that the Lord King lay with the Lady Alice, and that she has borne him a child that died. Her kin have risen up in anger, for the young lady was a hostage in the Lord King's household.'

At his words, Eleanor froze. Was there no end to Henry's betrayals? And when would he cease having the power to hurt her? She had liked to think that she was free of him, and that she was the stronger for it, but it was tidings like this that proved to her that she was still in some thrall to him.

She dismissed the messenger and withdrew to her bower, trying to seek solace in music and the chatter of her ladies. But however hard she tried, she could not dismiss from her imaginings the horrible, disturbing image of Henry getting Alice de Porhoët pregnant.

Sick to the heart, her delight in Richard's future being settled so unhappily deflated, Eleanor resolved to stay in Aquitaine for good. She told herself, firmly and adamantly, that she would never go back to Henry and live with him as his wife. From now on, they would be political allies, no more. She would henceforth invest all her love and care in her heir, her beloved Richard, and forget her faithless husband. Nowadays, she had come to the comforting realisation that her love for Richard was greater than what she had ever felt for Henry – apart from the passion that her husband had inspired in her physically. But that had died long ago.

Richard was now eleven, shooting up and developing strong muscles. She took great pride in his prowess, both in book learning and military exercises. She marvelled at his dexterity in Latin, and herself taught him to play the lyre and to compose verses in French and Provençal; his voice was high and true, and she thrilled to hear him singing with the choir of her private chapel. Tall, ruddy-haired and slender, he was, in most respects, his mother's son. He had her straight-nosed profile and fine bone structure. There was little of Henry in him – save for a streak of Angevin devilment and ruthlessness, already apparent. Never mind, she told herself: a ruler needed to be firm and establish his authority, and he must be fierce in battle. Richard had what it took, in abundant measure. He was her true heir in every way, for he had the south in his blood, as she did. He would do well: he was destined for greatness. She knew it in her bones.

For much of that year, Eleanor stayed in Poitiers, governing her domains with wisdom and firmness. Her presence in the duchy did much to heal the wounds dealt by decades of foreign rule by both her husbands in turn, and she was intent on making every effort to win back the love and loyalty of her vassals.

As soon as she had re-established herself in the duchy, she made a progress through her lands, her purpose being to greet and cultivate her lords, and be seen by them. If force had failed to establish central authority in Aquitaine, she would do it by love and peaceful persuasion. She travelled south, stopping first at the flourishing port of Niort, where she held court in the massive square fortress built by Henry, and was feasted by the locals with eels and snails from the nearby marshlands, and little cakes studded with angelica, a local delicacy. She promised that, in due course, she would grant the town a charter and new privileges, and was gratified by the delighted response of the worthy burghers.

Then she rode further south to Limoges, to repair the damage done by Henry, sixteen years before, when he had ordered the walls to be torn down. She admired the new fortifications, granted boons and received local lords, then moved on to the Périgord, land of the great rivers, the Vézère and the Dordogne, a region populated with flocks of plump ducks and grey geese. Here, she gloried in the deep-cut valleys nestling beneath limestone cliffs and caves, the lush dark woodlands, the fields of maize, the orchards of walnut trees, the bustling towns and hilltop villages, the mighty castles and humble churches, all basking in the golden sun. The people came with their gifts and their blessings, even the seigneurs who ruled these often lawless valleys bent the knee to her and swore fealty. She began to feel whole again, enveloped by the love of her people, cherished in the heart of her duchy, fêted by both the high-born and the lowly.

She swept westwards to Bayonne on the coast, near the foothills of the mighty Pyrenees, and then north again to Poitiers, lodging at castles, manor houses or abbeys on the way. Everywhere she went, her subjects came thronging, calling down blessings upon her and bringing her their humble petitions and grievances. She read them all, dispensing justice with fairness and humanity, and earning herself a reputation for wisdom and generosity. She had left Poitiers a sad, disillusioned wife struggling to break free of the past; she returned to it a happy, confident and jubilant woman, thankful to have won her independence.

Eleanor had written to tell Henry of her resolve to separate from him for good. It had been one of the most difficult letters she had ever composed in her life, but she felt better after she had set her mind down on parchment; in fact, she felt strangely liberated. Love for which one paid a high price in sorrow and humiliation was just not worth having. She might have feelings for Henry still, but overriding those, at least for the present, was relief at having distanced herself from the torment that their marriage had become.

He wrote back: 'I am as troubled as Oedipus about the rift between us, yet I will not oppose your decision.' Oedipus! Great Heaven! Did he now think of her as a mother-figure, no more? God's blood, she swore to herself, that trollop Rosamund was welcome to him!

There was balm to her hurt pride in the courtly adoration of the troubadours who had flocked to her court, overjoyed to be once more dedicating songs of love and beauty to their famed duchess. Their praises warmed her heart, for she knew she was no longer the glorious young woman who had inspired such chivalrous verse in the past; and yet still they sang of the incomparable loveliness of their noble Eleanor.

It was a luxury, after so many years of what now felt like exile, to be living in the midst of a civilisation that celebrated love in all its forms. Indeed, it was a delight to sit in a sun-baked arbour of an afternoon, discussing with her lords and ladies this most fascinating of subjects, with her courtiers gathered around, hanging on her every word.

'They do not speak of love in the kingdoms of the north as we do here in Aquitaine,' Eleanor told her astonished listeners. 'They think that love, as we honour it, is merely an excuse for adultery. My Lord Henry could never understand our culture.'

'Love,' declared the young troubadour Rigaud de Barbezieux, 'is the bedrock of happy relations between men and women.'

'There can only be true happiness when lovers meet on an equal footing, which is rare,' Eleanor said. 'For there is no equality in marriage, and our courtly code dictates that the suitor is always a supplicant to his mistress.'

'Then how can men and women ever come together as equals?' Torqueri asked, her smooth brow puckered in a frown. 'It can never be in a world in which we women are treated either as chattels or whores.'

'I thank God that our customs in Aquitaine favour women,' Eleanor smiled. 'Torqueri is right. In the north, women *are* just chattels. But here, thanks to our freer society, they live on pedestals! You see why I wanted to come home!'

'Did they not treat you with respect in the north, Madame?' a young lady asked, shocked.

'Yes, of course – I am the Queen, and they dared not scant their respect. But woe betide any troubadour who praised my beauty in a song, or dared to imagine himself in my bed! I tell you, they cannot understand that it is a harmless conceit.'

Bertran de Born, a wild and dangerous young man who was as skilled with the sword as with the lyre, bared his teeth in a wolfish grin. 'Whoever said it was harmless?'

'A lady is not supposed to condescend to give her favours to a man of lesser rank,' Mamille reproved primly.

'Then, since marriages are made for policy, how will she find love?' Bertran quizzed her. 'In truth, no man looks to find love in the marriage bed.'

'I would question that,' Eleanor put in, enjoying this discussion immensely.

'Madame, begging your pardon, I contend that true love cannot exist between husband and wife,' Bertran challenged. 'It must be looked for elsewhere. And I have to say that, although the object of one's desire is not supposed to condescend to a humble suitor, many do!' There were cries of outrage from the ladies present.

'Sir, you are lacking in chivalry, and breaking the rules of the game,' Eleanor chided.

'But Madame, you cannot agree that love can flourish within marriage,' Bertran persisted.

'I would not believe it,' Rigaud murmured.

Eleanor's smile faded. It was as if a cloud had passed over the sun. 'I do believe that love may be found in marriage,' she

270

said at length, 'if the partners be two kindred souls, which is rare, I grant you. But . . .' Her voice grew distant, her tone chill. 'But where the husband insists on being master, and has the right to take what he wants, rather than sue for it, love cannot flourish, for I truly believe, as I said before, that love must be given freely in a relationship of equals.'

'But that leads us back to the burning question. How can men and women ever enjoy such a relationship?' Bertran protested. 'In marriage, the husband is lord; in courtship, the mistress grants favours, if it please her.'

Eleanor laughed suddenly, and tapped him on the shoulder. 'You tell us, Messire de Born! What about all those ladies who have condescended – of whom you have just spoken? You must know all about love in a partnership of equals!' There was general laughter, as Bertran smirked and nodded, conceding defeat.

'Love?' Torqueri giggled. 'What does he know of it? All he thinks of is that unruly little devil in his *braies*!'

'I object to the word "little"!' Bertran roared.

'I should know,' retorted Torqueri archly, to more splutterings of glee. It was all very pleasant, Eleanor thought, sitting here, feeling completely at home and enjoying such idle discourse. Love, she reflected, was perhaps not the most important thing in the world, despite what the troubadours claimed; and there were many compensations for its loss. She knew now that she could live alone, at peace in her own company, and that she could face the future with equanimity. The battle had been a long one, but she had won it.

38 Caen, Normandy, and Poitiers, 1170

Henry had aged in the two years since Eleanor had last seen him. His red hair was streaked with grey, there were lines of strain etched on his face, and he had put on more weight. He greeted her formally with a kiss on the cheek, one prince to another, his face betraying no emotion; then, taking her hand, he led her into the grand Hall of the Exchequer in Caen, his courtiers bowing as they passed.

'I would not have summoned you north in the depth of winter, had it not been important for us to show solidarity on this issue,' he explained.

'You are resolved on having Young Henry crowned King of England now, I understand,' Eleanor stated.

'Yes. It is customary in England to wait until a ruler succeeds, but all the French kings back to Charlemagne have had their heirs crowned in their lifetimes, and I am of the opinion that it is a good way of safeguarding the succession. No doubt the English will grumble, as they dislike anything that breaks with tradition, but they will get used to it. There is but one obstacle to my plan.'

'Becket,' Eleanor said, without hesitation.

'Yes,' sighed Henry, 'but we will discuss that over dinner.' He led her into a fine vaulted chamber hung with tapestries portraying hunting scenes. 'Some wine?'

'Thank you,' Eleanor said politely, trying to recall the passion that had once existed between them, and failing, for it seemed that they had become two strangers. 'Did you have a pleasant Christmas?'

'Yes,' Henry replied. 'I kept it at Nantes in Brittany, with Geoffrey and Constance. It's a pity you were not there at Rennes last spring, to see Geoffrey invested with the ducal crown.'

'I am sorry I could not be there. I was on progress in Aquitaine. But Geoffrey told me all about it, and Constance was full of it, and puffed up with her own importance, the little minx.' She grimaced at the memory.

'Geoffrey will have his hands full with that one,' Henry chuckled. 'Thank God he won't be bedding her for several years to come.'

'So all is quiet in Brittany now?' she could not resist saying. It was ancient history, the rising of Eudes de Porhoët, but she wanted to make Henry sweat a little over it. He gave her a quizzical look, then turned away.

'You heard,' he said.

'All Europe heard!' she answered tartly. 'How could *I* fail to hear?'

'Eleanor, I did not ask you here to fight with you.' Henry's tone was almost pleading. 'You asked for your freedom, and you have it. At least allow me mine.'

'Naturally,' she said sweetly. 'I trust that Rosamund – "Fair Rosamund", as I hear they now call her – how charming that sounds! – wasn't too upset by it. She is still your mistress, I take it?'

'Vixen!' Henry barked. 'You haven't been here five minutes, and you're picking a quarrel with me.'

'Yes, but I've been storing up a few things to say to you over the past two years,' Eleanor riposted.

'Actually, it is good to see you,' Henry said. 'Don't spoil it.'

'How touching!' she exclaimed, smiling a touch too gaily.

'We need to work together now,' he told her, frowning. 'Shall we call a truce?'

'A truce!' The smile seemed to be fixed on her face. 'If you will.'

They dined in the solar, the servitors having withdrawn after laying out the food on a side table, from which they helped themselves.

When they were seated, Henry wasted no time in returning to the subject of Young Henry's coronation.

'What I want,' he began, 'is to see Thomas restored to his rightful place in Canterbury, and an end to this interminable wrangling. It is fitting that the Archchbishop of Canterbury perform the ceremony.'

'But I heard you had quarrelled again with Becket last year?'

Henry sighed deeply. 'Indeed I did. Louis had offered to mediate – once more – and, at his suggestion, I sent to tell Thomas that I would support his reinstatement if he would retract his condemnation of the Constitutions of Clarendon. And he agreed, Eleanor! He said he would do it.'

'So what went wrong?' She had heard several garbled versions of what had actually taken place, and had not known which to believe.

'He came to see me. We hadn't set eyes on each other for four years, so you can imagine how I felt. He fell on his knees, then prostrated himself fully before me, begging for mercy.'

'He was ever one for the grand gesture,' Eleanor observed acidly.

'You sound just like my mother, God rest her,' Henry objected.

'Your mother was a very wise woman – she had the measure of this man.'

'Look, I am trying to tell you what happened,' Henry protested.

'Go on then,' she said coolly.

'Well, I thought that would be it. We'd exchange the kiss of peace, he'd go home to Canterbury, and we'd all live happily ever after.'

'Henry, this is Thomas Becket we are talking about. Nothing is ever straightforward with this priest. What did he do?'

Henry flung her a hurt look, but resumed his tale without rising to the bait. 'He ruined it all. He said he would submit to my pleasure in all things saving the honour of God, and that it did not become a priest to submit to the will of a layman. By which I knew, beyond doubt, that we were back to where we'd started.'

'And what did you do?'

'I lost my temper. I swore at him and walked out, with everyone in an uproar, and Louis trying ineffectively to tell Thomas that he was being too obstinate. And that was that. Becket stormed back to his cloister, and has been sulking there ever since, God damn him.'

Eleanor rose, took her plate to the buffet, and speared two more pieces of chicken with her knife. 'So where do we go from here?' she asked.

'I propose – and I want your approval for this – to have our loyal friend Roger, Archbishop of York, crown Young Henry instead.'

Eleanor turned and stared at him. 'You know that Becket would see that as a gross insult?'

'I do,' Henry replied defiantly, 'and I know too that it would offend those who love tradition. But I cannot afford to let this infernal priest interfere with my plans. Do you agree?'

'Absolutely. It might be a way of bringing Becket to heel.'

But it was not.

'He has threatened me with excommunication if I order Archbishop Roger to officiate at the crowning,' Henry roared. 'What's more, he has complained to the Pope, and His Holiness has forbidden it, also on pain of excommunication. And any bishop or priest who takes part in the ceremony will also be subject to anathema. It is not to be borne, and by the eyes of God, I will defy them both! I am going to England now, to see the thing done, and I want you to stay here and govern Normandy in my absence.'

'You know you have my support,' Eleanor told him. He looked at her for a lingering moment, his expression warmer than she had seen it in years. But he said nothing; his mind was on practicalities.

'Close all the ports and keep them closed until you hear from me,' he commanded. 'We don't want our friend Thomas crossing the Channel and spoiling things.'

'What of your bishops?'

'Leave me to bully them. They know what's good for them. When all is ready, I will send for Young Henry. I leave it to you to ensure that he comes with a suitable escort. Add a couple of bishops for good measure, so that the people may believe this is done with the blessing of the Church. You'll know how to cozen your prelates.'

'You may safely leave all that to me,' Eleanor assured him. 'What of young Marguerite? Is she to be crowned too?'

'No. I dare not risk offending Louis at this time. He might be upset at my defying the Pope. Keep the wench with you. Tell her I will arrange a second crowning later, when Becket has come to his senses.'

Eleanor was convinced that Henry was doing the right thing, and she was touched that he now had such a good opinion of her abilities as a ruler that he trusted her to hold Normandy in his absence; but her heart grieved that she would not be there in Westminster Abbey to see her son, her golden boy, made a king. On the day appointed, Sunday, the fourteenth day of June, she had special prayers offered up for him at Mass, and spent hours on her knees, with Marguerite at her side, beseeching God to bless and direct him in his high office.

With the Channel ports open once again, messengers were able to bring her reports of the coronation.

'The Young King cut a fine figure in his crown and robes of

estate, my Lady! People were saying he was the most handsome prince in all the world.'

'He was debonair and gallant, every inch the King, and only a little lower than the angels!'

'Some called him beautiful above all others in form and face. He is blessed in courtesy, most happy in the love of men, and has found grace and favour with his future subjects.'

Eleanor's spirit soared when she heard these paeans of praise, yet there was one report that did not come to her directly by way of a royal messenger, but through the gossip of a lady betrothed to a knight who had been at the coronation banquet and had now come home to be married. Entering her bower, she overheard this damsel telling the others that the Young King had shown grave disrespect to his father. Then they suddenly realised that Eleanor had come upon them, and there was an embarrassed silence.

'Well?' Eleanor probed. 'Pray continue.'

'My Lady, forgive me, I should not be saying this to you,' the girl faltered.

'On the contrary, it is my son of whom you speak, and therefore my business. Go on!' she rapped.

'My Lady, my betrothed told me that the Lord King insisted on acting as servitor to the Young King, and when he carried the boar's head on a platter to the high table, he jested that it was unusual to see a king wait at table. But the Young King replied that it was no condescension to see the son of a count wait upon the son of a king – and – and he was not joking, my Lady.'

Eleanor concealed her dismay well. 'I suggest you cease spreading idle gossip like this, young lady,' she chided. 'Now, fetch my embroidery.'

The story rang true, though, and she decided to have a word with William Marshal, who was about to leave for England to head the new household that Henry had set up for the Young King, and tell him to exhort his charge, on her behalf, always to show the proper respect and deference for his father.

With Geoffrey and the Young King formally invested with the crowns and insignia of their future inheritances, it was now Richard's turn. As Eleanor's heir, he was to be installed as count of Poitou in Poitiers, and it was there that Eleanor travelled that summer. She thought she would burst with pride as she stood in the Abbey of St Hilaire and watched as the Archbishop of Bordeaux solemnly gave her twelve-year-old hero the holy lance and standard of the city's patron saint. Then she escorted Richard to Niort, where he received the homage of the lords of Poitou, holding himself with dignity and pride. Afterwards, she and he sat together on identical thrones at a feast to mark the occasion, which was followed by a series of tournaments that Eleanor had arranged for Richard's delight. Already, he was champing at the bit to take part in them himself, and his instructors told her that it would not be long before he was fully competent to do so. The prospect chilled her a little, for jousts were often brutal and bloodthirsty contests, but so great was her delight in her boy's prowess that she was determined to quell her fears for him. In a year or so, she promised him, he could have his wish.

39 Rocamadour, 1170

Eleanor knelt beside Henry in the dim church, her eyes dazzled by the multitude of candles that blazed before the shrine of the miraculous black Madonna. This was one of the most holy sanctums in her domains, a place of pilgrimage for countless numbers of the faithful. Perched on a sheer cliff, high above the straggling village of Rocamadour overlooking the River Alzou, the shrine could only be accessed by a steep stone stairway. In accordance with pious custom, the King and Queen had knelt on every one of its two hundred and sixteen steps as they made their slow ascent, in the company of their lords and ladies and many humbler pilgrims. They had come to venerate blessed St Amadour, who had escaped from his perse-cutors after the Crucifixion of Christ, then taken the Virgin Mary's advice and fled to this land of Quercy, ending his days as a hermit. His sacred bones lay beneath the floor of the *Chapelle Miraculeuse*, the holy of holies, and above his resting place had been reverently set the dark wooden statue of the Virgin and Child. Above that hung a bell, which was said to ring sponta-neously whenever a miracle was about to take place.

Henry and Eleanor were not looking for miracles. The time for that, Eleanor thought sadly, was long past, although she was grateful that they had at last reached a state of peaceable amity and accord. No, they had come, on this golden October day, to give thanks for Henry's recovery from the tertian fever that had very nearly killed him in August.

For this, Eleanor blamed Becket. Of course, the Archbishop could not have sent the fever itself, but by his conduct he had caused the King so much grief that he was more susceptible than usual to illness. For Becket and the Pope had been outraged at Henry's defiance, and for a time there had been fears that both the King and his kingdom would be placed under an interdict. But then Louis had intervened, and the Pope had changed his tune and insisted that Henry and Becket make up their quarrel. Henry had immediately declared that he was ready to make peace, and, through the good offices of King Louis, he had met with Becket in the forest of Fréteval, south of Paris, in June.

When the King's party and the Queen's joined up on the road to Rocamadour, a thinner Henry looking pale and exhausted after his illness, he had told Eleanor what had passed on that fateful day.

'I threw my arms around Thomas. I could not help myself,' he stated, looking at her as if he expected her to make some biting remark. But she was so shocked at the change in him, and by his apparent vulnerability, that she had no heart to criticise.

'Who spoke first?' she asked.

'I did. I gave him fair words. I told him that we should go back to our old love for each other, and do all the good we could for each other, and forget utterly the hatred that had gone before.' Henry's voice cracked with emotion. 'I admitted I had been wrong to defy the Church over the coronation, and I asked him to return in peace to Canterbury and crown Young Henry again, with Marguerite this time. And he agreed.'

'Was he conciliatory?' Eleanor wanted to know. 'Did he come in the same spirit of friendship?'

'Yes, I think so,' Henry answered. 'Although neither of us

referred to the Constitutions of Clarendon. We'll have to tackle that issue sometime, and until then, I have forborne to give Thomas the kiss of peace, although I have promised to do so when I return to England. I just haven't said when.' He looked at her with a trace of his former mischievous grin.

'So you gave him permission to return to Canterbury?'

'Yes, but before I could make any arrangements, I fell ill with that damned fever.'

Kneeling beside Henry now, and remembering how they had brought her piece after piece of ill news – that he was unwell, that his life was despaired of, that he had made his will – and how, for one long, dreadful day, she had believed a false report that he was dead, Eleanor shuddered. Confronting mortality had certainly had a profound effect on her husband: it had been he who had insisted on making this pilgrimage to give thanks for his recovery, and on her coming with him. Had he repented of his immoral life? Was Rosamund still his mistress? She dared not ask.

Their thanks offered, and feeling the better for it, they emerged into the sunlight and began the long descent to the valley below, where their horses waited. Then Henry rode with Eleanor north through Aquitaine, and at Poitiers he helped her to catch up on the business that had been left in abeyance during her absence. It was then that he told her he had broken their daughter Eleanor's betrothal to the son of the Emperor Frederick Barbarossa.

'The Emperor is no longer my friend,' he explained. 'It will be far more profitable to me to extend my influence south of the Pyrenees by marrying Young Eleanor to King Alfonso of Castile. She shall have Gascony as her dowry. Yes, I know, Gascony is yours,' he added hastily, seeing his wife's face. 'She shall have it only on your death.'

'Very well,' Eleanor agreed. 'It will be a good match for her.'

It was soon time for Henry to depart for Normandy.

'I will be arranging a safe-conduct for Becket to return to England,' he said. 'I will let Young Henry know that his reinstatement as archbishop has my full approval. Then I shall meet again with Becket before he departs – and try to avoid mentioning the Constitutions of Clarendon!'

'May God be with you, my Lord,' Eleanor said formally. In truth, she was sad to see him go.

'And with you, my Lady,' Henry answered, his eyes searching hers, and meeting only an unfathomable stare.

40 Chaumont-sur-Loire, 1170

When the Archbishop entered the great hall of the castle of Chaumont, shivering in the dank chill of a November afternoon, the King rose to his feet, walked forward and warmly embraced him. The two men gazed upon each other for a space.

'Welcome, my friend,' said Henry.

After they had talked of generalities for a while, Thomas looked directly at him. 'My Lord,' he confessed, 'I am afraid.'

'There is no need,' Henry reassured him. 'All is ready for your return.'

'It is not that,' Becket said quietly. 'My mind tells me that I will never see you again in this life.'

Henry stiffened. What was the man saying? His anger rose like bile.

'I told you, Thomas, I have smoothed the way for you. What do you take me for? A traitor to my word? Do you think I have plotted to have you done away with, and am sending you to your doom?'

'God forbid, my Lord!' Becket cried. 'Nothing was further from my mind. It was but a premonition of some evil.'

But Henry was barely mollified. 'Then give it no credence!' he snapped. 'I shall see you in England, make no doubt of it.'

'I hope so, my Lord,' Becket said. 'Farewell.' Henry just glared at him and watched him leave, a monk bearing his crozier in tow.

41 Bures, 1170

Henry had summoned Eleanor to keep Christmas with him at his hunting lodge at Bures in Normandy, and there she was, on Christmas Day itself, seated beside him at the high table, resplendent in her green fur-trimmed *bliaut* and her great mantle of crimson damask. Most of their children were present also, seated further along the board, above the salt, as was fitting. Richard was beside his mother, next to Geoffrey and Constance; decorous Joanna and even John, now a tousle-haired, unruly four-year-old, had been brought from Fontevrault for the occasion; Young Eleanor, sadly, had had to be left in the care of the nuns, for she was suffering from a winter ague and had been deemed unfit to travel. The Young King was, of course, not here: he was in England, holding his first Christmas court at Winchester.

It was late, and, seeing the King and his lords becoming rather the worse for wear after a surfeit of rich food and wine, the Queen signalled to the nurse to take the younger children to bed. 'You go too, Constance,' she said. The pert girl made a face, but dared not disobey. After she had gone, Richard and Geoffrey fell happily to squabbling over a game of dice, and Eleanor tried to join in the increasingly incoherent conversation at table.

She was just thinking of retiring for the night when the steward entered the hall and announced the arrival of the Archbishop of York and the bishops of London and Salisbury. 'They crave an audience, Sire. They have come all the way from England,' he said.

'In this foul weather?' Eleanor was immediately concerned to know what their arrival portended. Surely the bishops would not have attempted to cross the turbulent Channel unless they had urgent news to impart.

Henry had suddenly sobered up.

'Show them in,' he ordered, then, belching, rose to receive them.

The formalities briefly disposed of, the tall and cultivated Archbishop Roger spoke gravely for all three, with the whole court hanging on to every word.

'Lord King, we come to make a strong complaint about the high-handed conduct of his Grace the Archbishop of Canterbury.'

Henry groaned. 'What has he done now?' he hissed.

'He has excommunicated the three of us, this very morning, from his pulpit at Canterbury, for our part in the coronation,' the Archbishop announced. As the barons erupted in shouts of fury, Henry stared at him in shock.

'But that was all resolved,' he said.

'This is outrageous,' Eleanor murmured, appalled at Becket's duplicity. 'It is not the way to make amends!'

'Apparently it was not resolved,' Bishop Foliot of London growled. 'It seems he has been cherishing his anger against those who defied him. I never had much opinion of him, as you know, and it seems I was right to doubt him. Sire, the Pope should be told of his disobedience.'

'By the eyes of God, Becket shall suffer for this!' Henry shouted, his voice vibrating with ire and indignation. 'Is this how he repays my offer of friendship?'

'My Lord,' said the Earl of Leicester, sitting nearby, 'enough is enough. While Thomas lives, you will not have peace or quiet, or see good days.'

'By God, you speak truth!' Henry cried, furious and indignant. 'Becket has gone too far this time. He is doing this only to spite me, and yet he brazenly claims to be defending the honour of God.'

'It is his own honour he holds so dear,' Eleanor said, keeping her tone even, for she had realised that Henry was getting perilously close to a full-scale display of the famously ungovernable Plantagenet temper. 'He is puffed up with the sin of pride. My Lord, you must appeal to the Pope.'

'I will have him defrocked!' Henry spluttered, banging his fist on the table so hard that several goblets were overturned. 'And then, when his office can no longer protect him, I will proceed against him as a traitor!'

'Get His Holiness on your side first,' Eleanor urged, but Henry wasn't listening; he was so distracted with anger that he was beside himself, spewing a fiery stream of wild threats, to the point where his outraged courtiers ceased their indignant chatter and watched him in amazement. Presently, seeing he was the object of their incredulous stares, he ceased his tirade and stood there shaking in a menacing, deadly silence, raking the room with narrowed, bloodshot eyes. Eleanor shivered. She had never seen him so consumed with hatred. She ventured to lay a calming hand on his arm, but he angrily shook her off, and directed his terrifying gaze at his nervous court.

'What cowards you all are!' he hissed. 'I curse you all! Yes, a curse, a curse, on all the false varlets and traitors whom I have nursed and promoted in my household, who allow their lord and king to be mocked with such shameful contempt by a low-born priest!'

There was a stunned hush. No one dared speak. Clearly, no one knew how to respond.

'Will no one rid me of this turbulent priest?' Henry shouted, then sat down heavily, and slumped with his head in his hands, his shoulders heaving, as, all around him, people looked at each other helplessly.

Eleanor was up on her feet in an instant, folding her arms around Henry, all other considerations set aside in her desire to alleviate his pain. So engrossed was she in her efforts to console him that, like many others present at that fateful feast, she did not espy four stalwart knights slipping away from the hall, their faces alight with purpose, their hands grasping their sword hilts.

Henry came to her bed that night, for the first time in almost five years. He came for comfort, rather than for sex, although he would have died before admitting it. And she, knowing his need, welcomed him back, and they were gentle with each other, embracing tightly, not having to say anything. It felt strange – and unexpectedly delightful – to have Henry in her arms again. For this feeling, she was ready to forgive him anything. She was deeply moved that, at this moment of crisis, he had turned to her before all others. And so, when the need for comfort translated itself into the need for something deeper, and he moved towards her in the old familiar way, and entered her, she felt only joy, and a beautiful inner peace that made her want to weep.

Their lovemaking was not the explosion of lust and fire that it had once been – that was long ago, and they were both, quite obviously, older now – but it was gloriously satisfying, and her climax, when it eventually came – for she was quite out of prac-tice, she thought ruefully – was shattering. It was as if all the pent-up desire of the barren, loveless years had been released in one go.

When the waves of pleasure had ebbed away, Eleanor lay quiet with Henry's arm about her, thinking that the long separation had allowed time for her wounds to heal and for many matters to be put in perspective. The old saw, about absence making the heart grow fonder, was very apposite, she realised. And the sensual meeting of two skins between the sheets was sweetly conducive to full reconciliation. Rosamund or no Rosamund, if Henry wanted her, she was ready to go back to him.

But when at length Henry spoke to her, it was not about any future they might have together. 'Eleanor, something is troubling me. Just before I left the hall, the steward told me that four of my knights had left the castle not long before. He thought it strange that they should go abroad so late on Christmas night.'

'Do you know who they were?' Eleanor asked.

'Yes. William de Tracy, who was once Becket's chancellor, Reginald FitzUrse, Richard de Brito and Hugh de Morville. Hugh's done good work as my justice in the north of England. From what I could make out, they left just after . . .' Henry's voice tailed off. He could not find words to describe his fit of rage.

Eleanor was suddenly suffused with alarm. She sat up abruptly.

'Oh, no! I hope to God they have not taken you literally at your word!'

'At my word?' Henry raised himself on an elbow.

'You do not remember? You asked for someone to rid you of Becket! You called him a turbulent priest.'

Henry leaped out of bed and reached for his robe. 'I must summon the knights back!' he cried, and was out of the door before he had barely covered his modesty, shouting to his guards. But it was too late. The four knights had long gone.

Eleanor spent the next two days with dread in her heart. Henry was convinced that his unthinking outburst was going to have disastrous consequences, and privately she shared his foreboding. But her words were all of reassurance.

'My Lord, you have sent men after them, so rest easy. And surely no man would even contemplate committing violence on the Archbishop of Canterbury?'

Henry turned frightened eyes to her. 'They heard me denigrate his office. They might well be convinced that his removal would put an end to this interminable quarrel, and actually serve the Church's interests.'

'I hardly think they will go that far,' Eleanor reasoned, with more confidence than she felt. 'Mayhap they have gone to tell Becket a few home truths and frighten him into submission. After all, the Pope must support you; Becket cannot win. He is done for, this time.'

'Done for indeed, I fear,' Henry muttered. His face was shadowed with foreboding.

42 Argentan, 1171

Unable to bear the tension, the King abandoned the Yuletide festivities, dismissed his guests, and removed with the Queen to Argentan. It was here that Brother Peter, a young monk from England, mud-spattered and exhausted from a hard ride, found him, just as he and Eleanor were entertaining Bishop Arnulf of Lisieux to supper in their private solar.

'Lord King,' the monk gasped, falling to his knees for sheer weariness. 'I bring terrible, dread news.'

Henry went white and clenched his knuckles. The Bishop leaped up, scraping back his chair.

'What news?' Eleanor asked sharply.

'My Lady, Archbishop Becket has been foully murdered, slain in his own cathedral two days ago, as he celebrated Vespers.'

Eleanor was momentarily speechless, unable to take in the enormity of what she had just heard. 'Murdered?' she repeated stupidly. 'The Archbishop of Canterbury?'

'He was cruelly slain by four of the King's knights,' Brother Peter said, himself deeply distressed.

'Oh, God!' Henry wailed suddenly, beating his breast. 'Thomas, my Thomas! May God forgive me – this is my doing. I have killed him, as surely as if I strangled him with my own hands.' Tears were streaming down his face, and great sobs wracking his stocky frame.

'May God avenge him,' the Bishop murmured, crossing himself, appalled to the very core. 'This is surely the worst atrocity I have ever heard of. It is unbelievable that anyone should commit such sacrilege as to slay an archbishop, and in the house of God.'

Henry turned a ravaged face to him. 'It was done for me, at my behest. I am to blame. But as God is my witness, I *loved* Thomas, in spite of our quarrel. I spoke those words in anger. I did not mean them to be taken literally. I loved him!' His words were coming between short breaths; he was almost too paralysed by shock to say more, and the Bishop was staring at him, not quite comprehending what he was talking about. Eleanor went swiftly to Henry and would have comforted him, but he turned his back on her. 'No – I am not worthy of consolation,' he wept bitterly. 'Leave me to my terrible grief.'

She felt a pang of anguish at being rejected, but she thrust it away, realising that Henry needed time to come to terms with what had happened. This was a matter for his confessor, not his wife, although in time he might come to confide in her. For now, she turned her attention to the poor, shivering monk, and herself poured him a goblet of wine. She also handed one to the weeping Bishop, who gulped it back gratefully, then she offered another to Henry, but he was too distraught to notice.

'Now,' she said to Brother Peter, 'please sit down and tell us everything that has happened.'

The young man did as he was bid, and, piece by piece, the whole, tragic story came out. How Becket had gone back to England and, after all his fair words, defiantly excommunicated those bishops who had taken part in the coronation of the Young King. How the four knights had turned up at Canterbury and threatened the Archbishop with dire punishment if he did not immediately leave the kingdom. How Becket had calmly told them to stop their threats, as he was not going anywhere, and sent them away.

'All afternoon, they were hanging around the courtyard, plotting together, shouting insults about his Grace to us monks, and putting on their armour,' Brother Peter related. Once he had overcome his initial diffidence, and mastered his distress, the words had come tumbling out. 'Then, when we processed into the cathedral for Vespers, they followed us almost to the very doors. Truly, Sirs and Lady, we were terrified. When his Grace the Archbishop entered the church, we stopped the service and ran to him, thanking God to see him safe, and we hastened to bolt the doors, to protect our shepherd from harm. But' – and the homely peasant face crumpled at the memory – 'he bid us throw them open, saying it was not meet to make a fortress of the house of prayer, the church of Christ. And it was at that moment that the four knights burst in, with drawn swords ...' Brother Peter could not go on.

'Take your time,' Eleanor soothed, offering him more wine, and some bread to soak it up. She was horrified at what she was hearing, but still in control of her emotions. The time for weeping would come later, but with Henry seemingly in a stupor, still standing with his back to them, while intermittently emitting pitiful groans and cries, and Bishop Arnulf awash with tears, someone had to remain in control.

'I must tell it all,' Brother Peter sniffed. 'The world must know of this terrible deed.'

'We are listening,' Eleanor told him. 'And you may rest assured that justice will be done.' She saw Henry flinch.

'We were that frightened when we saw the devilish faces of those knights and heard the clanging of their arms,' the monk continued. 'Everyone was watching in horror – all save his Grace. He were calm, and when the knights asked where was Thomas Becket, that was a traitor to his king, he answered, "I am here, no traitor, but a priest." There was no fear in him. He asked why they sought him, then he told them he were ready to suffer in the name of his Redeemer. And he were that brave – he actually turned away and began praying!'

Eleanor held her breath as the monk paused, forced himself to chew on some bread, for which he clearly had little appetite, and went on with his tale.

'The knights came forward. They demanded that he absolve the bishops he'd excommunicated, but he refused. "Then you shall die!" they said. I will never forget those words. His Grace just looked at them, and told them he were ready to die for the Lord Jesus, so that, in his blood, the Church might find liberty and peace. The knights didn't like the idea of him being a martyr, so they tried to drag him outside, laying sacrilegious hands on him. But he resisted, accusing them of acting like madmen, and fell to prayer. Then one raised his sword, and smote the holy archbishop on the head, drawing blood. Brother Edward ran forward and tried to save his Grace, but they near sliced his arm off. Then it all happened very quickly. My Lord was clinging to a pillar, and they struck him again on the head, but still he stood there. They wounded him a third time, and he was bleeding badly when he fell on his hands and knees, calling us to witness that he was willing to embrace death for the sake of the Lord Jesus and the Church. He lay there on the paving stones; he were still alive and conscious, and then one of those devils went for him again, and sliced off the top of his Grace's skull with such force that the sword broke. He spilled his blood and his brains all over the floor, defiling our holy cathedral. It was the worst thing I have ever seen in my life. Then the knights scattered, and we were left to minister to the poor Archbishop, who was then beyond mortal help. He'd embraced his martyrdom with powerful courage, and truly, as I do believe, his blissful soul is with God.'

There was an appalled silence in the solar as Brother Peter fell silent. Then the King let out a strangled sound, as the Bishop wiped his eyes on his sleeve.

'This surpasses the wickedness of Nero,' Arnulf pronounced. 'Even Herod was not as cruel.'

'May God rest Archbishop Thomas,' Eleanor said. She was shocked by his murder, and shocked too to find herself wondering if it had been the greatest of Becket's dramatic gestures. It seemed he had almost welcomed martyrdom, had gone out of his way to court it. Yes, that would have appealed to his vanity! It would certainly have been the ultimate revenge on Henry . . .

Aghast at what she was contemplating, for it was unthinkable that she should be so uncharitable in the face of the terrible fate that had befallen Becket, she stood up, summoned the steward to arrange a bed and some food for Brother Peter, made it courteously clear to the Bishop that it was time for him to leave, and then, when they were finally alone, turned her attention to her husband.

Henry was like a broken puppet, his movements jerky and uncoordinated, his breathing ragged. Wrapped in his torment, he did not resist as she led him to the bed and herself stripped off his tunic and hose. Recumbent, he lay there with his face working in distress, moaning and sobbing. When she tried to hold him, he shook her off again. There was no reaching him.

Rapidly, the dread news spread throughout Christendom. The whole world was – like Henry – in shock. The murder was unanimously condemned as being equal in iniquity to Judas's betrayal of Christ, and King Louis loudly demanded that the Pope unleash the sword of St Peter in unprecedented retribution. Everywhere, Becket was hailed unreservedly as a blessed martyr, and universally, people laid the blame for his killing at the door of the King of England.

'In truth, Becket is more powerful dead than he was alive,' Eleanor complained to her son Richard, as they listened to yet another tale of the good people of Canterbury flocking to the desecrated cathedral to smear themselves with the blood of their slaughtered archbishop, or to snip pieces from his stained vestments as relics. 'Soon, they will be claiming that miracles are taking place at his tomb!'

'I heard him called "God's doughty champion",' the boy said. 'His murder was a terrible thing, but people now forget his long disobedience to his king.'

'It is your father who is the villain now,' Eleanor observed bitterly. 'I fear his fame will never recover. And the tragic thing is that he loved Becket, right to the end. He had no real wish to do him harm. And that, my son, is why you should always check yourself before uttering words in anger, words you do not really mean. Had your father done so, Becket would be alive today.'

Henry remained in seclusion for six weeks, refusing to attend to the business of ruling his vast domains. Shut away from the world, he put on a rough robe of sack-cloth that he smeared with ashes from the fire in penitence for his terrible sin, although nothing, he was convinced, could ever truly expiate it. For three days, he took no food, nor would he admit anyone to his chamber – not even his anxious wife. Soon, Eleanor was beginning to wonder if he had lost his reason; she even began to fear he might take his own life. It also occurred to her, although she begged

God to forgive her for thinking it, that he was feigning such excessive grief in order to convince people that he could not possibly have desired Becket's death.

In desperation, she summoned the Archbishop of Rouen, begging him to offer her husband some spiritual comfort.

'The King spoke quite lucidly to me,' the Archbishop told Eleanor after being closeted with Henry for some time. 'He is not going mad, so you may put your mind at rest on that score. But he is suffering from an excess of remorse. He holds himself entirely responsible for Archbishop Becket's murder, even though it had not been his desire or intent. Yet he knows he has brought upon himself the censure and condemnation of the whole of Christendom, and in my presence he called upon God to witness, for the sake of his soul, that the evil deed had not been committed by his will, nor with his knowledge, nor by his plan.'

'I believe that to be true,' the Queen said. 'I know him well, and I was there. I heard him say those words. They were spoken in the heat of the moment. Devious and quarrelsome he may be, a tyrant and murderer never.'

'You speak truth,' his Grace replied. 'The hard part will be convincing the rest of the world of it. But the King your lord has willingly agreed to submit, through me, to the judgement of the Church, and, showing great humility, he has promised to undertake whatever penance she should decide upon.'

'What more can he do?' Eleanor asked despairingly.

'What of the murderers, those satellites of Satan? Is there any news?'

'They have disappeared, by all reports, although I have ordered the King's officers in England to make a thorough search.'

'They are dead men already, or as good as,' the Archbishop commented acidly. 'The Pope will certainly excommunicate them.'

'I pray he will not excommunicate my Lord the King also,' Eleanor said.

'I hope not. The King has decided to send envoys to His Holiness, who will protest that he had never desired the sainted Becket's death.'

'Alas, I fear that His Holiness will heed the general opinion, which is much to the contrary,' Eleanor worried. Waiting for the Pope to speak would be like having the sword of Damocles hanging over their heads.

Underlying her fear was anger. Henry was a great king; he did not deserve such calumny. Even in death, Becket was hounding him.

Eventually, Henry emerged from his long seclusion, thinner and aged by several years. He had recovered his composure, though, and was ready to take up the burdens and cares of government again, but was still weighed down by remorse. Grief and guilt were eating at him, and made him short-tempered and difficult to live with.

Eleanor might have been a distant stranger. Henry had rejected all her offers of comfort in the time of his direst need, and he had nothing to give her now, nor did he appear to want even her companionship. He had withdrawn into himself, his emotions drained. With her fledgling hopes of a permanent reconciliation dashed, she felt that she had little to offer him, and that it might be better for both of them if she were to return to Aquitaine, at least for a short time. Maybe her absence would work its magic, as before. She was not surprised when Henry agreed to her going without protest.

'You are needed there,' was all he said.

As soon as the weather improved, and the roads were passable, she made her farewells, told Henry that he could be assured of her prayers, for the Pope had not yet spoken, and reluctantly rode south.

Part Three
The Cubs Shall Awake
1172–1173

43 Limoges, 1172

Eleanor thought it was a great pity that Henry was not here to see Richard invested as duke of Aquitaine. The sight of his fine, strapping son in his silk tunic and gold coronet, enthroned in the abbey of St Martial, would surely have gladdened his sad heart. It was a shame to be here alone, enjoying this triumph all by herself, watching the Abbot place the ring of the martyred St Valérie, the patron saint of Limoges, on the boy's finger, and then hearing him proclaimed duke, as he was presented to the cheering people of Limoges. And thank God they *were* cheering, she thought; it was as if they were aware that this ceremony, which she herself had devised, was a means of making a final reparation to them for the tearing down of their walls all those years before.

They had been in agreement, Henry and Eleanor, that Richard, now fourteen, was old enough to exercise power in Aquitaine as its ruler, although she herself, as sovereign duchess, would remain at hand to advise and assist him; they would govern her domains in association with each other – just as they had recently laid the foundation stone together for a new abbey dedicated to St Augustine.

Richard was now taller than his father, and showing signs of becoming a graceful, muscular man, with his long limbs and commanding appearance. In features, he resembled Eleanor, although he got his piercing grey eyes from Henry.

'The Young King is a shield, but Richard is a hammer,' Raoul de Faye perspicaciously declared, as they walked in the cloisters taking the late evening air after the feasting had ended. 'He will succeed at whatever enterprise he attempts.'

'He is single-minded enough to do so,' Eleanor smiled, knowing that, once her son's mind was made up, he was immovable – just like Henry. 'Of all my sons, he is the one destined for greatness.'

'I am impressed to see how he reposes all his trust in you,' Raoul said. 'Already, he strives in all things to bring glory to your name.'

'I am much blessed in Richard's devotion,' she replied proudly. 'He is inexpressibly dear to me. I am so sorry that Henry could not be here to witness this day, but he is busy in Normandy. At least he has made his peace with the Pope.' It had taken an oath, sworn by Henry in Avranches Cathedral, that he had neither wished for nor ordered the killing of Becket, but had unwittingly and in anger uttered words that had prompted in the four knights the desire to avenge him.

Eleanor could only imagine what it had cost Henry to make this public confession, humiliating in the extreme for a proud man such as he. Maybe being formally absolved of the murder by the Archbishop of Rouen had helped to alleviate his guilt and remorse, but it had come at a price. She had winced when they told her how the King, wearing only a hair shirt, had submitted to the shame of a public flogging by monks, in the presence of the Young King and the Papal Legate. It was not the most edifying example for a father to present to his son, still less for a king to show his subjects – and yet she knew it had been a necessary gesture. She still shuddered to think how painful a penance this must have been for Henry, in every way, and could have wept for the bloody lacerations inflicted by the whips and the hair shirt, and for the deeper wounds to her husband's soul.

Yet still, it seemed, God, the Church and the ghost of Becket were not satisfied, for the King had also vowed to undergo a similar public penance in England at some future date; in the meantime, he was to make reparation to the See of Canterbury and to those who had suffered as a result of supporting Becket. He was also to found three new religious houses, and – most galling of all, Eleanor knew – revoke the most contentious articles of his cherished Constitutions of Clarendon.

Of all this, she said nothing to Raoul, who knew it already. She was still incensed on Henry's behalf that Becket, in death, had won the moral victory, when Henry had had right on his side – she was convinced of this – all along. Unwilling to pursue this line of thought any further, for she had gone over it relentlessly in her mind, seething with indignation, and knew there was nothing to do but accept what had happened, she changed the subject.

'My Lord has new plans for our youngest son, John,' she said. 'He is not after all to be dedicated to the Church, which, I might say, is something of a relief.' She smiled faintly as she called to mind the unruly, lively five-year-old, whom all Abbess Audeburge's strictures had failed to tame. John, she had realised on her all-too-rare, conscience-appeasing visits to Fontevrault, was meant for the world, not for the spiritual life. 'Instead, he is to be married to the daughter of Count Humbert of Maurienne. As the Count has no son to succeed him, John will inherit his lands, and that will be of some advantage to Henry, because whoever rules Maurienne controls the Alpine passes between Italy and Germany.'

'What is the daughter like?'

'Alice? She's a mere child. As usual, my Lord is resorting to hard bargaining. I doubt we will see them betrothed for many a month.'

'And is John to stay at Fontevrault now that he is not to enter the Church?' Raoul looked at Eleanor searchingly.

'That is for Henry to decide,' she said firmly. 'I am more concerned about the Young King.'

She had been worrying about her eldest son for some time now. At seventeen, the younger Henry was ambitious and thirsty for power. He was a king, but he had no real authority beyond the superficial privileges that his father allowed him, and that had made him increasingly resentful.

'Geoffrey has Brittany, and Richard is to have Aquitaine, and both already have the freedom of their domains, yet I, the eldest, am ruled by my father,' he had complained, his eyes blazing, just before Eleanor had left Argentan. 'My titles are meaningless! I have asked him again and again to let me govern at least one of the lands I am to inherit – England or Normandy, even Anjou or Maine – Mother, I would even settle for Maine! – but he will not relinquish any part of his power, even to his own flesh and blood. I asked him if I could rule England as regent during his absence, but he appointed the justiciar instead.'

'I will talk to him,' Eleanor had said, but of course, there had been no way of approaching Henry at that time, not when he was suffering agonies of guilt over Becket's murder.

'It's not just that,' the Young King had added. 'He keeps me short of money. Even William Marshal thinks so. I have had to exist on what I can purloin from the Treasury or what profit I earn from tournaments. My father forgets I have a reputation for open-handedness to maintain. But what does he do? He bans tournaments in England, because he says that too many young knights have been killed. And he reserves the right to choose the members of my household. Mother, am I a king, or am I not? I cannot see why Father made me one, just to treat me like a child.' The boy was in anguish.

'It is hard for a father to accept that his children are grown up,' Eleanor soothed, 'much less that they will one day hold what is his. Your father takes great pride in his domains. No English king before him had such an empire. I counsel you, my son, be patient, and act prudently in all things. You are young yet, and must prove yourself worthy.'

After the Young King had gone away, sullen and unmollified, Eleanor reflected that her wise words had not been what he had wanted to hear. Yet she knew him well, and she knew too why Henry was keeping him on a tight rein. Young Henry was a restless youth, inconstant as wax. He was a spendthrift, and had shown himself to be lacking in wisdom and energy. He had not yet learned to control the violent temper he had inherited from his Angevin forbears, and probably never would. If the strong father couldn't do that, there was no hope for the weaker son. But Eleanor was confident, with a mother's instinct, that, given the privilege of adult responsibilities, Young Henry would quickly learn to live up to them. It was being treated like an incompetent child that was turning him into a wastrel. But Henry could not see that. He did not realise that he was driving a wedge between his son and himself.

'Henry is a doting parent,' she told Raoul now. 'He lavishes more affection on his children than most fathers, and takes it for granted that his love is returned. He cannot bear to acknowledge any faults in his offspring, and they know well how to deflect his wrath by bursting into tears. It never fails!'

'You are both indulgent and loving parents,' her uncle

pointed out. She accepted the implied criticism, knowing it to be justified.

'Yes, I know. We have spoiled our children, and as a result, they are too headstrong for their own good. And unfortunately they have been witnesses to much discord between us, so they have learned to compete for our attention, and to play off one parent against the other shamelessly!' She threw a mock grimace at Raoul. 'I have failed as a mother!'

It was a remark lightly made, but it masked an underlying anxiety. For all the balmy night, with stars studding the clearest of skies, Eleanor felt a sudden chill. She ripped off a leaf from a creeper and began crushing it in her palm.

'You may recall a curse laid by a holy man on your father, Duke William the Troubadour, my grandfather,' she said. 'He swore that William's descendants would never know happiness in their children. I told Henry about it once, long ago, and it quite upset him, because he could not imagine any of our brood causing us grief. Of course, they were small then, and easy to rule.'

'Does any parent ever know happiness in their children?' Raoul asked. 'We nurture them, we love them as our second selves, then they go away and leave us. It is the natural course of things. Every time they are hurt, we suffer. If they forget us, we suffer. Is that happiness?'

'What on earth did you do to your children, Raoul?' Eleanor exclaimed, trying to inject some humour into the gloom. Yet there was an uncomfortable degree of truth in what he had said, and she felt depressed by it. Then she remembered something else.

'There is another ancient prophecy, Raoul, of Merlin's. It has always puzzled me, and yet I have increasingly come to feel that it has some relevance for me and mine. It says that "the Eagle of the Broken Covenant" shall rejoice in her third nesting. Is that prophecy to be fulfilled in me? Am I the eagle? And the broken covenant? Is that my marriage to Louis?'

'It is too vague to say,' Raoul opined, dismissively, and began to walk towards the door that led to the abbey guest house. 'I should not concern yourself with it.'

'Yes, but if it is about me, then it portends well for Richard.

If you think of my living sons, then Richard is the third nesting, of whom I shall have cause to rejoice. I am almost convinced that he will be the fulfilment of the prophecy. It's what might be meant by "the broken covenant" that worries me.'

'Eleanor, you are worrying over nothing,' her uncle told her. 'Let it alone. I am sure that, prophecy or no prophecy, Richard will fulfil your every hope.'

The Young King had been crowned again, with Queen Marguerite, in Winchester Cathedral. Now, Eleanor hoped, Henry would permit their son to exercise more power. He had written to say that, since Marguerite had reached the age of fourteen, he had allowed the young couple to consummate their marriage and live together. That sounded promising; it was a start. But hot on the heels of that messenger came another from Young Henry himself.

He wrote indignantly that his father now insisted on keeping him under his eye at all times. He had dragged him from Normandy to the Auvergne to witness the betrothal of John to Alice of Maurienne, and when Count Humbert had asked what John's inheritance would be, Henry had promised to give him three castles. 'But they are mine!' the Young King had protested. 'They were to come to me.' He had made clear his anger to his father, but had been ignored. Instead, Henry had forced him to witness the marriage treaty that dispossessed him.

Henry was acting like a bull-headed fool, Eleanor thought. He loved his children, true, but when it came to inheritances he was back to his game of pushing them around like pawns on a chessboard, with no thought for their feelings. All was policy, and often there seemed no rhyme or reason to it! But what of the wider implications of his heavy-handedness? Did he not realise that a house divided against itself falls?

The next she heard, King Louis had invited his daughter Marguerite and the Young King to Paris. That in itself was worrying.

'Louis has long been trying to make divisions in Henry's empire,' she told Raoul one morning, as they rode out with their hawks. 'It would not surprise me if he has heard of the

Young King's dissatisfaction and is trying to exploit it to his own advantage. He fears that vast concentration of power in Henry's hands.'

'And the French have always liked to make trouble for the English!' Raoul observed. 'Maybe the King should have forbidden Young Henry to go to Paris.'

Eleanor agreed. 'Maybe he does not wish to offend Louis,' she said. 'After all, Marguerite is Louis' daughter. But I think it is folly for them to go to the French court now.'

Soon it became clear that the situation was worse than she could ever have expected. In his next letter, her son informed her that, before setting out for Paris, he had visited his father in Normandy and once more demanded to be given his rightful inheritance. But Henry had again been adamant in his refusal. 'A deadly hatred has sprung up between us,' the young man confided. 'My father has not only taken away my will, but has filched something of my lordship.' There was a palpable sense of grievance in his words – and it was entirely justified, Eleanor felt.

Her anger against her husband was mounting. How could he be so blind? It was unfair and unjust, the way he was treating their son – and it could be disastrous in the longer term. She almost hoped Louis would do something to provoke Henry into realising that he was acting destructively and forfeiting the love of his heir.

She wondered if there was anything that she herself could do to stop it. She felt so helpless, so impotent – and so frustrated!

44 Chinon, 1172

Christmas had arrived. Eleanor was keeping the festival with Henry at Chinon, and their three oldest sons had been invited. The King greeted her with unexpected warmth and one of his bear-like hugs, and complimented her on her rich attire. It was the green Byzantine robe that she had worn in the years of their passion, when the mere sight of her dressed in her finery had been sufficient to inflame his desire, but he seemed to have forgotten all that.

She had learned not to let herself get upset at his fitful interest in her; they were, after all, meant to be separated. She soon saw that, for all his bonhomie, put on for the season, Henry remained preoccupied with his own private demons and was impatient with everyone, and she suspected that he was building up to yet another confrontation with the Young King.

'I summoned Young Henry back from Paris,' he told her. 'My spies warned me that Louis was cozening him to demand his share of my dominions. I put a stop to that immediately!'

'I am glad that our son is coming here,' Eleanor said, trying tactfully to convey to Henry that there was more to this situation than a power struggle. 'I have not seen him for many months. And Marguerite has always been like a daughter to me.'

But the Young King did not come. He sent word to say that his friend, Eleanor's war-like troubadour Bertran de Born, had invited him to his castle at Hautfort, whither Young Henry had extravagantly summoned all the knights in Normandy named William to feast with him.

Henry exploded. 'God's blood! Is there no end to the cub's stupidity? Of all the pointless, frivolous things to do! What is he thinking of? And as for Bertran de Born, as you should know, he is a dangerous troublemaker.'

'Henry.' Eleanor laid a calm hand on his shoulders and looked directly into his purple-veined face. 'Our son indulges in frivolous and pointless pursuits because you force him to. His whole life is frivolous and pointless. You have made him a king, yet you allow him no kingly power, so the whole exercise was in vain. You keep him short of money and curtail his pleasures; you insist on appointing all the members of his household. You even dictated when he could sleep with his wife, who has been ripe for the marriage bed these past two years, as we both know. Henry, before it is too late, let him be the king he wants to be. Then he can prove his true worth. He needs to cut his teeth before he can rule an empire.'

The King stared at her as if she were mad, and shook her off angrily. Then she realised that he was looking beyond her, and she turned to see Richard and Geoffrey standing there. By the looks on their faces, they had heard what had been said.

'Mother is right,' said Richard defiantly. 'Why will you not give us any power, Father? I am duke of Aquitaine and Geoffrey is duke of Brittany, but they are empty titles.'

'Richard speaks truth, Father,' asserted Geoffrey.

'Shut up!' snapped Henry. 'You're only fourteen – what do you know? Are you all in this against me?'

'In what?' Eleanor enquired. 'A conspiracy? How could you think that, Henry? I am looking to the future, and doing my best to prevent a rift between you and our sons. I believe they have a just grievance.'

'Yes, we do!' echoed Richard and Geoffrey.

Henry faced them, a man at bay. 'It is written that every kingdom divided against itself is brought to desolation, and I cannot risk that happening. I have built up my empire, domain by domain, and I have spent most of my life fighting to hold it and keep it intact. One day, thanks to me, it will be your inheritance. *One day.* But if I now give England, Normandy and Anjou to Henry, Aquitaine to you, Richard, and Brittany to Geoffrey, what will I be left with? I might as well retire to Fontevrault and become a monk!'

'We ask only that you share your power with us, Father, and give us some proper responsibilities,' Richard said.

'No,' Henry told him. 'You are yet young and inexperienced. There will be time enough for that when you are older.'

'Henry, when you inherited Normandy, you were eighteen, only a year older than Young Henry is now,' Eleanor reminded him.

'Yes, but I did not consort with troubadours, or feast unworthy knights just because they bore a name that took my fancy. I had to grow up quickly, in the midst of a civil war, and I learned early on to fight in the field and pit my wits against my mother's adversaries. Thanks be to God, our sons have never had to deal with such difficulties.'

'Even so, you have overly protected them,' Eleanor retorted. 'Now you must let them be men, and stand on their own feet, and give them cause to be thankful to you. Heaven knows, their demands are not unreasonable.'

'I beg leave to differ. The courier who brought Young Henry's message was my own man. He had heard the cub boasting that he ought by rights to reign alone, for at his coronation, my reign, as it were, had ceased.'

Eleanor's sharp intake of breath pierced the stunned silence. The two boys looked at their feet, knowing themselves defeated by their brother's thoughtless stupidity.

'That is the kind of poison that your Bertran de Born has been dripping in my son's ear,' Henry snarled. 'I wonder where he got the idea.'

'Not from me!' cried Eleanor hotly. 'That is unjust! How could you think it?'

'You always take his part.'

'That is because you refuse to see things his way.' She was in a ferment, past caring if she offended or upset him. 'And now, clearly, it is too late. It is you who have brought us to this pass, Henry. You can never admit that you are wrong. Look what happened in Aquitaine? It's the same with your vassals all over the empire. They complain that you are too heavy-handed, too authoritarian. That's exactly what is wrong with your treatment of your heirs, and I will not stand by and see it!'

Henry hit her, hard, across the mouth. 'That's enough!' he roared.

'Mmmm!' she cried in pain, clapping her hand to her bleeding lips. This could not be happening, she thought. Henry had been that rarity among husbands: only once before had he used violence on her, that time she had unwisely taunted him about Becket – and that had only been a slap. Thus his lashing out at her now, and drawing blood, was shocking in the extreme. It was bad enough that he had struck her – worse still that he had done it in front of their sons.

Richard's hand had flown to his dagger, and Geoffrey, equally outraged, had sprung to comfort their mother. Henry glared at Richard.

'I am your king, and your father, to whom you owe all honour and obedience,' he said menacingly. 'Lift one finger in anger against me, and you commit treason, which I will punish accordingly, whether you be my son or no.'

'You hit my Lady Mother,' Richard replied through gritted teeth. 'You are no father of mine.' And, leaving Henry glowering and muttering threats, he helped Geoffrey assist Eleanor to her bower, where her horrified damsels flew to minister to her wound.

'There is no moving Father,' Richard said dejectedly.

It pained Eleanor to speak, and the pain in her heart was greater still — Henry had raised his hand to her; she still could not believe it — but she forced herself to clarify things for her boys. 'There is more to this than his obduracy,' she mumbled through her cut lip. 'He cannot see or comprehend what is happening right under his nose. He sees his word as law and expects it to be obeyed.' She sighed, fighting back tears. She must remain strong, for no one else would champion her sons' cause.

'You are aware that your father and I have lived apart for some time,' she said gently. 'That was our mutual decision. We had had our differences, yet we remained friends and allies. Today, that has all changed, for I will not have my children cheated of their rights. Plainly, we are in one camp, and your father is in another. That makes us enemies, although it grieves me to say it. But I promise you now, all of you, including Young Henry, that I will fight for your rights, and I will make the King see sense!'

'Will there be a war?' Geoffrey asked eagerly. He was desperate to prove himself in battle. But Richard's face remained grave; a year older, he had realised the true implications of the rift. Eleanor could guess what he was thinking — they were that close.

'Your father said that a kingdom divided would be brought to desolation,' she mused. 'Well, he has this day divided his kingdom, and if it all ends in desolation, he must bear the responsibility. By his stubbornness, he has laid himself open to the thing he most dreads. But I will not let it happen; there is too much at stake, for he is putting this empire we have built at risk. I have always been a true, loyal wife and helpmeet to my Lord, but I will not stand by and see my sons treated unjustly. He is wrong, utterly wrong, and we must make him face that.'

She regarded her boys unhappily. 'This saddens me more than I can say,' she admitted, her voice wistful, less strident. 'There should not be discord between father and son, or husband and wife. It is against the natural order of things.'

'What wonder if we lack the natural affections of mankind?'

Richard laughed humourlessly. 'We are from the Devil, and must needs go back to the Devil!'

What could she do to force Henry to his senses? Dare she write to Louis? It had been so long. Yet something told her that he would welcome her intervention. There was no doubt that he was of the same mind, although for different motives. She wanted justice for her sons, and for them to enjoy their right to a share of their father's power; Louis wanted Henry's empire disunited. He too had evidently read the Scriptures.

But what exactly did the Young King want? Was it sovereign authority, even if that meant the overthrow of his father? If so, then what she was contemplating was dangerous in the extreme. At its best it was rebellion – at its worst, treason.

She must talk to her oldest son as soon as she could, and find out what was in his mind. If it were indeed Henry's ruin, then she must try to talk some sense into the Young King. In the meantime – it could not hurt, surely – she would write to Louis, parent-to-parent, as it were, and confide to him her concerns. One word from him, threatening the peace that Henry had worked so hard to negotiate, might be all it would take . . .

And there was another thing. Louis was her overlord; she had every right to appeal to him for aid against her enemies. And, by his insupportable acts, Henry had now made himself her enemy. She herself had not created this terrible situation. She had been trying all along to find a peaceable solution.

Putting quill to parchment, she found her thoughts drifting hopefully back through the years to a young man with long yellow hair who had been so pathetically eager to please her . . .

45 Limoges, 1173

When Eleanor next saw Henry, he made no reference to what had passed between them; nor did he refer again to the rift with his sons. Yet he could not have failed to notice the frigidity of her manner towards him, or that she shrank from his touch. It seemed he no longer cared what she thought of him.

His striking her had changed everything. There was nothing

unusual in a husband beating his wife, of course: it was a man's right, and she knew of many women who had frequently to endure such chastisement. She also knew of several churchmen who wanted to limit the length of the rod that was used, but they had been dismissed as eccentrics. No, the issue here was that, in lashing out and wounding her, Henry had brutally demonstrated that his respect for her, and his love and regard, had died – and he had let her sons see that.

And something had died in her too. She could no longer bear to be in his presence.

He had insisted on her travelling south with him to Limoges, where he was to host a week of lavish banquets and festivities in honour of the betrothal of the Lord John to Alice of Maurienne. The guests of honour were to be Alice's father, Count Humbert, the Kings of Aragon and Navarre, and the Count of Toulouse. Richard was to be present, as duke of Aquitaine, and Henry had summoned the Young King from Hautfort; Geoffrey he had sent back to Brittany. Divide and rule, Eleanor thought cynically.

And that was how the great baggage train of the Plantagenets came once more to be wending its cumbersome way south through the Angevin territories. It was February, and cold, when they left Chinon, but Limoges, when they arrived, was mild, and the town was *en fête*. Although her heart was frozen, Eleanor mentally girded her loins and donned her most sociable mask, conducting herself as charmingly and wittily as ever towards her august guests. She warmed to the flattery of the Spanish kings, and revelled in the blatant regard of the black-haired Count Raymond of Toulouse, with whom, many years earlier, she and Henry had once been at war, each claiming that Toulouse belonged to them. Although Raymond had won the day, it seemed that he cherished no hard feelings towards his former aggressor. She wickedly hoped that Henry had seen him flirting outrageously with her. At fifty-one, it was balm to her broken heart and scarred lip to luxuriate once more in a man's frank interest.

'I had never believed the reports of your beauty until I met a man called Bernard de Ventadour,' Raymond told her as they sat at the high table, dining off gold plates and drinking from crystal goblets. 'He was a troubadour – you may remember him.'

'I knew him. He was once at my court,' she told him.

'He loved you, truly. Your husband the King had dismissed him through jealousy, and he sought refuge at my court. He pined for you greatly, did you know that?' Raymond's startling blue eyes, set in an angular, handsome face, were searching.

'I knew he had a regard for me,' Eleanor said. 'But, although I say it myself, all the troubadours claimed to be in love with me. I was the Duchess, and it was more or less expected of them.'

'But Bernard was special,' Raymond insisted. 'His songs were not mere flattery, but inspired by the heart. I judge him to have been one of the greatest poets of our age.'

Eleanor paused. 'You speak of him as if he were dead.'

The Count sighed and laid down his knife. 'Alas, Madame, he is. His grief was such that he sought refuge and peace in the abbey of Dalon in the Limousin, where he ended his days not long after.'

'I am sorry for that,' she said, feeling regret that she had so lightly dismissed Bernard's devotion.

'You could say he died for love of you – and most men, having seen you, would understand why.'

Eleanor recovered herself and frowned at Raymond in mock reproof. 'Do you know how old I am, my Lord?'

'If you tell me, I will not believe it. Madame, you rank among the immortals, your fame and beauty are legendary, and I can see for myself that the reports do not lie!' This was accompanied by increasingly animated gestures, and Eleanor noted with secret glee that Henry was looking at them suspiciously, and toyed mischievously with the idea of taking Raymond to her bed, to spite her husband further. It would not be difficult to seduce the amorous Count. Dare she do it? It might be all that she needed to quell her inner turmoil and pain.

The Young King arrived on the third day, shortly after a messenger from the court at Paris, who had brought letters of congratulation for the King and Count Humbert – and a secret missive for Eleanor.

Dragging herself away from her tower window, through which she had been hoping to espy her eldest son and his retinue approaching across the distant hills, she hurriedly broke the seal. It was from Louis, offering her and her sons his support against the unjust treatment of her husband. As Henry's overlord, he said, he had the right to demand the righting of the wrongs that her lord had done his heirs, and he, Louis, would pursue that even to the point of resorting to arms.

Her hands were trembling. She was horribly aware that, in invoking the King of France's aid, she had committed treason against her lord. Louis' response had forcibly brought that home to her. She had not meant Henry any harm, had wanted only to make him aware of the needs of their sons. But it was probably too late to retract now. The letter had been written, the damage done. She suspected that the Young King would have been in touch with his father-in-law and received a similar assurance anyway.

And here was the Young King now, his party just visible in the distance. His mother stilled her conscience and forced a smile. She had longed to see this oldest son of hers, yet realised that his presence here could only mean trouble. And that, with what she knew, and the heavy knowledge of what she had done, she would be involved in it up to her neck.

King Henry had gathered his family, his guests and his court in the great hall of the abbey of St Martial for yet another celebratory feast, and it was here that, with his face set hard like granite, he received the Young King and Queen Marguerite. To make matters worse, the younger man exchanged the kiss of greeting with his father in sullen silence, having barely bent his head in obeisance. His embrace of his mother was far warmer.

His disrespect did not go unnoticed. The Kings of Aragon and Navarre exchanged disapproving glances, while Raymond of Toulouse raised his elegant eyebrows at Eleanor. But she would not acknowledge him, and took her place between the two kings, her husband and her son, for the solemn banquet.

After the cloths had been drawn and spiced wine served, the company processed into the church for the betrothal of the Lord John to Alice of Maurienne. The future bride was an exquisite child of four with chestnut curls framing her sweet, round face; her father, the portly Count Humbert, looked quite distressed at the prospect of giving her away, for she was his only, cherished child. But soon, the deed had been done, and she was affianced to the six-year-old John, who could not have looked less interested. John's avid curiosity had been captivated by the wonderful luxury and excitement of this rare week away from his cloistered existence, and he saw his betrothal only as a means of escaping his frustratingly ordered world.

The ceremony over, the moment had come for Count Humbert formally to commit his daughter into the custody of the English King, and there were tears in his eyes as he lifted Alice up, kissed her, then set her down and gently pushed her into a wobbly curtsey. Henry patted her on the head.

'Queen Eleanor here shall care for her as if she were her own daughter,' he assured the anxious father, and Eleanor stepped forward and gathered the little girl up in her arms.

'As dowry, I give you the four castles stipulated in the marriage contract,' the Count confirmed, 'and I formally designate the Lord John my heir.' Henry glared at the fidgeting John, indicating with a sharp downward nod that he should bow in acknowledgement of his good fortune, which he belatedly did.

There followed a second ceremony, in which it had been decided that Count Raymond, now acknowledged by Henry and Eleanor as Count of Toulouse, was to pay homage to them as his overlords. But Henry had made a change of plan. He had the glowering Young King and Richard, as duke of Aquitaine in place of Eleanor, stand beside him, and obliged the Count to swear fealty to the three of them. That prompted outraged murmurs from Eleanor's subjects: what business had the Young King to be involved? It was Richard's right, alone of the sons of Eleanor, for had not King Louis recognised him as the overlord of Toulouse?

Eleanor, too, could not mask her fury. How dare Henry slight her, the sovereign Duchess of Aquitaine! But look at him! He was standing there beaming, happy to ride roughshod over everyone's sensibilities – as usual! In her fury, her resolve hardened. It was not the Young King's fault that he had been dragged into this; God knew, he had insupportable grievances enough of his own. But that Richard, her Richard, had been obliged ignobly to compromise his lordship – that she could not forgive. Henry must be stopped. If she had to commit treason to do it, then so be it – she would do it.

She guessed that, when the feasting came to an end and the guests had withdrawn, there would be a family bloodbath, and she was right. Before she and Henry could retire to their separate chambers – never again, she had vowed, would they share a bed – Richard had collared them in the stairwell and complained bitterly of the slight he had received.

'Your brother is my heir. Let that be an end to it,' Henry said dismissively.

'Yes, but not the heir to Aquitaine!' Richard stormed. 'He has no jurisdiction in this territory, nor ever will.'

'Henry, you were unjust,' Eleanor added coldly.

'Cease your complaints!' Henry growled. 'I'm going to bed.'

'Not so fast, Father!' It was the Young King, come up behind them. 'I have something to say to you. Do you want me to say it here, or shall we do it in private?'

Henry turned on the stair and scowled down at him. 'You had all better come to my solar, and we can get things straight, once and for all,' he said.

'Yes, we will,' his son promised, his eyes blazing with purpose.

Eleanor took her place in the carved chair by the brazier. Her two sons placed themselves firmly on either side of her, making it quite plain that they were all three allies. Henry stood facing them, feet planted firmly apart, arms folded across his chest, jutting his bull-like chin out defiantly.

'Well? Out with it!'

The Young King bristled. 'Why do you refuse to delegate any power to me and my brothers?'

Henry's eyes narrowed. 'Because you are not yet ready for it, as your hot-headed behaviour proves.'

'So John, at six, is ready to administer the castles you have given to him – castles that belong, by rights, to me! I had no wish to give them to him, and you had no right to dispose of them!'

'I have every right,' said Henry, abandoning his inquisitorial pose to pour himself some wine. 'I am the King. Everything is mine to dispose of. And I'm not dead yet.'

'You may not dispose of your lands here without the consent of your overlord, the King of France,' the Young King said, smirking nastily, 'and I must tell you that it is King Louis' wish, and that of the barons of England and Normandy, that you at least share your power with me, and assign me an income sufficient to maintain my estate.'

Henry stared at his son. 'You *have* been busy,' he snorted. 'Tell me, does it behove my son and heir to go behind my back, cozen my barons and consort with my ancient enemy?'

'That which you reap, you must sow, Henry,' Eleanor told him. 'There was no other way for him to receive justice, you must see that.'

'I'd give it another name, Madam.' The King regarded her with contempt. 'I'd call it treason.'

Her face must have betrayed her. Her sons looked alarmed as Henry bore down on her. 'What do you know of this, Eleanor? Have you been stirring up trouble too?'

'I but support my own blood,' she answered evasively.

Henry thrust his head forward until they were face-to-face, noses almost touching. 'But you would not go so far as to appeal to Louis for support, I hope!'

'I have no need to. It seems our Henry can take care of himself.'

Henry stood up, dissatisfied, yet not wanting to pursue the matter further for the moment. Surely she would not have gone so far!

'Out!' he commanded his sons. 'And don't come bothering me with your endless complaints and demands again. Go on, out! I wish to speak privately with your mother.'

Reluctantly, like naughty children, Young Henry and Richard left the room, their eyes smouldering, hatred burning in their breasts. Eleanor watched them go and grieved for them, but her attention was immediately demanded by Henry.

'If I find you have betrayed me,' he warned her, his voice deadly serious, 'I will kill you.'

'That would not surprise me, after the violence you have shown me,' she retorted, keeping her nerve. 'Henry, why have you come to hate me so? Is it because you can't bear it when I'm right?'

'It's because you have set yourself in opposition to me, when you should be supporting me,' he replied. 'You never show me the proper meekness of a true wife.'

'I never did!' she laughed mirthlessly. 'It didn't bother you in the old days. You liked my spirit – you often told me so. But I now speak a truth you do not want to hear.'

'Just stop interfering. You're a woman, and these are affairs for men.'

'Then why did you send me here to rule Aquitaine? Did you think me incapable of sound judgement back then? God's teeth, Henry, I could run circles around you!'

'You think you have some fatal power over me, don't you?' her husband sneered, his features contorted in what looked like loathing. 'Well, you don't. You are an irritation, that's all.'

'I am your wife and your queen!' Eleanor cried, incensed. 'You were lucky to marry me, for I could have had my pick of the princes of Europe. But I have always done my duty by you. I have been a true wife these many years, and a helpmeet when you needed it. I have borne you sons . . .'

'Yes, God help me!' Henry flung back. 'I wish I could get more and disown these ungrateful Devil's spawn . . .'

'Then perhaps you should marry one of your whores, and do just that! Mayhap Rosamund de Clifford would oblige, or did you abandon her long ago, as you abandon most of the women you've fucked?'

It was the first time in six years that the name of Rosamund had been uttered between them. For Eleanor, it had been a long shot, for she had heard nothing more of the girl since that terrible night when Henry had admitted his love for her – and had, indeed, not wanted to hear of her. He had rarely been in England since then, so she supposed the affair had died a natural death. But now she could see by his expression that she had been horribly wrong.

'I have never abandoned Rosamund,' he said, deliberately aiming to hurt her. 'She is here, in Limoges. She travelled incognito, with a separate escort, and I have slept with her every night since I arrived. There – does that satisfy your curiosity? I told you, Eleanor: I love her. Nothing has changed. I do not love you. I prefer to hate you.'

'It's the other side of the same coin,' she riposted, wondering why tears were threatening to spill down her face. 'Tell me, Henry, do you hit her as you hit me? Does she please you in bed as much as I did?'

He looked at her darkly. 'Rosamund would never give me cause to strike her. She is a gentle soul. And yes, she brings me much joy – more than you ever did! Look at yourself in the mirror, Eleanor, and ask yourself why I no longer lust after you. Look at the harridan you have become!'

He is doing this to bait me, she told herself. It is his way of being revenged for what he sees as a betrayal. I must not take it to heart – and anyway, what need have I to? I no longer love him, so why should I care? But she was honest enough to realise, to her dismay, that she did care – that she wanted to rake her nails down Rosamund's alabaster cheeks and ruin her beauty, that she wanted to fling herself at Henry and beat the breath out of his chest for being so cruel – and so *stupid*! Instead, she rose to her feet with immense dignity, picked up a candle and made to leave. But Henry stopped her, reaching out and taking hold – none too gently – of her arm.

'You and I are finished, but my sons are yet young,' he said. 'By reason of their age, they are easily swayed by their emotions and misplaced loyalty. I am beginning to suspect that a certain red-haired fox has corrupted them with bad advice and stolen them away from me. Isn't that so, Eleanor?' His grip tightened.

'You are a fool, Henry,' she told him with scorn. 'You delude yourself. You are the cause of this tragedy.'

'No, I am not a fool, or deluded,' he insisted. 'I can see clearly that my own wife has turned against me and told her sons to persecute me.'

'You are sick!' she cried and, twisting free, ran down the stairs.

She could not face going to bed. Instead, she found herself pacing up and down in those same cloisters where she had confided her concerns to Raoul de Faye. Within her, the tempest raged. They were destroying each other, she and Henry, and there was no help for them. Since Becket's death, he had changed, coarsened, become abrupt and unkind. He had betrayed her, abused her and slighted her; he had said cruel, unforgivable things. She would not believe them, she must not . . .

'Eleanor?' A man slipped out of the shadows. It was Raymond of Toulouse, his face full of concern – and something else that she recognised as desire. 'Forgive me for intruding, but you are troubled. Can I help?'

How long had he been there? Had he been waiting in the hope of waylaying her? He had been bold indeed to address her by her given name rather than her title. What could that betoken but amorous interest? And how had he guessed that nothing could have been more welcome to her wounded soul on this terrible night?

She went to him unspeaking, finding refuge in his arms, and sweet pleasure in his kiss. Lying naked on his bed, having stolen furtively up with him to his chamber, she watched his eyes roving over her body, and knew that she was not the ageing harridan that Henry had so cruelly called her. Ah, it was bliss to feel her body come alive again after so long, to shiver under a man's caress, and squeeze eager fingers around his virile member, surprising herself by the erotic response deep inside her. She could not be old if she felt like this, she told herself, as Raymond rolled and tumbled her on disarrayed sheets, riding her vigorously until she cried out in pleasure that was almost pain.

When it was over, and he had subsided, panting, beside her, she tried to tell herself that sex had been better with him than with Henry, but her self-delusion lacked conviction. Henry had been by far the more accomplished lover – she was honest enough to concede that. But what had most struck her had been the *strangeness* of it, the predominance of physicality and the lack of emotion. She was forced to admit to herself that there was nothing so erotic as the touch of a familiar, loved body, and the meeting of true minds.

She fought back tears, angry with herself for allowing sentiment to get the better of her. Why must she continually chase this fantasy of re-creating the past, when the past had probably never been as good as she remembered? Even Henry had told her that, in his usual brutal fashion. We can never go back, she said sadly to herself. There will be no more second chances for us. We are different people now, shaped and honed by our experiences, with scars that even time cannot heal. Where there was love, there can now only be hatred. Henry and I seem fated to destroy the good in our lives, and we will no doubt end up destroying each other. What happened to us, she cried silently, that we should have become such enemies?

'What was troubling you, sweet lady?' her new lover asked suddenly, snuggling up to her under the heap of furs. So emotional did Eleanor feel that she poured out the whole sorry tale of the rift in her family, even confessing how she had written to Louis. 'Some might call it treason, but truly I did not intend it that way.'

Raymond was silent for a moment. 'I understand,' he said at length, 'although many would not. Yet I think you are right to support your sons.'

'I suppose this night is another betrayal,' Eleanor smiled sadly. Her lover immediately sat up, his black-haired body lean and muscular in the candlelight.

'Don't tell me you have never lain with another,' he exclaimed. 'You, with your reputation.'

'This is the first time since I married my Lord,' Eleanor confessed. 'And the first time I have known a man in more than two years.'

There was a disconcerting pause.

'Why me, then?' Raymond seemed shocked.

'Nothing could have seemed more right at the time,' she told him, fearing that things were going badly wrong.

'But I assumed that you and the King had long had an arrangement to go your own ways in such matters. The way you flirted with me, and led me on . . . I thought he knew you had amours.' Already, he was moving away from her in the bed. 'God's blood, what have I done? I swore fealty to my overlord today, and here I am, already breaking my oath, and dishonouring my suzerain by bedding his wife. And you let me! My Lady, you talk of betrayals, but it seems to me you know not what the word means. Yes, this *is* betrayal – and you are to blame!' With that, Raymond leaped from the bed, pulled on his robe and held open the door. Furious and ashamed, Eleanor struggled into her gown, threw her cloak over it, and swept past him, her cheeks burning.

'I will say no more of this, on my honour,' he called after her.

'Who are you to talk of honour?' she muttered under her breath.

Having crept back to her bower and woken her sleeping ladies, explaining that she had been kept late with her lord – and how true that was! – Eleanor lay sleepless, hating herself for what she had done, and knowing in her heart that, after all these years of fidelity, she had now broken most of her marriage vows, and humiliated herself before a man who was one of her vassals. Worse still, she had revealed to him dangerous secrets. Could she count on Raymond to keep his word? Would he say no more of it, as he had promised? He would know that concealing treason was almost as bad as committing it. And if Henry found out any of this, his vengeance would be terrible, she knew it. She lay shaking in her bed, just thinking about it.

She was filled with self-loathing, yet she hated Henry more, for having been the cause of this unholy mess. And she hated Raymond too, for sinning with her and then holding her to blame. Yet deep inside her, she was secretly pleased that she had had her small revenge on her husband – even if he never got to hear of it. It would be her private triumph, proof that she could fight back – and that she still had what it took to seduce men, despite the cruel things Henry had said of her. And she was still convinced that she was right to take up her sons' cause, and that, if necessary, force – and any other means possible – must be used to make the King see reason.

Henry looked up from his book – it was a favourite, Geoffrey of Monmouth's *History of the Kings of Britain*, and he was in the habit of reading it again and again because it contained the stirring stories of King Arthur, which he loved. Today, Geoffrey's history was affording him a brief refuge from the maelstrom of troubles that surged around him, so he was irritated to hear a knock at the door.

'Enter!' he barked, and Count Raymond of Toulouse came in.

'Sire? I was told I might find you here. Might I have a private word with you?'

Cursing inwardly, Henry laid down his book. 'Sit down, my

Lord,' he invited grudgingly. Raymond obeyed, then sat there, looking uncomfortable – and curiously flushed.

'Yes?' Henry prompted.

'Sire,' the Count blurted out, 'the court is busy with gossip, and I am hearing strange things that I think you should be told. May I speak freely?'

Henry regarded him warily, but he believed Raymond to be a man of honour who surely would not speak lightly. 'Pray do,' he said.

'Then I advise you, Lord King, to beware of your wife and sons!' the Count said earnestly. To his consternation, Henry burst out in harsh laughter.

'Do not concern yourself,' he rasped. 'My sons are headstrong and led astray by those around them who preach sedition. My wife is a fond and foolish mother who should know better than to indulge them, and who has corrupted their minds with folly. This is not news to me, although I thank you for your care for my safety. But never fear, the situation is under control.'

He dismissed Raymond, who departed in evident relief, but when he was alone once more, Henry fell to brooding. Was Eleanor up to something? He did not think, after his threats, that she would go so far as privily to involve Louis – anyway, the Young King had done that openly, quite brazenly, in fact. He did not believe her capable of such perfidy, or of forgetting her nuptial vows.

It was his sons who were the culprits in this. In their rash ambition, they posed the greater danger. He was haunted by a prophecy of Merlin, which he had read in his book: *The cubs shall awake and shall roar loud, and, leaving the woods, shall seek their prey within the walls of cities. Among those who shall be in their way they shall make great carnage, and shall tear out the tongues of bulls, and their necks load with chains.* Were the cubs that the seer had foretold his own sons?

He would not wait to find out. They must be stopped, and now. Briskly, he gave orders that certain knights of the Young King's household be sent away; they, he believed, had been dripping sedition into his boy's ear. To the latter's howls of protest, he remained deaf.

The gathering broke up. The kings returned to their kingdoms, the counts to their domains. Henry himself planned to go north with Eleanor and their sons to Poitiers; when he had set the affairs of the duchy in order, he would press on to Normandy. The Young King he would take with him. He would not let the boy out of his sight. He would make sure that there was not the slightest opportunity for any intriguing.

'I am not a child!' shouted Young Henry.

'Then stop acting like one,' his father said tartly. 'Then I might begin to take you seriously.'

Henry genuinely trusted that his eldest son was the cause of all the present trouble, and the one to be watched. Richard could safely be left with Eleanor, to share control in Aquitaine. Kept apart from Young Henry, Richard would be harmless, he was convinced. Geoffrey he summoned, to keep them both company, and to divert Richard. And so, with his house in order, or so he believed, he departed from the duchy and dragged his seething heir off to Normandy.

46 Poitiers, 1173

Young Henry had escaped! Eleanor shook – she knew not with joy or fear – when she heard the news. He had endured his father's vigilance as far as Chinon, clearly aware that he would soon be breaking free of it. Then he had stolen out of the bedchamber that Henry had insisted they share, bribed the guards to lower the drawbridge, and ridden for Paris as if the four horsemen of the Apocalypse were at his heels. In vain did Henry send men in pursuit, and soon it dawned on him that his son's flight had been planned down to the last detail, no doubt with the secret connivance of King Louis.

One day, and that not far distant, men would point the finger at Eleanor, accusing her of being Young Henry's accomplice, yet she was as astonished at his escape as the rest of the world, and holding her breath to see what would come of it. She could not but rejoice that he had escaped his father's repressive vigilance, which had become so destructive, and prayed that Henry would now see sense. She had lost all patience with him.

She sent relays of messengers secretly to Paris. She had to know what was happening. They brought back momentous news.

'Lady, King Louis and the Young King have pledged themselves to aid each other against their common enemy.' That could only be Henry, she realised, although the sweating man on his knees before her had not dared to say so.

'Lady, the King has sent a deputation of bishops to Paris to ask the King of France to return his son. When King Louis asked, "Who sends this message?" he was told it was the King of England. "The King of England is here!" the French king said. "But if you refer to his father, know that he is no longer king. All the world knows that he resigned his kingdom to his son."' Eleanor could not resist a smile at that; she had not known that Louis had it in him to throw down the gauntlet in this manner.

'Lady, the Lord King is preparing for war; he is looking to the safety of his castles and his person. Many of the barons of England and Normandy have taken the Young King's part and declared for him!'

This was becoming serious.

'What of William Marshal?' Eleanor enquired. That wise man of integrity: how would he view all this?

'He is for the Young King.'

War! Eleanor could not believe that things had gone this far. Louis was making threats, Henry's barons were rallying to arms, and his sons were champing at the bit to teach him a lesson. And suddenly, with the malevolent Bertran de Born at his side, the Young King materialised in Poitiers, hurriedly embracing his mother.

'I am come in secret,' he told her. 'I need your aid, and that of my brothers.'

'Tell me truly, my son,' Eleanor asked seriously, 'what you hope to gain from taking up arms against your father.'

'I thought you supported me!' he flared.

'I do; I believe you have a just grievance. But we all need to be clear what the objective is. Do you intend to force the King to share his power with you, or do you mean – as report has suggested – to overthrow him and rule in his stead?'

'Would it make a difference to your supporting me?' Ah, she thought, so he does understand the moral issue at stake.

'It might have done once,' she said bitterly, 'but your father has since forfeited all right to my loyalty. I am as a widow; he has insulted and abandoned me, and he has treated you, his sons and mine, with contempt – and I will not stand by and allow it. A rotten branch must be cut off before it infects the healthy tree.'

'You are prepared to go that far?' Young Henry was staring at her in amazement.

'Yes,' she told him. 'Your father has forced me to make a choice between my loyalty to my husband and king, and my desire to protect the interests of my children. I am a mother. There can be no contest. Whatever love and duty he once had from me, as of right, he has killed, stone dead.' She stepped forward and hugged her tall son.

'What has he done to you?' he asked angrily.

'He struck me, that you know. I do not care to go into the rest.'

'You do not need to,' the Young King fumed. 'None of us are blind. We know about the *Fair* Rosamund.' The words were spat out with a sneer.

'It seems I was the only one who didn't,' Eleanor said lightly. 'But now we must forget about all that, and discuss this war with your brothers.'

She summoned Richard and Geoffrey to her solar. Constance arrived too, full of her own opinions, but Eleanor shooed her away impatiently. She did not want the silly girl meddling where she had no business to. The Young King's brothers were surprised to see him, and listened gravely, and in mounting fury, to what he and their mother had to say.

'It is up to you what you do,' Eleanor told them both. 'You are almost grown to man's estate, and I will not treat you like children.'

Richard got up and embraced Young Henry. 'I choose to follow my brother rather than my father, because I believe he has right on his side.'

'Well said!' Eleanor applauded. 'And you, Geoffrey, will you join with your brothers against your father the King?'

Geoffrey drew himself up to his full height; at fifteen, he was undergoing a growth spurt, but he would never be as tall as Young Henry and Richard, of whom he was intensely jealous. Unlike them, he was dark and saturnine in appearance, and it was rapidly becoming evident that he had a character to match. He was clever with words, perhaps the most intelligent of all Eleanor's brood, but untrustworthy and ruthlessly ambitious.

'Naturally, I support my brother,' he said smoothly. 'I too am a victim of our father's pig-headedness. I should be ruling Brittany without his endless interference.'

'Then we are of one accord,' Eleanor declared. 'Yet before we go ahead and make plans, I must ask of you all if you are aware of the implications of what you are doing, for you must go into this with your eyes open. By anyone's reckoning, it is treason.'

'Treason,' interrupted Young Henry hotly, 'is a crime against the King. I am the King, am I not? Even my father cannot dispute that. And King Louis says that, in making me king, he abdicated all sovereign authority.'

'That last is open to dispute,' Eleanor said, 'but it will serve for now. You do realise you are effectively declaring war on your own father, to whom you owe love and obedience?'

Geoffrey shrugged.

'Do you not know it is our proper nature that none of us should love the other? We came from the Devil, remember? So it is not surprising that we try to injure one another!'

'Our father has forfeited his right to our love and obedience,' Richard averred, his handsome face creased in resentment.

'Aye, indeed!' the Young King agreed. 'So you are both for me in this?'

'Yes!' the brothers chorused.

'You must go directly to Paris, to King Louis,' Eleanor urged them. 'He is your greatest ally, and will back you with military force. I will give you letters informing him and his council of my support. I will dictate them now, while you make ready.'

Within an hour, she was in the palace courtyard, kissing her sons farewell and wishing them Godspeed, wondering if she would ever see them again. Their departure was supposed to be a secret, but within hours, word of it, and excited speculation as to their purpose, had spread throughout the city of Poitiers, and within a week, the whole province of Aquitaine was in jubilation at the prospect of an end to the rule of the hated Duke Henry. Eleanor only became truly aware of this when a troubadour, Richard le Poitevin, visited her court and played before her and her company. His words, sung in a rich baritone voice, conveyed just how strongly her subjects really felt:

> Rejoice, O Aquitaine!
> Be jubilant, O Poitou!
> For the sceptre of the King of the North Wind
> Is drawing away from you!

Deeply moved, Eleanor turned to Raoul de Faye.

'We cannot ignore the voice of our people,' she murmured. 'It further strengthens my conviction that opposing Henry is the right thing to do.'

'I think many of us have been waiting a long time for you to come to that conclusion, Eleanor,' Raoul said with a gentle smile. She gripped his hand.

'Will you go to Paris for me?' she asked. 'Will you be my envoy, and convey a personal message from me to Louis, thanking him for his support for my sons, and begging him to have a care for their safety? He will appreciate such a personal gesture, and while you are there, you can send me word of my young lords' welfare, and perhaps contrive to have some say in making decisions.'

'I will go with pleasure,' Raoul agreed. 'I will be the voice of the Duchess of Aquitaine. You may depend on me.'

Raoul had gone, but now there came a letter, bearing the seal of Archbishop Rotrou of Rouen. What business had he, the Primate of Normandy, to be writing to her, Eleanor? Then fear gripped her. Could the Archbishop have written to tell her that something terrible had befallen one of her sons? With trembling fingers, she cracked open the seal and read, her jaw dropping in horror.

Rotrou had begun courteously enough: 'Pious Queen, most illustrious Queen . . .' But then he had gone on immediately to deplore that she, hitherto a prudent wife, had parted from her husband. It was not that which appalled her – she could deal with sanctimonous platitudes any day! It was the Archbishop's accusation that she had made the fruits of her union with the King rise up against their father. It was terrible, such conduct, he fulminated, before going on to warn her that, unless she returned to her husband at once, she would be the cause of the general ruin of Christendom.

He knew! Henry knew of her betrayal. He had made Rotrou, his Archbishop, write this letter, there could be no doubt of it. But how had he found out? Everything had been planned in secret. Had her letter to Louis been intercepted? Worse still, had Raoul been taken on the road and forced to confess what he knew? Worst of all, had Henry planted spies at her court? She tried to recall the names and appearances of those who had recently joined her household, and remembered that, before he left, the King had appointed four of her Poitevin countrymen to her chancery. She could not think that there had been anything sinister about that, but one never knew with Henry. He was a suspicious man. Of course, it might not be the Poitevins at all, but one familiar to her, who had been suborned into turning his coat. That was a chilling thought. Yet maybe her imagination was running away with her – Louis could well have implicated her in a letter to Henry.

Shaking, she read on, casting her eyes over pious exhortations to return with her sons to the husband whom she was bound to obey, and with whom it was her duty to live. 'Return, lest he mistrust you or your sons!' the Archbishop cried. Well, clearly, Henry did already mistrust her, and their sons. She did not believe Rotrou's assurance that her lord would in every possible way show her his love and grant her the assurance of perfect safety. This was the man who had sworn to kill her if she betrayed him! If she did as she was bid, she might be walking straight into a trap.

The letter continued: 'Bid your sons be obedient and devoted to their father, who for their sakes has undergone so many difficulties, run so many dangers, undertaken so many labours.' Might she infer, from this, that Henry did not yet know that she had sent the boys to the court of his enemy, Louis? It seemed to assume that they were still with her in Poitiers. If so, the

King could not realise the full extent of her perfidy, as he would see it.

Then came the threat. If she did not return to her lord, Rotrou warned, he himself would be forced to resort to canon law and bring the censure of the Church to bear on her. He wrote this, he protested, with great reluctance, and would only do it with grief and tears – unless, of course, she returned to her senses.

With what exactly was he threatening her, she wondered, feeling a little faint. Divorce? That had once held no terrors for her, but then she had happily instigated the process. It was bound to be a less happy experience when one was the person being divorced, especially as she knew she had much to lose, including her children. And the consequences for the Angevin empire would be dire indeed.

But 'the censure of the Church' sounded worse than divorce, although it might imply that too.

Excommunication. The terrible, dreaded anathema. To be cut off from God Himself, from the Church and all its consolations and fellowship, from all Christians, cast out friendless from the universal community, and condemned to eternal damnation. Surely Henry would never go so far? It was the thing he himself had most dreaded throughout the long quarrel with Becket.

She *could* not go back to Henry. Very soon, he would find out that she had sent their sons, and Raoul de Faye, to his enemy, Louis – if he had not learned that already. Even if she set out now, she would probably not reach the King ahead of that intelligence. And with proof of her treachery, Henry might very well carry out his threat to kill her. For her children's sake, and her own, she dared not return to him, not even at the risk of excommunication.

It dawned on her suddenly that she was not safe here, even in her own Aquitaine. Henry might have his hands full with his sons' rebellion, and war on all sides, but he would surely send men after her – and then what?

She must leave. She must get to Paris as soon as she could. She had never thought that one day she would be eager to seek refuge from Henry with her former husband, but now she realised that Louis was the only one who could offer her protection.

She summoned the captain of her guard and ordered him to

have a small escort party made ready. The fewer they were in number, the faster they could travel. Then she gathered together her ladies, Torqueri, Florine and Mamille, the three of her women whom she loved the best, who had been with her for years, and whom she would have trusted with her life; and she told them of her predicament.

'It is your choice entirely, whether or not you come with me. If you choose not to, I am not so handless that I cannot shift for myself, so do not trouble yourselves about that. I should welcome your company, of course, but this is flight, not a pleasure jaunt, and I cannot guarantee your safety, or when you will be able to return.'

'I'm coming,' said Mamille, without hesitation.

'You may depend on me,' Torqueri added.

'Did you need to ask?' Florine smiled. Eleanor hugged them all gratefully.

There was no time to lose. They packed hurriedly, taking only what was essential and could fit into saddlebags. Then they hastened downstairs and emerged into the May sunlight. Eleanor could not help looking around her at the dear, familiar surroundings of her palace and its beautiful gardens, just then bursting into bloom, and wondering when she would see it all again. But there was no time for sentiment. The horses and men-at-arms were waiting, and they had to make haste. Their departure went almost unnoticed, for they looked to all appearances as if they were off to visit a religious house or the castle of a local lord. Four men alone, watching from a tower window, registered that the Duchess was leaving and that this might be a matter worth reporting to their master.

Once clear of Poitiers, Eleanor and her party broke into a gallop and rode hard in a north-easterly direction, as if the hounds of Hell were at their heels – as well they might be, Eleanor thought grimly. She and her ladies were all expert horsewomen, and in other circumstances, the ride would have been exhilarating fun, but Eleanor was in fear that they would at any moment be intercepted or ambushed. She had been so hell-bent on fleeing that there had been no time to send word of their coming ahead to Louis, and anyway, no fast messenger could have covered the long distance as rapidly as they were doing now. They were bound for the Loire crossing at Tours, then for Orléans, whence it was seventy miles to Paris.

In all, more than one hundred and eighty miles lay ahead of them, a daunting distance in the circumstances. Their mounts would never stay it, of course, and they would have to rely on obtaining fresh horses at towns along the way. Eleanor had brought money for that purpose. She had even remembered to thrust a pot of salve into her bag, knowing they would all be suffering miseries from saddle-soreness by the time they reached safety.

Ten miles out of Poitiers, they heard the ominous sound of hoofbeats behind them, and Eleanor nearly froze with apprehension. If she was taken now, Henry could use her as a hostage for her sons' submission, and that would be an end to all they were fighting for. The captain heading the escort swung around in his saddle, his finger to his lips, and signalled that they should slow down and walk their mounts into nearby woodland, where they could conceal themselves behind the trees. As they obeyed his orders, they could still hear the thuds of distant galloping, which seemed to be gaining on them, but as they came to a standstill beneath the overhanging branches, and stayed there, holding their breath apprehensively, the noise faded, and soon all that could be heard was the rustling of the leaves and the twittering of birds.

'Let's press on,' the captain said brusquely.

'Stay a moment!' Eleanor ordered, and turned to her three ladies. 'Torqueri, Florine, Mamille: there can be no doubt that we are in danger, even of our lives. I realise that I have been selfish in asking you to come with me, for I have made you a party to treason. If we were to be caught, you would suffer for it, so I am commanding you to turn back and go home to your families until I am able to send for you.'

The ladies made to protest, and Mamille burst into tears, but Eleanor stilled them with a shushing finger. 'Go, I beg of you!' she urged. 'Now. Do not worry about me. I told you, I can shift for myself.'

'But, Madame, you cannot travel alone in the company of men!' Florine cried, shocked. 'It would not be fitting.'

'God's blood!' Eleanor swore. 'This is not a hunting expedition or a pilgrimage to Fontevrault!'

Florine dissolved in tears.

'Just go,' the Queen said to the other two. 'Take her with you and comfort her. I will take care of myself, never fear. I know we will meet again in happier circumstances.' How that would be achieved she had no idea, but one must always have faith in the future.

After brief farewells, she watched them ride back along the road they had travelled, then turned briskly to the men of her escort. 'Wait here a moment,' she bade them. 'I will not be long.'

She pulled her bag from her saddle and carried it some way off through the trees, to a place where she could not be seen. Then she stripped off her veil, jewels, girdle, gown and chemise and, standing there naked, bound her breasts tightly with some old swaddling bands, then pulled out of her bag some clothing that the Young King had left behind, and which she had brought in case it was necessary to disguise herself: *braies*, hose, a tunic, leather belt and shoon, and a caped hood clasped at the neck, under which she had bundled up her long plaits. Gloves and a dagger completed the ensemble, and when she emerged from the woods, having thrust her female attire under some bracken, she was confident that she made a very passable knight or gentleman. Certainly the astonished stares of her escort told her so. She suspected that they were a little shocked, for the Church taught that it was heresy for women to wear male clothing. Yet it seemed the only safe thing to do.

They rode on, pausing briefly to swallow some bread and cheese purchased from a farmstead, then made good speed through the afternoon. It was just as evening was falling, that golden dusk-time of the day that saw the blood-red sun sinking in an azure sky, when they again heard riders coming up behind. They were on a lonely road south of Châtellerault, and had been hoping to reach the town and change horses there before curfew, but now they deemed it wiser to turn aside along a hillside track that was shaded by trees and would provide some cover.

To their dismay, the hoofbeats followed them. They quickened their pace, but the terrain was stony, and Eleanor's horse stumbled. Looking around in dismay, she could now see the approaching party of riders, and knew without a doubt that it was Henry's men come for her.

'Escape! Scatter!' she cried to her escort. 'It is me they want. Go now, if you value your lives.' The soldiers hesitated, saluted her briefly, impressed by her courage, then cantered away. Alone, she turned to face her pursuers.

They had not recognised her at first. Of course, they had been looking to find a queen. Instead, they had been confronted by a strange knight on a white horse, holding up his hands in surrender. It had momentarily thrown them.

'Messire, we seek Queen Eleanor,' the sergeant called as they drew near. 'If you help us find her, we will not harm you.'

'I *am* Queen Eleanor,' the knight said, and the men-at-arms gaped, appalled at seeing her so attired. If she hadn't been in such peril, she would have found it amusing.

The sergeant recovered his equilibrium and swallowed. 'Lady, I am directed to apprehend you in the King's name for plotting treason against him,' he said gruffly. 'We have orders to take you to him in Rouen.'

They were not unkind to her. They did not insist on manacling or chaining her, but rode closely on either side of her through the long ride north, one always holding her bridle, so that she had no chance of fleeing from them. At Châtellerault, they stopped briefly to buy her a plain black gown and decent head-rail, then stood guard over the back room they had commandeered at an inn, so that she could change into these more seemly clothes. There was no mirror, of course, and she supposed she looked a fright, but at least they had let her bring some of the contents of her saddlebag, which mercifully included a comb and the pot of salve. Women's things, harmless.

When she emerged, the men looked at her furtively, and she even detected a touch of admiration in their faces. She could not have known – or cared – that she looked quite beautiful in the simple gown and veil, with her long hair in two braids, and her features drawn from anxiety but still arresting. Nor did she realise that, whatever she had done to injure the King, her daring flight held in it something of the legends and stirring tales on which these soldiers had been bred. Already, her own legend was in the making.

No, she did not care what became of her, she told herself, as they brought her some passable duck roasted in its own fat, and a flagon of ale, and locked her in the back room to eat it all by herself. What she did care about was what might be happening to her sons. She was in an agony to know that, and terrified lest any evil had befallen them. Were they even now shut up in a prison in Rouen?

When the sergeant came himself to take away her barely touched trencher, she tried to pump him for information.

'Please, Messire, do you have any news of my sons?' she asked. The tears in her eyes were genuine.

The sergeant was a personable, heavily muscled married man in his thirties, and stolidly committed to completing the duty assigned him, getting paid, then going home to his wife and stolid daughters in Angers. He was a reliable, moral soul without much imagination, unlikely to succumb to the wiles of a clever woman, and Henry had chosen him for this task for that quality alone. But when he looked at his queen, helpless and in distress, his upright heart softened and he was briefly tempted to bend the rules a little. But then he thought of the hoped-for promotion to captain that might be his by way of reward for this service to his king; it had been hinted at, and even if it never materialised, there was still a bonus in gold coins to be collected. So he pulled himself up, and said abruptly, 'My orders, Lady, are simply to convey you to the King in Rouen. I am forbidden to speak of anything but domestic matters.'

'Then I will be domestic,' Eleanor said, and it was in that moment that the sergeant realised that, given the chance, she might run rings around him. She stood up, wringing her hands, her expression pleading. 'At least tell me that my sons are in health. Please!'

The man hesitated. He remembered how his wife had been distraught when their five-year-old had gone missing for just a few minutes in the market place; how she had agonised that time the baby had been ill of a fever. He swallowed. It could do no harm . . . and it was, as the Queen said, domestic.

'I have not heard anything to the contrary,' he said, and left the room, impervious to Eleanor calling down blessings on him for his kindness.

Tours. Le Mans. Alençon. The trek north seemed endless, although they kept up a good pace. Eleanor got nothing more out of the sergeant, and she had dismissed the men-at-arms as being dull oafs, unable even to communicate coherently. She sensed that they were in awe of her and became tongue-tied in her presence, and took perverse glee in trying to get them to engage in conversation, and in making the occasional mild jest. Then, having provoked little response, she grew weary and gave up. Her heart was too heavy to brook any diversion for long. Soon, she was aware, she would be brought face-to-face with Henry. The prospect filled her with dread. What would he do? Would he carry out his threat to kill her if she betrayed him? If so, she was a dead woman – and then what would become of her sons? Her blood turned to ice in her veins as she confronted the very real possibility of Henry's vengeance having fatal consequences for herself.

Part Four
Poor Prisoner
1173–1189

It was growing dark as they approached the late Empress's palace outside the walls of Rouen. Eleanor had spent much of the journey imagining how Henry would receive her. Would it be in private, to spare her humiliation – and his? Or would he go so far as to parade her, his captive, before the whole court? She would not put it past him. Then again, Henry might not receive her at all. He might have her shut up in a dungeon, and she might not again see the light of day until she was brought to her judgement.

Her heart was racing as they approached the palace and the drawbridge was lowered. She was aware that she must look a sorry sight, travel-stained and no doubt haggard with apprehension, and that her gown stank with the sweat engendered by fear. Dear God, she prayed, give me the courage to face with dignity what may lie ahead!

Word of their coming had preceded them, and in the courtyard, one of the King's captains, with four men-at-arms at his heels, came forward to relieve the sergeant and his men of their illustrious charge. When Eleanor dismounted, the captain bowed stiffly.

'My Lady, you must come with me,' he said, and led her, his men following close behind, to one of the towers in which guests were usually accommodated. Momentarily, she was thrown by this, but after they had climbed the narrow spiral staircase to the topmost floor, she could see that the door to the single chamber had been fitted with a new lock. This, then, was to be her prison.

The captain opened the door and indicated that she should enter. She went warily, half-expecting that Henry would be waiting inside for her. But there was only a woman standing there in the candlelight, a stocky, hatchet-faced body of indeterminate age, wearing a grey wool gown, a snowy wimple and a hostile expression. Was this to be her gaoler? Her heart sank. Almost, she would have preferred to see Henry in a rage.

'Amaria is to be your personal servant, my Lady,' the captain told her, his face impassive, his eyes fixed at a point beyond her shoulder.

'My guardian, you mean!' Eleanor retorted, finding her voice. She sensed the woman bristling.

'No,' he told her. 'The King has appointed this woman to see to your needs. For your security, guards will immediately be posted outside this door, and at the outer door below. Amaria may come and go as she needs, to fetch necessaries, but I would advise you, my Lady, not to be so foolish as to attempt to escape. It will go harder for you if you do.'

'I could not imagine that things could ever be any harder for me than they are now,' Eleanor retorted. 'Tell me, do you know if I am to see the King my Lord?'

'I cannot say,' the captain replied.

'Is he here? I was told I was being brought here to see him?'

'I am not privy to the King's plans, my Lady,' the soldier said. 'My orders are to keep you safely under lock and key.' So saying, he produced the key from a chain at his belt, shut the door behind him, and locked it.

Eleanor sighed in despair, then looked about her. The woman Amaria was watching her furtively with unfriendly eyes. No doubt she has been told I am some kind of monster, Eleanor thought.

The room was circular. A single tapestry, so dull with age that it could have come from the Conqueror's old fortress in the city, graced one wall; she could not make out what it was supposed to depict, but there was a female figure at its centre. Some wicked woman of legend, no doubt; Henry might have chosen it himself, thinking it apt. There was a polished wooden chair, a stool, a table, a small chest carved with chevrons, an empty brazier, a pole on the wall for hanging clothing, and just the one wide tester bed, hung with heavy curtains of Lincoln green and made up with a comfortable enough bolster and striped cushions, clean bleached linen sheets and a thick green wool counterpane lined with what looked like sable. But there was no sign of any pallet bed beneath it for Amaria, just two chamberpots where such a bed would normally be stored.

She turned to the woman. If their confinement here together in such close proximity was to be in any way bearable, then she had best get off on the right foot – but there was the problem of the bed to be addressed.

'Good evening, Amaria,' she began. 'I suppose you are no happier to be here than I am, but for certes we must make the best of it. Tell me, what are the sleeping arrangements?'

The woman regarded her coldly, but she replied civilly enough. 'Lady, my orders are that I have to share the bed with you.'

Are they afraid I might seduce the guards while she's asleep? Eleanor thought angrily. It was a petty humiliation, and one that offended her innate fastidiousness. What if the woman, whose accent betrayed her rustic origins, smelt unsavoury or snored? Country people were used to whole families tucked up together in one bed, but Eleanor liked to choose her bedfellows, and, when alone, she liked to fantasise, and more . . . There would be no opportunity for that with Amaria in the bed.

But what could not be avoided must be endured. She supposed she had forfeited her rights to privacy and freedom of choice . . . or freedom of any kind, she thought sadly.

'Are you hungry, Lady?' Amaria asked.

'No,' said Eleanor, 'but a little wine would be welcome.'

Amaria rapped on the door, and when it opened, two gleaming spears could be seen across the doorway. That gave Eleanor a jolt, bringing home to her, more than anything else, the fact that she was a prisoner. She watched, dismayed, as the guards lifted the spears to let the serving woman through, then slammed and locked the door behind her. So this was how it was going to be from now on. She felt the walls closing in, stifling her . . .

But she must be strong, if she was to survive this – and practical. Grateful to be left to herself for a few precious moments, she quickly used the chamberpot, undressed down to her chemise – she must ask for more body-linen, as a matter of urgency – then climbed into bed.

When Amaria returned with the wine, Eleanor downed it

quickly, seeking oblivion, but it had no effect. She tried to sleep, yet sleep eluded her. She was tormented by thoughts of her sons in peril, and what the morrow might bring. When Amaria climbed heavily into bed beside her, she shuddered with distaste, moved as far to the edge of the mattress as possible and lay there weeping silently, her heart burdened with dread and sorrow.

The morning dawned bleakly, on all counts. Eleanor awoke to see a troubled grey sky through the window slit and, with a plummeting feeling in her breast, realised where she was. Beside her, Amaria still slept, her mouth slackly open, her breath foetid. Eleanor slid carefully out of bed and relieved herself as quietly as she could. It was going to be a problem, attending to the calls of nature and keeping her dignity as queen in the face of the serving woman's unwelcome scrutiny. She could see herself enduring agonies of discomfort as she waited for Amaria to disappear on some necessary errand.

Some water and holland cloths had been left on the table. She washed herself as best she could and donned the black gown and veil. No other clothes had been provided. She must demand some, along with the body-linen, as a matter of urgency.

Amaria woke up and rubbed her eyes as a church clock struck seven.

'Good morning,' said Eleanor, trying to be civil. Surely the woman must see that they each had to make an effort to make this bearable.

'Good morning,' said Amaria guardedly, getting up and pulling on her grey gown over her shift, with no thought for washing herself. Peasant! thought Eleanor. She watched the woman clear the table and empty the washing water out of the window into the courtyard below. '*Gardez l'eau!*' she cried.

'I will fetch something to break our fast,' she said, and rapped on the door. Once she had gone, Eleanor fell to her knees and tried to pray; she had always heard Mass before breakfast, but no provision appeared to have been made for her spiritual needs. That was something else she would have to ask for.

Prayer was difficult. The prospect of her imminent confrontation with Henry kept intruding, as did the memory of him threatening to kill her. When would he come, or summon her? Was he even here in Rouen?

She tried to focus her thoughts on Christ's sufferings. It had been easy to commune with her Redeemer in the richly furnished royal chapels or in the peace of Fontevrault and other great abbeys; but here, in this cheerless room, in the hour of her greatest need, He seemed to be elusive.

She made herself dwell on the five points of prayer. Give thanks – but for what? The ways of God were indeed inscrutable. What could be His purpose in inflicting this misfortune and suffering on her? Say sorry – but to whom? To Henry, the husband whom she was bound to love and owed all wifely duty – who was also the man who had betrayed her again and again, and who had fatally failed to do the right thing by their sons? No, rather should she say sorry to Young Henry, to Richard and to Geoffrey for failing them. Pray for others – God knew, when it came to her sons, and her other children, she did nothing but pray for them. And she prayed for her land of Aquitaine and its people, and for all Christ's poor, and for those who needed succour in this miserable world.

Pray for oneself. Her heart swelled with need. Help me, help me! she could only plead, for she could not focus her thoughts sufficiently to enumerate her troubles. God knew them, though. She trusted that He would be merciful.

Listen to God, to what He is saying. She tried – how she tried! – to still her teeming thoughts in order to clear her mind and let Him in. But she could not do it, and so, if there had been a still, small voice attempting to speak to her, she did not hear it.

What she did hear was Amaria returning with a tray of bread, small cuts of meat and ale. Eleanor was not hungry, but she forced herself to eat a little, as Amaria took the stool opposite and began stuffing the food unceremoniously into her mouth. Eleanor recoiled. Had the woman never been taught that meal-times were not just occasions for satisfying the needs of the body, but for good manners, courtesy, conversation . . .

She tried. 'Do you live near here?' she began.

Amaria stared at her coldly, chomping noisily on her bread.

'No, Lady,' she said.

Eleanor tried again. 'Do you have family nearby?'

'No.'

'Then where are you from?'

'Norfolk.'

'So what are you doing in Normandy?' Eleanor's natural inquisitiveness was beginning to assert itself.

'My husband were one of the Lord King's captains, and went with him everywhere. I missed my man, so I got a post as a laundress in the King's household, so as I could travel with him.'

'Is he here with you, your husband?'

'He be dead,' came the flat reply.

'I am sorry to hear that,' Eleanor said kindly. 'Have you been a widow long?'

'Three months. Anyway, what's this to you, Lady?'

'I just thought that, if we are to bear each other company all the time, we might try to get along in a friendly manner, so that it will be more pleasant for us both.'

'For you, you mean.' There was contempt in the rustic voice.

'Of course. But you would benefit too.'

There was a pause as Amaria thought about this. 'I'm not supposed to talk much to you, Lady,' she said, 'just to see to your needs.'

'I will not ask you to talk about why I am here,' Eleanor promised. 'Just about yourself and matters of general interest. I am interested to know how you came to be in attendance on me.'

'When the Lady Alice de Porhoët was here as hostage, my husband had charge of her, and I helped look after her. That were some years back, but since then, I've acted as waiting woman to other visiting ladies, on occasion.'

'Were some of them hostages, like the Lady Alice?'

'I don't know. All I were told was that I had given satisfaction and that the Lord King were pleased with me. I reckoned that were why I were sent for the other day and told as I was to have charge of you, Lady.'

'Did they tell you why I am here?' Eleanor asked.

'No, just that you were the King's prisoner.'

'But you have heard rumours, yes?'

The surly look was back, the woman's lips pursed. 'I can't talk about that.'

'Fair enough,' Eleanor said evenly, anxious not to kill off this fragile rapport before it had gone beyond the budding stage. 'Tell me, do you have children?'

'I have the one boy, Mark, who's twelve. He be in the cathedral school at Canterbury. He's a clever boy. Going into the Church.' Amaria's eyes suddenly softened with pride, and she looked quite different. Eleanor could even see that she might have been pretty once.

'You must be so proud of him,' she said. 'I am a mother too, so I understand how you must feel. Our children are the most important thing in the world, aren't they?' She wondered if Amaria was astute enough to get the message she was trying to put across, if she realised that Eleanor was trying to tell her that, whatever she had done, it had been for her sons.

Amaria was regarding her with a puzzled yet concerned frown, but quickly looked away when Eleanor smiled hopefully at her. 'I must clear these things,' she said, and began piling up the breakfast clutter.

'I need some necessaries,' Eleanor said.

'In the chest,' said Amaria. Eleanor knelt, lifted the lid, and found a pile of clean clouts for the monthly courses that, in her, had long since ceased, fresh chemises, headrails and hose, all strewn with fresh herbs, and two gowns, one of Lincoln green, the other of dark-blue woollen cloth, both plain and serviceable. Nothing regal or grand here – being stripped of the trappings of her rank was clearly all part of her punishment. She wondered, with sinking fear, which gown she would wear to her execution.

'I can see that you had a hand in preparing these,' she said appreciatively to Amaria. 'Thank you.' The woman looked nonplussed; plainly, she did not know what to make of her queen. Maybe she had been expecting a monster, Eleanor thought, and has been surprised to find that I am a creature of flesh and blood much as she is – and that I love my sons as much as she clearly loves hers. That, at least, was something upon which she could build.

'There is one other thing,' she said, getting to her feet. 'I should be grateful to have the consolation of faith in this my ordeal. Might it be possible for a priest to be sent to me?'

'I will ask, Lady,' said Amaria, and rapped again on the door. She was back within a quarter hour. 'Father Hugh will come tomorrow morning to hear your confession and say Mass,' she told Eleanor. Already, her manner was warmer.

As Amaria busied herself with making the bed, Eleanor sat down in the single chair, and wondered what on earth she was going to do during the long hours that stretched ahead. She desperately needed something to occupy her, to keep her mind from wandering down fearful paths. But there were none of the things with which she was used to passing the time: no books, no musical instruments, no embroidery, no ladies to challenge with games of chess or riddles – and, of course, no possibility of riding out for the hunt, or even walking in the gardens. Her imprisonment, although it was not as bad as she had anticipated, felt suffocating; she could not bear it a moment longer.

But she must. She must do *something*.

'Tell me, Amaria, how do you like to pass the time?'

'I sew,' said Amaria. 'And I used to like tending my little garden, but the cottage is gone now. No need for me to keep it on.'

'Do you think I could help with some sewing?' Eleanor asked. 'I have nothing to do.'

'There's a pile of sheets need turning,' Amaria said.

'Then let's set to,' said Eleanor gratefully.

'I'll fetch them.' The woman's face creased into what could have passed for a smile. 'Strikes me I never thought I'd see the day when I'd be sitting mending sheets with the Queen of England!'

It was the afternoon of the second day, and the pile of sheets seemed only a fraction lower than it had been the previous morning. Eleanor was sitting there wishing that she had something more mentally stimulating to take her mind off her predicament, but she was thankful that at least Amaria had grown, if not exactly friendly, then more amiable. They had managed to keep a steady conversation going, touching on food, childbirth, travel and a host of other mundane things. Eleanor was desperate to confide in the woman, but dared not risk compromising the delicate accord between them. Yet she needed to unburden her fears to someone. The priest had been no good; he was an old man, doddery and deaf, and had heard her whispered confession with sage weariness, then mumbled some undemanding penance. She had performed it immediately, reciting her hail Maries as she bent to her needle. It was a tough challenge, she realised, sitting here sewing with nothing else to distract your fevered mind, and thinking you might go mad.

Yet she was not to fret in idleness for long. Suddenly, the door opened and the captain of the guard entered.

'Make ready, Lady, the King comes this way,' he announced, then backed out of the door. 'You, woman, follow me,' he said to Amaria, and suddenly Eleanor found herself alone, facing her destiny. Dread filled her soul as she heard Henry's spurs clinking at a brisk rate up the stairs, then the spears parted once more, and he burst into the room, a portly figure in his customary plain hunting gear, his bull head thrust forward, his red curls and beard threaded with iron grey, his eyes icy with fury and hatred. Eleanor took one look at him and knew that this was not going to be easy. Had she ever hoped it would be?

She curtseyed and bent her head, observing the proper courtesies. Of course, it might have been more politic to kneel, or prostrate herself, as a supplicant, but she was not the one at fault here, she reminded herself. Not that maintaining that position would help her, she knew, but she could not accept that she was in the wrong.

'There are no words to describe what I think of you,' Henry growled, without preamble. She looked up, but he would not meet her steady, hostile gaze. 'This is the bitterest betrayal of my whole life,' he declared, his face puce with anger and distress.

'There was no reasoning with you,' Eleanor said evenly. 'You could have seen it coming. God knows, I tried to warn you what might happen if you persisted in your unjust treatment of our sons. Did you really expect me, as their mother, to stand by and let you do it?'

'Do you know what you have done?' Henry snarled. 'Half of Europe is up in arms against me, and that includes your whoreson vassals of Aquitaine! They make this quarrel their excuse to rise in protest at what they like to call my oppressive rule.'

'Look to yourself, Henry!' Eleanor flung back. 'Look who is really to blame.'

'Don't try to excuse your conduct,' he spat. 'You have offended grievously, and you are trying to shift the blame onto others. Thanks to you and your sons, my kingdom is under threat; why, I could even lose my crown! Is that the act of a dutiful and loyal wife? It is outrageous, beyond belief! I tell you, Eleanor, you could look at all the old chronicles and find numerous examples of sons rising up against their father, but none of a queen rebelling against her husband. You will make me the pity and laughing stock of Christendom. They are even saying that this is God's punishment on me for entering into an incestuous marriage. Incestuous? Diabolic, more like!'

He was beside himself; there could be no reasoning with him, so it was not even worth trying.

'What are you going to do?' she challenged, trying to keep her voice steady. 'Are you going to put me on trial, to be judged by your twelve good men and true?'

He glared at her. 'By rights, I should have you hanged as the traitor you are. But count yourself extremely fortunate that I have no wish to parade my shame – or yours – in public. I have made no announcement of your arrest, nor do I intend to proclaim your disaffection. I want no more scandal, as you have caused scandal and damage enough. The whole of Europe will no doubt be whispering of it by now – I hope you realise that. God, Eleanor, did you really want to hurt me so much?'

'Hurt you?' she echoed. She was safe, she was safe – and could therefore speak out. 'I think the boot was rather on the other foot. What of all your women over the years, all the times you betrayed me? What of your foolish thraldom to Becket, on whom your love was wasted, and for whose counsel you forsook mine? What of the way you rode roughshod over my advice on how to rule my domains, with consequences you now have to deal with? And, worst of all, what of the injustice you have shown our sons?'

'I never realised you hated me so much,' Henry said, his face working in rage and self-pity. 'By the eyes of God, I have been nourishing a viper in my bosom!'

'I *loved* you!' cried Eleanor. 'But you destroyed that love, and I had to watch you do it. I can never tell you how deeply you have injured me. All these years . . .'

She buried her face in her hands and began to sob, all the pent-up tension and fear of the last days finding its release in a flood of tears. 'Alas, it is too late for us!' she wailed.

'None of my so-called betrayals justifies your treachery,' Henry said brutally.

'So punish me!' she screamed, wanting there to be an end to this horrible wrangling between them, wanting to hurt him where he would feel the most pain. 'Do your worst. Ask yourself how deep my betrayal went! Put me to death, and then spend the rest of your life wondering.'

Henry thrust his face into hers. 'What do you mean by that?' he demanded, his tone menacing.

'Ah, so you do care!' Eleanor pounced. Henry gripped her arms.

'Tell me!' he barked. 'Have you been playing the whore, Eleanor?'

'No more than Fair Rosamund has, or the Lady of Akeny, or Rohese de Clare, or any of the legions of other sluts you have bedded, Henry!'

'You will tell me!' he roared.

'And have you make war on a great lord?' She was enjoying having her revenge, in a bitter sort of way; it was as if it was her last chance to do so, as if it no longer mattered what she said or did.

'Who was he?' Henry was beside himself. '*Tell me!*'

'Ah! You'll just have to keep guessing – and wondering if I found him a better man than you!'

The taunt went home. Henry was almost foaming at the mouth. In a moment, he would be thrashing on the floor, chewing the rushes.

'Oh, but he was a well-endowed stallion!' she baited him.

'You've done it for yourself now,' he seethed, baring his teeth.

'So what will you do to me? Hang me now?'

'No. That would be too easy for you.' His breath was coming in short pants. He was almost out of control. 'You must hate being shut up here. It's true, isn't it? I can see from your face. Well, my faithless Lady, I'm going to leave you locked up to think on your sins while I deal with the God-awful mess you have caused. And, Eleanor,' Henry added, his bloodshot eyes narrowing, 'I hope you rot here.'

His pronouncement almost winded her; all sense of triumph fled. He had the power, she did not. It was as simple as that. She was to be confined here, in this miserable room, for God knew how long. The prospect was grim, ghastly . . . She could not breathe, she was stifling. Shut up, imprisoned, never to walk in God's fresh air, never to smell the scent of growing flowers, never to hunt, to feel the wind in her hair, the thrill of the chase. Cut off from her children; exiled from her beloved Aquitaine. It was too cruel a punishment. It would kill her. Already, the world was dimming . . .

As Eleanor collapsed to the floor in a faint, Henry looked down pitilessly on her and barked for her servant.

'Lay her on the bed,' he commanded Amaria, as he flung himself out of the room, desperate to be gone. 'She'll come round soon. Or she's faking it, which wouldn't surprise me.'

But Eleanor wasn't faking it. For a few, blissful moments, she was dead to the world, unaware of the darkness and oblivion closing around her.

48 Barfleur, the English Channel and Southampton,
    1174

The Queen had been suffering her terrible imprisonment for more than a year when the summons came for her to be conducted to the King at Barfleur on the Norman coast.

'The King has summoned me?' Eleanor repeated incredulously, when the captain of the guard informed her of his instructions.

'Make ready,' he told Amaria, ignoring the Queen's question.

She could not believe it. The dragging months of her confinement had been the worst time of her life; she had thought they would never end, that Henry meant to keep her immured here for ever. She had not seen him since that catastrophic day when he had condemned her to be shut up here, nor had there been any message from him. It had been as if she were dead and buried – as well she might be, she had thought bitterly. It had changed her, this year of extreme trial; it had made her feel as if she had suddenly become anonymous, as if the living, breathing entity that was Queen Eleanor had ceased to exist and that, in her place, there was only a barely existing shell of the woman she had once been. She felt demoralised and isolated, starved of lively conversation and of all the things that had made life pleasant and joyful.

For a long time, she had burned with resentment at the injustice of her punishment, and with hatred for Henry, fanning the flames with thoughts of vengeance, and what if . . . Yet after a while, she had discovered that it was best not to nurture her grievances, unless she wanted them to destroy her. That was when she had learned a kind of acceptance, and become able to adapt to her circumstances and take pleasure in small, everyday things, and to shut her mind to thoughts of what could or should have been. The worst of it had been not knowing when – or if – she would ever be free.

But now, at long last, Henry had sent for her. Did this mean that he had made peace with his sons, and that they had insisted on her liberation? God, let it be so! she prayed.

Two of the most awful aspects of her captivity had been not receiving any news of, or communications from, her children, and being cut off from the rest of humanity. She missed her sons dreadfully, more than she could ever have expected; she could not bear even to think of her beloved Richard. It was torture to her, not knowing if he was safe, or well. Would Henry even inform her if he had died? She could not quite bring herself to believe that he would not, but the Henry who had shut her up here was a vengeful man; he was no longer the idealistic prince she had married, but a king who cared nothing for the sensibilities and opinions of others. So she agonised over her sons, fearing that their father might have turned them against her, or that they were wounded, even dead in the fighting, and no one had told her. But surely, if that had been the case, she would have known it in her bones, or at least picked up some hint of it from Amaria.

She knew virtually nothing of what had been going on in the world beyond her window, just the odd bit of information that she had been able to glean or extract from the waiting woman. Against all her expectations, Amaria and she had become almost friends during the months of living in close proximity to each other; it could not have been otherwise, or they would have been at each other's throats. Yet there remained some unbridgeable distance between them, for it had soon become clear that Amaria was an uneducated woman of few words and fewer ideas. It was also plain that, however much Amaria might privately sympathise with her mistress, she was in fear of her superiors and the King, and therefore determined to obey her orders to the letter, refusing to discuss with Eleanor anything beyond domestic and mundane subjects. And Eleanor was, of course, the Queen, a fact of which Amaria was still slightly in awe.

Amaria's initial hostility had quickly evaporated, Eleanor had been quick to realise, yet to begin with, she had embarked on her task with the feudal peasant's resentment towards those of higher rank, and her inverted snobbery had made her suspicious from the first, especially after she had heard gossip about what the Queen was supposed to have done. But Eleanor had subtly won her around, not by overtly protesting her innocence, as many prisoners in her situation might have done, but by letting slip the odd, telling remark, or occasionally betraying the depths of her anguish for her sons; and by and by, Amaria had come to realise that the situation was far more complex than she had at first surmised.

And Amaria, to her astonishment, had soon found herself liking the Queen, very much indeed. So now she was pleased for Eleanor that the King had summoned her, although she felt a touch anxious that her services would no longer be required once the Queen was set free. She had served her mistress well, and with as much kindness as she dared – there were now four books, a chess set, a lyre and three more gowns in the over-flowing chest – but my Lady might not wish in the future to be reminded of this dark period in her life, or of the servant who had shared it with her.

'Do not look so worried, Amaria,' Eleanor said, catching her mood. 'When I am restored to court, I promise you I will make you one of my waiting women. I shall always be grateful for your kindly treatment of me in this my prison.'

Dared she let her heart sing at the prospect of freedom? She kept looking at the slit of blue sky, thinking that she would soon be out in the world again and able to enjoy the rest of the summer. But what did Henry really intend? After all that had passed between them, he surely could not want her to live with him again as his wife. If he meant to continue as before, with her ruling Aquitaine and him the rest of his empire, then he would not be summoning her to Barfleur. Barfleur was one of the ports from which they had often taken ship for England. It was years since Eleanor had seen England. England, for her, was now and for ever associated with that terrible visit to Woodstock and the miserable birth of John that followed it.

But if Henry wanted a reconciliation of sorts, and for her to accompany him to England as his queen, then so be it. She would go, and meekly do as she was bid – and make the best of it, avoiding all occasion for conflict. Anything would be prefer-able to this. Her heart leaped at the possibility that she might see her sons again soon.

Watching the Queen standing at the window, deep in thought, Amaria reflected sadly that these months of confine-ment had aged her. Eleanor was fifty-two, and looked it. Her greying red hair had faded to the colour of straw and gone thin on the skull; her eyes and the corners of her mouth were circled by fine lines; her skin had paled through lack of expo-sure to sunlight. Yet she retained – and always would – that exquisite bone structure that lent her her peculiar beauty. The King would find his wife changed, but still, despite every-thing, attractive.

*

Eleanor's spirits sank rapidly when she saw that she was to be accompanied by a heavily armed escort. There could be no doubt that Henry meant for her to travel as a prisoner, under guard. Unless he was bent on making some dramatic gesture such as liberating her before the eyes of their sons, she had to face the fact that her future still looked bleak. She toyed feverishly with the idea of making a dramatic personal appeal to Henry, of debasing herself before him and promising anything – *anything* – to regain her freedom.

It felt strange to be on horseback again; she was stiff and out of condition, she realised. But, expert rider that she had been all her life, she soon became acclimatised to being back in the saddle. Yet her pleasure in once more feeling the heat of the sun and the soft breath of the July breeze was subsumed by her inner dread and bleak disappointment. She could take no pleasure in the flowers that bedecked the hedgerows, the green fields peopled by villeins stripped to the waist and singing as they toiled on their strips, the sparkling rivers and streams, or the rich, golden countryside in all its summer beauty. It was as if her life was being held in suspension until her fate had been revealed to her.

As they rode into Barfleur, Eleanor could see a great fleet of at least forty ships waiting in the harbour. So they were bound for England, as she had anticipated. But why so many ships? Then she saw a great company of soldiers waiting to board some of the vessels anchored at the further end of the quay. So Henry was taking an army with him. Surely he could not *still* be at war? She began to feel even more uneasy.

Her escort led her past the squat fortified church tower where she had once waited with Henry for a tempest to cease, so that he could cross to England and claim his kingdom. That had been all of twenty years ago. Where had the time gone? And look where it had brought them! But there was no leisure to reflect, as the captain was leading them towards the quayside, where she could see a large gathering of people, many of them well-dressed women, waiting while their baggage was stowed on board the flagship. As she drew nearer, she recognised many familiar faces.

There was Henry, his face weather-beaten and tanned,

standing with his hand on the shoulder of a stocky boy with dark, copper-gold curls. It was John, grown up fast, she realised with a jolt, looking around anxiously for his older brothers. But there was no sign of them. In fact, it looked as if Henry had rounded up all the females in his family. She caught her breath as she espied her daughter Joanna, pretty as a partridge, looking apprehensively in her mother's direction; it was such a joy to see Joanna again; she hoped that her daughter did not think ill of her, that Henry had not poisoned her young mind with calumnies.

There was Queen Marguerite, sixteen now, and the living image of Louis; Alys, her younger sister, Richard's betrothed, a willowy brunette who must now be about fourteen, and surely ripe for marriage. The insufferable Constance was staring at Eleanor with undisguised contempt; already, even at twelve years old, she was posing provocatively, her clinging white *bliaut* accentuating every detail of her wide, curvaceous hips and small breasts; unlike most girls, she kept her hair cropped short, which gave her an elfin appearance, but did not, in Eleanor's opinion, look attractive or suit her. But Constance always was one to be different and draw attention to herself. Gentle Alice of Maurienne stood with her, casting wistful glances at the oblivious John, her betrothed, and watching over them all was the King's bastard sister, Emma of Anjou, a capable matron in widow's garb who looked the image of her father, Count Geoffrey. Eleanor supposed that she had been summoned by her brother to take the place of the mother who had been shut up in prison. A little way off, a cluster of noble girls and ladies chattered excitedly; no doubt they had been summoned to attend on all the King's womenfolk.

As the Queen's escort dismounted, the captain holding Eleanor's bridle as she climbed off her horse, the King broke away from his party and walked slowly towards them, his face impassive. Eleanor curtseyed formally, then rose in trepidation to face him. He looked at her blankly, with no trace of emotion.

'I will not say you are welcome, Eleanor,' he began, his voice husky. 'You'd know I didn't mean it. But I trust you had a good journey.'

'Why have you summoned me, my Lord?' she asked. There

was no point in continuing with the pleasantries, even though everyone was watching them with avid interest.

'I am taking you – and these young ladies – to England. Thanks to your efforts, we are still at war.' He glared at her. 'Even the Scots are joining the fray now, as if Louis and our beloved sons are not making enough mischief. They are all threatening England with invasion, and my justiciar there is bombarding me with appeals for help. No doubt it pleases you to hear that, Madam.'

Eleanor could not ignore the barb. 'I am very sorry for your trouble,' she said, 'but you only brought it upon yourself.'

'So you had nothing to do with it?' he sneered, his manner icy.

'I never incited anyone to invade England. And I don't see how my presence there will help your cause.'

Henry grinned at her nastily. 'Did you think I would leave you in Rouen, with war breaking out on all fronts, and Paris not that far off? One of our sons – nay, Louis himself, possibly – might take it into his head to free you and exploit once more your treacherous heart. I'm not a fool, Eleanor. You are going to a more secure prison in England, where you can stay out of trouble.'

It was as if a dead weight were pressing on her chest. She feared she might faint again, as she had when he had last told her what her fate was to be. To have her hopes of freedom suddenly raised, and then as speedily dashed, was devastating. But she managed to maintain her composure.

'Where are you sending me?'

'I am thinking about it. Where would you least like to go?'

She almost said Woodstock, and stopped herself in time. Any prison, however grim and gloomy, would be preferable.

'While my sons are in peril, I care not where I go,' she answered. 'But what of these young girls, their wives?'

'They will be well looked after. I am sending Marguerite, Constance and Alys to Marlborough Castle, as hostages for the good behaviour of their lords and King Louis. My sister will have the care of them.'

'And Joanna and John?'

'Joanna goes with them. John stays with me from now on. Of

all my sons, he is the only true one.' Henry's face had softened at the mention of the youngest of his brood.

'Might I be permitted to embrace my children?' she ventured.

'You weren't worried about embracing them when you packed them off to Fontevrault,' Henry retorted.

'*You* packed them off there,' she threw back.

'Be honest, Eleanor: you couldn't wait to see the back of John, baby that he was.'

She was taken aback. 'It is another thing for which I have you to blame,' she accused him.

'Me? What have I got to do with it?'

'It's a long story, and you would never understand it,' Eleanor said wearily.

Henry shook his head in exasperation. 'Eleanor, I don't have time for this. We must board our ship soon, to catch the tide. Tell your woman to bring your gear.'

It was 1154 all over again, except that one would not have expected the voyage to be so rough in July. As soon as they put to sea, the waves swelled, heaving so violently that the ship was pitched and tossed to within a timber's breadth of breaking up.

The women, Eleanor included, were all confined to a cabin in the forecastle; some were seasick, most were very frightened. Nine-year-old Joanna crept warily to her mother's side and clung to her.

'There, there, sweeting,' Eleanor murmured, glad beyond measure to be able to embrace her child, and grateful for this small blessing amidst all the fear and misery. But when she tried to comfort the wailing Constance, the girl shook her off rudely. Eleanor recoiled; she would do no more for Constance, she vowed.

Outside, they could hear the sailors shouting warnings. The rain came, pattering furiously against the wooden walls and roof. The terrible motion of the waves was relentless. Eleanor tried to pray, but could not focus her mind. Did she really want God to spare her? Would it not be best for everyone, herself included, if she drowned and sank to the bottom of the sea?

Then they could hear the King's voice, roaring above the storm, addressing the ship's company: 'If the Lord in His mercy has ordained that peace will be restored when I arrive in England, then may He grant me a safe landing. But if He has decided to visit my kingdom with a rod, may it never be my fortune to reach the shores of my country!'

God was merciful. Soon afterwards, the sea calmed, and they sighted Southampton by nightfall. But Henry had less mercy than his Maker. As soon as they had disembarked, and the royal party had been given bread and fresh water for their saddlebags to stay them on the journey, he turned to Eleanor, whom he had contrived until now to ignore, and bade her walk a little way off with him.

'I am for Canterbury, to do my penance at last at the tomb of the holy blissful martyr, as they now call my late lamented Thomas,' he told her. 'You did know that he had been made a saint?'

Eleanor did. She experienced a wicked pleasure at the thought of the monks of Canterbury lashing Henry's back; God knew, he deserved it, and not just for his unwitting part in Becket's murder!

'Yes,' she replied, 'That was before you locked me up.'

He let that pass, his mind racing ahead. 'I have decided to send you under guard to Sarum Castle, where you will remain during my pleasure. Be clear, Eleanor, that this is your punishment for jeopardising my crown – and for wilfully destroying our marriage.'

'For that, you have only yourself to blame!' she cried, stung to anger.

'All the world condemns you as a traitor to your lord and king, Eleanor. You should hear what they say about you! Do you think that, after what you did, I could ever trust you again?'

'Trust is a mutual thing,' she said bitterly. 'You broke mine years before. Your contribution to our marriage was one long betrayal! You were destroying it long before I came out in support of our sons.'

'Men sow their wild oats,' he shrugged. 'What makes you think that you were so special among wives, that you should expect fidelity? You had my love, God knows – and you killed it.'

'Ah, but that was after Rosamund had stolen that love. You didn't love me any more; you loved her – you told me so yourself. It was quite affecting!' She spoke the words with scorn, but deep inside the wounds were yet tender: she could still feel the pain. And the prospect of her continuing imprisonment was terrible to her. 'Henry, how long do you mean to keep me shut up?'

Henry had been about to make some tart response to her remark about Rosamund, but her sudden changing of the subject put that out of his mind. He wanted to hurt her, wanted to pay her back for the long and bitter year of struggle, strife and hard fighting for which she, in part, was responsible.

'For as long as you live!' he said venomously.

49 Sarum, Wiltshire, 1175

The forbidding stone keep of Sarum sat solid and four-square in a windswept position on a grassy mound atop a hill. The hill was in fact an Iron-Age fort, but no one knew much about 'the old ones' who had built and occupied it. There were vague rumours that those humps on the top of various hills in the vicinity were their burial mounds, but no one wanted to go near them for fear of the evil shades that might be lurking there, protecting the dead. Later, the site had been colonised by the Romans; bits of masonry and pottery surfaced in the soil from time to time, and once a fragment of a mosaic pavement, which had the town dwellers shaking their heads and murmuring about heathen spirits. Sarum – or Salisberie, as some now liked to call it – was the source of many legends, and the latest ones were already in the course of being embroidered from the gossip about the Queen of England, who was shut up in the castle.

Nobody had seen her, although she had been there for many moons. She had arrived in secret, at dead of night, and – rumour had it – was kept locked in a secret chamber high in the gloomy keep. Why she was there, no one knew for sure, so discreetly had the business been handled, but the word in the taverns was that she had somehow been responsible for the terrible wars that had raged in England and over the sea for the past year and more. A ferocious conflict it had been, between the King and his sons, who had throughout been abetted by the King of France – and God knew, the French were never to be trusted. It had been an unnatural war, with son against father, husband against wife – if rumour spoke truth. But what could you expect, when the King and all who were of his blood were descended from the Devil?

It was over now, the war, and the quarrel. That was all thanks to St Thomas the Martyr! No sooner had King Henry done penance at Canterbury for his part in the saint's wicked murder, than – God be praised – the holy, blissful Becket had won for him a victory against the Scots. The Scottish King, William the Lyon, had been taken prisoner, even as King Henry lay smarting from his stripes, a sure sign of Heaven's forgiveness and approval. With God and St Thomas as his allies, Henry FitzEmpress had been seen to be invincible; and King Louis had taken fright and made the Young King and his brothers call off their invasion – the news had been all over the market place, brought by carriers in their carts and a man with a dancing bear, lately come from London.

Next the townsfolk heard, King Henry had returned to Normandy in triumph, the craven French king had sued for peace, and the English princes had made their submission, on their knees, to their father, who had given them the kiss of peace. A treaty had been signed, and they had promised never again to rise against him. My, there had been such a ringing of bells throughout the land in celebration as never before!

Eleanor had heard the bells, clanging deafeningly from the tower of the half-built cathedral that stood, dark and squat like a crouching beast, on the hill beneath the castle mound. She knew those bells must betoken something momentous, some great victory – but whose? Had Henry triumphed over their sons at last? Or had he been defeated, and – joy of joys – would her sons soon come to free her?

Her heart ached for freedom. This was a bleak, inhospitable

place – and a dirty one, for water was scarce. Isolated on its hill, and surrounded by strong walls and a deep, wooded ditch, Sarum was cut off from most civilised amenities. And the wind! It roared. Amaria had told her that, in the cathedral, a clerk could not even hear the man next to him singing. Even in summer, the blasts whipped and whistled around the castle and its battlements, rattling doors and shutters; in winter, the wind came in gales, lashing the walls and howling mercilessly through the window slits, repeatedly extinguishing the fires they tried to keep blazing in the inadequate braziers. Eleanor's first winter here had been a martyrdom. She had been so cold, colder than ever before in her life. She had suffered miseries with chilblains, and could only thank God that she had not yet fallen victim to the rheumatism that was chronic in this benighted place.

Otherwise, she had to admit that she had little cause to complain. Far from being immured in a dank prison, as the townsfolk imagined, she was housed and served as befitted a queen. The chambers assigned to her were no worse than those in her palaces, and equipped with luxuries such as the cushions and rich hangings to which she was accustomed. That had been a welcome surprise until she realised that it betokened the permanence of her confinement. All the same, it was good to enjoy once more the privileges of her rank, even if she was deprived of her freedom. She was served reasonable fare, on silver plates, and the good wines of Bordeaux in jewelled goblets. She had even been provided with illuminated books from the treasury at Winchester, an ivory chess set and the finest silks for her embroidery. For all this, though, the allowance allocated by the King for her household was small, and did not allow for the employment of more than the one maid.

She was grateful that Amaria had been allowed to accompany her to Sarum, yet exasperated that they were still required to share the same bed. At least she had tactfully succeeded in educating Amaria in the necessity for washing herself daily and changing her body linen, but all the same, they faced an uphill struggle to maintain hygiene in the face of the meagre supply of water, and the sometimes brackish mess that passed for it in their washing bowl. She never ceased complaining that they were forced to go about smelling of damp weeds.

Her custodians were men of standing, much trusted by the King: the lawyer and diplomat, Ranulf Glanville, was the very man who had captured the Scottish King the previous year. He had told her so himself: it was one of the few items of news she had been permitted to receive. Glanville was an energetic, versatile man, wise and well spoken. He had assisted Henry in his legal reforms, and had even written a treatise on the laws and customs of England. Eleanor liked him, for all she suspected that his fidelity to the King precluded him from entirely approving of her, and she had early on taken the initiative in inviting him to dine with her. To her surprise, Glanville had readily accepted, and his presence at her table was now a regular arrangement. Their lively and witty conversation, which never, by unspoken mutual consent, strayed to contentious matters, helped considerably to enliven the dreary monotony of her days.

Her other custodian – she was rather impressed to find that Henry had deemed two necessary to keep her under lock and key – was one of the royal chamberlains, Ralph FitzStephen. He was more taciturn than Glanville, yet although he never scanted his respect towards her, she knew he was wary of her, and could not warm to him. She knew instinctively that, if she wanted any favours, it was Glanville whom she should approach. And indeed, he did his best for her. He allowed her to take the air on the battlements, when the wind permitted; otherwise, it was dangerous to go up there, and she – and the guards who had to accompany her – would run a very real risk of being swept over the parapet if they defied the elements.

When the weather was clement, she would climb to her high eyrie and gaze out across the mighty ramparts and the teeming, overpopulated town they protected to the vast sweep of the Avon Valley beyond, with its gentle hills that led to the eastern edge of the New Forest, invisible in the far distance. Then she would turn and look wistfully southwards, where – hundreds of miles distant – lay Aquitaine. It pained her to think of the land of her birth, which she feared she might well never see again, yet her heart was drawn towards it inexorably. In her mind, she often travelled the hidden, lushly wooded valleys, the sun-drenched hilltops and narrow gorges, and feasted her eyes once more on the mighty castles on their craggy heights, the mellow stone churches and pretty villages, the ranks of vines and the glittering rivers. Aquitaine was a constant ache in her heart.

Did her people feel grief and anger at the cruel way in which their duchess had been treated? Her imprisonment must have had an unwelcome and brutal impact on their lives, for Henry, in the wake of the war that – she guessed – had almost succeeded in toppling him from his throne, would not scruple to lay his heavy hand of authority on his domains. (No one had thought fit to tell her that Richard now sat in her place in Poitiers, accepted by her subjects and acclaimed as the doughty warrior he had proved himself to be. Richard, who was there at Henry's command, and subject to his vigilance . . .)

Perched in her lofty refuge, her useless veil in her hand, ignoring the wind whipping the tendrils that had escaped from her plaits, and with her face pressed forlornly against the rough stone of the crenellations as she stared fixedly into the distance, Eleanor had often reflected that the prophecies had been misleading. The 'King of the North Wind' – that was Henry – still wielded his sceptre over Aquitaine, but the 'Eagle of the Broken Covenant' – that had to be herself; she was beginning to understand its meaning now – had yet to discover why she should especially rejoice in her third nesting. The cubs had awakened, and roared loud, as Merlin had long ago predicted; but the only person who remained loaded with chains, as the seer had described, was their mother.

Her inner torment was ceaseless. Her harp was turned to mourning, she told herself, reverting in her distress to the language of the troubadours, on which she had been reared. 'My flute sounds the note of affliction; my songs are turned to lamentations,' she grieved.

There was only Amaria to whom she could unburden herself, although Amaria was still scared of her superiors, and usually just sat and listened, clucking sympathetically here and there.

'I had a royal liberty!' Eleanor told her, over and over again;

she was remorseless with herself. 'I lived richly, I took pleasure in the company of my women and delight in my music. I was a queen with two crowns! I had everything. But now I am consumed with sorrows – my heart is ravaged with tears. I cry out unanswered!'

Then she would grow defiant, her old spirit burgeoning. 'Never fear, I will not cease to cry!' she assured Amaria. 'I will not weary; I will raise my voice like a trumpet, so that it may reach the ears of my sons. They will deliver me!'

Hearing the bells, her breast was filled with hope surging anew, and she was in a ferment, desperate to know what they betokened. She could not sit, but got up and paced about, up and down, up and down the chamber, hugging herself tightly, as Amaria watched her, dismay all over her face. She had been in the cathedral this morning; she had gone, as she often did, to be shriven, not liking that snooty chaplain who had been charged with the cure of the Queen's soul. And she had heard of the King's victory. But, as usual, she forbore to say anything of what she heard beyond these walls.

Eleanor was well on the way to convincing herself that Richard and the Young King – and perhaps even Geoffrey – were coming to free her. 'The day of my deliverance is here, I know it!' she breathed. 'And then I shall come again to dwell in my native land. Please, O God, let it be so!' Amaria looked away, unable to bear much more of this.

The door to the chamber opened. Ranulf Glanville stood there, his attractively craggy, clever face wearing a look of jubilation. For one blissful moment, Eleanor thought he was going to tell her that she was free. She even got as far as thinking that she would be bountiful towards him when she was restored to power, for he had been a considerate gaoler . . . But with his first words, her hopes were savagely dashed.

'My Lady, I am commanded by the King to inform you that your sons have submitted to his authority, and that King Louis has conceded defeat. The bells you can hear are being rung in celebration of the peace that has been agreed. They are being sounded everywhere, for the whole of England rejoices!'

Eleanor sank down into a chair, feeling as if she had been winded. She could not speak, so great was her disappointment.

Glanville was looking at her, not unsympathetically. No fool, he would have guessed that she might misunderstand the reason for the rejoicings.

'Are you able to give me news of my sons?' she managed to ask.

'I am at liberty to say that the breach between them and the King has been healed; he has excused their treason on account of their youth. In the circumstances, the King has been very generous, although I am not allowed to discuss the terms of the peace settlement with you, my Lady. What I can say is that, out of affection and love for the princes, he has proclaimed a general amnesty.'

Eleanor rose to her feet, hope springing again.

'So I am to be freed after all?' she asked eagerly.

'No, my Lady, I am afraid not.' Glanville's face was pained.

Eleanor almost reeled at his words, as did Amaria, who burst into noisy tears. This was altogether too much to bear.

'Then how can it be a general amnesty, if I am excluded?' Eleanor shrilled.

Glanville looked uncomfortable. Clearly, he was debating with himself how much he dared say to her. 'I am probably exceeding my orders,' he said, 'but the King made known his belief that his sons had been led astray by troublemakers. He named the King of France . . . and yourself.'

Of course. Someone had to take the blame and be punished. Henry needed his sons: they were his heirs, although she suspected that he had conceded them even less than before as the price of making peace. It was politic, indeed necessary, to restore good relations with them as soon as possible. But for that to happen, there had to be a scapegoat, someone at whom people could point a finger and think: *she* was the evil genius behind their rebellion. They were not to blame.

She could never, in her worst nightmares, have envisaged that Henry could be so vengeful.

The King had triumphed, and for a time the talk in the market place and inns of Sarum was all of that. Good King Henry, the people called him, forgetting their horror at the murder of Becket and how they had vilified him then. All that mattered to them now was that he had been victorious against his enemies, as kings should be. Some could remember the trials of the weak Stephen's reign, and knew how to appreciate a strong ruler like this one. For weeks, the taverns resonated with the sound of ballads bawled tunelessly in honour of the King's real – and imagined – exploits.

Clearly, Queen Eleanor, the one who was shut up in the castle and had not been freed – heads nodded significantly over that – was much to blame. *She* had caused the war, beyond any doubt, *and* that devil, Louis of France. She was an unnatural woman, betraying her lord like that. But no one was really surprised. There had been other rumours over the years, scandalous ones at that, *and* probably all true, given what they knew now. The people fell to whispering . . .

Yet as time passed, in its normal seasonal cycle for the good folk of Sarum, but dismally slowly for Eleanor, incarcerated in her tower, the mood of the people changed. By varied and circuitous routes, other rumours had reached them, rumours that offended their peasant sensibilities and their ingrained sense of right and wrong.

'The King is living openly with his leman!'

'He flaunts his paramour for all to see!'

'They call her the Rose of the World. My eye! Rose of Unchastity would be a better way of putting it!'

Henry was again the object of rank disapproval and derision, and the women were even more censorious than the men. 'Since the world copies a bad king, he sets a bad example,' they complained. 'Why, our husbands might think to follow it!' And tongues clucked in outrage.

Eleanor did not hear any of this, although Amaria could have told her a thing or two. She refrained, of course, not because she had been specifically instructed to keep quiet about such matters, but because she felt sorry for her mistress, whose emotions were very fragile where the King was concerned. The poor lady had troubles enough, and Amaria was not about to add to them.

But Eleanor was not to be kept in ignorance for long.

Unexpectedly, she had a visitor, the ascetic Hugh of Avalon, Henry's good friend and mentor. Eleanor had always liked and respected Hugh, that saintly man, that good and fearless man, who never shrank from speaking his mind, and whose unbounded charity was famous. Of a noble Burgundian family, and a monk of the Grande Chartreuse, Mother House of the austere Carthusian Order, he had just arrived in England at the King's urgent request to head Henry's new monastic foundation at Witham in Somerset.

Kneeling to receive Prior Hugh's blessing, Eleanor wondered what had brought him here. She did not think it was merely to offer her some spiritual consolation, although she would be glad of that for, try as she might, she could not warm to the chaplain whom Henry had appointed. She feared that Hugh of Avalon might be the bringer of bad tidings – another blow from Henry – and she was right.

'My daughter,' the Prior said, in his deep, commanding voice, 'I am come on a somewhat delicate but necessary mission.'

Oh no, Eleanor thought, but she observed the courtesies and invited her visitor to sit down.

'This is very sad and regrettable, this estrangement between you and the King, my Lady,' Hugh began, regarding her with great warmth and humanity.

'It is no mere estrangement. I am his prisoner. He cannot forgive me for taking my sons' part against him.'

'Of that, in charity, I will forbear to speak,' Hugh told her, seeing her distress, and knowing that anything he could say would only add to it. 'But I must open my mind to you plainly, and tell you that I have always held the union between you and King Henry to be adulterous and invalid.'

'Adulterous?' echoed Eleanor, her mind rejecting the wider implications of what he was saying, and thrusting to one side the memory of Geoffrey in her bed, and the secret, shameful barrier to her marriage with Henry that her trysts with his father had created. What would the holy Prior say if he knew about that? But she could never speak of it, and Henry knew it. Nor, she realised, could he, because he had married her knowing of the impediment. To admit that would be to declare their children bastards.

She had feared for a moment that Hugh of Avalon had somehow found out about her affair with Geoffrey. But he could not have done, she told herself. Even Henry would not be so rash or vicious as to endanger his sons' rights. But it had been a nasty moment, and she waited in trepidation to hear what the Prior had to say.

'The annulment of your first marriage was, in my opinion, on questionable grounds,' Hugh told her. 'You had married King Louis in good faith. A dispensation could without difficulty have been procured, and penances undergone for the lack of it. Yet you chose to leave your husband and take another, to whom you were even more closely related in blood. Because of that, no good could have come from that second union – which time, indeed, has proved. And therefore, the King wishes to end it by entering a plea of consanguinity.'

Eleanor listened to all this in shock. End their marriage? But of course, it was the logical thing to do, the *coup de grâce*, for it was finished already, all but dead from several mortal blows, a mere memory from the past. Yet she had never anticipated that Henry would actually try to divorce her. And why now? The time to have done it would have been when he learned of her fateful disobedience.

She shook her head disbelievingly. 'And where do I stand in this?'

The Prior took her hand and held it as he did his best to make the unpalatable palatable. 'The King will claim that both of you entered into the union in ignorance of any impediments; that being so, your children will continue to be regarded as legitimate, and the succession will not be endangered.'

Eleanor was doing some quick thinking. If Henry was arguing that theirs was no marriage, then he had no claim to her lands – or on her person! Freedom was beckoning . . .

'If I was never married to the King, then I am not his subject, and cannot be accused of committing treason against him,' she said. 'If I give my consent to this divorce, then he will have no grounds for keeping me here, and must free me. Wait, good Prior! Let me speak.' She held up her hand to still his objection. 'I am sovereign duchess of Aquitaine. Once I agree to this, my domains must be restored to me, and I must be freed to go back and rule them as an independent prince; and on my death, they will pass to my sons. It will mean the empire being broken up now, but in time all our domains will be reunited.'

'Ah,' enunciated the Prior, and in that one syllable managed to make it very plain that things would not be as simple as that. 'The King also wishes to object that you have committed adultery, by your own admission.'

'If I am not his wife, how can I have committed adultery?' Eleanor was quick to object.

'It is a technicality, my Lady. At the time you rebelled against the King and committed adultery, you believed you were his wife. Anyone who deliberately takes an action that threatens the King's safety and the weal of his realm is either his enemy or commits treason. By your adultery, you could have impugned the succession.'

'At my age?' she cried.

'Well, maybe not,' Prior Hugh conceded with a faint smile. He did not relish this unpleasant mission. 'But the Pope will take a dim view of your conduct, of that there can be no doubt. He may be of the opinion that the King is right to keep you as his prisoner.'

Eleanor was furious. 'Henry wants it both ways! He doesn't want me as a wife any more, but he's prepared to play any trick to keep my lands, to which, when our marriage is ended, he can have no lawful claim.'

'He proposes that Duke Richard can continue to rule Aquitaine in your stead, as your heir, as he is doing now. I believe that was what you wanted anyway.'

Richard! Eleanor was overjoyed to hear any news of him, let alone such good news, but the injustice of Henry's purpose rankled bitterly.

'Richard was to share power with me; *that* was what was agreed, not that he should rule alone. He is but seventeen.'

'Old enough to have reached man's estate,' Prior Hugh observed. 'He has gained renown as a great warrior, but one could wish that he had learned more wisdom. Alas, I fear he has brought nothing but strife to that untamed land of yours. I should not be telling you this, but the people erupted in anger when they learned that you were not coming back, and Richard has been exacting a terrible vengeance to bring them to heel and establish his rule.'

This was not what she had expected to hear. Richard had been brought up to have all the knightly virtues: to strive to be valorous, to protect the poor, the weak and the innocent; he was a well-educated young man, a troubadour reared and nurtured as a true son of the south; and she had done her very best to instil in him a great love of his heritage.

'What has he done?' she asked tremulously, forgetting for a moment the proposed divorce and her grievances against Henry.

Prior Hugh looked pained. 'You could not say he has been inefficient, for Aquitaine is quiet now, and in subjection to him. Yet it is small wonder, as he has been ravaging the land with great savagery, reducing castle after castle, and sparing not man, woman or child. The details of the atrocities that were committed by his men do not bear repetition.'

'Tell me!' Eleanor urged, unable to believe what she was hearing. Richard was her son – she could not credit that he had done these things. Surely he had done them at the command of his father – he could not, of himself, have inflicted these wrongs on the domains he had claimed to love, or on its people. They were her people. She wanted to weep for them, and for the land of her birth; they had, after all, been fighting for the return of their duchess, and protesting at the imposition of an overlord who had no right to usurp her place entirely. If they had borne these cruelties, then she could bear the telling of them.

Hugh's fine-boned face betrayed great emotion as he spoke. 'Those who opposed the Duke were mutilated: some had their eyes gouged out, others had their hands cut off. It is said that their women were raped – forgive me, my Lady – by Richard and his soldiers. By all reports, he was merciless. Aquitaine has been ruthlesly quelled, and now lies under his iron gauntlet.'

And this was my own son, my beloved, Eleanor thought, unable to speak. 'May God forgive him – and comfort the afflicted,' she murmured at length, deeply moved. She could not come to terms with the idea of her Richard as tyrant, torturer, rapist . . . This could only be Henry's doing. She had to believe that.

'You realise, Father Prior, this makes me even more deter-mined to fight for my rights,' she declared. 'Aquitaine needs me, and I should be there.'

'You must do as your conscience dictates, my Lady,' Hugh replied gravely. 'I have conveyed the King's wishes to you, as I was bound to do, and told you my opinion. I might add that you will have a battle on your hands, for he is determined to keep you here. The last thing he wants is for you to return to Aquitaine. He says he cannot have you free to plot more mischief against him with your sons and your vassals. He fears that you might remarry – and that to a lord hostile to him.'

'So he seeks a way to set me aside without any loss to himself,' Eleanor fumed. 'But if it will prove so difficult to divorce me, why is he doing it?'

'I do not like to tell you this, but he wishes to remarry,' Hugh of Avalon said gently, although his words came like a slap in the face. It was too much to take in; it had all been too much to take in, after months of quiet, uninterrupted monotony.

'Who?' she asked, thinking of Rosamund. Was Henry really going to marry his mistress, the daughter of a mere knight? He must have lost his wits completely!

'The Princess Alys of France,' the Prior said, his mouth turned down in disapproval.

'But she is Richard's betrothed!'

'Aye, but betrothals can be broken as well as marriages,' Hugh reminded her. 'Already, the King has sent to Pope Alexander, asking him to despatch a legate to England to hear his case against you. The matter is being kept secret, of course, and the King insists specially on your discretion, since annulling your union is a serious step and may have far-reaching conse-quences.'

'And I suppose that, if I try to proclaim my objections to the world, although there's little chance of my being heard, then he will withdraw my privileges!' Eleanor said scornfully.

'He has not said so, and I should hope that he would never go so far,' Hugh replied, as he got up and made to leave.

'Father Prior,' Eleanor said quickly, 'you are a wise man, known for your integrity. What would you counsel me to do? If I agree to this divorce, might things go better for me?'

'My Lady, I would advise you to pray for guidance, and to await the Pope's pronouncement. He will deal with you fairly, you may be sure. He is not the kind of man to be bought by kings.'

When Hugh had gone, she did as she had been bidden, sinking to her knees, praying for herself and Henry, praying for Richard, whose immortal soul was surely in peril, and seeking a way forward in her present dilemma. She had long accepted that her marriage had ended, and could understand the necessity for Henry to remarry, but she was surprised to find herself near to weakening tears at the realisation that he wanted to set her aside for this young girl of – what was it? – fifteen! Dear God, she thought, could You not at least have spared me this?

She knew that Henry's love for her was long dead. He hated her: he had proved it again and again. Why, then, did she sometimes, in the dark wastes of the night, find herself still wanting him, still nourishing the smallest of hopes – against all reason, and in spite of all he had done to her – that they might be reconciled in the future? Why?

The answer was not far to seek. Because no man had ever stirred her as Henry had, or inspired such violent emotions in her. No man could touch him. There would always be something between them, some vestige of the great passion they had once shared. And, even in the face of all that had happened, she still wanted him in her bed. That was almost the worst of it; in fact, it had been one of the worst things about her imprisonment, being shut away from the company of men – and of one man in particular. Even now, she would find herself aching for his touch, for the feel of him inside her, for the joy he had brought her . . .

She was growing older: the years were passing relentlessly. Soon, her juices would run thin and she would be an old woman, and her powers of seduction, of pleasuring a man and receiving pleasure herself, would diminish. Isolated here, she was aware that, for her, time was running out, but that there was no means of fulfilling that surging need in her. She had thought that, deprived of any stimulus, it would lessen, and that she would learn to focus more on things of the spirit, as she had not done in her reckless youth and turbulent married life; that she would discover that inner peace that enables one to open the mind and heart to the love of God – but she had been wrong, so wrong. It had got to the point where she had even toyed with the idea of trying to seduce the handsome Ranulf Glanville, who was such a congenial supper companion, and who might not be impervious to the suggestion that he stay a little later . . . But it was not Glanville she wanted.

It was Henry, but Henry wanted to divorce her. And if he had his way, she would never bed a man again. And now her tears did flow at that dreadful prospect.

Four months she waited for further news. Four long, unending, miserable months, during which she wore herself out speculating what the Pope might say or do. Then, at last, Prior Hugh returned. She forced herself to be calm when she received him, and resolved to deal with whatever news he brought with calm reason and as much wisdom as she could muster.

It was November, and cold; the wind was howling across the plateau that was Sarum, and whistling through the window slit, and it was impossible to keep the brazier alight for long. So Eleanor sat shivering, swathed in her furs, and Prior Hugh gathered his inadequate woollen cloak about his habit as they talked.

'His Holiness sent a legate, the Cardinal of Sant' Angelo, ' he told her. 'He came on the pretext of resolving a dispute between the sees of Canterbury and York. He met with the King at Winchester, and your husband raised the matter of the annulment. Regrettably, he also tried to bribe the Cardinal with a large sum in silver coin, but the Cardinal would not take it. Nor would he even listen to the King's pleas. He merely warned him that divorcing you would involve great risks, and refused to discuss the subject further. He left for Italy soon afterwards.'

Eleanor let out a long sigh of relief, but her gratification at the Legate's rejection of Henry's plea was tempered by the awareness that, even though she remained entrenched as his lawful wife, Henry did not want her, and would almost certainly feel even more resentment towards her now, regardless of the fact that she had not actually opposed him – although that was not to say that she would not have done so, had she been pushed to it.

'I am content, of course, but I suppose the King is angry,' she said.

The Prior gave her another of his sweet smiles. 'Need you ask? He does not like to be thwarted.'

'He will not give up,' she observed lightly. 'He will find another way to be rid of me.'

'He may appeal to the Pope, but I fear it will be a waste of time.'

'You do not approve of the Pope's decision, do you, Father Prior?' she challenged.

'Our Lord speaks through His Holiness. Who am I to question that?'

'It's not easy for you, is it, acting as mediator between Henry and me?' Eleanor smiled at the Prior.

'I do not look for ease in worldly affairs,' he told her. 'I hope I have dealt with you fairly and with humanity.'

'I wish the King my Lord had been as considerate,' Eleanor told him, as he rose to take his leave. 'No doubt we shall meet again.'

'I would it could be in happier circumstances,' he told her kindly.

50 Sarum, 1175–6

It was a terrible winter. The crops had failed and famine bestrode the land, resulting in a dearth of good food even on Eleanor's table, for everyone in the castle was on short rations. The cost of a bushel of wheat had gone through the roof, and bread, that staple of the diets of rich and poor, was scarce. The destitute had been reduced to eating roots, nuts, grasses and even bark stripped from the trees. There was meat, for most farm animals had been slaughtered and their carcases salted for winter fare, but the hungry folk in humble cottages saw little of that. People were dying of starvation in the streets, or of plague. It was only the onset of bitterly cold weather that saw off the pestilence.

Eleanor sent what food she could spare from her table to succour the needy.

'I am no longer able to dispense charity as a queen should,' she told Ranulf Glanville, 'but this little I can do for them.' And went hungry herself. It was freezing in her chamber, and she and Amaria spent their days huddled in furs, their gloved hands icy at the fingertips, their noses pink with cold. Christmas was a dismal affair, with no festive fare or revelry, and Eleanor spent much of it confined to bed with a cold.

She was surprised therefore, early in the new year, to hear Glanville announce the arrival of Hugh of Avalon. She guessed, with a sinking feeling, that, if the Prior had braved the snow and ice to see her, he must bring news of some import, and wondered wearily what it might be. Something to do with the divorce, she wagered to herself.

He greeted her with his gentle smile, giving her his blessing as she went on her knees before him, then came straight to the point.

'My Lady, the King has sent me to ask if you would consider retiring from the world and taking the veil at Fontevrault, a house for which he knows you have much love.'

Retire from the world? When her heart cried out for freedom and she was bursting with life, body and soul?

'He has offered to appoint you abbess of Fontevrault, which, as you are aware, is a most prestigious and respected office.'

'And what does he ask in return?' Eleanor replied, knowing that this was just another clever ploy on Henry's part to get rid of her – and retain her lands.

'Nothing, my Lady. If you expressed the desire to take the veil, the Pope would assuredly annul your marriage. He would see it as a happy solution.'

She walked to the window and stared out unseeing at the narrow, limited view of snow-covered hills. What prestige was there in being an abbess when one had been a queen? And there was another thing . . .

'I have no vocation,' she said.

'I had not imagined that you had,' Prior Hugh told her, with wry humour. 'In my experience, large numbers of those who enter religion have no vocation. They are dedicated to God by their families. In time, they learn acceptance in the cloister. Some make a great success of their lives, and become shining examples of the monastic rule.'

'Can you see me as a shining example of the rule?' Eleanor asked.

The Prior had to smile. 'No, my Lady. But an abbess's role is not merely spiritual. She is a governor, a leader, an administrator, with her opinion sought by great men. In charge of such a house as Fontevrault, you would have status, autonomy, and the opportunity to use your considerable talents and your experience of statecraft. Think on it. Fontevrault is a peaceful place, a powerful house of prayer, and your family has enjoyed a long association with it.'

Eleanor was silent as she thought. Maybe Hugh was right. It was better to enjoy a degree of power and independence than none at all, certainly. And as abbess of Fontevrault, she would enjoy many freedoms. She knew she could make a success of it. But there was the longer-term future to consider. Not only were the stakes higher, but she wanted more, far more than Fontevrault could offer her.

'Do not think I am not tempted,' she told him. 'Believe me, I would do much to get out of this prison. But I am certain that I still have much to do in the world. I have no intention of retiring from it, or giving up my crown – or my inheritance. Because, Father Prior, that is what this is all about. It's the only way Henry can divorce me and retain possession of my lands.'

'Are you sure you wouldn't like time to think more on this?' Hugh asked.

'No. Please tell the King my Lord that I have no vocation for the religious life.'

'Very well, my Lady,' the Prior said, and made to depart, but Eleanor persuaded him to stay for dinner and overnight before he embarked on his long, cold and difficult journey.

It was something he said over the rather spartan meal that gave her cause for alarm.

'Henry cannot force me to become a nun?' she had asked.

'I should like to be able to say no, but there have been cases of husbands immuring unwanted wives in convents, and intimidating the communities into keeping them confined. Knowing him, I do not think the King would go as far, but there is much at stake in this case.'

'And just one ageing, obstinate woman standing in the way,' she added.

She fretted, she worried. At length, she thought of approaching the Archbishop of Rouen, that Rotrou who, on the brink of the fatal rebellion, had exhorted her to return to Henry. Unlike Hugh of Avalon, he believed that her marriage was valid. A plea to him might help. So she wrote, appealing to him against being forced to enter the cloister against her will, and gave the unsealed parchment to Ranulf Glanville for inspection. He looked a little troubled at its contents, but agreed to despatch it. She wondered if he would really do so.

But Glanville was as good as his word, and presently, a reply came from the Archbishop, assuring her that he would refuse to consent to her becoming a nun at Fontevrault against her wishes. Rotrou added that he had made his position known to the King, and warned her that Henry had said he would appeal again to the Pope to have their marriage dissolved. Ah, she thought, but that way, he won't get my lands! She might, she dared to think, have her freedom yet.

51 Winchester, 1176

'Make ready, my Lady,' beamed Glanville, entering Eleanor's chamber one blazing August morning. 'You are summoned to Winchester.' It was clear that he was pleased to have some good tidings to impart, at last.

Eleanor looked at him blankly. She could not take this in. Had Henry at last relented and granted her her liberty?

Glanville seemed to have read her thoughts. 'The Lord King has betrothed your daughter, the Lady Joanna, to the King of Sicily. She is staying in Winchester, where preparations are being made for her departure from this realm, and the King has given leave for you to visit her there and make your farewells. You will, of course, travel under guard.'

This unexpected kindness on Henry's part nearly took Eleanor's breath away. Was he finally thawing towards her? Was this the first step towards a reconciliation? For three years now, she had been cruelly cut off from her children, deprived of the pleasure of watching them grow to maturity and playing her proper maternal role in their lives. Heaven only knew what effect this deprivation could have had on the younger ones, those poor, innocent victims; Henry hadn't thought of that, had he, in his need to exact vengeance on her? Yet, in the wake of this one kind gesture from him, she was willing to put all that behind her. In the joyful anticipation of seeing Joanna, she was prepared to meet him more than halfway on anything.

The royal apartments in Winchester Castle were abuzz with activity, with damsels scurrying about with armfuls of rich garments and chests full of jewels, merchants displaying their luxurious fabrics, and seamstresses stitching away furiously at the eleven-year-old bride's trousseau. In the midst of it all sat Joanna, a slightly less brilliant mirror image of the young Eleanor, her fresh young face rosy with excitement. At the sight of her mother appearing in the doorway, she rose and swept a deep curtsey, her pearl silk skirts fanning over the floor.

'My dear child!' Eleanor cried, unable to contain her emotion, and suddenly mother and daughter were in each other's arms, formality and the intervening years forgotten as they embraced each other with tears and laughter.

'So you are going to be married,' Eleanor said, when she had managed to compose herself. It did not do for this girl to be burdened with the undamming of the floodgates of her own sorrows.

'I am to take ship for Palermo and marry King William, my Lady. My Lord my father says he is a great prince, and that Sicily is a fair land.'

Eleanor's heart almost bled for her daughter's innocent hopes. She prayed fervently that this marriage would turn out to be far happier than her own had been. Then she noticed Joanna looking at her blue *bliaut*. It was fine but old; all her gowns were old, for Henry had not thought fit to replace them, and the hem of this one was looking a little frayed. She could tell what Joanna was thinking, that it was unseemly for a queen to be clothed so meanly. But her daughter began prattling on happily about the wondrous wedding robes that Henry had provided for her, at enormous cost to himself. Clearly it mattered to him that his daughter impressed the world.

'I will ask him if he will purchase some fine robes for you too, my Lady,' the girl said touchingly.

'No matter,' Eleanor said. 'He has been kind enough, in allowing me to visit you here.'

'Oh, but I shall!' cried Joanna, her eyes shining. 'And I will make him let you come and visit me in Sicily. Have you ever been there, Mother?'

Eleanor's heart sank. Had Henry not seen fit to instruct anyone to break it to this poor child that her parting from her parents might be final? She was going a long way off, to a distant kingdom, and there was no guarantee that they might ever meet again. Such was the fate of princesses who were married off to foreign princes. Look at Matilda, in far-off Germany; Eleanor had no idea when, or if, she might see her eldest daughter again; she missed her still, and always would – it was a sadness that would never leave her. It was always easier for the one going away, for they were embarking on their life's adventure; it was those left behind who felt the loss most keenly.

'I went to Sicily when I was queen of France,' she said lightly. 'It is a beautiful country, with wondrous scenery and many ancient ruins, and Palermo is a fair town. King William is Norman by descent, as you are. But Daughter, do not look to have me visit you there. As you know, your father is displeased with me. It is a miracle that he has let me come here. I should not like you to look for my coming in Palermo, and then be disappointed. But we can write to each other,' she added quickly, seeing the sweet face about to crumple. 'Now, are you going to show me your wedding gown?'

*

The days spent with Joanna were precious, golden days that passed all too soon. The imminent parting lent them piquancy and brilliance. It was tragic to be restored to her daughter's company just when she might be separated from that daughter for ever, but Eleanor did her best to keep happy and cheerful. Why waste this gift of time with lamentations? Joanna should take with her a joyful image of her mother, one she could cherish and hold in her heart for ever.

'Will Father send you back to Sarum?' the child asked one day, as they took the air in the castle garden, two guards hovering discreetly in the background, as they always did. Eleanor had long since learned to get used to that, but she sensed that Joanna found it disconcerting.

'Yes, I'm sure he will,' she said lightly.

'Why did he lock you up?' The naïve question gave her a jolt.

'We had a difference of opinion as to the amount of power that the King should allow your brothers,' she answered carefully. 'Unfortunately, it led to war, and although I never intended that, your father holds me partly to blame.'

'I heard him say he can never love or trust you again,' Joanna said innocently, her little voice mournful.

Eleanor was shocked. No child should ever have to listen to one parent saying such things of the other!

'*Were* you to blame, Mother?' Joanna's look was searching.

'I did not think so at the time,' Eleanor sighed. 'I thought I was right. But now I'm no longer sure. I just want the wounds to be healed.'

'I want that too,' the child declared, 'but I don't think my brother the Young King does.'

'Oh?' asked Eleanor. This was news indeed. She had thought Henry and their sons reconciled, and had imagined the boys living in subjection to their father's heavy hand.

'The King my father kept his Easter court here. My brothers came too, but they were arguing all the time. Young Henry was angry about being kept idle in England while Richard and Geoffrey were allowed to rule Aquitaine and Brittany. He accused the King of trying to oust him from the succession, but Father wouldn't listen, so he asked leave to go to Spain, to visit the shrine of St James at Compostela, although I think he just wanted to go and meet his friends and cause trouble, or so Father said. He wouldn't let him go. Since then, he has let Young Henry go to Aquitaine, but I think he has been stirring up the people there against Richard. Oh, and I heard he was taking part in a lot of tournaments.'

So, Eleanor realised, all was clearly not well between Henry and his heir. If anything, if Joanna had it right, matters were worse now than they had been before the rebellion. Of course, Henry would find it impossible to trust his sons after what had happened.

'What of Richard? Do you know anything of him?' Eleanor asked.

'No. He went back to Aquitaine. The people there hate him. Geoffrey seems to be all right in Brittany, apart from having to live with Constance!' Mother and daughter exchanged knowing smiles, although Eleanor was disturbed to hear that her subjects hated Richard.

'And Eleanor? And John?' she enquired.

'Eleanor is still at Fontevrault, Mother. She is going to marry the Infante of Castile, but I don't know when.' Another daughter lost, Eleanor thought sadly. 'And John is betrothed again, to Hawise of Gloucester.'

'But he was betrothed to Alice of Maurienne!'

'She died of a fever,' Joanna told her. 'He says this new marriage will make him even richer.' Another heiress, Eleanor thought, with a doleful pang for that sweet child Alice, dead before she had a chance to taste life's joys. This new marriage seemed a godsend, a sensible solution to the problem of John's lack of an inheritance.

'My father keeps John with him,' Joanna was saying. 'He calls him his favourite son. But actually, he likes Geoffrey best.'

Geoffrey? Surely not! Then Eleanor realised that Joanna was talking about Henry's bastard son. He had ever favoured the boy, she thought sourly.

'Geoffrey fought for him in the war,' Joanna was saying. 'He was very brave. My father said . . .' Her voice tailed off and she flushed a deep pink.

'Yes? What did he say?' Eleanor prompted.

'He said that Geoffrey alone had proved his true son, and that his other sons were really the bastards.'

'I see,' said the Queen. She saw all too clearly.

It was gratifying to have the freedom of the castle, even if there were guards posted at every door. One day, wandering through the deserted state apartments, Eleanor stepped into the famous Painted Chamber, so-called because of the wondrous murals that Henry had commissioned for its walls, and found herself gaping in surprise. For where there had been a panel left blank, there was a new and disturbing picture of an eagle, freshly painted, and on its outstretched wings and back were three eaglets, with a fourth, the smallest, sitting on its neck, looking for all the world as if it might, at any moment, peck out its parent's eyes.

As Eleanor stared, she heard a footfall behind her. It was Ranulf Glanville.

'Pardon me, my Lady, but dinner is about to be served. Oh, I see you have noticed the painting.'

'The King commissioned it?'

'Yes, my Lady.'

'The eagle is himself, I gather, but what does it all mean?'

The custodian spoke evenly, not relishing what he had to say. 'When some of us asked the King the meaning of the picture, he said that the eaglets were his four sons, who ceased not to persecute him even unto death.'

'But John is just a child! How can he include him in this?' The rest she could understand, but at this crass folly, she was aghast.

'That is what some of the King's courtiers said, my Lady. But he answered that he fears his youngest, whom he now embraces with such affection, will some day afflict him more grievously and perilously than all the others.'

'That is nonsense,' snapped Eleanor.

'I think one has to understand the King's frame of mind when he said it, my Lady. He observed that a man's enemies are the men of his own house.'

And the women, she thought, remembering her own part in

her sons' revolt. But John! John would never betray the father who spoiled him so and lavished so much love on him.

Joanna had gone, trotting off in her gay cavalcade to Southampton where her ship was waiting to take her across the seas. Saying farewell and standing there at the castle doors, watching her go, had been hard, but Eleanor had fought to maintain her composure. She had long grown used to dealing with sorrow, had coped with far worse ordeals than this, and kept her resolve to say goodbye to her daughter with a smile on her face.

She had expected to be taken back to Sarum immediately, but Ranulf Glanville was temporarily absent on the King's business, and no one mentioned her leaving. So she stayed on at Winchester, rattling around the luxurious royal chambers with just Amaria for company and her two sentinels on the outer doors. Henry, she reasoned, must be preoccupied with other, more pressing matters. For her part, she could only thank God for this welcome respite from the tedium and discomforts of Sarum.

Michaelmas; and she was still at Winchester. Through her windows, she could hear music and dancing and the cathedral bells ringing to celebrate the bringing in of the harvest. September drew mildly to a close. The weather turned colder with the coming of October, and still there was no summons back to Sarum. Then, one morning, the steward arrived with a leather travelling chest.

'My Lady, this has come from the Lord King. It is for the use of you and your serving woman.'

Eleanor, who had assumed that the arrival of the chest betokened that she was to pack and depart, gaped at him – and the iron-bound case – in astonishment. Could this really be a gift from Henry? Was it another peace offering? Had God at last turned his heart?

When the steward had gone, and there was only Amaria to see, she lifted the lid in a fever of speculation, and drew from the chest, in some amazement, two scarlet cloaks, two capes of the same colour, two grey furs and an embroidered coverlet. Amaria let out a sigh of wonder.

'I think I know whence these proceeded,' Eleanor said, her heart full. 'I think I have my daughter Joanna to thank for them.' Of course. Dear Joanna, who had seen her poverty, must have appealed to Henry. That in no way diminished his gesture, she told herself, for he could have ignored the appeal. Instead, he had sent these fine clothes, and he had remembered Amaria too. It rankled a tiny bit that he had not thought to distinguish in status between his queen and her servant, for whom he had supplied identical garments, but he was a man who liked to dress plainly himself and cared little for the trappings of estate, so maybe it would not have occurred to him that Eleanor should have clothing of greater richness than her maid. At least he had sent it. That was something indeed, and they would now have good warm robes for the winter.

52 Godstow Abbey, 1176

The abbey nestled on an island between streams gushing from the River Thames. It stood solid and grey amidst green fields, in which the good sisters could be seen toiling diligently. The work of the hands, Henry reflected, was almost as important to the Benedictine Rule as prayer, the work of God.

He had ridden over from Woodstock on this special pilgrimage. Going to Woodstock had been a torment: he had barely been able to bring himself to climb the stairs to the dusty, deserted tower rooms, or walk past the overgrown labyrinth with its sinister tangles of briars. He'd realised almost at once that he should never have come, that being in the place that had housed his love would conjure up memories too painful to confront.

So he had come instead to Godstow, to seek peace in the abbey where she had sought refuge. Well he recalled that awful day, two years before, when Rosamund had come to him, anxiety written clear on her sweet face, her cherry lips trembling . . .

She had found a lump in her breast, she said, and she was scared because her granddame had died of a canker in that very part of her body.

Henry had thought that she was making much out of nothing. He had felt the lump, declared it nothing but a spot, then, as lust asserted itself at the soft swell of his beloved's exposed bosom, had taken her without further ado, and stilled her fears – or so he had believed.

But the lump had not gone away. Over the months, it had grown, and the place had become sore and nasty, and increasingly painful. Rosamund had become tearful and at times hysterical, declaring that this was a punishment for the great sin she had committed in loving him. They must no longer bed together, she cried. Thoroughly alarmed by that, and by the state of the lump, Henry had summoned his doctors, who had frowned, clucked on about an imbalance of the humours, and bled his dear love, applying leeches; but none of it did any good. Rosamund had steadily lost weight and grown frail. In the end, there was nothing more the physicians could try.

'This is a judgement on me,' Rosamund had said again. 'I have sinned grievously, not only against God but against Queen Eleanor. What we have done is wrong.'

'You can cease worrying about the Queen,' Henry had told her roughly. 'She is a traitor to me, and not my lawful wife.'

'No, Henry,' she answered sadly. 'Queen Eleanor is your true wife, and the mother of your children, whatever she has done. The Pope knew it, which is why he would not annul your marriage. And in committing adultery with you, I have wronged her deeply – and I am being punished for it.'

'This is a vain fancy!' he had stormed, but there was no moving Rosamund. No longer was she the laughing girl he had loved, but a sick woman consumed with remorse.

'I wish I could make amends,' she wept. 'I cannot go to my rest with this great wrong on my conscience.'

'Just confess it and have done!' Henry growled, his voice gruff with emotion.

'Let me send a letter to her, please. Just to explain my folly and say I am sorry for it.'

He turned on her, shocked. 'No. I absolutely forbid it. She does not deserve your guilt or your apologies. When I think of what she has done to me . . .'

'*Please*, Henry!'

'I said no.' And he had got up and left her.

After that, Rosamund's condition had deteriorated rapidly. His heart breaking, Henry had agreed that she should go to Godstow, the nunnery in which she had been raised, where the sisters could care for her; it would be convenient for Woodstock, whence he could visit her. He had insisted on escorting her as she was carried to the abbey by litter; their progress had of necessity been slow, since she had become so weak by then. Once she was tucked up in her narrow bed in the infirmary, the Infirmaress let him see her briefly. He could hardly bear to look upon Rosamund's wan, wasted face as she lay on the coarse pillow, her fair tresses curling across it.

He had blundered back to court, for there could be no shirking the manifold duties of a king. Ever a plain, practical man, he faced the fact that his beloved was dying, and that he might never see her again, would certainly nevermore lie with her. His nights were a martyrdom, and in the end, he could bear it no more, and took to his bed a serving wench, a nameless, forgettable hussy who lay there mute with awe as he slaked his need and his desperation on her body. After that, true to form, he had repeatedly fallen prey to his lusts. His most notable conquest was Ida de Toesny, an aristocratic girl of good family, who was already growing heavy with his child.

It was not that long since his wife – he could not bring himself to say her name – had betrayed him. The hurt was still raw. What she had done had near cost him his crown, and a lot else besides. Well, she was paying for that, and she would pay more dearly yet, he thought in his grief and bitterness. Although he had banned her from receiving any news, he hoped mercilessly that someone had told her how, after her incarceration, he had lived openly with Rosamund, blatantly flaunting her as his mistress for all to see. As for Rosamund begging to make amends to Eleanor – well, the poor lady was not in her right mind with this terrible illness. The guilt should all be his wife's. And as for Rosamund writing to her . . . The very idea!

Once Rosamund was gone from his daily life, and like to die very soon, Henry found himself wanting to cry out his agony to the world. He needed desperately to be comforted. The pain he suffered was unbearable, exacerbated by the eternal gnawing craving to be revenged on Eleanor. It was then that the desire to take another wife flared again in him. He had been toying in earnest with the idea for a year now, ever since he had looked anew at Alys of France, Richard's betrothed, and realised that she was growing into a graceful beauty, with high breasts and voluptuously rounded hips and thighs. He had now convinced himself that Alys would make the most suitable wife, with her royal blood and a figure fit for breeding. She could never replace Rosamund, of course, but marrying her might help to ease the pain of his loss. And, from the first, he had known that it would be a magnificent way of getting back at his faithless queen!

But Alys was a princess, the child of King Louis, who was now supposed to be his ally, and – to make matters infinitely more complicated – she was affianced to his own son. Despite the outward appearance of peace and amity that he had worked hard to establish, Henry was still sufficiently resentful towards Richard to take some pleasure in depriving him of his bride. By God, he was so disappointed in all his elder sons that he had even considered naming John the heir to all his domains!

Now he decided that he wanted Alys, and knew he must act soon, before Louis started making more noises about the much-discussed marriage ceremony taking place.

There was just one obstacle: Henry had a wife already, of course. But both Eleanor and the Pope had proved obdurate, to his chagrin. Neither bribes nor veiled threats could move His Holiness, and that bitch at Sarum was determined to hold on to her lands, come what may. Small good they would do her, shut up as she was, he thought vindictively.

He went to see Rosamund, although it caused him infinite pain to do so; he visited as often as he could get away, and each time he found her in worse condition. He realised she had gone from him for ever, the woman he had loved, and in her place was a wraith whose mind was focused on repentance and the hope of Heaven to come. That much, and no more, had the nuns done for her.

Each time he left her, he was in a ferment of grief and longing for what he had lost. Back at court, seated restlessly at his place at the high table, or departing for the hunt, he would catch sight of Alys, alluring and sinuous in her clinging silk *bliauts*, and feel the old familiar excitement burgeoning. After a time, he became aware that she was watching him too with her cat-like eyes, and posing provocatively to catch his attention. Richard, he knew, had little time for her; Richard was too pre-occupied with fighting and whoring, and Alys meant little to him, beyond the fact that she was a great prize in the royal marriage market.

The Pope had not spoken in his favour; Eleanor had refused to go into a nunnery. Henry was as far from remarrying as he was from growing wings and taking flight, but he wanted Alys in his bed, and no longer cared whether she was there legally or sinfully. And neither, it seemed, did she.

He had stolen to her chamber one night after she had spent the evening sending him significant glances across the teeming, noisy dining hall. He found her waiting for him in the firelight, clad only in a chemise so fine in texture that it was diaphanous. He took one look, and was damned.

Barely had he caught his breath, it seemed, than Alys too was pregnant. Of course, he had to send her away, to a convent in the wilds of Norfolk, while warding off eager enquiries from Louis as to wedding plans. It was at that point that the news he most dreaded to hear came from Godstow. Rosamund was dead.

So here he was, approaching the church door in trepidation, come to mourn his love in private. The Abbess had been waiting to greet him at the gatehouse, and given him permission to enter the enclosure, marvelling at how the King had aged since he had first come here with his lady love. He was now a broken man of forty-three, grizzled of hair and portly of body, his ravaged face grooved with the lines of care and sorrow. Whatever the right and wrong of it, he had truly loved his mistress – no one could doubt that.

Henry found himself alone in the church. A single lamp burned in the chancel, signifying that God was here in His house. The King bowed his head in respect, then paced slowly towards the altar and the freshly laid tombstone before it. She was there, beneath the chancel pavement, his Rosamund, no longer fair but food for worms. The thought broke him. He sank to his knees before the grave, weeping uncontrollably, vowing that he would build a fine stone sepulchre to the memory of his beloved, and have it adorned with silken palls and lit by candles. It should be lovingly tended by the nuns; he would pay them handsomely, he swore, and grant many favours to the abbey.

So lost in anguish was he that he did not see the sad-faced, cobweb-fine grey shadow glide slowly up behind him with its filmy arms outstretched, and hover there for a long, wistful moment before vanishing into the gloom of the vaulted chapel – but he felt even more bereft.

53 Winchester, 1180

Eleanor was fifty-eight, and she had been a prisoner for seven long and difficult years. Yet nowadays, her prison was a gilded cage appropriate to her rank, for after her visit to Winchester, the security that surrounded her had been relaxed by degrees. The monotonous tedium of Sarum had been gradually ameliorated, as the King had been increasingly pleased to permit her to lodge at different places – in Northamptonshire, in Berkshire, and at the royal castle at Ludgershall in Wiltshire. Always, she was in the custody of the charming Ranulf Glanville or the taciturn Ralph FitzStephen, and attended by the faithful Amaria. Henry had never allowed her any additional personal servants.

Now she was comfortably installed at Winchester again, in greater state than hitherto, occupying luxurious chambers, with the choicest food on her table, and with a newly appointed chamberlain to order her small household.

By and by, the rules had been relaxed, and she had been permitted to write the occasional letter – although not to her sons; Henry still did not trust her enough for that – and to receive news of the outside world. Ranulf Glanville, whom she now accounted a dear friend, often imparted snippets of information at the dinner table. Amaria, in her forays into market and through seemingly idle chatter with the castle servants, picked up a lot more, which, these days, she was less reluctant to repeat to her mistress. Thus it was that Eleanor had learned of Rosamund's death, although not of the strange rumours that had begun to circulate about it, or of the whispered gossip about the King living in fornication with their son Richard's betrothed; both Glanville and Amaria were anxious to protect the Queen from anything that might cause her pain and distress. Yet the gossip on both counts was rife throughout the kingdom and beyond.

Eleanor had indeed wondered why Richard's marriage to Alys had not yet taken place. Both were of age, and ripe for bedding – and Aquitaine needed an heir. The Young King had sired a son on Queen Marguerite three years ago, although sadly his little William had died soon after birth. Eleanor felt deeply grieved that she had never seen any of her grandchildren; it was a continuing sorrow to be cut off from her flesh and blood.

Had Louis been pressing for Alys's marriage? He had good reason to chafe at the delay, but Eleanor suspected that Henry had some devious reason of his own for putting it off. And Richard seemed to be in no hurry. She had heard that he was still much occupied with enforcing his authority in Aquitaine – and shuddered to think what that might mean.

By all reports, Matilda was contentedly producing baby after baby in Germany, and Joanna seemed to have settled down happily in Sicily, although something Ranulf had let slip had disturbed Eleanor a little.

'They say that King William has adopted many of the customs of his Moorish subjects,' he'd told her, 'and that Queen Joanna lives entirely in seclusion.'

'Don't tell me he has a harem!' Eleanor had interjected sharply. She had seen harems in Constantinople and the lands of the Turks during the long-ago crusade, and knew what ills they concealed.

Ranulf looked ill at ease. 'I did hear something of the sort,' he disclosed, 'but the Queen his wife has her own apartments.'

So poor Joanna had had to deal with her lord's infidelity right from the first, Eleanor thought, dismayed. If she had been given her head, she would have hastened across the seas and snatched her daughter back, but there was no hope of that. She must endure the knowledge of Joanna's situation, just as Joanna herself was having to learn to bear it. But how uncivilised of King William, to expect his wife to tolerate a harem in the palace! Eleanor was fuming inside.

It was Ranulf Glanville who informed Eleanor when John was made nominal king of Ireland and her daughter Eleanor was sent to Castile to marry King Alfonso. It was hard to believe that little Eleanor, with her heart-shaped face, was nineteen and a bride. How the years had flown – and so many of them, latterly, wasted. She felt weary with the futility of it all.

'The Lord Geoffrey has been knighted by the King,' her custodian told her one rainy July evening.

'I rejoice that my Lord now enjoys good relations with our sons,' Eleanor replied, remembering that Henry and his three eldest had kept such a magnificent court together last Christmas at Angers that it was still spoken of with wonder.

'God be thanked, they are at peace at last.' Ranulf's sentiments were genuine. 'I hear that the Young King has been rushing around all over France fighting in tournaments and carrying off the prizes. His fame is sung everywhere.'

'Henry will like that,' Eleanor observed.

'Indeed he does. In fact, the King has been so delighted by the Young King's many triumphs that he has restored to him in full all the lands and possessions he had taken away.' It did Eleanor's heart good to hear that, but – as always – there was, underlying her pleasure, a nagging sadness and resentment that she herself was never embraced by Henry's evident desire to set things right.

Richard, she later heard, had achieved great victories in Aquitaine.

'He is now acknowledged one of the great generals of our age,' Ranulf told her proudly.

Yes, she thought, but at what cost? What violence and bloodshed has he committed, at Henry's behest, to earn that reputation? Her heart bled for Aquitaine, and she could take little joy in Richard's fame, although she was gratified to hear that he, like the Young King before him, had been received with honour by his father. Please God, matters were now mended between them.

'My Lady, the King of France is dead,' announced Amaria, coming into the royal lodgings with a basket of autumn herbs for the simples she liked to make, swearing by her own remedies for aching joints and blistered heels.

A great wave of sadness engulfed Eleanor. Whatever his failings, Louis had once, many years in the past, been her husband. She had done him many wrongs, and there had been some bitterness between them, but he had been a kind and devout man, who had stood by her and her sons in their hour of need, and done many good deeds in his days – and now he was no more.

She went to her chapel and sank to her knees to pray for Louis; he had been a saintly man, and surely his soul was even now on its winged flight to Heaven. She had known he was ill. The year before, he had come to England on a pilgrimage to St Thomas's shrine at Canterbury, in company with the thousands who now flocked to keep vigil at Becket's tomb, hoping for one of the miracles that the saintly archbishop was widely reputed to work. Louis had needed such a miracle. He was in poor health, and not really fit enough to make the journey. But Henry had afforded him a splendid reception, and they had gone together in procession to the cathedral, where Louis made offerings of a great ruby ring and other precious gifts.

Then he had hastened back to France to prepare for the crowning of his heir, Philip Augustus, now grown almost to manhood. Louis had not been there to see it. A massive apoplexy had suddenly struck him down, and effectively ended his reign. He had lingered for more than a year, as his crafty and ambitious son had seized the reins of government – and now, poor shadow of his former self, he had gone to his much-deserved rest. His former wife paid him the compliment of her tears as she looked back on his virtues and tried to forget that he had once been a timorous young man who had driven her to distraction because he had been better suited to the cloister than to wielding a sceptre and doing his duty by her in bed.

*

'It's odd that all that talk of divorce suddenly died down,' Eleanor reflected as she and Amaria sat at their embroidery in a window embrasure, enjoying an unseasonably warm breeze. Over the years, she had painstakingly taught her maid the art of plying her needle to decorative effect, and Amaria had proved a willing pupil. They were now working on an altar frontal for the chapel.

Amaria remained silent, but that was nothing unusual. She had the peasant's way of few words.

'The last I heard, Henry had appealed to the Pope, but that was years ago,' Eleanor went on. 'He must have thought better of it. Nevertheless, being thwarted by His Holiness should not stop him from marrying Richard to Alys. They should have been wed long since.' She rethreaded some red silk through her needle, then looked up. To her consternation, she saw that Amaria's eyes were filled with tears.

'What's the matter?' she asked.

'Nothing,' muttered the woman.

'No one weeps for nothing,' Eleanor said. 'Have you had bad news?'

Amaria shook her head. 'Really, my Lady, 'tis nothing.'

'Now you have me worried!' her mistress declared. 'Tell me what troubles you. I command it!'

'You won't like it,' Amaria said in a low voice.

'Tell me!' ordered Eleanor, really worried now. 'Has someone died?' Her heart was instantly pounding. If it was one of her children, she did not think she could bear it.

Amaria braced herself. 'There be rumours that the King has got the Princess Alys with child.' She omitted to mention that these rumours had been increasingly fuelling the public imagination for years now.

Eleanor caught her breath. So . . . Everything suddenly became clear. She instinctively knew that rumour spoke truth – or something like it. How could Henry have stooped so low? To compromise the honour of a princess of France was bad enough, but when that princess was his son's betrothed – that was another matter entirely! Disgust consumed her.

When she had regained her composure, another thought struck home. How long had this been going on? Was it the reason why she had heard no more of a divorce? And had she been the only person left in ignorance of what was going on? If Amaria had heard these rumours, then it was a certainty that most of England had too.

She wondered if Louis had known, if he had spoken out. But surely not. He would hardly have gone to Becket's shrine with Henry in the circumstances. And Richard — where did he stand in all this? She was outraged on Richard's behalf, and incensed against Henry.

She turned to Amaria, who was concentrating furiously on her sewing.

'What more do you know of this matter?' she probed.

'Only what that rumour said, Lady,' Amaria lied. She was not about to repeat the gossip that accused Alys of having borne the King at least three children that died, or the shocked expletives of people scandalised to hear of Henry's vile behaviour. Nor would she say anything of those other rumours . . . Had it been the King who had put them about, perhaps seeking yet another pretext to put Eleanor away — this time for good?

But Eleanor was ahead of her. 'Talking of rumours,' she said, resolutely moving on from the horrible gossip about Henry, 'I overheard Fulcold' — that was the chamberlain — 'talking with Master FitzStephen the other day. They were in the outer chamber, but the door had been left open. I could not catch everything they said, but I am sure that I heard Fulcold say, "All the world knows that Queen Eleanor murdered Rosamund." And Master FitzStephen, dour old fellow that he is, actually laughed, so I supposed the remark to have been made in jest. But what an odd thing to say. How could I murder Rosamund, shut up as I have been these seven years?'

Amaria mentally girded her loins; Eleanor could almost see her doing it.

'There have been tales to that effect,' she said at length.

'What tales? How could there be?' She could not credit it. Why should people always believe ill of her, especially when there was not the slightest justification for it? This really was too much!

'Aye, there be all kinds of silly stories. I took little notice of them, they was so far-fetched, and because I knew them to be false – and I said so often, mark ye, my Lady! But folks likes to believe such things.'

Eleanor knew that. They livened up the daily round of ordinary people's lives, provided the excitement that was lacking elsewhere. But she hated the idea of herself being the focus of such stupid and unjust calumnies.

'Tell me what they say of me!' she demanded, her anger rising.

'They say the King kept the Lady Rosamund – the Fair Rosamund, they call her—'

'Putrid by now, I should think!' Eleanor interrupted.

'They say you hated her, my Lady, and that the King kept her shut up in a tower at Woodstock, for fear you would discover her, and had a maze put around the tower, so that you could never find the way in.'

'There was a maze, but it was built for her pleasure,' Eleanor said. 'This is just nonsense.'

'Aye, it is nonsense, I know. Then you are supposed to have found a clue of thread or silk from the lady's sewing basket, and followed it through the maze until you discovered her in her tower.'

'And then I supposedly murdered her!' Eleanor sniffed furiously. 'I should like to know how!'

'Saving your pardon, but there are lots of gruesome stories,' Amaria admitted. 'Some even say you stripped her naked and roasted her between two fires, with venomous toads on her breasts; some say you let her bleed to death in a hot bath, some that you poisoned her, and others that you stabbed her with a dagger after putting out her eyes. I say some people have a vivid imagination.'

Eleanor had been listening to all this in mounting horror. 'How could people think these things of me?' she cried. 'It is all lies, vile lies. Yet they believe it, against all logic. I dare say some think this supposed murder is the cause for which I am still shut up.'

'A few do,' Amaria confirmed. 'Although I have heard other people scoff at the rumours. Not everyone believes them, mark me.'

'But some do, and that is what offends me!' Eleanor cried.

'How am I to defend myself against such slanders? I am powerless. Surely people realise that I could not possibly have had anything to do with Rosamund's death.'

As the words were spoken, a salutary inner voice reminded her that she had once taken pleasure in imagining herself doing vengeful violence on Rosamund's body – and that she had rejoiced in the most unchristian manner on hearing news of her rival's death. But I would never actually have done her harm, she told herself; God knows, I shrink from bloodshed. And when I was told of her sufferings before she died, I realised that what is written in Scripture is true: Vengeance is mine, saith the Lord: I will repay. And then I felt remorse for my unseemly joy in her death, *and* a belated pity for her.

'I will write to the King,' she vowed. 'I will acquaint him of these terrible calumnies and demand that he publicly refute them. He must know that, even had I had the opportunity, I do not have it in me to do such a thing.'

Ralph FitzStephen looked dubious when the Queen asked for writing materials so that she could send a letter to the King. She had never ventured to write to Henry before, and he wasn't sure if it was permitted or not; but, in the absence of specific instructions, he grudgingly gave his consent.

Eleanor's message was to the point:

'Eleanor, by the grace of God, Queen of England, to her Lord Henry, King of England, greetings,' she began. Then she simply said it had come to her notice that rumour unjustly accused her of murdering Rosamund de Clifford, and asked him to issue a public proclamation declaring her innocence. Left like that, it looked a bit abrupt, so she added two short sentences: 'I trust you are in health. The Lord have you in His keeping.' Then she signed her name, showed it to a suspicious FitzStephen, and sealed it.

There was no response.

Geoffrey and Constance were married – it had been a summer wedding – and Henry had gone straight back to England afterwards and made his bastard son, the other Geoffrey, lord chancellor of England. Eleanor shook her head in dismay at both pieces of news. Devious her Geoffrey might be, but Constance was worse, and was probably running circles around him. As for the bastard, the King was heaping far too many rewards on him: he was archdeacon of Rouen, treasurer of York Minster, and the proud owner of two castles in Anjou. She could foresee jealousy poisoning his relations with his legitimate siblings, and of course there was no telling where the young man's ambition might lead him. Henry, she feared, was making a rod for his own back.

Recent news from over the sea was not good. Joanna had borne, with great difficulty, a son that had died at birth. And Matilda was in exile with her husband, who had quarrelled with the Emperor and fled from Germany; the word was that the couple might seek refuge in England. Eleanor wept for her daughters, and prayed for Matilda to come home, that she might comfort her. It was thirteen years since she had set eyes on her daughter, and she hungered to see her. She longed to see all her children. Her heart quailed at the thought of another lonely, unhappy Christmas.

She would have thought that eight years of imprisonment would have taught her patience and resignation, but it had not. She had relived the events leading up to her sons' rebellion a thousand times, and still she felt, deep within her, that she had been right to support them. She knew that, if she had her chance again, she would make the same choice, because it had been the only, the right choice. A mother's instinct was to defend her young. Yet what a terrible price she had paid for it. Never hearing from them, by Henry's express order, she wondered if they still cherished the same affection for her – or if she was now but a distant memory in their young minds.

Thank God her spirit was still strong, unquenched by adversity, even if her body was ageing. She had lost weight, and her mirror reflected a haunted face with the skin stretched tightly over the bones beneath; it was too pale from her long confinement, even if she was allowed to take the air in the garden these days. And there was always a yearning look in her eyes.

Of Henry, she rarely thought these days, unless it was with sadness, or in passing. There was no room left in her for bitterness. She had prayed often for the grace to forgive, and with the long passage of time, found that such grace had been accorded her.

Occasionally, at night, when she lay awake with Amaria snoring peacefully beside her – she had got used to that, but God knew it had taken all her patience – she would imagine that it was her husband who lay there in the darkness, and would remember his hand reaching across to claim her, and the weight of his body as he mounted hers. Those were the worst moments, for, even now, she could feel the surge of desire, almost to the point where she feared she might go mad if she could not assuage it. Henry had been such an exceptional lover that she could never forget the joy and sense of liberation that she had experienced in his arms. But then she would find herself back on the old treadmill, remembering that he had never been faithful to her, and that all the loves they had shared had not counted for much in the long run. Why, he was probably rutting with Alys at this very moment, if rumour spoke truth. Her memories were for ever tainted; it was best not to think of the past, but to dwell on the mundane round of her daily life and the things of the spirit. But oh, how she yearned for a man to warm her bed in the darkest reaches of the night!

55 Caen, 1182

Henry's eyes swept over the packed hall of the Norman Exchequer in the castle of Caen with satisfaction. They had come, in response to his summons. His sons were here, and together, in this fine new building, they would preside over a glittering Yuletide court that had been deliberately arranged to rival any that that ambitious puppy, Philip of France, might hold in Paris.

The festivities were in full swing, the hall smoky from the

fire that blazed merrily in the central hearth, and lit by giant circular iron candelabra, suspended from the roof between the high, arched windows. It was the early hours of Christmas morning, and the court, having attended Midnight Mass, was in high spirits, tucking into the traditional feast known in the duchy as *Le Réveillon.*

Henry was keeping a wary eye on his sons, who were ranged on either side of him at the high table. It was not going to be a happy gathering. The Young King had arrived in the company of Bertran de Born, whom Henry did not like or trust, and was in a foul mood; the King watched him sitting there sulking, and pointedly ignoring his wife, whose homely face bore a strained, troubled expression. Henry thought it odd that, for once, his eldest son had not brought William Marshal with him; the two were normally inseparable, and the King approved of William's influence on his hothead of an heir.

For Young Henry had not only upset Queen Marguerite, but had fallen out spectacularly with Richard, who was glowering heatedly at him down the table – their father had had to ensure that they were seated as far apart as possible. The quarrel had erupted back in the spring, in Aquitaine, where the young Duke Richard's harsh rule had finally provoked his volatile vassals to open rebellion. The evil genius behind this was the malicious adventurer Bertran de Born, who saw Richard's oppression as the rape of his land, and had incited the Young King to join the rebels. Resentful of his brother having more power than himself, that rash young man had been easy to persuade. Not to be left out, Geoffrey, greedily anticipating the spoils of fighting, had hastened to join him. Aquitaine had been abruptly plunged into war, with one brother against the other two.

For some months, Henry had had no choice but to let them get on with it, having his hands full in Normandy, but as soon as the campaigning season came to an end in the autumn, and he had summoned the Young King north, meaning to divert him from the bloodbath in the south, the arrogant young fool had loudly demanded that his father cede to him Normandy and Anjou; and when Henry had angrily refused, the Young King had stormed off in a temper to Paris, where that puppy

Philip – who would soon need to be firmly muzzled – had welcomed him with sympathetic arms and fallen to plotting with him.

Back had stormed Young Henry to Rouen, demanding to be given the power that should be his. He would take the Cross and go on crusade, he threatened, if the King refused his reasonable demand. Indeed, he would prefer banishment to being treated like a subordinate. He was a king, was he not? Or had he imagined those coronations at Westminster and Winchester?

Henry had ignored the sarcasm. He had also ignored his heir's demands, which left the young fool threatening suicide. In the end, worn down by the pressure, the King had bought his son off with a generous allowance and sent him to live with his sister Matilda at Argentan Castle, where Henry had offered her and her husband and children refuge during their exile. Having given his oath not to make further demands, the Young King, with Queen Marguerite in tow, had gone off to join her household. Henry had hoped that Matilda might talk some sense into him; she had a lot of her wise grandmother and namesake in her. But it seemed that his hopes had been in vain.

Henry had insisted, in the interests of restoring peace, that all his sons attend the Christmas court. Matilda was present too; she had grown into a handsome matron of twenty-four, and was now the mother of a large brood, of whom Henry was inordinately proud.

Dark-haired Geoffrey was exerting his usual charm, his ready flow of words smoother than oil, but Henry knew him to be slippery, grasping and dangerous. He had few scruples – there had been disturbing reports of him plundering abbeys and churches at will – and although he was of tireless endeavour, he was a hypocrite in nearly everything that mattered, and certainly not to be trusted.

Where did we go wrong with our children? Henry sighed to himself, as his gaze lighted on each of his three elder sons in turn. Of course, Eleanor was much to blame, for seducing them into believing that they could seize their father's domains, and then encouraging them in their treasonable rebellion – but Henry believed that the rot had set in well before then. We both spoiled them, he reflected. I was as much to blame as Eleanor in that respect. And now we reap what we have sown.

Richard, seated to his father's right, was reining in the famous Angevin temper and taking pains to avoid his brothers. Only fifteen-year-old John sat stolidly enjoying the rich food and imbibing too much wine, while basking smugly in his father's love and approval. It was good to be the favourite, adored son! But the atmosphere was tense, and it became tenser still when William Marshal arrived on the Feast of St Stephen and, ignoring the venomous glares of Young Henry and the embarrassed fluster of Queen Marguerite, presented himself immediately before the King, his fine face flushed with indignation.

'Sire,' he cried, so that all the courtiers could hear, 'certain persons are spreading calumnies about me, which touch my honour and that of this blameless lady here!' He bowed to the blushing Young Queen. 'These foul lies accuse me of having cast amorous looks on her. In your presence, I challenge all those who have spread these falsehoods to let me prove my innocence and hers by ordeal of combat! If I win, I ask no reward but the vindication of my honour and hers. If I lose, then I will be hanged for my crime.' So saying, he drew off his heavy gauntlet and threw it on the floor before the King's high seat.

No one spoke. Marshal was staring hard at Young Henry, as if daring him to respond. At length, the younger man had the grace to look away. Beside him, Marguerite was weeping silently.

'Will no one take up this noble knight's challenge?' Henry asked. No one did.

'And you, my daughter, what have you to say to these calumnies?' Henry demanded, fixing a stern eye on Marguerite.

'William spoke truth, my Lord. They are malicious lies,' she insisted, casting a sideways glance at Bertran de Born. Henry nodded, satisfied, then turned back to Marshal.

'It seems that those who have slandered you are craven, and afraid to defend themselves,' he observed.

Marshal knelt before the King, his face a mirror of distress.

'I had hoped that God would make my innocence manifest,' he declared. 'Forgive me, Sire, but I cannot remain in a place where my enemies hide their faces. I beg leave to depart. I shall make a pilgrimage to the shrine of the Magi at Cologne.'

'In truth, I am sorry to see you depart, old friend,' Henry said, glaring at his eldest son and the smirking Bertran, who had clearly seen off the rival who would have counselled prudence rather than pursue some hot-headed scheme.

But Bertran had not finished stirring up trouble. He played on the Young King's insecurities and grievances.

'There goes the Prince of Cravens,' he sneered, when Richard was within earshot. 'Did you know he has built a castle on your land?'

Richard threw him a menacing look, but, respecting the season, walked on without comment. But he was obviously seething inside, and determined to settle the score as soon as the opportunity presented itself.

'If Geoffrey had been made count of Anjou in your place, *he* would have known how to enforce his rights!' Bertran whispered, his words dripping like poison into Young Henry's ear until, in the end, he could bear it no more, and, seeking out his father in private, exploded in a furious outburst, much to the secret amusement of Richard and Geoffrey, who were looking on.

'Father, I swear I will renounce my titles and take the Cross if you refuse to allow me more power!' he shouted.

'When you have learned discretion and wisdom, I might reconsider,' Henry said calmly, leaning back in his chair.

For answer, the Young King burst into hot, angry tears. 'At least make Richard dismantle the castle he has built on my land!' he cried.

Henry's brow creased in a frown. He was aware that Philip of France was waiting for an opportunity to make trouble between the Angevin princes, and fearful that a disaffected Young King might seek Philip's support, much as he had sought King Louis' eight years ago. And look where that had led! Good statesman that Henry was, he saw the necessity of appeasing his son and warding off the threat.

'Henry, you are my heir,' he said in a steady, placatory tone.

'Your brothers come after you in the succession, and therefore they shall do homage to you as their overlord. Will that content you?'

'Yes, Father,' the Young King sniffed.

'Richard, Geoffrey, will you now render homage to your brother?' the King demanded.

'Yes,' muttered Geoffrey.

'No, by our Lady, I will not!' Richard snarled. 'It might have escaped your notice, Father, that I hold Aquitaine of the King of France, and to him only do I owe homage. And,' he went on, as Henry opened his mouth to protest, 'might I remind you that I had my domains as a gift from my Lady Mother, whom you have unjustly held prisoner these many years!' The venom in his voice was frightening. 'If my brother the Young King wants land, let him go and fight for it, as I have had to do!' With that, he picked up his lyre and slammed out of the room, uttering threats and defiance, and leaving Henry looking at his remaining sons in perplexity. One glance at the Young King's face told him that all his efforts to reconcile his feuding brood had been for nothing. Young Henry's blood was up; war was in his heart.

As for Eleanor, despite what Richard had said, Henry had no intention of freeing her. The thought of what havoc she might wreak in this present conflict and chaos was enough to deter him from even considering it. In fact, her presence in Winchester, the ancient capital of England, was now a matter of concern to him. Security must be tightened . . . That meddling woman must go back to Sarum!

56 Sarum, 1183

Eleanor was awakened by the dream, and sat bolt upright in the bed in alarm, disturbing Amaria.

'What is it, my Lady?' she mumbled, rubbing her eyes.

'Nothing. Go back to sleep,' Eleanor whispered, breathing deeply to still her thudding heart. She needed privacy and quiet to work out what the dream might mean. For in it, she had seen, as in a vision, her son, the Young King, lying recumbent on a couch, his hands pressed together as if in prayer. It struck her, with a chill, that he had looked not unlike an effigy on a tomb. But what puzzled her were two things: one was the ring, a great sapphire, that had twinkled and flashed on his finger. It was a ring she had never seen before. The sapphire, of course, symbolised the sky, God's Heaven and His protection; in the East, she had heard, people believed it warded off the evil eye. Was there some portentous meaning to be divined from this?

The other thing that troubled her beyond measure was the remembrance of two crowns hovering in the air above her son's white face. One she recognised as the crown Henry had had made for his son's coronation; the second was no earthly crown, but a circle of pure, dazzling light that shone with the incomparable brilliance of the Holy Grail itself.

She knew in her heart what the dream must mean, yet her reason and her terrified soul rejected it. She rose from the bed and fell on her knees before the window, gazing up at the narrow view it afforded her of the starry summer sky, and prayed as she had rarely prayed before that this dream would prove to be but a warning of what might pass if this bitter war between her sons did not cease, and not a preparation for news that she must shortly have to hear.

The morning brought with it a strange calm; it was as if she was being cradled in a cocoon of peace and security, from which she would emerge strengthened and ready to take on lions or wolves. The dream now seemed a distant, unreal memory, born of the fears that come by night. In the dark, everything seems more frightening, she told herself, and by and by, the memory faded, until her fear had dissipated. In its place, she was left with the uplifting feeling that, even if her dream foreshadowed the worst, death was merely the gateway to unimaginable bliss and joy, and should be a matter for rejoicing, not sorrow.

Her calm mood persisted, even when Ranulf Glanville, his face grey, announced the arrival of Thomas Agnell, Archdeacon of Wells.

'The King has sent him to you, my Lady,' he told her, his voice unusually tender.

Even before Agnell entered, she knew the tidings he had come to break to her. The dream had foretold this; and Henry himself had sent this man to her.

The Archdeacon came in unwillingly. He was a devout and compassionate man, and his placid face was lined with distress. He bowed low, not just out of respect to one who was queen, but with deference to one who was about to have cause to grieve. Eleanor stood to receive him, marvelling that she should feel so serene. God, she believed, was succouring her, holding her in His loving hands. That feeling, and the vivid memory of the dream and its promise, sustained her.

'My Lady,' Agnell said quietly, 'I am asked by the Lord King to inform you that your dearest son, the Young King, has departed to God.'

She had known it.

'I was prepared,' she said simply. 'I had a dream.' She told him about it.

'What other meaning than eternal bliss can be ascribed to that brilliant second crown, that perfect circlet with no beginning and no end?' she asked. 'What can such pure and resplendent brightness signify, if not the wonder of everlasting joy? That crown was more beautiful than anything that can manifest itself to our senses here on Earth.'

The Archdeacon marvelled. This was not the wicked queen to whom rumour attributed all manner of scandalous deeds, but a brave and venerable lady honed by adversity, strong in her faith. He looked on her in admiration.

'God in His goodness has vouchsafed you the tiniest glimpse of what Heaven must be,' he told her. 'He was surely offering you divine comfort against your sad loss.'

Eleanor could not even think of what that loss would mean for her. The time for that, and for grieving, would come later. But she was fortified by her belief that her son was in a better place and that there was no real need to mourn him, only to await the time when she could be reunited with him in Paradise.

'I have had my epiphany,' she told Agnell. 'As the Gospel says, *Eye hath not seen, nor ear heard, neither have entered into the heart of Man the things which God hath prepared for them that love Him.*'

'My Lady, I can but praise your courage in meeting this great sorrow with such staunch faith,' he replied. 'I am humbled by the way you have fathomed the mystery of the dream, and by the discernment and strength with which you are bearing your son's death. May God comfort and console you.'

'Thank you,' Eleanor said simply, suddenly feeling grief welling like an unquenchable tide within her. 'I would be alone now, by your leave. Come to me later. I will be ready to hear what happened to my son.'

After he had gone, the tears came flooding. Young Henry might be in Heaven, and exulting in its eternal glories, yet he was gone from her on this Earth, and never more would she see his handsome face, or hold him in her arms. Her calm had deserted her. She cursed Henry for keeping her from her son for ten wasted years. She had never seen him grown to full manhood, and now never would. And Henry had treated him so unjustly, promising him power, yet always keeping it tantalisingly out of reach. If the Young King had turned out feckless, quarrelsome and ruthless, Henry had made him so. She could not but remember that dear little boy with the angelic golden curls, playing with his wooden horses and his toy dagger. What hopes she had had for him! And now they were all come to dust, as was he.

Her grief went very deep. Always, she knew, she would be tortured by the memory of this beloved son.

'He had fought his father and brothers,' Agnell began. 'He even shot twice at the King when the royal troops were drawn up before Limoges. He sent a messenger to apologise and explain that it had been an accident, but it was widely bruited that he secretly lusted for his father's death.'

Where did we fail, as parents, that our son should be driven to that? Eleanor asked herself in remorse. She closed her eyes in misery.

'The King stopped his allowance,' the Archdeacon went on, 'and of course the Young King ran out of money. He and Duke Geoffrey began sacking and looting monasteries and shrines, and holding villages to ransom. He became a leader of outlaws and excommunicates. I hesitate to tell you this, but only last month, he and his men desecrated the holy shrine at Rocamadour and stole the altar treasure and the famous sword of Roland, as the horrified pilgrims looked on.'

She could not bear to think that her son had been such a monster. Yet if he had been past all redemption, why had God vouchsafed her that dream? Was it to show that His forgiveness was boundless? Had Young Henry truly repented at the last?

'Then the Young King's life was suddenly cut short,' Agnell recounted. 'He fell violently ill with dysentery and a fever. They carried him to a house in the town of Martel, and, he being *in extremis*, the Bishop of Agen was summoned hastily, to whom he made fervent confession of all his sins.'

Eleanor sent up a silent prayer of thanks.

'His case being hopeless, he asked that his father the King be summoned. But, as the King told me himself, he suspected a trap, so he sent the Young King a message expressing the hope that, when he had recovered, they would be reconciled. And with it he sent, as token of his forgiveness, a sapphire ring.'

Agnell's eyes met Eleanor's. A sapphire ring!

'I never knew Henry to wear such a ring,' she said, marvelling, 'yet I saw it in my dream, as clearly as I can see you now.'

'He had taken it from his treasure; it had belonged to the first King Henry.'

'Truly, I am astonished,' she told her visitor. 'If I had thought before that my dream was sent by God, then I am utterly convinced of it now, for how could I have known about that ring?'

'The ways of God are indeed mysterious and wonderful,' declared Agnell.

'I feel a little better now,' Eleanor said, her voice gaining strength. 'I think I can bear to hear the rest.'

'There is not much more to tell, my Lady. At the end, the Young King was so overcome with remorse for his sins that he asked to be clothed in a hair shirt and a crusader's cloak, and laid on a bed of ashes on the floor, with a noose around his neck and bare stones at his feet, as became a penitent. As he lay there, his father's ring was brought to him, and he begged that the

King would show mercy to you, his mother, whom he had held so long in captivity, and he asked all his companions to plead with your lord to set you at liberty.'

His last thoughts had been for her, his mother. With his dying breath, he had asked for her to be freed. Eleanor's heart was full. She could not speak.

'He gave up his spirit later that evening,' the Archdeacon concluded. 'The end was very peaceful.'

'He was only twenty-eight,' Eleanor murmured, choked.

'Young in years, but full of time when measured by the experiences of his life,' Agnell observed. They were silent for a few minutes.

'Henry must bitterly regret not going to him when he lay dying,' Eleanor said at length. 'Tell me, how did he take the news of his death?'

'He was inconsolable, my Lady. He threw himself on the ground and pitifully bewailed the loss of his son. He was so distraught that his secretary, in some alarm, was moved to reprove him for his excess of grief.'

Eleanor found herself inexplicably wanting, needing, to comfort Henry. This was our son, flesh of our flesh, bone of our bone, she thought desperately; we conceived him in love and joy, and we should mourn him in love and compassion. We should be sharing our grief together. Alas, it was clearly not to be. If Henry had wanted to heal the breach in the hour of their terrible sorrow, he would have come here. There was no point in torturing herself.

'Good Father, where has my son been laid to rest?' she enquired.

'His body has been interred by the high altar in the cathedral at Rouen, clothed in his coronation robes. His entrails lie, at the King's request, at the monastery of Grandmont, which, regrettably, the Young King had recently sacked. I am happy to say that the brethren received them in the spirit of forgiveness.'

Eleanor knew Grandmont well. It was one of Henry's favourite monastic foundations. He had spoken of being buried there himself one day.

*

404

There was no doubting, she told herself later, as she knelt in prayer, forcing herself to face the facts, that the Young King's death would leave Henry more secure, and Richard the undisputed ruler of Aquitaine and, now, of course, heir to England. Agnell had told her that, on hearing of the tragedy at Martel, the rebels had immediately disbanded and fled. So Richard, her Richard, would have all except Brittany when Henry died. Maybe, in the end, the eagle *would* rejoice in her third nesting.

She prayed for her daughter-in-law, the widowed Marguerite, now bereft and childless. No doubt Henry would want to keep his hands on the Vexin, her dowry, although Eleanor doubted that King Philip would be happy about that. At least Marguerite was young and like to marry again; her life lay mostly ahead of her. Unlike me, poor prisoner, Eleanor thought mournfully. I am sixty-one, and my autumn is upon me. What is there left to me?

A letter came for her from a grief-stricken Bertran de Born; renowned troubadour that he was, for all his treacherous soul, he had couched it in picturesque and evocative language that moved Eleanor deeply, for it evoked the spirit of her native land and sang to her grief. 'Youth stands sorrowful,' he wrote. 'No man rejoices in these bitter days. Death, that mortal warrior, has harshly taken from us the best of knights.'

The parchment fell to the floor. Eleanor could read no further.

57 Sarum and Normandy, 1183

The first inkling Eleanor got that things were going to be different from now on was when the royal messenger was ushered into her presence. Normally, Ranulf Glanville or Ralph FitzStephen would convey whatever instructions they had received or news the King wanted her to hear. But now, she was suddenly being accorded all the respect due to a queen.

Her head spinning with speculation, she sat in her high-backed chair as the man, his clothes dusty from what had evidently been a long ride, knelt before her.

'My Lady,' he said, 'I am commanded by the Lord King to request your presence in Normandy. He asks that you make ready with all possible haste, as we are to leave for Rouen without delay.'

Henry was requesting? Asking? For the past ten years, all he had had to do was send his commands to her custodians, and she had been taken here and there without any deference to her own wishes.

Could it be that grief over their mutual loss had brought him to his senses? Had he realised, as she had, that they two were the ones best placed to help each other through their mourning for the life they had created together? Was his need for comfort as urgent as hers?

'I will be ready within the hour,' she told the messenger, then effortlessly slipped back into her regal role and sent him off to the kitchens to find food and drink, as if she had never been prevented from extending such courtesies and the past decade had never been.

Ranulf came to her as she and a beaming Amaria – who was much gratified to see that Henry had come to his senses at last – were hastily gathering their possessions.

'Am I to travel under guard?' Eleanor asked him warily.

'No, Madam, with just the normal escort. I have come to tell you that you are no longer a prisoner.'

So. At last, she was free. Free! It was what she had been praying for all through these long, weary years of her incarceration. She could not quite take it in, nor begin to conceive what it would mean to her. Had it happened at any time prior to that terrible day in June, she would have been shouting exultantly for joy, but now it was a bitter-sweet triumph. For it had taken the death of their son to bring Henry to this decision, and Eleanor would have traded her freedom for the Young King's life any day, yea, even though she remained shut up here until the hour of her death.

It was good, nevertheless, to be in the saddle again, clopping along the sun-dappled lanes of England, revelling in the soft late-summer breeze and the azure-blue sky. It was exhilarating to be on a ship once more, gliding in stately fashion across the smooth waters of the Channel, and then – joy of joys – to sight the coast of Normandy. From there, it was only a few days' ride to Aquitaine . . . and Richard!

Ranulf Glanville watched Eleanor as she stood high on the forecastle, her cloak billowing out behind her, her profile straining towards the continent where lay her own lands, far to the south – and where the King her husband awaited her. Ranulf knew that Eleanor would find him sadly changed.

He was going to miss her. He had become pleasantly accustomed to her charming company at dinner, to their long and lively conversations, the quicksilver agility of her mind and the ready mother-wit of her tongue. He would miss those flashing eyes that invited conversation, and the grace and unconscious allure that even encroaching age could not dim. Imprisonment had not defeated Eleanor: she had emerged from it as vital and energetic as ever, and the weight she had lost in recent weeks had left her looking much younger, with her fine features as elegantly chiselled as if a master mason had crafted them.

Ranulf was aware – had been for a long time – that he had come dangerously close to falling in love with his prisoner; that his infatuation had increased to the point where he had been in peril of losing that objectivity that all conscientious gaolers need to maintain. Privately, he thought his king a fool. Eleanor was an intelligent woman, amenable to reason; a year in prison would have been enough to curb her rebellious spirit. And the situation had been far more complex than Henry would seem to have believed – anyone could see that.

He pulled himself up, reminded himself that this woman had betrayed her lord and king, and that society justly condemned her for it. He reminded himself, as he had done countless times, how he would feel if his faithful Bertha had done such a thing – but of course, it would never enter her head, for she was as docile and biddable as a cow. And Eleanor was not Bertha – *more's the pity*, said the treacherous little devil in his soul. But after the expiation of sins there must come forgiveness. It was sad that it had taken the Young King's death to bring Henry to that point, but fitting that he should take his wife back unto himself. All the same, Ranulf was going to miss her.

Amaria was revelling in her mistress's new-found liberty, but as they journeyed the roads of Normandy, passing apple orchards and lush swathes of fertile farmland, with here and there a stern castle, a bustling town, a soaring abbey or sleepy hamlet, her excitement was increasingly tempered by a festering anxiety. When the Queen was restored to her proper place, would she still want a peasant for a serving woman when she could have the greatest ladies in the land to attend upon her?

For the truth was that Amaria had grown to love Queen Eleanor. What had begun in disapproval and suspicion had ended in deep affection and loyalty, for never once had Eleanor done anything to confirm Amaria's earlier opinion of her. And she had suffered so much . . . and all for love of her children – that much was abundantly clear. Amaria knew what it was to love a child, and she knew too that, if her Mark had ever been treated unjustly by his late-lamented father, she would have sprung like a lioness to his defence.

She had asked herself again and again if she dared question Eleanor about what was to become of her now, but the truth was that she feared to hear the answer. The Queen had made her a promise, but what if she now wished to forget the woman who had shared her long imprisonment? That would be wholly understandable, of course, but did loyalty and friendship count for nothing? And there *had* been friendship between mistress and maid – Amaria had not imagined it; every day she had marvelled that she, a humble miller's daughter, should be the friend of the King's own consort, the woman who, by rights, should be queening it over half of Christendom!

Not long now to Rouen. Amaria would be glad of a soft bed, after hours of jolting in an unfamiliar saddle – and she no horsewoman, by anybody's reckoning! But what would happen when they got to Rouen? Amaria dreaded to think of that.

Eleanor, riding beside her, turned and smiled.

'Is it not wonderful to be away from that dreary castle!' she cried. 'Cheer up, Amaria – we are free! There is no need to look so dismal. I promise you, when we get to Rouen, I will order us both some fine *bliauts*. I expect mine will have rotted away by now.' Most of her wardrobe had been left in Poitiers.

'My Lady, what use would I have for fine *bliauts?*' Amaria asked, but her heart was welling with excitement, for already she knew the answer.

'For wearing at court, of course!' the Queen replied. 'I cannot have my ladies attending me in plain woollen gowns and wimples. I had three chief damsels – Torqueri, Florine and Mamille – and now I will have four, including you. I only hope that the others can come back to me – I know you will like them!'

Amaria's cup ran over.

It was dark by the time they approached Rouen and clattered into the courtyard of the ducal palace beyond the city walls, and torches lit Eleanor's way as she was escorted up the spiral stairs to the royal lodgings in the great tower. The King had dined alone, she was told, and would receive her in private. Her spirits lifted in relief. She had been dreading this moment more than she would even admit to herself, and was supremely thankful, much as she had been ten years earlier, that her reunion with Henry was not to take place in public with the whole court looking on.

Through a window slit on the stairwell she briefly glimpsed the tower where she had first been held. *If I had known then what lay ahead, I might have tried to kill myself in despair,* she thought. *Thank God we are not vouchsafed the knowledge of what is in store for of us.* She wondered, with hope and dread in her soul, what lay ahead now.

The door opened into a barrel-vaulted chamber lit with candle sconces and hung with tapestries in vivid hues; above them she glimpsed painted friezes with scarlet and gold roundels, and at one end of the room there hung a majestic canopy embroidered with the lions of Anjou and Poitou. Beneath it stood a golden throne with its carved arms and back painted bright indigo. Evidently Henry lived in greater state these days than he had used to. All this Eleanor took in with one glance before her eyes met those of the man who had risen from the long table in the centre and come limping towards her.

She was shocked to her core. This was not the Henry she remembered so vividly, but an *old man.* In the brief glimpse she had of him before she sank in a deep and graceful curtsey to the floor, she took in the iron-grey hair, the stocky, corpulent body, the bowed legs, no doubt made so by years of hard riding around his vast empire, and that painful limp. His face was lined and drawn with care and grief, his grey eyes wary and blood-shot – he did not look a well man. And he must be, what, fifty? He looked far older. She was astonished to find herself feeling pain – and another, deeper emotion – at the sight of him, which was incredible indeed after all that he had done to her. *All that we have done to each other*, the voice of her conscience corrected her.

Henry stepped forward, stretched out his hands – his familiar, calloused hands, much rougher now than in former days – and raised Eleanor by the elbows. Then he let his hands fall and they stood there appraising each other, neither of them knowing quite what to say. What *does* one say to the wife one has kept a prisoner for so long? each was thinking.

Henry had rehearsed this scene over and over again in his mind. He had resolved to be business-like and tell Eleanor that her presence in Normandy was needed in order to counteract King Philip's demands for the return of lands she had assigned for her lifetime to the Young King, but which Philip was now insisting belonged to Queen Marguerite in right of her late husband. But, seeing his queen now, he could not say it. Philip's demands had been a pretext: he had known that all along, if he were honest with himself. The truth was that, since the terrible news had come from Martel, he had felt differently about Eleanor. Instead of the arch-traitress who had betrayed her lord and king, and who must be kept under lock and key for everyone's safety, he could conjure up only images of her as a young mother, swinging Young Henry up in the air, happily arranging a birthday celebration for him, kissing his hurts better, pleading with himself, as the boy grew older, to give him what she'd called his rightful dues. *Had* she been so wrong to support her son? Had her shattering betrayal been motivated by nothing worse than mother love?

Yet she had hurt him, her husband, irrevocably, rocked his throne more dangerously even than had the murder of Thomas, and had seemed to be doing it purposefully to bring him to ruin. But now all he could see was the woman who had borne him the child they had lost, the only one who really knew what he was suffering. And when he saw her, in the flesh, standing before him at last, after a decade of absence, there stirred in him, along with pity and the need for comfort, some vestiges of the feelings that he had long told himself were dead and buried – killed off brutally by her faithlessness.

For still she was beautiful. He did a quick reckoning. Sixty-one? Impossible. But yes, she was eleven years older than he. Tall and dignified in her elegant mourning robes, with her gossamer-thin black veil falling from a black coif, her heart-shaped face was framed in the most flattering manner by the matching barbette that creased in linen folds under her chin. Her eyes were clear, if questioning, her skin smooth and pale as marble, her mouth bow-shaped yet. But it was the expression on her face that struck him most: there was a new serenity about her, the promise of hard-learned wisdom in those eyes, and an indefinable aura of spiritual peace. It occurred to him suddenly that this woman might no longer be a threat to him.

'My Lady,' he said at length. 'Welcome. I trust you had a good journey.'

'Wonderful,' she answered. 'I cannot tell you how good it felt to be out in the world, enjoying God's good fresh air again.'

Was she baiting him already? He looked at her sharply, yet could detect no malice in her, and could only deduce that she had but spoken from the heart – as well she might, he conceded.

'Pray sit down,' Henry invited, pulling out the nearer of the two carved chairs that stood at each end of the table. Bread, fish and fowl had been laid out, along with a fruit tart and the good sweet wine of Anjou, but it looked as if Henry had barely touched the food.

'Are you hungry? Have you eaten?' he asked.

'Some wine would be welcome,' Eleanor said. She could not face food. All she could think of was that she was here, with Henry, her lord, after so long, and that his presence still had the power to move her, as it always had.

Henry poured the wine, moved his chair next to hers, and sat down. 'I don't want to shout down the table,' he jested, breaking the tension a little. 'Now, I expect you are wondering why I asked you here.'

'I was a little surprised to receive the invitation,' Eleanor returned. 'Henry, please – I have to ask, before we go any further.

They told me I was no longer a prisoner. Does that mean that I am forgiven?'

He stared at her, nonplussed, then swallowed. 'Yes,' he said hoarsely. 'Yes, provided you behave yourself in future.'

'Oh, you can count on that,' she assured him, her tone light. 'I am not likely to risk your walling me up for another decade. I am coming to the end of my natural span, and the years I have left are precious to me.'

'I am relieved to have your assurance,' Henry declared, with the hint of a wry smile.

Was that it? she asked herself. The subject, her long years of imprisonment, the breakdown of their marriage, disposed of in a few words? Am I forgiven? Yes, as long as you don't do it again. No, I won't. And yet, what else was there to say? Was she to dwell, in accusatory detail, on the miseries she had suffered? Henry must have some idea of what he had put her through. Should they disinter and pore over the horrible conflict between them that should long since have been laid to rest? What was the point? What mattered was the present, and the future. They must move forward. If they dwelt too long and hard on how calamitously they had made mistakes and broken faith in the past, they would surely destroy each other.

'You were going to tell me why you sent for me,' she said resolutely, reaching for her goblet.

'Ah,' Henry responded, clearly relieved to be back on safer ground. 'It concerns certain lands in Normandy that that young fox Philip is claiming were given to his sister Marguerite. He wants to lay his grubby hands on them, of course, but I reminded him that in fact they belonged to you, and that you had assigned them to Young Henry only for his lifetime, after which they were to revert to you.' At the mention of his dead son, his face tautened. For a heartbeat, the mask slipped, and it became clear that Henry was suffering greatly – just as she was. But she was not feeling quite ready to confront their common grief just yet. She had had too much to deal with already this day.

'Yes, I suppose those domains will have reverted to me,' she said. 'I fear I am long out of touch with my landed and financial interests.'

'That's neither here nor there,' Henry interrupted impatiently. 'What matters is that I retain control of those properties that are rightfully mine, as your lord. Young Philip is dangerous; he has grandiose ideas about expanding the might of France. He has his eye on my empire. Were he to gain possession of these lands, we'd have French troops infiltrating Normandy and ... well, you can imagine the rest. I have my hands full as it is, trying to keep my domains under control.'

'I see your point,' Eleanor conceded. 'It would indeed be fool-hardy to give Philip what he wants. So what can I do for you?'

Henry looked at her with admiration. She was actually willing and ready to co-operate with him, after long years of being bitterly at odds, fighting, quarrelling and worse. And Eleanor marvelled that they were sitting here discussing politics much as they had done in the old days – the early days. This was surely one of the best aspects of her new freedom, this being restored to the centre of affairs.

'I want you to visit those domains, each in turn,' Henry said. 'I want it to appear that you are reasserting your rights to them. Show yourself friendly to the local lords, grant charters and privileges, endow churches, found markets – you know the kind of thing that wins hearts.'

'You want me to do all this?' she asked in wonderment. 'I, that was so lately your prisoner? You trust me to do it?'

'There is no one else who can,' Henry said, and grinned, and in that moment, his guard fell. The grin faded, and in its place there appeared on his care-worn features a look of such anguish that it nearly broke Eleanor to see it.

He reached out his hand to her, the movement jerky and tenta-tive. His face was a grimace of agony.

'Help me, Eleanor!' he muttered, his voice strangled. She rose without hesitation, and grasped that outstretched hand, pressing it to her lips, her ready tears salting it, her own need for conso-lation welling urgently. 'I did not ask you here just to discuss Normandy,' Henry gasped. 'I asked you because there is no one else I can turn to, no one else who loved him as I do.' And with that, he clasped his arms about her waist, buried his head in her belly and howled like a baby.

*

When the storm of weeping had passed, and Eleanor felt she had no more tears left in her, they were gentle with each other, sitting quietly in the candlelight, sipping the restorative wine and talking without rancour of the events that had led them both to this place.

'Henry, I long to see our other children,' Eleanor said suddenly.

Henry turned his ravaged face to hers, and took her hand. 'I knew you would want to,' he told her. 'They are here. I summoned them for the purpose. Come, you will be reunited with them now.'

As he led her downstairs to the lower chambers, Eleanor feared that she could not cope with so much grief and joy in such a short span of time. She was to see her children, at last, after so long! They were here – and Henry had bidden them come specially to see her. She felt a little light-headed with emotion and anticipation. Would they have changed beyond recognition? How would they react to seeing her? And – most crucial of all – did they still love her? She was in anguish to know.

When she entered the princes' lodgings hand-in-hand with Henry, three young men and a young woman rose at once and bowed low. For a confused moment, Eleanor hardly recognised any of them, and then she knew them all for her own – much older, of course, and grown to adulthood, but still her children, those she had left to her, and still inestimably loved.

In an instant, they were embracing and kissing her, overjoyed to be reunited with their mother, and there were, inevitably, more tears, but happy ones this time. How, she thought, could she ever have doubted their love for her?

'Let me look at you all!' Eleanor cried in delight, as Henry watched them, a wry smile on his face. With the conversation flowing excitedly, she could not take her eyes off Richard, now a magnificent golden giant of almost twenty-six who towered above everyone else. 'My great one!' she breathed, all his cruelties and depredations forgotten; she had long since convinced herself that reports of them had been greatly exaggerated, and that it had been his father who had really been to blame. She was thrilled to find that Richard, in manhood, had such natural authority and presence, and seeing him so powerfully built and charismatic, she did not doubt that his reputation as a warrior equal to Mars was well deserved. He was a born leader, who clearly had the ability to prove himself superior to all others.

Geoffrey, a year younger, had not fulfilled his earlier promise of maturing into a handsome man. The only dark-haired one of her sons, he was short of stature and blunt of feature, and his bearing lacked a certain princely grace. But his fair words to his mother belied his appearance; she had always known that this son was blessed with acute intelligence and mental agility, and yet . . . and yet, she also had a stronger impression than ever that there was a darker Geoffrey, a devilish Geoffrey that lurked only a little way beneath the clever and urbane front that he presented to the world.

She could not believe that John, the youngest of her children, was the young man who had now grown as tall as his brothers, who seemed still to treat him as a child to be humoured, whereas Henry behaved towards John with affectionate indulgence, clapping an arm around his shoulders and ruffling his hair; indeed, the light seemed to shine from his eyes whenever he looked on the youth, which was an obvious irritation to Richard and Geoffrey. Eleanor could detect a certain jealousy . . . It was evident that, despite their outward bonhomie, these three sons of hers would always be rivals.

John was courteous to her, yet holding a little aloof from the rest. She could not blame him for that. She suspected that he resented her for having effectively abandoned him at Fontevrault in his infancy; she perceived in his conversation – the diffident conversation of a young man who thinks he knows everything – a certain antipathy towards the Church, which she guessed might have had its roots in his early experiences. Yet she knew that she could never explain to John why she had left him in the care of the nuns. Such things were better put firmly behind them all and consigned to the past. If we allow the past to blight our lives, we will never make a success of this reunion, she told herself again. At least she could now look with warmth on John, with his dark-red curls and his strongly built body that so favoured his father's, and actually care about what happened to him, as became a natural mother. That was a significant blessing.

She rejoiced to see Matilda; it was a special delight to be reunited with this daughter she had thought never to set eyes on again, although nothing – nothing – could equal the joy she felt at seeing Richard after all the hard, cruel years of separation; and her cup was full when Matilda summoned a nurse, who escorted into the room a procession of seven little Saxon children to greet their grandmother – the first of her grandchildren that Eleanor had ever seen. One of the girls, she was touched to hear, had been named in her honour. She bent and hugged the sturdy little boys, Otto and Henry, lifted the baby Lothar into her arms, and made much of the pretty daughters, especially Richenza – who told an amused Eleanor that she would really rather be called Matilda while she was in England; then there was Gertrude, Ingibiorg and tiny Nell, her namesake.

She looked on Matilda's brood with pride, while reflecting that it was sad that none of her other children had been similarly fruitful. The Young King's son had died, as had Joanna's and Eleanor's firstborn. So far, there was no whisper that Geoffrey's Constance, who had now joined the gathering and was fawning possessively all over her husband, might be *enceinte*, and Richard and John were as yet unmarried. Both were betrothed, of course, but, John being only sixteen, it was Richard's situation that perturbed the Queen more than anything. So far, she had encountered neither sight nor sound of the Princess Alys. Was it really true that Henry had at one time meant to marry her himself? If so, he had abandoned the idea, years since, for Eleanor had never heard any more of it. Had he really made the girl his mistress, as gossip had long-ago claimed, and gotten children on her? She was not so sure that she believed that now, although she would not have put it past him. When the opportunity arose, she promised herself, she would tactfully raise the matter of Richard's marriage with Henry. It must take place soon.

But for now, that could wait. There were more pleasant matters at hand, and so much news to catch up on. It was enough that, tonight, she was feasting her eyes at long last on her children, with Henry at her side. Lord Jesus, she prayed, let all our strife and troubles be firmly behind us. And with a radiant smile that captured all the love and hope in her heart, she raised her goblet in yet another toast to this wonderful reunion.

Once more, Eleanor assumed her rightful place as queen. When Henry led her out before the court the following evening, and they took their seats at the high table for a celebratory feast, there were cheers and applause as the company rose to its feet. It was all quite overwhelming. She had not imagined that her husband's courtiers would have thought so kindly of her.

She was pleased to find Hugh of Avalon seated at her right hand. Although she knew he did not approve of her marriage, she liked and respected him as a man of integrity and holiness, and she could sense that he was happy to see her here.

'I am more than glad to see good relations restored between you and the King, my Lady,' he told her warmly.

'God has answered my prayers,' she said fervently, and then, with a touch of mischief, added, 'I am to be on my best behaviour now, if I am not to incur Henry's hatred once more.'

Hugh gave her a long look. 'I think you have both learned wisdom, which means that something good has come out of this whole sorry business. And this reunion does not really surprise me. Those whom the King once loved, he rarely comes to hate. And he needs you, my Lady, more than he realises. God works in ways that are incomprehensible to us, but He has brought you together, and taught you both to forgive. Would it could have been in happier circumstances. This has been a sad time for you both. I am deeply sorry for your loss.'

Eleanor inclined her head, not wanting to go there. 'What I want to achieve is a good working partnership with my Lord the King.'

'I believe he desires that too,' the Prior told her. 'He no longer wishes to give his sons cause to criticise him for treating you harshly.'

'And did they so criticise him?'

'Oh, indeed – constantly!' Hugh smiled. 'Your children are very loyal to you. It is a happy day for them, to have their parents reconciled.'

'Indeed it is,' said the Queen, her heart full. But we are not fully reconciled, she thought. She should not have expected it, of course, yet she had wondered, briefly, last night, if Henry, having poured his heart out to her earlier, would come to her bed and cement their reunion with his poor, ageing body in which, she suspected, the old Adam doubtless still lurked. Despite everything, she would very much have liked him to, for she desperately needed the comfort of that unique close union with another human being – and to prove to herself that she could still experience sexual pleasure, which would have enabled her briefly to distance herself from her grief. But he had not come, and she had lain there – blissfully alone for the first night in years – thinking how foolish she had been even to imagine it.

Overjoyed to be at liberty and free to ride where she would at will, Eleanor set off on her travels to the disputed fiefs. She was received everywhere with honour and acclaim, and found herself slipping back effortlessly into the queenly role that had once been a way of life for her. It was very gratifying, and moving, and she was proud to find that she had not lost her common touch, and that the efforts she was making on Henry's behalf were going a long way towards restoring her own popularity.

Then came the summons to Angers, which had been preceded by rumours that trouble had broken out yet again between the King and his sons. Immediately, she hastened south, determined to do all in her power to put things right; but almost as soon as she had dismounted in the castle bailey, Richard was there at her elbow, his handsome face dark with anger.

'Father is out hunting. I need to speak with you urgently,' he muttered.

'At least let me get my breath back,' she chided, then beckoned him to follow her to her lodgings. As Amaria – an Amaria whose bulky figure was now encased in a stylish green *bliaut* – bustled about in the inner chamber unpacking her gear, a job she had to do by herself, as Henry had demurred about recalling Eleanor's other ladies (no doubt they were tainted with suspicion too, and he thought they incited me to rebellion, she told herself), she poured some wine and bade Richard sit down with her in the solar.

'Now, tell me what is going on,' she ordered.

Richard eased his long body onto a settle and looked at his mother, frowning, as if weighing up how much to reveal to her. 'It's about Alys, my betrothed,' he said at last. 'Father is keeping her under guard at Winchester. I have asked time and again for him to let us be married, but he will not. Now Philip is insisting that Father honour the betrothal treaty and arrange the wedding without further delay, but still he stalls.'

The door opened and Henry walked in. 'Plotting rebellion again?' he asked his son nastily as he came over to kiss his wife's hand in greeting.

'That's unfair, my Lord!' Eleanor protested. 'I know nothing of what has been going on. Richard was acquainting me with the facts.'

'You mean, he's been telling you his one-sided view of affairs,' Henry growled, sitting down heavily and rubbing his lame leg, which Eleanor now knew was the casualty of a well-aimed kick from a horse. 'Richard, would you leave us, please.' Richard glared at his father mutinously, but bit back the protest and stalked out, slamming the door. Henry's eyes narrowed, but he said nothing.

'Philip wants to divide my empire and weaken it,' he told Eleanor. 'To that end, he seeks to drive a wedge between me and my sons. If I marry Richard to Alys, Philip will almost certainly use that alliance to bind Richard closer to him and turn him against me.'

'That's a fair argument,' Eleanor observed. 'By all accounts, Philip is a slippery character, not like his father at all.'

'He's crafty and greedy, and suspicious too – they say he sees an assassin hiding behind every tree. But never underestimate him: he's as shrewd and calculating as they come. Dangerous too. An enemy to reckon with, and believe me, I've seen off a few in my time.'

'Can you not break the betrothal?'

'And lose the county of Berry, Alys's dowry?'

Eleanor remembered Henry's glee at having secured that rich prize, all those years ago. But what of Alys herself? she wondered.

Is it because he still lusts after her himself and cannot bear to send her back to Paris?

'No,' Henry was saying, 'I have enough to deal with just now with Richard and John quarrelling, and I don't want Philip exploiting it.'

This was news to their mother. 'Richard and *John?*' Was there no end to this family strife?

'Yes,' Henry sighed. 'Richard is now my heir.' They were both silent for a moment, remembering why. 'And yet,' he continued, with an effort, 'it seems unfair that he should get England, Normandy, Anjou and Aquitaine while John has only a few scattered estates and Ireland. The Irish don't like the idea, but it might be helpful to have a royal presence in Dublin and the Pale surrounding it to keep their native kings in order. What I was saying was that John will inherit very little, and I want to redress that, if people are not to call him "John Lackland".' He laughed grimly at his own joke, then got up and began pacing restlessly around the room. Eleanor could sense his discomfort, and that what he was about to say might not be what she would want to hear.

Henry turned to face her. 'I have called both Richard and John to make peace between them, and a settlement that is fairer to John – and I've brought you in because I want your approval.' It concerns Aquitaine, she thought, in alarm.

'I want Richard to cede Aquitaine to John, and have John swear fealty to him as his overlord,' Henry said.

'No!' Eleanor said unhesitatingly.

'Be reasonable,' Henry wheedled. 'What does it matter if Richard or John has Aquitaine?'

'It matters to me!' she retorted, rising to face him. 'I nurtured Richard as my heir. The south is in his blood. John neither knows nor cares about Aquitaine.'

'He would quickly learn to, if he were its duke. Eleanor, you're not very good at concealing the fact that Richard is your favourite and that you have very little love for John. That blinds you to all other considerations.' Henry's gaze was challenging.

'Ask Richard what he thinks of this plan, then!' she flared. 'You know you will dispose of Aquitaine regardless of what I say – but he is the one most nearly concerned. And, I warn you, Henry: alienate him over this – and you will drive him into the arms of Philip!'

'Very well, we will have him here!' Henry said, and shouted down the stairwell for someone to go and fetch the Duke of Aquitaine.

Richard could not speak, he was so enraged. A look of thunder suffused his chiselled features.

'Well?' Henry prompted.

'Are you going to ride roughshod over us both?' Eleanor asked him.

'Richard?' his father barked. 'My son, you must see that this is an altogether fairer disposition of my domains.'

Richard thrust his furious face into the King's. 'I am a southerner. My Lady Mother raised me from my infancy to be her heir. I love that land of Aquitaine. I have spent years fighting to hold and keep it, and you ask me to relinquish it to John? To that light-minded, lazy, greedy wastrel who has barely set foot in Aquitaine, let alone learned how to govern it? Pshaw! The place will be a bloodbath within a week without a firm hand in control of it!'

'I will give you Alys – now,' Henry said, as if he were dangling a carrot before a donkey. Richard threw him a look that Eleanor could not quite interpret.

'Leave her out of it for now!' he snapped. 'Tell me, Father – do you mean to make John your heir? Will it be Aquitaine now, and Normandy next, and then Anjou, Maine and England – the whole bloody empire for the son you love best?' Eleanor caught her breath – that had not occurred to her.

Henry's face darkened. 'No,' he spat. 'How could you think that? Has Philip been whispering treason in your ear?'

'He has good cause, with my marriage being continually postponed!' Richard was beside himself with rage. 'He thinks you delay the wedding because you mean to marry Alys yourself, so that she can bear you sons and dispossess us.'

Eleanor's hand flew to her mouth. 'Is this true, Henry?' she cried, appalled at the terrible prospect opened up by her son's harsh words.

'Of course not,' Henry answered, a shade too quickly. 'It's some nonsense that Philip has fed him. Besides, have I not just said he can marry Alys now?'

'He has said that several times and retracted it,' Richard said, his tone bitter. 'I wish I could believe him this time.'

'You can have Alys if you surrender Aquitaine to John,' Henry offered brightly.

'No!' said Eleanor.

'I should have her anyway!' Richard roared. 'We've been betrothed since we were children.'

'Go away and think it over,' Henry told him.

'I'll go to Hell first!' his son riposted. 'And I'll appeal to the Church to support me, see if I don't!'

'If you won't marry her, I'll give Alys to John,' Henry threatened.

'You *are* plotting my ruin!' Richard yelled, and stormed to the door. 'I knew it. Well, you won't have to endure the sight of me any longer. I am for Poitiers. Don't think to see me back!'

Eleanor looked coldly upon Henry. 'And you think *I* caused the divisions in this family?' she asked scathingly. 'You say you want peace between your sons, but it's always only on your own terms. Do you want them to resent you? Do you want the years of your age to be overshadowed by endless discord and strife, so that you can find no abiding happiness or enjoy any peace and security?'

'Peace, woman,' Henry growled. 'Had you supported me, this would not have happened.'

'Oh, I think Richard spoke for himself – he does not need his mother's approval!' she retorted.

59 Berkhamsted, Woodstock and Winchester, 1184

Henry sent her back to England in the custody of Ralph FitzStephen. She knew he feared she might stir up more trouble in Richard's defence, and smarted with the unfairness of it all. Although she had been promised her freedom, she was effectively a prisoner once more, presumed guilty until time should prove her innocent. The cage would be gilded, but it was a cage no less.

She was forced to brave the turbulent January seas, then a hard ride to Berkhamsted Castle, Becket's former luxurious residence, which was looking a little worn and frayed after years of neglect. Here, in company with the ghosts and remembrances of the past, she kept Easter with her daughter Matilda, who was pregnant yet again. Afterwards, Matilda returned to the lodgings that had been assigned her in Winchester Castle, and Eleanor was removed to Woodstock.

She did not want to go there, to that place with its painful, unhallowed memories, but she had little choice in the matter. The King had sent orders, and that was that. She wondered if he had done it to spite her. At least she was not required to sleep in Rosamund's tower – that was now locked up and deserted – but in the Queen's chambers in the hunting lodge. Her high window looked out upon the labyrinth – now an overgrown wilderness abandoned to Dame Nature.

She would have liked to ignore it, but it drew her, remorselessly, almost supernaturally, and one early June evening, bored by the tedium of her dreary leisure hours, she felt an urgent need to take the air, and found her steps tracing the bracken-strewn paving stones that led to the entrance of the maze. She had to untangle some branches to get in, and tore her veil on a briar, but soon she was through, and able to make her way along the weed-infested paths. Fortunately, whoever had designed the labyrinth had laid them out broadly, so that the encroaching foliage did not impede her progress too greatly. Soon, by keeping her wits about her, she found the wide arbour at the core – which was actually, although she did not realise it, to one side – and sank down thankfully on a lichen-covered stone bench.

So this was where the gossip had her hunting out her rival, following the thread of silk to the forbidden door. The things people were prepared to believe! If only they knew . . . Yes, she had been deeply hurt to hear Henry say he loved Rosamund; yes, she had rejoiced, God forgive her, to learn of the young woman's early death. But that she would have stooped to violence to rid herself of her – Heaven forbid! Rosamund had been – outwardly, at any rate – beneath Eleanor's notice: a queen had her dignity to preserve, and she had fought many battles with herself to do just that.

She wondered if Rosamund, that pretty, arrogant little whore, had taken much pleasure in her labyrinth; if she had walked here often. It had been the most touching gift from a besotted king, so surely she had cherished it?

The sun was setting in a golden glow behind the black silhouette of the castle walls, leaving the skies a brilliant clear pink-tinged azure in the dying rays of the light. The shadows were lengthening. As the glow dimmed, the labyrinth began to seem a different, darker place. Eleanor shivered, aware of old, primeval forces at work. Here, Dame Nature was alive and hard at work, having reclaimed her kingdom; the soft rustlings and crackles from the stirring bracken made it easy to believe in all those ancient tales of the Green Man, which the English loved to tell. He was one of the 'old ones' they spoke of, and he went by many names – Robin Goodfellow and Jack i' the Wood were two that Eleanor had heard from Amaria. He was a fertility god or a monster, whichever story one believed, and his power had never been bridled by church or state. In the twilight, it was easy to imagine his cunning face peering out eerily from the foliage.

As the Queen sat there, feeling increasingly uncomfortable in the gathering gloom, and bracing herself to retrace her steps – she *thought* she knew which way to go – she heard what sounded like a soft footfall. *Crunch.* There it went again, to her left; someone stepping on bracken! It might be a squirrel or a fox, she told herself sternly, but nevertheless, she stood up and hastened along the path back to civilisation, negotiating her way between the high ragged hedges.

Crunch. It was behind her now. *Crunch.* Again! Someone was in the labyrinth, someone who was approaching by stealth and had not thought fit to announce their presence by calling out to her. She was almost running now, scared to look behind her, her spine tingling with fear, expecting at any moment to feel a hand clamp itself on her shoulder or – horror of horrors – a stab of pain as a dagger pierced her back. If Henry really did still mean to marry Alys, her removal would be all too convenient. Yet she could not, even *in extremis*, imagine Henry being the kind of man who would send an assassin to kill her. But Henry, she knew, was prone to saying violent things in his ungovernable rages, things he did not mean – look what had happened with Becket! Supposing he had said something similar of her: 'Who will rid me of this turbulent queen?'

She was lost and desperate to get out, but she had to pause for breath or she would collapse. She came to a halt at a corner, her chest heaving, and looked both ways. Nothing stirred. There was only the sibilant rustling of leaves and the occasional twitter of a tiny bird. Then she heard it again. *Crunch*, this time followed by a faint moan that could almost have been a sob. Ahead of her. There was no rhyme or reason to it. Did the person stalking her know where they were going?

She would not run this time. She would tread silently, and keep her wits about her. She crept furtively along the paths, steeling herself to take her time and breathing shallowly. Then, turning another corner, she glimpsed, ahead of her, the trail of a grey gown disappearing into the briars. And that sound again, faint but distinct, and definitely a sob. A woman, then! But what woman? Her fear abated a little. She was equal to besting a woman! It was the brute strength of a man she had feared.

She followed carefully, keeping her distance, and noticing that she was very near to the edge of the maze, for beyond stood the high wall of the hunting lodge. *Crunch*. It was behind her again, on the path she had just walked – but how could that be? She would have had to pass whoever it was, surely?

Eleanor was becoming a little weary of this game of cat and mouse, and increasingly chilled in body and soul. The light was fading fast, the moon rising, and all she wanted was to get back to her bower and the down-to-earth common sense of Amaria, so it was with enormous relief that she suddenly espied the entrance to the maze ahead of her. Yet, once through it, she did not immediately hurry back to the hunting lodge. She could see the two guards who always trailed her standing to attention by the garden door, so, taking courage from their presence, she concealed herself behind a straggling mulberry tree to watch for her pursuer emerging from the labyrinth – for, without doubt, they must soon do so. There was no other way out, and they could not remain there all night.

She waited, in increasing puzzlement, for nigh on half an hour, but no one appeared. Nor did she hear any more footfalls or other noises that might betray the presence of someone in the maze. The night was quiet, its peace unbroken. Then, just as she was deciding to go indoors, her attention was captured by the dim but unmistakeable flicker of a candle in the upper room of Rosamund's tower. She caught her breath. Someone was indeed playing games with her! Were they deliberately trying to frighten her? Tomorrow, she vowed, she would get to the bottom of this, and that person would be made to account for their purpose in disturbing the Queen!

Once back in the safety of her bower, she told a surprised Amaria and a sceptical Ralph FitzStephen of her experiences. FitzStephen had the maze searched, and the tower unlocked and inspected, but found nothing to account for what Eleanor had heard and seen. It was not until two mornings later that she was given a less-than-satisfactory explanation for what had happened, when Amaria brought the local laundry woman to see her. They had fallen to chatting on the banks of the River Glyne, as the woman washed sheets, and Amaria had told her of the Queen's fright in the labyrinth.

The laundress was nervous of speaking to so great a lady, but determined to tell Eleanor what she knew.

'That baint no 'uman soul in that there maze,' she declared. '*She* walks. Some has heard her, heard her footsteps. They be all around, no rhyme or reason to them.'

'Who walks?' Eleanor asked gently. The laundress's words had chilled her.

'Why, the Fair Rosamund, o' course, Lady, her as people say was murd—' She stopped in mid-flight, remembering to whom she spoke. 'Begging your pardon, Lady, it's only what fools say. But *she* walks, no doubt about it. And *she*'ve been seen up in that tower. *She* weeps for her sins! And another thing, young Matt, the miller's boy, he's seen her, in the maze! Well, not her, so to speak of – but he caught a glimpse of her gown; it were grey!'

Eleanor froze. She had not mentioned that detail.

*

She still did not quite know if she believed what the laundress had said when permission arrived for her to remove to Winchester, so that she could be present at Matilda's confinement. If the tale was true, then why should Rosamund appear to her rival, Eleanor, the woman she had wronged in life?

'Stop thinking about it,' Amaria counselled in her blunt way. 'It's just silly gossip.'

'I'm not so sure,' Eleanor said thoughtfully. 'It was a nightmarish experience, and I did not dream it. Can malice survive the grave? I can hardly believe Rosamund was trying to seek my forgiveness – it was an odd way to go about it, scaring me half to death like that.'

'It's all nonsense!' snorted Amaria.

'I know what I heard, and saw,' Eleanor insisted. 'You were not there. But we will say no more of it.'

'Mayhap, my Lady,' interrupted FitzStephen, staggering into the bower with a pile of cloth-wrapped bundles in his arms, 'there is no reasoning behind the appearances of spirits, and it means nothing at all – or you were mistaken in what you heard and saw; it could have been a shadow, or some small creatures of the night. Now, here are some parcels for you from the Lord King.'

Eleanor temporarily forgot her puzzlement, as she unwrapped the gifts and exclaimed delightedly over the bold scarlet *bliaut* lined with grey miniver that she found in the first, the saddle worked with gold and trimmed with fur in the second, and the embroidered cushions in the third. Nor had Henry omitted to send a gift to Amaria, of whom he soundly approved: for her, there were fine linen headrails and an amethyst brooch.

Peace offerings, Eleanor told herself. He won't admit that he has again treated me – and our sons – unjustly, so he sends presents instead. Her spirits lifted, and she had to smile. It was so typical of Henry – and it augured well for a happy resolution to all the quarrelling.

As for that strange Rosamund business, she knew she would never convince herself entirely that it had not been a supernatural experience. And the appalling thought occurred to her that Rosamund had not yet found the eternal peace that is every Christian soul's hope and desire, and that her shade was condemned to a relentless earthly purgatory in expiation of her sins. The notion chilled her immeasurably, for she herself was no longer young, and Divine Judgement could not be far off! Might she too be condemned to walk this Earth for eternity, at Poitiers, the place where she had plotted her husband's betrayal – or, worse still, in the grim keep of Sarum? Heaven forbid! She had best start ensuring that she lived wisely and virtuously from now on. That would make a change, she thought, with the hint of a darkly humorous smile playing on her lips.

Matilda, with the minimum of fuss, had a healthy little boy, to Eleanor's joy, and called him William in honour of the Conqueror and the Queen's father. Eleanor had arrived at Winchester just in time to greet her new grandchild as he emerged from his mother's womb, and she was thrilled to be able to spend the following weeks in her daughter's company, taking pleasure in the infant's progress.

This happy interlude was marred by the arrival one morning of two more packages, both of identical size.

'For the Queen!' announced the steward, placing them on the chest. 'A gift from the Lord King.'

Henry *was* trying to make amends! Eleanor smiled and unwrapped the first package. It contained more costly items of clothing: a lightweight summer cloak and hood of the deepest blue samite, and a good few yards of colourfully embroidered trimming for edging garments. Suitable peace offerings! It was gratifying to know that Henry was thinking of her, and that her good opinion counted for something with him; and, of course, such gifts might well signal that she was soon to be set at liberty again.

She opened the second bundle to find, to her astonishment, that it contained exactly the same items. Why would Henry send two of everything, and in separate packages? Then her eye was drawn to a tiny scroll of parchment that lay on the floor; it must have fallen out of one of the bundles. She picked it up and saw that it was a receipt of sorts, written by some clerk who had obviously intended to file it away in the royal accounts, but had mistakenly wrapped it with the gifts. He would be looking for it, no doubt. But what was it that he had scribed? *'£55.17s. for the clothes of the Queen and of Bellebelle, for the King's use.'*

Who was Bellebelle, and why had she been provided with exactly the same gifts of clothing as the Queen? Looking at the final phrase, her heart sinking, Eleanor suddenly knew the answer. The garments could not be for the King's use, of course – but the mysterious Bellebelle obviously was.

Her mind disquieted, she made it her business, whilst at Winchester, to seek out Alys, Richard's betrothed, telling herself firmly that any plan of Henry's to divorce her and take Alys as his wife in her place could not have been Alys's fault. Nor had Alys been in a position to resist any less-honourable propositions made by Henry. But when she saw Alys, now a beautiful, buxom young woman in her early twenties, she was not so sure.

Alys's welcome was muted; Eleanor supposed that she was permitted few visitors, since Henry was still keeping her under guard, no doubt fearing that Richard might descend on the castle and spirit her off to the altar, thereby depriving his father of a valuable bargaining tool in his tortuous power games with Philip. And of course the poor girl had suffered so many turns of fortune that she had probably given up all hope of ever getting married. No doubt she anticipated that the Queen had come with news of yet another unwelcome development, or simply to gloat at her luckless rival; hence her understandable wariness.

She found Alys hard work. All her questions met with monosyllabic replies, and in the end, Eleanor almost gave up. Clearly, Alys bore a deep resentment towards her, and small wonder, she thought grimly: but for herself, Alys would have been queen of England these nine years. Instead, she was shut away here, wasting her youth to no purpose.

What had there been between this princess of France and the King? Had Alys actually loved Henry? Did she love him still? Eleanor had to know. She needed to reassure herself that this had not been the kind of grand passion that Henry had shared with the ill-fated Rosamund, that Alys was no real threat to herself.

'Your life cannot have been easy, child,' she ventured. 'You should have been married to Richard years ago, and become the mother of a fine brood by now.'

Alys flinched. Her recoil was unmistakeable.

'I should have been *married* years ago,' she said pointedly.

'You can forget about that,' Eleanor retorted. 'My marriage is valid. The Pope would not countenance its annulment.'

'You could have retired gracefully to Fontevrault!' It was an accusation.

'For which I have no vocation,' Eleanor replied calmly, although her ire was rising like bile in her throat. 'It was all a ruse by Henry to gain possession of my domains.'

'It was far more than that!' Alys countered, her eyes flashing fire. They were green, like a cat's, and full of venom. 'You just didn't want to lose your husband to another woman – a *younger* woman. You couldn't accept that it was me he wanted for wife, not you.'

'Next you'll be telling me that he loved you!' Eleanor said scornfully. 'Well, let me assure you I have heard it all before, with Rosamund.'

'He did love me – he loves me still!' Alys cried.

'How sweet!' Eleanor sneered, resolutely ignoring the flicker of fear that the girl's words had ignited in her. 'My, you are an innocent! Love indeed! What does that have to do with royal marriages made for profit and politics? Do you think, you foolish child, that love ever dictated Henry's policy? I thought you would have more sense.'

Alys jumped to her feet, and as she did so, the folds of her *bliaut* rippled over her figure. She was, quite obviously, pregnant. Eleanor stared at her in horror.

'Is this not the fruit of love?' the girl cried triumphantly, smoothing her hands over her swollen belly.

'Any trollop can get a man to bed her,' Eleanor observed tartly, but her voice came out hoarsely through dry lips. 'Love rarely comes into it. I suppose you are going to tell me that that is the King's.'

'It is!' insisted Alys.

'Tell me also, how could you so dishonour Richard, the man to whom you are betrothed?' Eleanor cried, rising, scandalised beyond measure. That Henry had not scrupled to take his son's betrothed! It was true, horribly true, but still she could hardly believe it, even of him, with his voracious appetites. 'Shame on you for a harlot!'

Alys was weeping now. 'He loves me! *You* will not stand aside and let us marry. It's your fault!'

Eleanor ignored that. The desire to wound her rival was strong in her, and she could not resist it. 'Did you know he has another mistress?' she taunted.

The barb went home. Alys gaped at her. 'You're lying – to spite me. I will not believe it.'

'Nor did I until yesterday afternoon,' Eleanor said, 'and if it wasn't for some clerk's silly mistake, I would be in happy ignorance now. But how I found out is neither here nor there. Her name is Bellebelle. She sounds like a harlot. But you would know, of course. And you would know too that Henry is incapable of staying faithful.'

As Alys collapsed in tears, Eleanor looked down on her with distaste. 'What matters most in all this is that my son, your betrothed, is spared any hurt,' she hissed. 'If he knew of your shame, he would surely kill you – and his father too, and the world would applaud him for it.'

'He does know,' sobbed Alys, a note of defiance creeping back into her voice. 'He does not care. He wishes only to wed me to spite his father and deprive him of the person he loves most. And he means, through me, to ally himself with my brother.'

Her words took Eleanor's breath away. Richard knew. Of course he did. She remembered that strange look he had given Henry.

She left the girl weeping, and stumbled blindly back to her apartments, her thoughts in turmoil. What have we come to, as a family, that Henry and Richard should effectively collude in such vile, underhand dealings? she asked herself. Was there no honour left in the world? And what of the silly, deluded girl – a princess of France, no less – who had been the unwilling pawn in it all? Philip would declare war if he heard of it!

But maybe, just maybe, he did know. He was capable of dissembling with the best of them, and maybe he was playing them at their own game, meaning to have the last laugh.

She began to make excuses, not for Henry – he was past redemption where women were concerned, in thrall to that unruly and mischievous member between his legs that seemed to have an independent life of its own, in defiance of all sense

431

or morality! But Richard . . . Richard, she told herself, was merely being pragmatic – and chivalrous too, yes, in standing by his compromised betrothed. It took a very special man to do that. Most would have abandoned Alys, or demanded satisfaction from her seducer. But Richard was not most men: he was a lion among mortals.

Having consoled herself with such reasoning, Eleanor decided that she would say nothing of this to anyone. If that meant she was colluding too, then so be it. She could find it in herself to feel pity for Alys, unpleasant chit though she was, and as for Henry – well, what should she feel but disgust, that old, familiar revulsion at his concupiscence, but far more strongly this time, because he was injuring not only herself, and Alys, but – far more importantly – her adored Richard? Yet even that she would conceal, for Richard's sake.

Had she really wanted Henry in her bed again? She must have been mad! Something had died in her this day, and she feared it might never be revived.

60 Westminster, 1184

It was on St Andrew's Day that Eleanor arrived at Westminster to be reunited with her husband and sons. Her presence, and theirs, had been required by Henry in the wake of the war that had broken out in Poitou that autumn between Geoffrey and John on the one side – Geoffrey being ever ready to assist in the stirring up of trouble – and Richard, valiantly defending his lands, on the other. It was only after a stern command from their father that the brothers had lain down their arms and come north to England. They were already uneasily installed in the Palace of Westminster when Henry came to greet Eleanor at the river stairs.

'Greetings!' he called chirpily, as she stepped out of the boat. He took her hand and pressed it to his lips. 'My Lady, welcome. I have long looked for your coming.'

Instantly, she was wary. He wanted something from her. Aquitaine for John, no doubt! To what else could she attribute these fair words and cozening smiles?

'Greetings, my Lord,' she murmured, thinking of Alys and the unknown Bellebelle, and disengaging her hand from Henry's. She could not bear him to touch her at this moment. 'So our boys have been fighting again. Do you really think they will make peace when you keep inciting them to war?'

'I incite them?' Henry threw her a sideways glance. She was going to be difficult. 'They must learn to obey me.'

'They are grown men now, and have their own sense of what is right and just,' Eleanor told him. 'Might cannot always triumph over right, Henry.'

'Why do you always like to make out that I'm in the wrong?' he asked aggrievedly, his good mood rapidly dissipating.

'If the cap fits . . .' she smiled.

'You and I need to have a little talk,' Henry told her brusquely. 'I have summoned you to help me bring about a concord between our princes, not to join in the quarrelling. I have summoned the Great Council as well, as we also have to confirm the election of the new Archbishop of Canterbury. Baldwin's the man. A saintly soul he is too, a gloomy bag of nerves, in fact, and I've no doubt he'd prefer to remain a monk, but he'll be useful to me.'

'You mean he won't defy you as Becket did,' Eleanor murmured.

'Hardly!' Henry grinned. 'Not with all his wavering and lack of guile. Just the right man for the job! There'll be no obstinacy from this one.'

When Eleanor had refreshed herself and rested after her journey, a page came to summon her to the council chamber. There, she found the King and her sons waiting for her, with the new Archbishop, who quavered a greeting, and the barons of England, resplendent in their fine tunics and heavy furred mantles of scarlet, blue, vermilion or tawny.

Henry handed her to the seat of honour next to his – he *does* want something, badly, she thought – and then, the company being also seated, called upon their three sons to come forward and publicly make their peace before her. They stood forward, Richard's and Geoffrey's faces set, John's triumphant – and stiffly gave each other the kiss of peace.

Then they stood facing their parents, waiting to see what would happen next.

Henry turned to Eleanor. He had given her no formal warning of what he was about to say – but she had guessed! 'My Lady,' he said, in ringing tones, 'I now ask you to approve the assignment of Aquitaine to the Lord John.'

Eleanor stared at him, fury mounting within her breast. How dare he! How dare he do this to Richard, to her, publicly, in the face of his entire council! She could see the flush of anger on Richard's handsome face, hear his sharp, indrawn breath, sense Geoffrey's secret enjoyment of this human drama being enacted before him – and catch John's complacent, gloating smirk.

'My Lord, we should discuss this privately,' she murmured, her profile rigid. She could not look at Henry.

'There is no need for discussion, my Lady,' he countered. 'I only wish to make a fairer distribution of my empire. Surely you can understand that?'

'All I understand is that you are depriving your rightful heir of his lawful inheritance in favour of your favourite son, who has yet to prove himself,' she muttered.

'Richard, always Richard!' Henry muttered, fuming. Then, in a louder voice, he reiterated his demand for Eleanor to approve the transfer of Aquitaine to John.

'No, my Lord, I will not approve it,' Eleanor stated firmly.

The barons leaned forward, to a man. This was going to be interesting!

'I call upon you all, my Lords of England,' the Queen went on, 'to tell my Lord the King if this is indeed a fair division of his domains.'

'I say it is not!' thundered Richard, who had been itching to speak.

'And I!' echoed Geoffrey. John glowered at him.

'Shut up,' Henry said brutally, his face puce with rage. Eleanor would pay for her defiance! By the eyes of God, she would pay! 'Well, my Lords?' His jutting jaw brooked no opposition.

The lords, who had been conferring perplexedly amongst themselves, looked at their sovereign warily. None of them wanted to see that spoilt brat John in control of Aquitaine, and none of them wanted to offend the man who might well be their future king, for Richard's reputation was fearsome indeed; yet they were all afraid of Henry's notorious temper.

The quavering voice of the new Archbishop broke the silence, to everyone's astonishment. 'Lord King, I say this cannot be a fair division,' the saintly Baldwin opined, and if an angel from Heaven had come down and voiced his view, Henry could not have been more shocked.

'And you thought he'd be useful to you!' Eleanor mocked quietly under her breath.

Some of the barons took courage from the brave old man's stand, and added their voices to his. Much gratified, Eleanor turned to Henry. 'You must know, my Lord,' she warned him, 'that I can appeal this matter to King Philip, of whom I hold Aquitaine. And if I do, you know as well as I that he will support me, if only to discountenance you and drive a wedge between you and your sons.'

Henry threw her a murderous look. 'I see I am defied on all sides. Very well. My Lord Archbishop, a word in private, if you please!' With that, he rose and stalked out of the council chamber in high dudgeon, with the faltering prelate scuttling in his wake. Poor old man, Eleanor thought, having to face the King's wrath, and so soon after his election.

But she had won, she reminded herself exultantly, as she went to embrace her two eldest sons, John having flounced off in a sulk. It was some small, sweet revenge for Alys and Bellebelle!

61 Windsor, 1184–5

When Eleanor arrived at Windsor Castle for the Christmas court, wondering why Henry had bothered inviting her after their spectacular falling out at Westminster, after which he had sent her summarily back to Winchester with not a word of farewell, the first person who came to greet her was Constance, a Constance now grown tall and proud, bearing a tiny infant in her arms. Yet her face bore no trace of the serenity and joy of young motherhood; instead, the winged brows were creased in a petulant frown, the wide, bee-stung lips pouting in a disagree-able grimace. Barely had the Duchess of Brittany risen from her curtsey than she was complaining.

'Madame the Queen, I beg of you, go to the King for me. He will not permit me to join Geoffrey in Normandy for Christmas. It's so unfair!'

'Daughter,' enjoined Eleanor, a touch sharply, 'will you not allow me a moment to get my breath after braving these treach-erous roads?' She sank thankfully into a cushioned chair. 'And first things first! May I not greet my new grandchild?' She held out her arms. Plainly irritated by this distraction, Constance placed the baby in them, then opened her mouth to have her say . . .

'Oh, you are gorgeous!' Eleanor cooed to the tiny pink and white face blinking up from the swaddled bundle. 'Is it a boy?'

'No,' said Constance flatly, smarting with disappointment, for she had been convinced she was carrying an heir to Brittany – and perhaps to more than that, if her own and Geoffrey's ambitions were to be fulfilled; she was convinced that her instincts would prove correct in regard to that.

'A little girl! How delightful!' Eleanor baited her, tracing the soft cheek with her finger. 'And what is she called?'

'She is named after you, my Lady,' Constance said grudgingly, recalling how Geoffrey had insisted, despite her protests.

'I am most touched. How kind!' Eleanor smiled sweetly, and handed the baby back. Immediately, Constance called for the nurse to take her, at which Eleanor deliberately prolonged matters by calling for wine and comfits.

'Now,' she said comfortably, when they had been brought, 'what's all this about Geoffrey and Normandy?'

'The King sent him to take charge of Normandy while he himself was in England,' Constance told her, with the air of one throwing down the gauntlet.

Eleanor was surprised. 'Indeed,' she managed. Was this some new ploy of Henry's to discountenance her and Richard? Could it – surely not! – even mean that the King was now grooming Geoffrey to succeed to his empire? One look at Constance's smug face was enough to tell her that it could – or at least that

Constance herself, and therefore probably other people, were interpreting it that way.

She mastered herself. 'And you want to join him there?' she enquired, neatly deflecting the subject in favour of something far less contentious.

'Yes, my Lady, that's why you must go to the King for me!' Constance insisted.

'Must?' Eleanor lifted her eyebrows. 'I should have thought that, with you so lately delivered and barely up on your feet, braving the conditions out there would be foolhardy. The King has made a very sensible, and considerate, decision in keeping you here. You must rest, child, and then you can join your lord when the weather is improved.'

'But, Madame!' Constance protested. Eleanor cut her short.

'That's enough!' the Queen reproved, raising a hand in warning. Constance scowled at her and subsided.

Henry was remote but polite, Richard studiedly courteous to his father and overly attentive to his mother, John mutinous and foul-tempered. The court held its celebrations in an atmosphere as hostile as it was tense, making a mockery of the holy season of Christ's birth. Not all the lavish outlay on fine wines, meats, spices, choice fare and gifts could compensate for the rifts that had opened up within the royal family, and as soon as Twelfth Night had come and gone, Richard hared off south to Poitiers. A day later, with a perfunctory kiss on her hand and a lowering look of dislike, Henry despatched Eleanor back to Winchester.

62 Normandy, 1185

Eleanor was glad to leave England. After that mighty earthquake, which had been heard and felt throughout the whole realm and had brought the mighty cathedral at Lincoln crashing to the ground in a storm of dust and masonry, she had not felt safe there. Cracks had even appeared in the walls of Winchester Castle. She had lain there at night tormented by fears that the building would collapse over her, crushing her as she slept.

But now she was bound for Normandy, on Henry's orders, with Matilda and her husband for company. Could it be that the King too was concerned for her safety? She would have liked to think so, but she suspected it was something other than that. And, as so often before, her intuition was right.

No sooner had Henry received her, as coldly as he had left her all those months before, than he raised the matter of Aquitaine. They were alone in his solar this time; he was not about to risk any more public outbursts of disobedience.

'I have decided that Richard must surrender the duchy to you, Eleanor, and that you will rule it once more,' he said, his tone brooking no defiance.

She sank down wearily into her chair, bone-tired after the long ride, and momentarily defeated. Oh, but he was clever! To offer her the one thing that meant so much to her, the chance to return to her beloved lands after so many long years of exile, and the liberty to rule them as sovereign duchess – but only in return for the dispossession of the person she loved best in the whole world, her lion-hearted Richard. It was an exquisitely cruel choice. How her husband must hate her! Yet *did* she have a choice? One look at Henry's face gave her the answer to that.

'And if I refuse?' she challenged.

'Then you go back to Sarum,' he replied brutally. It was like a blow.

'I suppose you will dispossess Richard anyway, whether or not I agree?' she said. At least let Henry bear the guilt for injuring his son, rather than herself.

'No, *you* will do it,' the King said. He was being deliberately vengeful.

'Ah, but I will not,' she declared, her old spirit flaring. 'You are only doing this to show Richard who is master. How low of you!'

'I think you *will* agree, Eleanor. You have no choice. You are my wife, and have vowed obedience to me. I could make a public example of you. Already your faithlessness is notorious. You had your way at Christmas, and made me look a fool. You will not defy me again. Now, say you agree to demand Aquitaine back from Richard, or you go straight back to Sarum, and I warn you, you will not be so comfortably accommodated!'

It was at times like these that Eleanor found it hard to reconcile the nasty, brutish Henry of recent years, the Henry who was descended from the Devil, with the Henry who had desired her, who had bedded joyfully with her, bred children on her and cried out his grief to her, the one person who could console him. It was as if he possessed two souls in his one body, and the one she was dealing with now was certainly not the one to whom she had once jubilantly given her heart and her body. Because her insubordination had rankled so deeply, and publicly humiliated him, this ferocious Henry was taking his revenge – she could see it, very clearly. It was his pride, his stubborn pride that drove him – and his usual talent for walking roughshod over people's sensibilities. How tragic, though, that they should have come to this – and how tragic that he should no longer have the power to break her heart with his cruelty, and that all that was left of her for him to arouse was her anger and contempt!

She really had no choice – she saw that too, and prayed that Richard would understand her predicament.

'Very well, as you insist so persuasively,' she said drily.

'Good! I'm glad you've seen sense at last.' There was a hint of relief in Henry's steely eyes. He called immediately for his clerk to bring parchment and writing materials, and then began dictating a letter to Richard. She listened in mounting consternation as he instructed his son to surrender without delay the whole duchy of Aquitaine to his mother, Queen Eleanor. The only reason he gave for this was that it was her heritage – as if that would satisfy Richard as an excuse for robbing him of the inheritance he had fought bloodily to secure. But there was worse to come. If the Lord Richard in any way delayed to fulfil his father's command, the King went on, he was to know for certain that his mother the Queen would make it her business to ravage the land with a great host. Eleanor gasped aloud at that.

'As if I would set myself up in armed opposition to my own son!' she cried.

'You did not scruple to set yourself up in armed opposition to your king and husband!' Henry reminded her. There was, of course, no answer to that.

She spent the next weeks agonising over what Richard might think of her when he received Henry's orders, and grieving for him, knowing that they would come as the heaviest of blows. Secretly, she smuggled out a letter explaining how his father had suborned her and advising him to surrender with all meekness, laying aside his weapons. She never knew whether he received it, but was utterly relieved to learn, in due course, that Richard had wisely ceded Aquitaine into her hands and was on his way north to Normandy. Later still, she stood looking on as Henry received him with open arms, and saw incredulously that – for the moment at least – the lion had been tamed.

Towards herself, Richard betrayed no shred of animosity or resentment. She was a woman, subject to her lord's will, and the King's prisoner. She had had no choice – his manner indicated that that much was clear to him.

Soon, though, it became perfectly clear that Henry meant to rule Aquitaine himself.

63 Bordeaux, 1186

Things had not turned out as badly as she had feared, Eleanor reflected, as she stood on the ramparts of the Crossbowman, the tall keep of the Ombrière Palace, looking down with pride on the beautiful courtyards with their tiled fountains playing in the sunshine and the gardens with their exotic plants and flowers, spread out before her like a carpet of jewels in myriad colours. It was heaven to be back in Bordeaux, her southern capital, to feel once again the summer's heat warming her ageing bones, and the soft breeze from the ocean breathing new life into her, making her feel young again, and deliciously aware that the familiar air once more held a promise of something wonderful and precious.

Thus she had felt long ago, a young girl standing on these

very battlements, imbibing the heady scent of the sea and the flowers, and sensing in the gentle winds that teased her hair and her skirts some joyful anticipation of the life she had yet before her, and the love that she was sure would be hers one day.

She frowned. She was sixty-four now, and rather old to be dreaming wistfully about love. That was all behind her now. Yet some trace of yearning remained, for Henry as he had once been, young and magnificent in all the vigour of his early manhood, before time and strife had soured and changed him. She did not want the man he had become, but she would always mourn the loss of the man he had once been.

To be fair, despite his thuggish means of wresting Aquitaine from Richard, Henry had treated both Richard and herself with consideration, seeking their counsel on various matters concerning the duchy, and even allowing them each a share in its government. He had also granted them the right to issue charters. It had been Eleanor's particular pleasure to bestow gifts and concessions on the abbey of Fontevrault, where she had stayed on her way south, exulting in its long-missed spiritual peace and tranquillity, which was such a balm to her troubled soul. One day, she had resolved, she would be laid to rest here. She could not think of a better sepulchre.

Yes, it had felt good to come home, after twelve years of exile – so good that, even now, months later, she could not stop thanking God for it. Every place she visited was utterly dear to her, every old acquaintance inestimably precious. The realisation that her people remembered her with affection and love had been sheer joy; and in this expansive and thankful mood, she had continued to help rule them with increasing wisdom and kindness.

Then there had come the never-to-be-forgotten day when Henry, impressed by the way she had used the power he had given her, relented, granting her humble request and allowing her to cede all her rights in the duchy once more to Richard, leaving their son effectively ruler of Aquitaine once more. Henry's reasoning was often fathomless, but on this occasion Eleanor suspected that his iron determination to keep Aquitaine had gradually been softened and tempered by Richard's prolonged display of filial devotion and her own conformity to his will. Besides, it had become abundantly clear that Richard could rule the duchy better than anyone – and that it was in everyone's interests for him to continue to do so. Henry had even, at Philip's insistence, agreed that Alys could be married to Richard as soon as the wedding could be arranged, although there was no sign of him hurrying to give orders for that. He was too busy calculating how to keep Alys for himself, or as a useful bargaining tool, Eleanor thought dourly.

Nevertheless, she reflected, looking down and smiling as she espied her damsels playing hide-and-seek amongst the trees, things had improved greatly. Yet, although relations between them and their sons were far more cordial these days, she still did not trust Henry. The matter of the disposition of his empire was still unresolved, and she suspected he had plans that he was keeping to himself, which no amount of oblique probing could prompt him to disclose. She feared that the future would see a resurgence of the rivalry that had blighted their House, but knew herself powerless to forestall it.

John, clearly, was not going to live up to Henry's high expectations. The petted favourite had been despatched to Ireland with plain instructions to establish good relations with the Norman barons who had fought to colonise the English Pale around Dublin and with the Irish kings who still reigned supreme in the wild and beautiful lands beyond that. But Henry had made the fatal mistake of allowing John to be accompanied by his giggling young cronies, and when the native kings had come, with gifts, to pay homage to their new overlord, John and his silly friends had outraged their sensibilities by pulling on their long beards and making fun of their strange attire and time-honoured rituals that seemed outlandish to the newcomers. To compound these insults, John had enraged the Norman barons by seizing their hard-won territories and bestowing them on his worthless intimates. John was, even now, on his way back to England in disgrace. Henry had had enough of his crassness, and had had to appoint a viceroy to go and sort out the mess his son had created.

John was impossible. Henry had spoilt and indulged him, and they were all now suffering the consequences. By contrast,

Eleanor had few worries about her daughters. Matilda and her family had at last found it safe to return to Germany, where a new Emperor ruled, who was amenable to making peace with the exiles. Eleanor and Joanna were, it seemed, reasonably happily settled in their distant kingdoms. Only John and Geoffrey were giving Eleanor real cause for concern.

Geoffrey had gone to Paris, where he was even now fraternising mysteriously with that menace Philip, and no doubt plotting some fresh mischief. You never knew with Geoffrey. Reports had it that he was as close as a blood brother to the French King. Eleanor had some time since concluded that he was dissatisfied with being merely Duke of Brittany and wanted more. Not so long ago, he had thought he had Normandy within his grasp. Now he was making noises about Anjou. It was all a great annoyance to the King, and doubtless Philip was relishing abetting Geoffrey in his ambitions. Anything to discountenance Henry!

The Queen sighed. Soon, to her great sadness, she would have to leave this beloved city and travel north, for Henry was for England and wanted her to accompany him. They were to lodge for a time at Winchester. She did not want to go, really she didn't. How could she forsake the golden lands of the sunny south to waste the coming summer in a castle that would be forever associated in her mind with her long captivity?

But of course, she had, as usual, no choice in the matter.

64 Winchester, 1186

Eleanor could have cried over the unjustness of it all! The situation with Geoffrey and Philip having become increasingly a matter for concern, she had thought to write to her son, urging him to come to England, where she hoped to talk some sense into him. But Henry had intercepted the letter – she had not realised that her correspondence was still subject to the scrutiny of his officers – and his suspicious mind had interpreted it as evidence that she was involved in a plot against him. After all, had she not schemed with King Louis, on that earlier, fateful occasion when her sons had sought refuge and support in Paris?

Nothing she said could fully deflect Henry's mistrust. He muttered that he accepted her explanation, but his eyes told a different story. And now she had a new custodian to replace Ralph FitzStephen, whose services had been dispensed with some time before. She would have liked Ranulf Glanville, but he had been deployed to more pressing duties of state. At least Henry Berneval was an upright, amiable man of little imagination, and he treated her with great deference and kindness; but he was her gaoler, nonetheless, and tailed her, two guards at his heels, wherever she went, even with the King in residence, which he was all that summer.

Eleanor was still smarting from the unfairness of it all when the messenger from France arrived at Winchester and she received a summons to the King's lodgings. There she was confronted by an ashen-faced Henry, slumped in his chair, a wine goblet lying in a pool of liquid on the rush matting, where he had evidently dropped it.

Shutting the door on Henry Berneval and his guards, so that she could be alone with her husband, she knelt down before him in alarm.

'Henry! What has happened? Is it war? Has Geoffrey allied with Philip against you?'

The King looked at her dully. His eyes were bloodshot; he had been drinking a lot lately. He was quite drunk now, she realised.

'Worse. I know not how to tell you,' he mumbled, slurring his words slightly. 'Geoffrey is dead, killed in a tournament in Paris.'

'Oh God!' Eleanor cried. 'No!'

A tear slid down Henry's weathered cheek. He leaned forward and placed one tentative hand on her shoulder in a gesture intended to comfort. She barely noticed it in her distress.

'What happened? Tell me – I must know!' she wept, unable to believe that God had been so cruel as to take yet another of her children to Himself. And Geoffrey, like the Young King, had been but twenty-eight years old. Yet, unlike what had happened with the Young King, three years earlier, there had been no warning to prepare her, no vision vouchsafed of the bliss that lay ahead for the precious departed. This, by contrast, was a brutal shock.

'He had a fever,' Henry related, his words coming slowly and unevenly, for he too was dazed from the blow, and somewhat befuddled by alcohol downed too quickly. 'Even so, he insisted on taking part in that damned tournament, but he was unsaddled in the mêlée and . . .' He could not go on. Eleanor could imagine the scene in its full horror: the merciless sun beating down on the jousting ground, the stands packed with baying spectators, the deadly clash of swords, the ferocious, heaving fray of fighting men engaged in frenzied combat, the screams of horses, the cries of the wounded . . . and her son, her Geoffrey, lying there in the bloodied dust, his body broken and trampled . . .

It tore her apart, and she moaned in her misery, rocking back and forth on her haunches. Weeping freely, Henry drew her to him, and in that awkward embrace, and the violent tempest of their grief, they drew some small comfort from each other.

When he at last disengaged himself from Eleanor, Henry seemed embarrassed; it was as if he had somehow compromised himself by exposing his raw emotions, or betraying any need for her; as if the fragile truce between them was in danger of being subverted by the acknowledgement of a bond that had long ago been thought severed. But Eleanor did not care. She was too immersed in her sorrow to give much thought to Henry. He had comforted her when she had been in desperation: she would read into his kindness nothing more than that. He need not worry.

They sat in the quiet intimacy born of years of marriage as he told her haltingly of Geoffrey's burial in the cathedral of Notre-Dame in Paris.

'Philip has sent to offer his condolences and to tell me that he is building him a fine tomb in the choir. The messenger said that Philip was so mad with grief that he had to be forcibly restrained from throwing himself onto the coffin in the open tomb.' He stopped, choked.

'If I had been there, I would have done the same!' Eleanor cried passionately. 'Henry, we *should* have been there.'

'It was too late,' he replied heavily. 'The hot weather . . .' His voice tailed off. 'At least God has spared us two sons.' His voice was bitter. 'And Constance is pregnant again. There may yet be an heir to Brittany.'

'She must be taking this hard,' Eleanor said, without much conviction.

'I dare say.' Henry's ravaged face bore a sardonic expression. He knew, as well as she, that Constance would not grieve overly for Geoffrey.

'What will you do?' she ventured to ask. 'Will Richard still be your heir?'

'As long as he is faithful to me,' he replied. 'I have sent for John to join me. I leave for Guildford tomorrow.'

Henry had sent for his favoured son to be his comfort. He was abandoning her to her grief. Eleanor could not believe that he could be so selfish and callous. 'Let me send for Richard,' she urged. If he could have his favourite, then she had need of hers.

Henry looked at her as if she had lost her wits. 'Richard is needed in Aquitaine,' he said dismissively.

65 Sarum, 1188

Henry had done it at last, the thing he had always threatened: he had sent her back to Sarum, and now he was coming, presumably, to gloat on her predicament.

She supposed she could not blame him. Richard's long-festering resentment towards his father had finally driven him into the open arms of Philip, and the result had been a bloody war, with Henry on the one side, backed by John and the bastard Geoffrey the Chancellor, and Richard and Philip on the other.

'Philip wants a foothold in Brittany,' Henry had said, quivering with anger and the need for action. 'He dares to claim young Arthur as his ward. It wouldn't surprise me if Constance had something to do with that. Ever since the brat was born, she's not stopped making mischief.'

That was true. It had all begun with the naming of the baby. Henry had wanted Geoffrey's heir to be called after himself, but Constance and her Breton councillors had insisted on baptising him Arthur, in honour of the legendary hero-king who had once ruled Brittany – and as a gesture to demonstrate that duchy's desire to be free of Angevin rule. Henry had been hurt – and angered.

'I have never liked or trusted Constance,' Eleanor had warned, and he had roundly agreed.

'I shall find her a new husband,' he'd declared, 'one who will keep her in check.' And he had done just that: the Earl of Chester was one of his most loyal vassals, and Constance, her protests ignored, had been speedily pushed into his open arms.

Then there had been the contentious matter of Alys. Again and again, Philip had tried to force Henry's hand and have her wed to Richard. When Henry had stalled, Philip had threatened to take back the Vexin and Berry and break the betrothal, demanding that Alys be returned to Paris. Then Henry had cheerily suggested that Alys be married to John instead – and it was at that point that Philip saw red. Indeed, that had proved the final straw, and it had provoked him into raising an army and marching into Berry with the intention of seizing it – which was when Richard had deserted his father and gone over to the enemy.

Reports of what happened next had troubled Eleanor deeply, and her concerns still bedevilled her even now in the dark reaches of the hours before dawn. Duke Richard had ridden to Paris, and there he had been so honoured by Philip that every day they had eaten at the same table and shared the same dishes; and at night, the bed did not separate them. Those were the very words the King's spy had written. *The bed did not separate them.*

Eleanor had never until now doubted her son's sexual in-clinations. Those terrible revelations of savagery and rapine in Aquitaine had been enough to confirm that Richard had inher-ited the lust of his race. She had known that there had been women in his life, for he had acknowledged two bastard sons; her unknown grandchildren were called Philip and Fulk, Fulk being one of the favoured names of the old Counts of Anjou. She grimly guessed whom Philip was named for. Of course, she would not have expected Richard to confide details of his amours to his mother, but now she realised that she had never heard any of his mistresses mentioned by name, which she had always taken to mean that they had been casual encounters of the kind in which his father indulged. She realised too that Richard had never shown the slightest affection for Alys, or any inclination to wed her – but there was nothing odd about that: many men were reluctant to marry the brides chosen for them. It was what Alys represented that mattered to Richard. That was completely understandable.

But then Henry had shown her that confidential report revealing that Richard was sharing a bed with Philip. He himself had not commented; it was she alone who had been a little disturbed by it. But what nonsense! she told herself; Richard and Philip were like brothers, by all accounts, and many brothers shared the same bed. Yet that wording had been disturbing, almost as if some sinister meaning had been intended. Her imagination began to run amok. As with Henry, years before, she could not bear to think of Richard preferring the love of his own sex, enduring a barren life, being cast out from, and despised by, the normal run of men, and risking the scandalised censure of the Church, or even charges of heresy for having offended against the natural order of God's creation. She would not be able to bear it. He was her favourite son, her cherished one, and she wanted to see him happily settled in marriage with a brood of thriving children at his knee.

By day, she could dismiss her fears; by night, they came to torment her. She told herself she was being silly, irrational and womanish. But the anxiety would not leave her. She dared not confide her concerns to Henry; she remembered how he had reacted to the implied suggestion that he and Becket had been lovers, all those years ago, and could imagine him exploding with wrath, and venting that wrath either on Richard or herself, or bringing the whole matter out into the open and making things infinitely worse. So she kept quiet, nursing her worries and letting them fester. Soon, she was alert for any snippet of gossip that would confirm or demolish her fears. It was exhausting, wearing herself into the ground like this.

'I'm worried about what's going on between Richard and Philip,' Henry had suddenly said one day, seeming to confirm Eleanor's worst terrors. She drew in her breath sharply, then waited in agony to see what he would say.

'I'm alarmed at what they might be plotting,' he went on, to her massive relief. 'These reports of this great friendship between them concern me greatly. I want to know what lies behind it.'

So do I, she thought desperately. So do I!

'Philip thinks to sow discord between me and my sons, and thus weaken my power.'

Is that all you think it is? Eleanor wanted to ask. But Henry's thoughts were elsewhere.

'An uprising in Aquitaine might be what is needed to divert Richard – and perhaps one in Toulouse. What say you, Eleanor? I believe I might orchestrate these risings to drag Richard away from Philip.'

'Yes!' she said, a shade too enthusiastically. 'Yes, indeed!'

Henry had not noticed her vehemence. He was far too preoc-cupied with plotting strategies. 'Then, with Richard out of the way, I'll meet with Philip and agree a truce. The Pope is urging a new crusade, so I've the perfect pretext. We can't have the rulers of Christendom squabbling amongst themselves while the Turks are occupying Jerusalem.' Eleanor winced, wishing he would not be so flippant when the Holy Places were under threat; she, like most people, had been horrified to hear news of the fall of the Holy City, and applauded the Pope's initiative. It made the quarrels between Henry, Richard and Philip seem so petty. She had been thrilled to hear that Richard had taken the Cross, and prayed that it would divert him from plotting hostil-ities against his father.

But despite the truce and the plans for a crusade, the war had dragged spitefully on, and Henry had again grown fearful that Richard would attempt to enlist his mother to his cause. Thus it was that Eleanor had found herself commanded back to Sarum, to live once more in miserable captivity. The only difference was that, this time, she was assigned a more spacious suite of chambers on a lower floor that were not so open to the violent assaults of the ever-blowing winds; and she was served in more suitable state, although her damsels had been dismissed and she was once again attended only by

Amaria – faithful Amaria, now grown stiff in her joints and exceedingly stout, but as plain-spoken and common-sensical as ever.

Eleanor's heart was heavy, therefore, and her mood resentful when Henry arrived, limping pronouncedly, on a wet July day. But she was shocked out of her ill will by the change in him, a change that a mere year and a half had wrought. He had aged dreadfully, and become grossly corpulent, and he seemed to be in some pain and physical distress, which was evident from the taut unease with which he carried himself.

'I came to bid you farewell, my Lady,' he told her, after kissing her hand briefly on greeting. 'I am bound for France, to make an attack on the French and trounce that cub Philip once and for all.'

Fear gripped her. 'But what of Richard? You will not take up arms against him too?' she cried. 'That would be terrible.'

Henry's eyes narrowed. 'Once, you did not think so,' he reminded her. He could never forget her treachery. 'Yet calm yourself. Richard and Philip have quarrelled.'

Thank God, she thought. That was one thing less to worry about.

'Richard has risen against him and driven the French out of Berry,' Henry was saying.

'Then, if Richard is for you, why are you keeping me here?' she burst out.

'I do not trust Richard,' Henry stated, 'and, forgive me, Eleanor, but I do not trust you either. When this thing is settled to my satisfaction, I will set you at liberty. Until then, you stay here. I have given orders that you are to be afforded every comfort.'

'I wish, for once and for ever, that you could put the past behind us!' she burst out. Henry regarded her warily.

'If I cannot, you have only yourself to blame,' he said heavily.

'Henry, it's been *fifteen* years, and in all that time, I have done nothing to your detriment or my dishonour! Doesn't that prove to you that you need no longer fear me?'

'I can't help it,' he told her. 'I dare not trust anyone now. I am suspicious of my own shadow. You, and our sons, I hold responsible for that. I was betrayed by those whom I trusted most. I cannot forget it.'

'Then there is no help for us,' Eleanor said sadly, rising and walking over to the window, standing with her back to him so that he would not see how deeply his words had affected her. 'At least say you have forgiven me, even if you cannot forget.' So saying, she turned around and slowly stretched out a tentative hand to him. Henry stood there for a moment, hesitating, then he too reached out, and clasped it in his familiar calloused grip.

'I do forgive you, Eleanor,' he said simply. 'Forgive me if I cannot forget. I thought I would never be able to forgive even, but I find myself growing old and not in the best of health, and I cannot risk going to my judgement without granting you the absolution that Our Lord enjoins in regard to those who have wronged us.' His grasp on her hand tightened. 'I want you to say you forgive me too. I have not been the best of husbands.'

Eleanor was filled with a sudden sense of foreboding, as if this might be her last chance to make things right with Henry – or as right as they could ever be now. 'I forgive you, truly I do,' she said, meaning it wholeheartedly.

'My Lady,' he answered, in a choked voice, and, bowing his head, raised her hand to his lips and kissed it again. The thought came unbidden to her that here they were, two people who had once worshipped each other passionately with their bodies, now reduced to the chaste contact of hands and lips. It was an unbearably poignant moment. What was it about this man, she asked herself, that tied her to him against all reason, when he had done so much to destroy the love she had cherished for him, and she had tried again and again to liberate herself from her thraldom?

Henry recovered himself first, raising sick grey eyes to her. 'I will free you as soon as I can,' he said gruffly. 'All that remains now is for me to resolve my differences with Philip, by force, if necessary,' he said, swallowing.

Eleanor looked at him fearfully. Having established this new, forgiving rapport with him, with the dawning hope of perhaps a happier reconciliation to come, she could not bear the thought of anything evil befalling him. 'You are in no fit state to go to war!' she told him. 'Have you looked at yourself in a mirror recently? Henry, what exactly is wrong with you? I know you are not well. Tell me!'

'It's nothing. A trifle,' he shrugged.

'I'm not blind,' she persisted. 'You are in pain.'

Henry sighed. 'I have a tear in my back passage,' he admitted. 'It bleeds all the time, and festers, as I cannot keep it clean.'

'Then you should not be riding a horse, still less going on long marches,' Eleanor reproved. 'Can the doctors do nothing for you?'

'No, they're useless,' he said, frowning. 'I'm sorry, Eleanor, but I have to settle matters with Philip. Then I can rest and give myself time to get better. Don't look at me like that! I'll be all right!'

'Then may I at least give you one piece of advice, Henry?' she asked gently. 'If you would keep Richard on your side, let him marry Alys without any further delays.'

Henry frowned. 'I cannot,' he said at length.

'Why?' she persisted. 'Is it because she is your leman?'

He looked like a trapped animal, furtive and wanting to bolt. 'You know?' he asked incredulously.

'I have known for some time. Alys told me. I noticed that she was pregnant.' Eleanor paused.

'You knew, and you never said anything?'

'What was there to say, beyond warning you of your great folly and the magnitude of your sin, but I doubt you would have heeded me, of all people.' Her eyes, clear with sincerity, met his. 'Henry, we were finished. The days when I lay with you wondering if another woman had enjoyed your body were long gone. I was shocked, yes, but mainly for Richard's sake – and that silly girl's. Alys did not come between *us*.'

'Richard knows,' Henry said.

'The whole world will have to know, if he marries her,' Eleanor warned. 'Their union will be incestuous without a dispensation.'

'As ours was,' Henry reminded her. 'You had known *my* father. I often ask myself if we were cursed as a result. What else could explain all the evils that have befallen us and our issue?'

'The fact that you are descended from the Devil might have something to do with it!' Eleanor smiled. 'But Henry, not everything has been touched with evil. Look at the great empire that our marriage created!'

'That too, Eleanor,' Henry said, shaking his head. 'It's been well nigh impossible holding it together; I have worn myself out trying to do so. It has caused nothing but strife and jealousies, and it will go on doing so, mark my words, maybe for hundreds of years, even. Any fool should have seen that trying to unite such large domains would bring unique problems of its own, even without a cat like Philip waiting to pounce.'

He looked at the hourglass. 'I must go, if I'm to get to Southampton by nightfall.'

'God go with you then, my Lord,' Eleanor prayed, knowing that further protests about his health would fall on deaf ears.

'And with you, my Lady,' Henry said briskly, and, planting a brief kiss on her lips this time, was gone.

66 Winchester, 1188–1189

At first, the reports that filtered through to England were encouraging. The King was winning – a great victory over the French was almost a certainty! And hot on the heels of that news came Henry's order for Eleanor to move to the greater comfort of Winchester; yet no sooner had she gratefully settled into her lodgings there, with Henry Berneval fussing about to make sure she had everything she needed, as the King had commanded him, than there came the news she had dreaded to hear. Richard had succumbed to Philip's blandishments and utterly deserted his father.

She wept, she raged at her son's perfidy. But then she learned of the peace conference at Bonmoulins, where Richard, backed by the French King, had demanded that Henry name him as his heir, give him Anjou and Maine now, and let him marry Alys forthwith, without further prevarication. All reasonable requests, of course, and naturally it made sense for Richard to shoulder the burden of governing some of Henry's domains, given the King's state of health. But the stumbling block was, and always would be, Alys.

When Henry had refused, Richard had defiantly knelt before

Philip and done homage to him for Anjou and Maine, and the French, incensed at the old King's obstinacy, had attacked him and his men and driven them away from the negotiations, against all the laws of chivalry and diplomacy.

Eleanor wept again, this time for Henry's shame and ignominy, picturing him being forced to take refuge in some crumbling, godforsaken castle, which was what appeared to have happened. Fortunately, the winter rains had set in, drawing to a close the campaigning season, and a truce had been agreed until Easter. Henry wrote to say that he was at Le Mans and in good health, but Ranulf Glanville, who was with him, sent to Eleanor privately to warn her that his master was ill and in low spirits.

Concerned, she wrote to Henry, pleading to be allowed to join him for Christmas, but he refused, saying that he was not planning any great festival. That was unusual in itself, for Henry had always observed the major feasts of the Church with all due ceremony and revelry, and she perceived by his answer that he was indeed unwell. She considered going to him unbidden, but that would mean evading the vigilance of the conscientious Henry Berneval and finding sufficient money and means for a journey in the depths of winter, which might prove a virtual impossibility. No, all she could do was pray for Henry's recovery. So she spent hours on her knees before the statue of the Virgin in the castle chapel, almost bullying the Holy Mother into interceding for the King; and, for a few quiet weeks, it seemed that her prayers had been heeded.

Easter came, and with it news of another peace conference. Clearly the princes did not want all-out war if they could help it. Eleanor was on her knees again, praying for a peaceful settlement, when another letter from Ranulf Glanville was brought to her, in which she read, to her dismay, that the conference had had to be postponed because the King was too ill to attend. After that, it was back to hectoring the Virgin Mary, often with tears and bribes of Masses and manifold good deeds.

June, and the King was better. Eleanor's heart rejoiced when she heard that he had met with Philip and Richard, but it plummeted again when she was told that Henry had persisted in his determination to marry Alys to John, and that Richard, maintaining that this was the first step in a sinister plot to disinherit him, again threw in his lot with Philip and declared war on his father.

War. A dreadful thing in any circumstances, but when son was fighting against father, it was especially terrible. Eleanor lived through her days in horrible suspense, for there could be no praying that one side would win, because there could be no winners in this conflict. It was either her husband or her son. Once, she had made that choice. She would not do so again. She gave up going to the chapel, could not constrain herself to pray. God, the protector of the just, would surely show the way to a peaceable solution. She could not believe that He had abandoned the House of Anjou entirely.

But God, it seemed, had His attention elsewhere. Philip and Richard had advanced inexorably into Angevin territory, taking castle after castle; so fearful was their might that Henry's vassals, long alienated by his oppressive rule, had, one by one, deserted him. The King, meanwhile, had withdrawn again to the city of Le Mans, his birthplace, and when the French army appeared before its walls, he gave orders that a suburb be torched to create a diversion and give him the chance to attack when the enemy's attention was elsewhere; but he had not reckoned with the wind, which fanned the flames until much of his favoured city was ablaze and Philip was able to breach its defences. Once again, Henry and his knights were forced ignominiously to flee. In yet another letter, Ranulf Glanville disclosed to Eleanor how Henry had railed bitterly against the God who had abandoned him: 'He warned that he would pay Him back as best he could, and that he would rob Him of the thing that He loved best in him – his immortal soul. He said a lot more besides, which I refrain from repeating.'

Eleanor could imagine it all, could see Henry seated painfully on his horse, silhouetted against the burning city, crying out his impotent anger to an unheeding deity. Her soul bled for his – and yet she could do nothing to ease his sufferings of mind or body. How could it be worth praying, she wondered, when God had turned His face from the King? Was it worth appealing to Richard? But that could – and probably would – be miscon-strued. She shuddered to think what might happen if Henry found out. It might be better to get back on her knees and constrain herself to prayer.

Waiting for news was agonising. She would wonder, a hundred times a day, if Henry and Richard might even now be confronting each other in battle. A letter from William Marshal, whom she had always accounted her champion, brought her a little relief. The King had gone north to Normandy, he informed her, and had deputed him to take a force and guard his back. Not far behind, Richard had come marching at the head of a French army, and he, Marshal, had levelled his lance in readiness for battle. 'The Duke cried out to me not to kill him, for he wore no hauberk. I answered that I would leave the killing of him to the Devil, and had the pleasure of unseating him instead. That gave me the chance to ride away and warn the King of his approach, and thus I enabled him to avoid a direct clash of arms with the Duke his son.'

Maybe it could be avoided for good, if only each side would give a little, Eleanor thought, as the horrendous waiting went relentlessly on, and June dragged itself into July.

It was unbearably hot. Within the sun-baked walls of Winchester Castle, Eleanor and Amaria wore their lightest silk *bliauts* and avoided walking in the gardens until the heat of the day had subsided. In the lands of France, it was reported, the armies on both sides were suffering miseries from sunburn, fatigue or dysentery. Henry wrote privately to Eleanor, complaining that he was enduring torture from an abscess, and that sitting in the saddle would soon be beyond him if those damned fool physicians didn't do something to remedy it quickly.

Hard on the heels of this came another missive from William Marshal. The King had been forced to retreat to Chinon to rest, and had gone alone, with only his bastard Geoffrey for company, travelling by back roads to evade the enemy forces. 'He can neither walk, nor stand or sit without intense discomfort,' William wrote. 'We are all worried about John, who has disappeared. It is feared that he may have been taken for a hostage by Duke Richard or King Philip. If so, Heaven help the King.' Reading this, Eleanor redoubled her prayers, beseeching God and His Mother to hear her. Let there be peace, was her earnest cry.

She was listless, not knowing how to fill the hours of waiting for the next letter or report. It took a fast courier up to five days to cover the distance from Chinon, depending on the Channel winds, so anything could have happened. Amaria tried to entice her to games of chess or thinking up riddles; she went to market and bought embroidery silks in the brightest hues, hoping to inspire Eleanor to make new cushions or an altar frontal; she had Henry Berneval send for minstrels, to while away the evenings, and herself spent hours in the kitchens baking exquisite little cakes to tempt her mistress. But none of these pleasant distractions could alleviate the Queen's fears or anxieties.

Having little appetite, Eleanor lost weight. She looked drawn and her skin took on an ethereal quality. She was sixty-seven, but she knew without vanity, when she peered in her mirror, that she appeared and felt younger; her greying hair was hidden beneath her headdress and veil, her fine-boned face was only delicately etched with lines, and she had the energy of a woman half her age. That restless energy was pent-up now, surging within her breast; she was desperate to be at the centre of affairs, not cut off from them here at Winchester. If she had her way, she would be riding into battle with the rest of them, like the Amazon that she had once pretended to be, long ago, on that distant plain of Vézelay, when they had preached the fatal crusade that had ended in disaster for both the Christian hordes and her marriage to Louis. She had been young and reckless then, and afire to show off her crusading zeal in the most attention-seeking way possible; and she would unhesitatingly take the field again, for real this time, if given the slightest chance. But, of course, it could not be: she was a woman, and a prisoner, and all she could do was wait here for news. Wait, wait, wait! They could carve those words on her tomb: *She waited.*

There had been another summit meeting between the chief combatants. Eleanor had the news from both William Marshal and Ranulf Glanville. The King, she learned, had dragged himself from his sickbed towards Colombières, near Tours. On the way, complaining that his whole body felt as if it were on fire, he had been forced to rest at a preceptory of the Knights Templar, and sent his knights ahead to tell Richard and Philip that he was detained on account of his illness. But Richard had not believed it. His father was feigning, he insisted; he was up to no good, plotting some new villainy; they should not trust his word.

When news of this had been carried back to the King, ill as he was, he had had his men prop him up on his horse, then rode in agony through a thunderstorm to the place where his enemies waited. King Philip had actually blenched at the sight of him, and, moved by pity, had offered his own cloak for him to sit on. But Henry had refused it; he had come not to sit, he'd declared, but to pay any price they named for making peace. And so he remained on his horse, his knights holding him upright. He had looked ghastly.

Philip's compassion had ended there. He'd laid down the harshest terms. Henry must pay homage to him for all his lands. He must leave his domains – even England, which Philip had no right to dispose of – to Richard. He was to pardon all those who had fought for Richard. He was to give Alys up to Philip at once, and agree to Richard marrying her immediately after the planned crusade. And, as further tokens of his good faith, he was to pay a crippling indemnity and surrender three of his chief castles to Philip.

Henry had agreed. He had given in without any argument, and wheeled his horse around preparatory to riding away. But Philip had stopped him, and demanded that he gave Richard the kiss of peace. Henry had done so, his manner frosty, his eyes as cold as steel, and when the distasteful deed was accomplished, and Richard had had the grace to look suitably chastened, Henry had said to him: 'God grant that I may not die until I have had a fitting revenge on you.' By then, blood was seeping out of his breeches and down his horse's rump, and he had had to be lifted from his horse and carried back in a litter to Chinon.

Eleanor laid the letters on the table. Her thoughts were in turmoil. The peace she had prayed for, and the securing of

Richard's inheritance, had been agreed, but at what cost? The utter subjection and humiliation of a sick king who was too ill to fight back. Would to God it had been done in any other way! She would even have preferred Henry and Richard to have met in battle, and have the differences between them resolved in a fair fight, whatever the dangers, rather than this. To know that Henry, whose empire stretched from Scotland to Spain, had been brought so low, with his pride cast in the dust, was unbearable. He had been a strong king, a respected king, even a great king – and now he was a defeated king. And he was laid low with this pitiful complaint, poor wretch. How her heart ached for him.

But there had been that threat he had uttered. He *would* have his revenge on Richard, never doubt it. Almost she was glad that he was confined to his sickbed. How could there ever be real peace between her husband and her son after this? And yet . . . Her thoughts winged back to the aftermath of that earlier rebellion that she herself had helped to foment. He had forgiven his sons then, after all their treachery. Hugh of Avalon, that wise, saintly man, had said that those whom Henry had loved he rarely came to hate. It was no less than the truth! She must hold to that, she told herself, as she waited – waited again – in suspense to see what would happen next.

For a week or so there was no news. Of course, she should not expect any yet. Henry was resting up at Chinon, waiting for that abscess to heal. Ranulf Glanville, having some business in England, came to see her, but he could tell her nothing that she did not know, as he had left Anjou some time before.

The weather turned, and became unseasonably changeable. Hailstones were clattering against the castle walls on the day when Henry Berneval knocked at the Queen's door and found her measuring lengths of linen with her maid. Eleanor looked up. Something in the custodian's face checked her smiling greeting. It seemed ominous that he had brought Ranulf Glanville with him, and Ranulf's mournful expression gave her further cause for alarm.

Berneval bowed low, lower than she had ever seen him bow.

'My Lady, I bring grave tidings,' he told her, in a choked voice. Eleanor rose and stood before him, quiet and dignified, bracing herself to hear the worst. But what could the worst be? Did it concern Henry, or Richard – or one of her other children?

'My Lady, I grieve to tell you that the Lord King has departed this life,' Berneval said quietly. 'He died at Chinon four days ago. My Lady, I am so very sorry to have to give you this news.'

She supposed she had half-expected it. Henry had been ill, and had not been getting better. But that he was dead, that vital autocrat who had bestrode half of Christendom, and had been her husband these thirty-seven years, God help them both, seemed inconceivable . . . But as she stood there, trying to understand and accept her loss, the great bell of the cathedral started tolling in the distance, and other churches nearby in turn picked up the dread message, signalling to all England that its king was no more. Fifty-six chimes in all, one for every year of the King's life . . . That ominous sound would be heard across the length and breadth of the land, as word spread of Henry's passing.

'Do you know what happened?' Eleanor asked.

'No, my Lady. We had the news from the carter who came up from Southampton. All he knew was that the King had died at Chinon. No doubt messengers will come soon with further tidings.'

Eleanor said nothing, but stared unseeing through the window, dry-eyed, her mind conjuring up the image of a magnificent young man with a straight, noble profile and unruly red curls, who had swept her off her feet, bedded and wedded her, to the scandal of all Europe. Henry had been so vigorous, so lusty! It was impossible to comprehend that all that vitality was now dust, that the virile hero who had shared with her such passion and, later, such blistering discord, was gone from her for ever.

Occasionally, during these sixteen difficult years of her confinement, and even before that, when their marriage was crumbling and seemingly beyond redemption, there had been times when she had sensed that they might put all the pain and betrayal behind them and salvage some spark of their former ardour, some semblance of the close affinity they had once shared; but the moment had never been right: always, some fresh trouble had intervened. And yet, when she had taken what was to be her last farewell of Henry – a year ago, now – and they had readily extended their forgiveness to each other, and been kind together for once, she had truly believed that some real chance of a reconciliation lay in the future. And now it was not to be. The realisation should have broken her, but she only felt numb.

Amaria's face was set in stone; the two custodians still stood before their queen, respectfully unwilling to intrude on her silence. Beyond the windows, the bells clanged mournfully. Soon, they would ring out in rejoicing for a new ruler, and life would move on, consigning Henry FitzEmpress to history. It was then that Eleanor realised that Richard was now king of England and undisputed ruler of the mighty Angevin empire. The realisation brought a mixture of triumph and pain. If only her beloved son's rightful inheritance had come to him in any other circumstances than these, with his father dying while they were so bitterly at odds!

She had been plunged suddenly into mourning, but even so, she knew she had more than one cause to rejoice, and she looked every inch the Queen as, her voice steady, she addressed her gaoler. 'Master Berneval, I command you, in the name of King Richard, to set me at liberty at once.'

He had been wondering if he dared free her without a mandate. The late King had commanded him to keep her secure until he received further orders, and he had carried out those instructions faithfully. He was unsure now how to respond, and looked helplessly at Glanville for guidance.

The latter did not hesitate. 'It is well known that King Richard has much love for his mother, and, bearing in mind his fearsome reputation, it might be as well to obey the Queen's just command,' he declared. At that, Henry Berneval fell to his knees, detached the keys from the ring at his belt, and laid them in Eleanor's outstretched hands. She bestowed a warm look of gratitude on Ranulf.

She was free, yet her freedom was an empty thing in such

circumstances, and she had no desire to go anywhere. Again, she must wait on developments.

'I pray you will attend me until the King comes,' she said to both men. 'And now, I desire only to go to the chapel and pray for the soul of the King my late Lord.'

Later that day, William Marshal arrived, soaked to the skin after his breakneck ride to bring the news of King Henry's death to the Queen, along with King Richard's orders for her release. He was astonished, therefore, to find her already at liberty and waiting to receive him at the castle doorway, with a nervous Henry Berneval and a respectful Ranulf Glanville at her side.

Eleanor, garbed in her black widow's weeds and a wimple crowned with a simple golden circlet, greeted Marshal with a smile, putting on a courageous mien and extending her hand to be kissed.

'Madame, I am overjoyed to see you free,' he told her, thinking that she looked more the great lady than ever. 'King Richard was most anxious that you should not be held captive any longer than necessary. He has much need of you at this time.'

Henry Berneval relaxed. He was not going to be censured for disobeying his instructions. That terrifying man who was now his king would be grateful to him for anticipating his orders. Berneval was indebted to Ranulf Glanville for his wise counsel.

'We are just about to eat, William,' Eleanor told Marshal, having reverted effortlessly to her former accustomed role as royal châtelaine. 'There is time for you to change and refresh yourself, and then I should be grateful if you would join me and give me all your news.'

Marshal was gratified to see that many lords and ladies had hurried to join the Queen's hastily assembled court, but relieved to learn that he would be her guest at a private supper that night, for what he had to tell her was best recounted away from the public gaze. When it came to it, only the maid was present, the one who had attended Eleanor throughout her long captivity; also wearing mourning, she moved discreetly around the solar, serving food, topping up the wine and removing dishes, then making herself scarce. William could not have guessed, from her calm manner, that Amaria was beside herself with exultation that her mistress had been freed from her captivity, and from her long purgatory of a marriage. As far as Amaria was concerned, the Queen was better off without that bastard to whom she had been chained in wedlock – chained being an apt word – and she was glad that the good Lord had called King Henry to his reward. She knew what she would have liked to reward him with! Yes, she was wearing black, but only out of deference to custom. As soon as King Richard came, she was buying herself a fine scarlet gown!

'Tell me what happened,' Eleanor said, when she and William Marshal were alone.

He had been dreading this moment. Yet she must be told.

'The King was in a terrible case when we got him back to Chinon. He felt his humiliation deeply, and kept cursing his sons and himself, rueing the day that ever he was born. He uttered dreadful blasphemies. He asked why he should worship Christ when He allowed him to be ignominiously confounded by a mere boy. He meant Richard, of course.'

'I cannot bear to think of his state of mind,' Eleanor said, deeply moved. 'He surely could not have meant those blasphemies. He was ever one to say all kinds of rash things when his temper was aroused, and then regret them afterwards. What happened to Becket was a prime example. Henry suffered agonies of remorse over that.'

'He repented of these utterances too,' William told her. 'Archbishop Baldwin was waiting for him at Chinon, and when he heard what the King was saying, he braved his anger and made Henry go to the chapel and make his peace with God. And he did, for all that he was near fainting with pain; and so he confessed his sins and was shriven. Then he took to his bed.'

'Could not the doctors do anything to help him?' Eleanor was shaking her head. Her meat lay congealing in its gravy on her plate, forgotten.

'I doubt they could have done very much,' William said, then took a deep breath. 'Besides, he lost the will to live.'

'He must have been sorely grieved at Richard's hostility, although really, he had only himself to blame for it,' Eleanor said sadly.

Marshal swallowed. 'Richard had wounded him deeply. His pride was in the dust. But that was not what finished him. His vassals, vile traitors, had deserted him in droves, and gone over to Richard's side, and towards the end, they brought him a list of those traitors, so that he might know who was to be spared punishment under the terms of the peace treaty, and whom he could not trust in the future. The first name on the list was that of the Lord John.' William was near to tears.

'John!' Eleanor exclaimed. 'John betrayed his father? But John was his favourite, the one he loved above all his other children. Why would John have abandoned him?'

'I imagine that Richard and Philip offered sufficient inducements,' William said heavily.

'Thirty pieces of silver, no doubt!' Eleanor cried. 'That John, for whose gain Henry broke with Richard, should have forsaken him – I cannot credit it.'

'That was more or less what the King said. And it was at that moment that he lost the will to live. He turned his face to the wall and dismissed us, saying he cared no more for himself or aught for this world. Then he fell into delirium, moaning with grief and pain. His bastard Geoffrey kept watch over him, cradling his head and soothing him. At the last, Henry cried, "Shame, shame on a conquered king!" and fell unconscious. He died the next day without having woken again.'

It had been two days now, and Eleanor had not yet wept for her loss. The numb feeling had persisted, yet she had been conscious of a great tide of emotion waiting to engulf her. Now it broke forth, and she bent her head in her hands and sobbed piteously while Amaria hastened to hold her tightly, and William, unmanned by this display of grief to the point of weeping himself, placed a tentative hand on her heaving shoulders.

He would not tell her the worst of it, he decided. She had enough to bear without that. Of course, she would find it out eventually, but by then she would hopefully be stronger.

He himself had stayed at Chinon only to hear Mass and make an offering for his late master's soul; he knew he had to make all speed to convey to King Richard the news of his father's death. But when he had gone, after a hurried dinner, to bid a final farewell to his old master before taking the road north, he had been shocked by what he found, for King Henry lay there naked, with even his privities left uncovered, and the room was bare of all his effects. It would have been his servants, he deduced afterwards, finding that they had fled. They must have invaded the death-chamber the moment Geoffrey left it, and, like scavengers, they had stripped the body and stolen all the dead man's personal belongings, even his trappings of kingship.

William, in a fever to be on his way, had enlisted the help of a young knight, William de Trihan, and together they had made the body decent and laid it out for burial. They had shifted as best they could in the circumstances. A laundress found them a filet of gold embroidery to serve in place of a crown, and they managed to find a ring, a sceptre and a sword, and some fittingly splendid garments, including fine gloves and gold shoes. He shuddered at the memory, for the body had not been a pretty sight, and this last duty had been a great trial for both himself and de Trihan. It had been high summer, and hot, and the King had been suffering from a noisome complaint . . .

No, Marshal would not tell Eleanor any of this. She was still crying, her head against Amaria's ample bosom, but the storm of her weeping had subsided now, and she was recovering herself, taking deep, gasping breaths. It was a relief to know that she *could* weep, he thought. It was a significant step on the hard road to coming to terms with her loss and the tragedies that had surrounded it. No doubt she would weep again, many times. But she would heal, for she was strong. She had weathered many tempests in her time, and this latest one would not crush her.

'Forgive me,' Eleanor said, sniffing. 'I am forgetting myself.'

'Not at all, my Lady,' he assured her.

'If anyone's entitled to do that, it's you!' Amaria said tartly, but with affection. William Marshal noted, and approved, the familiarity. It was good to know that the Queen had someone like this sensible, homely woman to help her through this difficult time.

Eleanor reached for her goblet and took a gulp of the sweet vintage it held.

'That's better,' she said, essaying a weak smile. 'You have seen the King?'

For an awful moment, William thought she was referring to Henry, but then realised that she meant Richard.

'Yes, my Lady. I brought him the news of King Henry's passing.'

'And how did he take it?'

'He hastened to Chinon and bade me ride with him there. When he looked down on the late King's body, his face was unreadable. I could not tell if he felt sorrow or grief . . .'

'Or even joy or triumph!' Eleanor put in. 'I know my son, as I know myself. I am sure he would have experienced very mixed feelings.'

'I am sure of that too,' William agreed. 'He did pray awhile before the bier.' He omitted to add that no sooner had Richard got to his knees than he was up again, much to the disapproval of many who saw it. And there was no way that Marshal would tell Eleanor how, as the new King rose to his feet, black blood began to flow from the nostrils of the corpse. Or how there had been gasps and cries of horror from the observers, who later voiced the firm opinion that Henry's spirit was angered by his son's approach and hurried prayers. It had been a ghastly thing to witness, and Marshal still shuddered at the memory of it.

Still, he could tell Eleanor how Richard, no doubt belatedly racked by guilt, had been weeping and lamenting as he followed the body to Fontevrault, which the new King had deemed a more fitting resting place for his father than Grandmont, where Henry had long ago expressed a wish to be buried.

'Is that where he lies?' Eleanor asked.

'Yes, my Lady, they laid him to rest in the nuns' choir.'

'It is more fitting than that austere abbey at Grandmont,' she observed. 'Richard could not have chosen a better sepulchre, for

Henry loved Fontevrault. That is where I myself mean to be buried when my time comes. Has Richard said anything about raising a tomb to his memory?'

'Yes, my Lady. Already, he has sent for masons and commissioned an effigy to lie upon it.'

'It seems strange,' she brooded, 'that a man to whom many realms were subject should be brought, in the end, to lie in a few feet of earth. But it is our mortal lot, and it does us good for God to remind us of the narrowness of death. Yet a tomb, even a fine one, hardly seems to suffice for a man like Henry – – for whom the world was not enough.'

She smiled at him, all trace of her tears gone. 'Forgive me, old friend. I am pondering aloud.'

'Your pondering was very profound,' he told her, returning the smile. 'You are a great philosopher, my Lady.'

'Ah, but I never benefit from my own wisdom, William!' She sipped the wine again and reflected. 'There was much I did not like in Henry. He could be oppressive and unjust, and his morals were appalling. I hope he repented at the last. I should hate to think of him suffering the torments of Hell for his sins.'

'He did repent,' William assured her.

'I thank God for that,' Eleanor went on. 'I am sure that many will remember Henry as a wicked man, but he was never that simple. I loved him with a passion – and came to hate him as fervently, and in our later years I hardly recognised the young man I had so joyfully married. But I could never forget what had been between us, and just occasionally I was afforded a rare glimpse of the old Henry, the one I had loved – and that is why I say to you that he was not truly a wicked man. And when all is said and done, he was, in many respects, an excellent and beneficial ruler.'

'He was a great king, and I will miss him,' Marshal said simply.

'And I too, immeasurably,' said Eleanor. 'For all the unkindness between us, and our terrible betrayals of each other, I think I still loved him to the last. I can't explain why, and God knows I had little reason to love him. But there was something about him, something about us, that kept me in thraldom, even when

I wanted to free myself. It's very complicated, and I couldn't expect anyone to understand it.'

Clearing the buffet cupboard behind her, Amaria made a face.

William Marshal, flouting protocol, laid his hand on Eleanor's. His kind eyes were warm. 'I know what you mean,' he said. 'I loved him too. I would have died for him.'

Part Five
The Eagle Rejoices
1189

67 Winchester, 1189

Later, after the tablecloth had been lifted, William came to the chief purpose of his visit.

'My Lady, we must get down to business. This cannot wait. I have come here, not just to set you free, but to inform you that the King has entrusted you with the power of ruling England as regent. I carry in my saddle pouch instructions to the princes and lords of the realm that your word shall be law in all matters.'

Her heart was suddenly singing. This was the measure of Richard's love and trust, she knew. And, please God, she would be equal to it. Not many men, let alone women, were called at the advanced age of sixty-seven to such responsibility and honour. She gave thanks that her years of durance had taught her a degree of wisdom, despite what she had self-deprecatingly said to William Marshal; and that she was as energetic as she had ever been, and had all her faculties about her. She knew, for she had learned in a hard school, how to rule well, and how to command the respect and obedience – and the love – of her people. Her new authority, for which she thanked God most humbly, would sit easily upon her.

She was eager to be gone from Winchester, to grasp the reins of government and wield power for the common good. She would make sure that she exerted a sage and benevolent influence over her son the King, who was going to need all the help and support he could get to rule his great empire. His subjects in England hardly knew him, for he was a stranger to them. Well, she would do all in her power to win him their love.

Her head was full of plans. She would go to Westminster and make every free man in England swear to bear fealty to their new liege lord. Then she would make a progress through the shires, dispensing justice and disposing of all things as she sought fit, cozening the obedience of the nobles. She would transact the business of court and chancery in the King's name, but using her own seal.

She was bursting with great plans. She would reform the harsh forest laws, which were so injurious to the poor who tried to scratch a living from the vast swathes of woodland that kings had hitherto regarded purely as their personal hunting grounds. She would legislate for honest weights and measures, and a coinage that would be legal tender anywhere in the kingdom; and she would found hospitals, and free prisoners. If any protested against that, she would remind them that she had found prison to be a terrible thing, and that those who were released from it experienced such a delightful refreshment of the spirits that they would make sure never to risk such punishment again. She would make herself exceedingly respected and beloved, to her son's benefit and that of the whole kingdom.

With God's help, she would do all this and more, with wisdom and compassion, and in her own name: Eleanor, by the grace of God, Queen of England.

Envoi: Winchester, 1189

Eleanor thought her heart would burst with joy when she beheld Richard, in all the golden beauty of his manhood, striding towards her across the vast length of the great hall in Winchester Castle. As she stepped forward from the dais, and he caught her in his strong arms and embraced her, the whole court burst into cheers and applause. Then, in all humility, the King knelt for his mother's blessing, which she gave with gladness.

With due state and ceremony, Richard ascended to his throne; there were in fact two thrones, side by side, with nothing to distinguish one from the other in precedence or importance. Eleanor saw by this that her son was resolved to treat her as an equal.

But he had not yet sat down in his high place; he had remained standing before her, facing the assembled throng. 'My Lords and Ladies!' he cried in ringing tones. 'I wish to express now, before you all, my deepest gratitude to my Lady Mother the Queen for so ably securing this kingdom for me. I cannot sufficiently do her honour, but I would ask you now always to remember how especially dear she is to me, and treat her accordingly.'

Eleanor's eyes brimmed as she rose and curtseyed before the acclaim of the people. It was a while before she could see clearly to watch the great ceremonies that were being enacted to welcome the King to his realm.

'And now, my Lady,' Richard said, much later, in a lower voice, 'let us be private, for I would unburden myself to you.'

As soon as they were alone in his great chamber, which she had had done up so gorgeously against his coming, he turned and grasped both her hands, gazing down on her with a troubled countenance.

'My Lady, I am aware that, through rebelling against my father, I have earned the disapproval of good and wise men,' he confessed, his strong, handsome face flushing a little. 'Do you, too, censure me for it?'

He looked for a moment like a little boy again, seeking his mother's forgiveness for some silly prank. But this was no childish silliness; he had cruelly made war on his father, against all the laws of God and Nature, and Eleanor had found that difficult to reconcile with her cherished notions of her son, however just his cause had been. She had reminded herself, often, that had not Richard rebelled, John would have stayed faithful, and Henry would have been spared that last, bitter betrayal. But, of course, Henry had been wrong in the first place . . .

'I make no judgement until I have heard what you have to say,' she said carefully.

'Then know this, Mother. I crucify myself every day for what I did to my father − and yet, I know that, if I had it all to do again, I would do the same. I had the right of it, you see. But he is gone now, and I cannot mend things between us. Instead, to make up for my past wrongs, I will do all I can to show honour to you as my mother. He would have wanted that. And I hope that my obedience to you will atone for my offence against my father. Will that suffice? Can you forgive me?'

Eleanor gazed lovingly into his eyes. 'Yes, Richard, of course. Our Lord teaches us that to err is human, to forgive divine. Before he left me for the last time, your father and I pledged our forgiveness to each other. I can do no less for you, his son and mine. Yes, I forgive you, with all my heart. And I am sure that, if Henry has attained Heaven and is looking down on us, he would forgive you too.'

She sank into a chair, overcome by the emotion of the moment. 'This reminds me of a prophecy of Merlin that I never thought to see fulfilled,' she said. 'He foretold that "the Eagle of the Broken Covenant" should rejoice in her third nesting. I puzzled over that for years. But now I know for certain that I am indeed that eagle, and that the broken covenant was indeed my marriage to your father − I suspected that much long ago, but I knew that the latter part of the prophecy had yet to be fulfilled. And now it has. It is you, Richard, my third son, who is my third nesting. It is in you that my heart rejoices. You are the one who will raise my name to great glory, as the seer foretold.'

The King turned to look at her with those arresting, ice-blue eyes.

'No, my Lady,' he said. 'If anyone has raised your name to glory, it is yourself.'

Epilogue: Abbey of Fontevrault, 1 April 1204

The old lady stirred restlessly in her sleep, and the young nun seated beside the bed looked up anxiously from her book of hours. It was hard to believe that this frail, papery-skinned, aged woman was the fabled Queen Eleanor, wife to two kings and mother to two more: great Eleanor, whose fame – or notoriety, depending on what you believed about her – spanned Christendom and beyond. Great Eleanor, who was now a humble bride of Christ.

Sister Amice rose, straightened the fine wool coverlets and bleached cotton sheets, rearranged the old lady's veil on her pillow, and murmured a prayer for her. Eleanor was very old, all of eighty-two, a great age for anyone, and her superb health and vigour had finally yielded to time. She existed as one dead to the world, tended by her sisters in religion in her beloved abbey of Fontevrault, that blessed retreat nestling in its luscious wooded valley in the heartlands of the River Loire.

Mother Abbess Mathilde de Bohème peered around the door.

'How is our sister?' she enquired. The young nun fell to her knees.

'Sleeping, Mother, thanks be to God.'

'She will not wake again,' Mathilde predicted. 'It is a mercy. She will never know that her son, that iniquitous King John, has lost Normandy to the French. We must thank God for this kindness.' Raising her hand in blessing, the Abbess glided away to her other manifold duties.

They think I cannot hear them, Eleanor thought, that I lie here senseless, waiting for eternity. The truth is, I am too weary for human company. I have made my peace with my Maker and am ready to be called to His judgement seat. I am confessed and shriven, ready for my journey. It will not be long now. All that are left to me are my memories. So much to think back on, over the course of a long life fully lived, and not always wisely. It took a long and bitter imprisonment and the advancing years to teach me true wisdom. I learned it the hard way. Oh, but it was sweet to be young and foolish, to love and be loved, to lust . . .

She stirred again, her old body, even now, remembering.

There is much to regret too, she reflected, thinking of the consequences of her follies. I could wish a lot of my deeds undone. I was impetuous, governed by my desires, unheeding of the needs of others. Poor Louis . . . I led him a merry dance, timid, monkish prince that he was. And Henry . . . what did we do to each other? How could it have ended the way it did? Then Richard, my golden, lion-hearted son, favourite of my brood and love of my life – but dead too soon, cruelly sundered from me by an assassin's arrow. We will be reunited very shortly, my beloved prince . . .

What sounded like a sob came from the figure on the narrow bed, and the young nun looked up. But Eleanor seemed to be lying there peacefully. Richard was in God's hands, as she herself would be soon. It was the memory of Henry that held her. There had been so much bitterness that it was easy to forget how it had once been between them, before faithlessness, bloody murder and rebellion had riven them apart. Yet now, at the last, she wished to remember, to savour, how glorious it had been in the beginning, how it had all started; and, for the thousandth time, to make herself understand what had gone wrong. Yet she doubted she ever would.

Who would have thought, she mused, as a faint smile played upon her sunken lips, that we would have fallen for each other as headily as we did, and in so doing, shocked the world? Even now, it was hard to believe. No poet or troubadour even could make sense of it. But then there is no accounting for the ways of the heart – or the responses of two healthy bodies to each other. She had never forgotten that day in Paris, more than half a century before, when she had first set eyes on Henry in his magnificent prime . . .

Heady memories, but crowded now by sad ones. They were always with her. Not just the tragedy of her marriage, but the pain and unending grief of loss. Eleven children she had borne, and nine she had lost: they came to her often, a sad procession of cherished ghosts: Marie and Alix, whom she never had seen again after her divorce from Louis, both gone to their rest these six years now, leaving her full of regrets for having failed them dismally as their mother; little William and baby Philip, sweet, fleeting, poignant memories; Henry the Young King, and Geoffrey, her fine strapping sons, dead before their time, their bitter rivalry vanquished only by death; beloved Matilda, snatched away in childbirth that same summer that Henry had died; tragic Joanna, scarred by a violent marriage and the burns that had marred her beauty in a terrible fire and left her too weak to survive a brutal confinement; and Eleanor's adored Richard, who was to have been the staff of her old age, gone from her too. Having suffered the failure of his great crusade to free Jerusalem from the Turks, and then captivity by the treacherous Emperor – how she had slaved and cajoled to raise that ransom! – he now lay here quiet at Fontevrault, his lion heart stilled, in the choir, at the feet of his father, as Richard in humility and penitence had requested. And soon, if God was merciful, she herself would be laid to her rest near them both.

After Richard's death, the light had gone out of her life. A shell of her former self, she had girded her loins and done her best to secure John's inheritance for him, but her heart had not been in it; it was broken and could never be mended. Yet even after that, aged as she was, she had been afforded no rest, but had traversed the inhospitable Pyrenees to fetch her grand-daughter, Young Eleanor's child, from Castile, to marry the Dauphin Louis, Philip Augustus's son. Then there had been the rebellion led by her grandson, Arthur of Brittany, who had contested John's crown, and even had the impertinence to besiege his eighty-year-old granddame in her castle at Mirabeau. It had been John, perfidious John, who had shown his mettle and come vengefully to her rescue, riding at breakneck speed to raise the siege, her champion on a white charger. She had almost loved John on that occasion. It was the nearest she had ever come to it.

But after Mirabeau, John had murdered Arthur. He had never confessed to it, and it was not the kind of thing people spoke of other than covertly, but she had known. There were awful tales being whispered. Some said the King had ordered the boy's gaoler to have him blinded and castrated; others that John himself had killed Arthur and had his weighted body thrown into the Seine. Eleanor herself had pleaded with her son for her grandson's life, but John had not been able to meet her eyes. That was when she knew. Again, it seemed that the Angevin family was cursed, as Bernard of Clairvaux had long ago declared, and that its scions, those hapless descendants of the witch Melusine, must forever be destroying each other. Was there to be no end to it?

And now they were saying that John had lost Normandy, that proud heritage of the Conqueror, that jewel in the Angevin crown. As the Empress Matilda had once warned, there would be a reckoning one day, for her son's marriage was accursed. It would fall, the empire, Eleanor knew it; if Philip's successors were as ambitious and tenacious as he, they would claw it away, inch by inch. It might take hundreds of years, but the great empire that she and Henry had built would crumble in the end, and its legacy would no doubt endure to trouble Christendom for centuries more. That much we achieved! she thought grimly, thanking God that Henry and Richard were not here to see this day. Yes, Henry, we built a great empire, she reflected, but it may well leave a bloody legacy.

Had her life been worthwhile? Not in human terms, she felt. When all her passion had been spent and her hopes dashed in the dust, what was left to show that she had made the best use of her time on Earth? The great dynastic marriage that she had schemed and sinned to make had brought neither happiness nor peace, even if it had invested her and Henry with a fleeting greatness. Instead, they were leaving a bitter heritage to those who came after them. Already, the reckoning was due.

But Normandy, and the problems of the empire, could not concern her now. God had other priorities. True greatness lay in existing in harmony with Him, and in living wisely and exercising power with humanity. Often, she knew, she had signally failed, but in the main she had done her very best, even if her motives had not been the purest. You could not say much more for anyone than that. The book of her life was almost written, and nothing could now be changed. She was done with earthly things, had put them firmly behind her. John must go to Hell in his own way . . .

*

By the time of Arthur's disappearance, she had had enough. She was old and weary, and her task was done. All she sought was the peace and tranquillity of the cloister, and a quiet mind. She had benefited from the former, but doubted she would ever achieve the latter. Had it not been said, by someone very wise – she forgot whom; she was very forgetful these days – that the blood of the wicked would not thrive? Had she and Henry been so very wicked? She feared to answer that question, with death and Divine Judgement fast approaching. And yet – whatever she had done wrong, she had done her best to atone for it and seek forgiveness. In the final accounting, God Himself would be all-merciful. She must do as the Abbess said and put her trust in Him, and wait for death with serenity, embracing it rather than fearing it.

So here she was, shrouded among the shrouded women. She shifted a little in her narrow bed, causing the young nun to look up from her book. Still dead to the world, the girl thought. She did not know that, in the old lady before her, a subtle change was taking place; but Eleanor was herself suddenly, joyously aware that a golden door had burst open, that it had opened to receive her and that she was drifting towards the brilliant light that was streaming from it, dazzling her with its splendour. She had one last, lucid thought, that we none of us know exactly what lies beyond the door to eternity, but, if Our Lord is kind, our loved ones will be waiting there for us, in His tender care, and we will be in a Paradise far beyond our earthly imaginings.

If she had had a voice, she would have cried out in rapture, for, suspended in the light, she saw again, as she had seen in a dream all those years before, a circlet of blazing gold that shone with incomparable brightness, a crown with no beginning and no end, so gloriously pure and resplendent with its assurance of everlasting joy. And in that wonderful moment, as the candle beside her bed flickered gently and went out, and the young nun called in alarm for the Abbess, Eleanor felt her soul suddenly take wings and fly, south to Poitiers, Bordeaux, Aquitaine . . .

Author's Note

This novel is based on historical facts. However, Eleanor of Aquitaine lived in the twelfth century, and contemporary sources for her life are relatively sparse, as I found when I was researching my biography of her in the 1970s and 1990s. It was while I was writing that book that I first conceived the idea of writing historical novels. Essentially, the nature of medieval biography, particularly of women, is the piecing together of fragments of information and making sense of them. It can be a frustrating task, as there are often gaps that you know you can never fill. It came to me one day, as I realised I could go no further with one particular avenue of speculation, that the only way of filling those gaps would be to write a historical novel, because – as I then thought – a novelist does not have to work within the same constraints as a historian.

But is that strictly true? What is the point of a historical novel (or film for that matter) based on a real person if the author does not take pains to make it as authentic as possible? You can't just make it up. I know, because my readers regularly – and forcefully – tell me so, that people care that what they are reading is close to the truth, given a little dramatic licence and the novelist's informed imagination. For lots of people – myself included – come to history through historical novels, and many will never make that leap from such novels to history books; they rely on the novelist to tell it as it was, and to set the story within an authentic background, with authentic detail. Of course, historical sources are subject to a wide variety of interpretations, but they are the only means we have of learning what happened centuries ago, and it is crucial that a historical novelist, just like a historian, uses them with integrity. Otherwise a novel must lack credibility.

But what of the gaps? How should they be filled? Yes, it is

liberating to be able to use one's imagination, but you can't simply indulge in flights of fancy, and what you invent must always be credible within the context of what is known. Making up wild, unsubstantiated stories will always fail to convince, and sells short both those who know nothing about the subject and those who know a great deal. There should always be a sound basis for writing anything that is controversial, and any significant departure from the historical record should be explained in an author's note like this one.

Hence, because this is a novel, I have taken some dramatic licence. Eleanor's sexual adventures, for example, have been the subject of much learned conjecture among historians, but I think there was some substance to the allegations, as I have shown in my biography. The Rosamund legends – the tales of the labyrinth at Woodstock and her murder by Eleanor – belong to much later periods, and are unfounded, yet I have made use of them here.

Elsewhere, for dramatic purposes, or to add descriptive colour to the story, I have taken a few liberties. The 'Hall of Lost Footsteps' in Poitiers, where Eleanor receives Henry in Chapter 6, was not so called until four decades later, when she remodelled it. Although Eleanor was in fact duchess of Aquitaine and countess of Poitou, in order to avoid confusion, I have generally referred to her simply as duchess of Aquitaine.

We know that Eleanor could read, but there is no extant example of her handwriting, so it is not certain that she could write. In this novel, I have assumed – credibly, I think – that she could.

Readers may find the descriptions of Henry II's rages a little hard to believe, but the Plantagenet temper was notorious, and these scenes are just as they are described by contemporary chroniclers.

Eleanor's sister Petronilla is sometimes called Aelith in contemporary sources; I have opted to use the name by which she is more commonly known. There is no record of the date of Petronilla's death, so I have made up my own tale about her fate, suggested by the regular payments in the Exchequer records for generous sums of wine for her.

There is no evidence that Eleanor visited Woodstock in December 1166, when she was travelling in Oxfordshire, but I have made use of the conjectures of some biographers that she did indeed do so, and that she encountered Rosamund de Clifford there.

Nor is there any historical evidence for any homosexual relationship between Henry II and Thomas Becket, although theirs was certainly an exceptionally close friendship. The attitudes expressed in the book in regard to homosexuality are very much those of the twelfth century. Accounts vary as to the exact words that Henry II used on the occasion when, in great anger and distress, he castigated his courtiers for allowing him to be mocked with contempt by Becket, and so inadvertently prompted four knights to go secretly to England and murder the Archbishop. Traditionally, he is said to have cried, 'Who will rid me of this turbulent priest?' Although those words do not appear in any contemporary source, I have used them in this novel because of their dramatic effect.

Some of the dialogue in the book comes from original sources, although I have modified it in parts to make it compatible with a twenty-first-century text. My inspiration, in writing the dialogue, comes largely from the film *The Lion in Winter* (1968 version) and Jean Anouilh's *Becket*, in both of which pithily modern idioms combine with more archaic forms. This kind of language chimes well with translations of contemporary sources from Latin or Norman French. Such translations can sound surprisingly modern when compared with (for example) Tudor sources in old English.

Writers familiar with my Tudor books may have noticed that I have 'borrowed' from that period with my paraphrasing of Sir Thomas Wyatt's verse on page 98. 'If all the world were mine', the song sung by the German minnesinger on page 150, was one of a collection of medieval goliardic songs that were adapted by Carl Orff for *Carmina Burana*, his collection of secular songs for orchestra, soloists and chorus, which was first performed in 1937.

Those with an eye for detail might wonder why the jacket illustration for a book about Eleanor's years as Queen of England shows her wearing a blue gown patterned with fleurs-de-lis, the

French royal arms. Although the fleur-de-lis symbol was used by her first husband, Louis VII, and had been associated with Frankish kings back to the Dark Ages, it was not used exclusively in France, and does not appear there as a royal heraldic symbol until 1211. In fact, it may not even represent a lily; there has been some debate as to whether it is meant to be a broom flower, the *planta genista* that gave Henry II's dynasty its name. As heraldry was in its infancy in the twelfth century, and the fleur-de-lis was a popular symbol with several European dynasties at that time, it is credible that Eleanor of Aquitaine might have worn such a gown.

Readers may also notice that I have incorporated descriptions of the reinterpreted rooms at the Great Tower in Dover Castle where the jacket photographs were taken.

The shields on the part-title pages show the arms of Henry II, and incorporate Eleanor's Lion of Poitou.

When I was researching my biography of Eleanor, and first conceived the idea of writing a novel, it was Eleanor whom I really wanted to write about. For obvious reasons, I couldn't do so at that time, and therefore I opted to write about Lady Jane Grey instead. That was in 1998, more than a decade ago, and I am delighted that I have at last been able to fulfil my original ambition. The wheel has come full circle!

It was a deliberate decision not to write a fictional account of the whole of Eleanor's life. Again, one of my chief inspirations was that incomparable film, *The Lion in Winter*, and what I really wanted to explore in this novel was the marriage between Eleanor and Henry II – not just their dynamic interaction over one explosive Christmas, but the whole course of their relationship over a period of thirty-seven years. In doing so, I feel I have been able to achieve insights into what might have gone wrong between them, and to explain what drove them to act as they did. That has been the real challenge.

I should like to extend my warm thanks and deep appreciation to my brilliant editors, Anthony Whittome, Kate Elton and Caroline Gascoigne at Hutchinson and Arrow, and to Susanna Porter at Ballantine in New York, for the tremendous support that they have all given me during the preparation of this book; to my agent, Julian Alexander, who is always marvellously kind and encouraging; to Sarah Eastall and Garry Newing for permitting us to shoot the jacket photographs in the Great Tower of Dover Castle, and for making us so welcome; and to all my family and friends, for putting up with a frantic maniac who is seemingly on an endless mission to meet deadlines! Lastly, thank you, Rankin, my dear husband. I've said it many times, but it's the plain truth: I couldn't do it without you!

ALISON WEIR
CARSHALTON, SURREY
AUGUST 2009